Select praise for
New York Times bestselling author
Maisey Yates

"Her characters excel at defying the norms and providing readers with...an emotional investment."
—*RT Book Reviews* on *Claim Me, Cowboy*
(Top Pick)

"A sassy, romantic and sexy story about two characters whose chemistry is off the charts."
—*RT Book Reviews* on *Smooth-Talking Cowboy*
(Top Pick)

"This is an exceptional example of an opposites-attract romance with heartfelt writing and solid character development.... This is a must-read that will have you believing in love."
—*RT Book Reviews* on *Seduce Me, Cowboy* (Top Pick)

"Their relationship is displayed with a quick writing style full of double entendres, sexy sarcasm and enough passion to melt the mountain snow!"
—*RT Book Reviews* on *Hold Me, Cowboy* (Top Pick)

Books by Maisey Yates

The Carsons of Lone Rock

Rancher's Forgotten Rival
Best Man Rancher
One Night Rancher
Rancher's Snowed-In Reunion

Gold Valley Vineyards

Rancher's Wild Secret
Claiming the Rancher's Heir
The Rancher's Wager
Rancher's Christmas Storm

Copper Ridge

Take Me, Cowboy
Hold Me, Cowboy
Seduce Me, Cowboy
Claim Me, Cowboy
Want Me, Cowboy
Need Me, Cowboy

For more books by Maisey Yates,
visit maiseyyates.com.

You can also find Maisey Yates on Facebook,
along with other Harlequin Desire authors,
at Facebook.com/HarlequinDesireAuthors!

NEW YORK TIMES BESTSELLING AUTHOR

MAISEY YATES

Rancher's Snowed-In Reunion

MILLS & BOON

CONTENTS

Rancher's Snowed-In Reunion

CHAPTER ONE

After

FLINT CARSON HAD to hand it to his brother. His recent move in life had inspired Flint. And he couldn't say that he was often inspired by his little brother. Not that Jace wasn't a decent guy, it was just that Flint, in general, didn't want what Jace had. He had settled down recently, and that wasn't in the cards for Flint.

But when his brother had become a part owner of the hotel that his fiancée bought, it had gotten Flint thinking. And then he had done more than think. He had been content for a long time competing in the rodeo. Working his family ranch, giving to them in a way that he could. His father recognized rodeo triumphs, and he took them as credits to who he was as a father, as the rodeo commissioner.

He also recognized contributions to the ranch. His mother appreciated that his father felt appreciated. He didn't do emotions, so that kind of physical involvement was what he had to give, so he gave it.

At least until a couple of years ago. It had started being profoundly not enough.

And after…

There was just so much anger in him. There had been, for

a long time. For a lot of reasons. But after that song had come out…

He gritted his teeth. It infuriated him every time.

But what didn't infuriate him was his brand-new purchase. Pine Creek Resort. Nestled in the mountains of central Oregon, a couple hours away from his family home of Lone Rock.

He'd seen it and just felt drawn to it. He didn't give much credit to fate or feelings—not these days. But he believed a man ought to trust his gut.

So, he was trusting his.

It was practically off-grid, and solar panels, generators and other things kept it going with the iffy power running to the place. But it was pretty seamless, and he had done his due diligence on that. Because while he thought it was great that Jace and Cara were running the hotel at the end of the main drag of Lone Rock's main business center—which was just a few businesses, surrounded by mountains—he wanted more. Bigger.

The thought made his mouth curve into a smile as he looked around the highly polished lobby area. It was all logs and wooden beams. Rustic sort of luxury.

He could remember back when he'd said he didn't have ambitions or dreams at all.

But that was before.

Back then, everything he'd done had been to burn the rage out of his blood. To push himself to the edge so that he could ride out the simmering hatred that turned his blood to poison.

He'd chased adrenaline because it made things feel clear. Pure. Clean.

Could have been worse.

Could have been heroin.

Maybe it wasn't all that different now. Maybe this wasn't all that different. Maybe he was still trying to climb impossible mountains, just with more financial risk than physical.

With the weather being what it was, almost every guest had canceled their reservation for the weekend. There was a huge storm coming in, and while usually the hotel was accessible year-round, there had been some warnings and questions about whether or not it would be possible over the next couple of days. He didn't mind. A little bit of quiet in his newest acquisition while he looked to the next one was fine by him.

And since there was only going to be one guest, he'd let the staff go as well. The guest had declined maid service, and there was enough food that all he would have to do was heat and deliver. And he didn't mind that.

A little bit of manual labor didn't bother him at all. In fact, he thought it was good. Another way to burn out that rage. He had to do it.

And as if just thinking had brought it all to him, he suddenly became aware of the fact that there was music playing in the lobby. And not just any music.

You were the cowboy my mama warned me about
And I thought I listened, I thought you were different
I gave you my heart, and you gave me good-luck charms
I gave you my body, and you kept my scarf
I gave you my body, and you kept my heart

For God's sake. Was it destined to follow him everywhere? Even when he quite literally owned the damn place?

He growled and stalked toward the reception desk. The guy had told him how to control the music, but as his own personal level of hell played around him, he couldn't quite remember how.

I gave you everything to the sound of crashing waves
You knew you were the first one
I wanted you to be the only one

It made him think of her.
The song always made him think of her.

The way she'd looked at him, like she was searching his eyes for the answers to all of her questions. Wordless questions he'd wished he hadn't understood. Questions that still echoed inside him.

In the end, she'd said that he was right. She had said that they needed to finish the whole damned thing.

She was the one that had called it a fling.

She said she loved you too.

Yes. She had said that. And then she had taken it back. She had said that it was just because of the sex. And he'd been more than willing to believe it because hearing her say that she loved him had done things to him. Terrible, intense things that made him feel like his chest was being cut into.

He needed to find the volume. Or a sledgehammer.

Before the next part.

But then it was the next part, and it was in his head, his heart, his soul.

You took the clothes off my body
I gave you my yes and I love you
You took the skin off my bones
You gave me nothing at all
I prayed for our sin to disappear
But I didn't mean for it to end in blood

He found the speaker right then. He found it just a lyric too late. He crouched down, reaching for the knob on the speaker behind the desk. And as he did, he heard the door to the lobby open. He hit the off button on the speaker just as the next part of the song started.

He couldn't explain the way it made him feel.

He could remember where he was the first time he heard it. The first time he'd heard his ex-girlfriend—was she his ex-girlfriend? He'd never had a girlfriend in his life. And they weren't supposed to be that, but he'd also never ended a physical relationship with someone and felt like their connection was still there. And yet.

The simple truth was, he'd gotten in deeper with her than he ever had been with anyone else. Much deeper than he'd intended to. And he wasn't going to say he'd covered himself in glory at the end of all things. But she had seemed to accept it. He'd been up-front with her, from the beginning, about what they were, about what they could be.

So imagine his surprise the first time he'd heard that song. Documenting everything. The most personal, deep feelings he'd ever had in his whole life turned into a sing-along.

Even if no one else had ever heard it, it would have felt too raw and personal for him to listen to.

But people had heard it. So many people.

To make matters worse, her fame and his own niche notoriety in certain circles had made it so there were theories out there on the internet about who the song was about.

Her fans were nuts. They spent all day weaving together theories about what every lyric meant. And he knew that because he'd googled it, because he'd wanted to know what the lyrics meant too.

Dammit.

The terrible thing was, her fans made points. Points he didn't like, but points nonetheless.

That would have been bad enough. But it didn't stop there.

Strangers sometimes accosted him on the street and asked him how dare he break Tansey Martin's heart? Country music's sweetheart. Barrel-racer-turned-overnight-singing-sensation.

She was beautiful and beloved, and he was the expertly cast villain in her narrative. Set to music, which meant that people could hum his humiliation as a catchy tune.

He could remember clearly the way that she had looked up at him. The way that she had looked up at him when he'd said all those things. The awful sort of things that he'd warned her he would say. As everything had broken apart inside of him, the walls that he had erected around himself beginning to crumble, she had looked up at him, and she had said that he was right.

That he was right, and they shouldn't be together. That he was right and they should forget everything.

Yeah. He knew that. Because he knew his limitations. And then... And then four months later, completely and totally blindsided by this song. And he'd known it was about them. That it was their story.

It was like she had crawled beneath his skin with those song lyrics. Like she had described his own pain. Like she'd dug into his soul and carved clear arrows to his own motives. To things he'd denied even to himself.

He'd pretended that he wasn't hanging on to her scarf for any particular reason, and she had immortalized it in song and made it impossible for him to pretend.

But it was the pregnancy scare.

That was what destroyed him the most, because it shone a light on the way that he had fallen apart most profoundly.

The worst, cruelest way he'd failed her.

When something like that happened, you had to take a good look at yourself. Even though there hadn't been a baby in the end, it had been a come-to-Jesus moment. A look-hard-at-the-man-he'd-become moment.

He didn't like that man.

It was one reason he'd changed everything. One reason he'd started...working. Really working. Not just on his father's land, not just on being rodeo champion yet again. But building something that was entirely his.

And he couldn't let that song into his head. Not now. Because it was the only thing that could get beneath his skin, just like *she* was the only thing that ever could.

He was pretty good at staying stoic in the face of difficult things.

It wasn't the fans yelling at him. That was actually fine. That made him *mad*. Anger, he had found, was fantastic fuel.

It was the pain.

The pain he wasn't supposed to be able to feel anymore. The pain that ambushed him when he didn't expect it. When he was alone. The pain that took him right back to the place that he'd been when he was a boy, a place he couldn't even think about, much less fully remember or relive.

And so he pushed the song to the back of his mind, and he stood up. But then he froze. The predator spotting prey. That was what it felt like. Like everything in him went quiet. And the edges of the empty lobby blurred.

Her.

There she was. Standing there at the center of the room, strawberry blond hair curling and cascading past her shoulders.

She looked like he remembered her.

Not the way that she dressed up for the public. All fake eyelashes and red lipstick.

This was just her.

The way that he had seen her that first day. Coming in from barrel racing, her cheeks bright red, her smile exuberant. Though she wasn't smiling now. She looked storm tossed, her hair full of snowflakes, and a couple of twigs. Her face was wet, likely from melting snow, and it forced him to remember how hot her skin could be when he put his hands on it.

She looked just like she had the first time…

Before

SHE WASN'T HIS type.

Flint Carson had interacted with more than his fair share of the sort of women you met at a rodeo. From rodeo queens to buckle bunnies, and everything in between. He tended toward the queens and the bunnies. Soft, pretty rhinestones. The sort of glamour that wasn't necessarily subtle or classy, but he liked it. He was a man, dusty, hard and full of grit. He liked a woman who was the opposite of all that.

That was the point of women, as far as he was concerned.

Bring on the glitter, the lip gloss, the long fingernails. Flashy, maybe even bordering on what some would call trashy. He didn't think it was trashy.

He liked it.

Now, some of the barrel racers had a little bit of flair to them, but they still weren't his thing. Felt too much like coworkers, really. He didn't like it.

He was also very careful to choose women close to his age and level of experience. He didn't have forever in him. Hell, he didn't even have more than a couple of nights in him, so it didn't do any good to go after a woman who was expecting something more. To go after the kind of woman who wanted something more. He needed the women that he hooked up with to want exactly what he wanted.

Which was why, when the pint-size, barefaced barrel racer tripped on unsteady legs on her way out of the gate after a ride, and landed right in his arms, the first thing he told himself was, she wasn't his type.

She had freckles all over her face. Her eyes were green. Her hair was strawberry blond, curly, he could tell; even though it was in a braid, there were wispy tendrils that had escaped. She was thin but athletic, wearing a plain white tank top and a pair of torn blue jeans. She was young.

And something in him burned.

He set her back on her heels.

"Careful there."

"Thanks, Ace," she said, brushing some dust off of her jeans. "I'll do my best to be more careful."

"Darlin', I just saved you from doing a face-plant, and you're going to get sassy with me?"

"A face-plant never hurt anybody."

"Neither has spending a few minutes in my arms. You can ask around."

She laughed. But it wasn't a particularly kind or warm laugh. "Of course. Somehow that doesn't surprise me."

"What's your name?"

"Tansey," she said. "Tansey Martin. You're Flint Carson."

She knew who he was. He supposed he shouldn't be surprised. She was…young. He was sort of an elder statesman of the bull-riding circuit, and in addition to that, his dad was the rodeo commissioner. Practically everybody around these parts knew the Carsons.

"Guilty," he said.

"Of quite a lot of things if the gossip is anything to go by."

She could walk away. That was the thing. She could walk away, but she was antagonizing him instead. *He* could also walk away.

Neither of them were doing that.

It would almost be interesting except she wasn't his type.

She wasn't his type, and wasn't charmed by his whole facade. Which made him wonder if there was any point to the facade at all. Made him tempted to drop it. And he never dropped it, not ever.

"Now," he asked, "did your parents ever teach you not to listen to gossip?"

"My mom taught me that gossip could be useful. If something is said often enough, there's probably some truth to it. And maybe a person should listen to it. All my daddy taught me was the way 1999 Ford pickup taillights look going out of the driveway."

"Sounds like a country song," he said.

She smiled, and it was unreadable. Not flirtatious. Not friendly. He wanted to know what the hell it meant. "Yeah. It kind of does."

She was standing with her horse. He had kind of only just noticed. The big animal that was right next to her. Funny.

It was like she took up all the space.

"Nice," he said, patting the animal on the flank.

"Thanks. Cinderella has a thing for cowboys that are too charming for their boots."

"I take it her owner does not."

"No, she doesn't. Like I said. Taillights. I'm familiar. With cowboys. Do you know what they're good for?"

"What?"

"Leaving."

That made him want to do something. Surprise her. Climb a mountain.

Stay.

"That is true. We are very good at that."

Except, he didn't leave. Neither did she. Neither of them pointed that out. They just stood there and marinated in the irony.

"You want to get a drink?" he asked.

Her lips twitched, like she was pondering that. "Sure. I'm not having sex with you. To be clear."

The way she said it was a gut punch. And good thing she wasn't his type, or his mind might have wandered somewhere it shouldn't.

"I'm not asking," he said. "To be clear."

Her face went scarlet. Well. He'd succeeded in getting something other than a cool, snarky reaction out of her.

Though, he had no idea why he was asking her for a drink. Except they were standing there, right near the gates, cluttering up the space, taking up too much room.

So, obviously they needed to move to another venue. It was the last night in this particular stop on the rodeo tour, and he didn't know how he hadn't noticed her before. He didn't really stand around watching all the other events. He had once, when he'd been new to the game. When things had been shiny and bright and he'd been excited.

At least, in his memory he was excited. It was entirely possible that he was painting the whole thing with a varnish that had never actually been there.

Always easier to look back on the glory days.

Mostly, he had been young and angry, and the adrenaline had felt good.

Now he was old and angry, and the adrenaline made his muscles hurt.

Okay. He wasn't old. He was thirty-four, but that was getting on in rodeo years. And that was a fact.

Especially when you'd been doing it since you were eighteen years old. It was a lot of years of abuse. More than not.

"Are you old enough to drink?"

Her face went red. "Yes."

"Okay. I don't want to be out there buying alcohol for a minor. I don't have a criminal record, which is a miracle to be honest. So I'd rather not get one now."

"That's kind of a surprise. I thought all you guys had a slew of DUIs."

"Sorry to disappoint."

"Well. I'm happy to be surprised. I didn't think your kind could surprise me."

"What exactly is my kind, Tansey?" He started to follow her out of the arena area and toward the stalls where the horses would be kept until they were ready to load up and head to the next event.

"Smooth talker. Probably never met a woman you couldn't con out of her clothes."

"Now, that sounds vaguely predatory. This here being the modern era, I am a huge fan of consent. I don't con anyone out of anything. Now, if they get a look at me and decide they'd like to take their clothes off, that is another story altogether."

"Good to know. A respectful womanizer. But a womanizer nonetheless."

"You do have my number. But then, I don't go around claiming to be anything other than a bad bet. I assume your daddy did."

"He thought he'd try to be a family man for a little bit. Didn't work out."

"Well. There's a difference between me and your father, right off the bat. I'm never going to pretend to be a family man."

"Well, I suppose that's something."

He watched as she took all the tack off of her horse—he didn't figure she was going to accept any help from him. She probably had a million reasons for it too. Something about being independent, he was sure. And while it would be fun, maybe, to engage in that banter, he figured he would keep going in the direction of the unexpected banter. Because he liked it.

He liked talking to her.

And hell, he'd had a great idea how this night was going to go. He'd won his event, kept his top spot on the leaderboard, and he'd been planning on going out to the bar with all the other guys, including his brother Boone, and having drinks. Which would probably devolve into taking shots, which would inevitably end up with him finding a woman to hook up with...

He'd go back to his motel room, they'd have sex, she'd go her way and he'd sleep for a few hours before getting on the road the next morning.

He could see it all play out in his mind. And it bored him.

Tansey didn't bore him.

And anyway, she wasn't his type.

So it wasn't like it was going to be anything but a conversation. He couldn't remember the last time he'd wanted to engage in a conversation with anybody after an event.

He didn't engage in a lot of conversations, really. He did a lot of drinking, a lot of physical things.

Didn't talk all that much.

This felt like a novelty. And... Hell. He was in the market for one. Hadn't known that he was until she'd fallen into his arms. But then, maybe that was a sign.

Not that he believed in that kind of thing.

Still, he found himself jerking his head toward where he parked his truck. "Want to take a ride with me?"

"I'll drive myself," she said. "Which bar?"

"Cactus," he said. "It's right across the street from the Okay Motel. That's where I'm staying."

"Me too," she said.

"How about we drive there, park across the street. Then nobody has to watch the drinking."

"I don't get drunk," she said.

"Why not?"

"Because. I like to have my wits about me."

"Well. There is the difference between you and me. I prefer to make my wits a bit blurry."

She looked at him, for a long moment, and he had the uncomfortable feeling that her green eyes could see more than just his face, his shirt, his jeans. He had the feeling that she could see something deeper in him than he even knew was there. And he didn't like it.

And still, he wanted to go get that drink with her.

"Okay. Meet you there."

After

SHE WAS STANDING completely still. Like she was the prey. Like she knew it. Like she knew that she had been scented.

Like she knew exactly what he felt.

Because hadn't she always?

Until that last moment.

And hadn't he always? Until then.

When they had both pretty spectacularly lied to each other's faces and broken down the world.

He stood by it.

Because the fallout had proved that he was right. His own behavior after the fact, and hers.

He would never have said he was sensitive. Far from it. He

was a man who didn't do feelings in the slightest. But he felt like she had taken a layer of his skin and peeled it off with a paring knife, pulled it back and showed the world everything that was inside of him. And he didn't even like to look at all the things that were inside of him.

Hearing the pain in the song was like being stabbed through the heart.

Because as much as it was about her own pain, it was about his. As much as it was about him breaking them up, it was about him breaking himself. As much as he was the villain to her...

He'd been that for himself too.

If he believed in fate, he'd have been certain it had come for him today.

He didn't believe in fate.

It was just that life was a bitch.

So he had to be a bigger bastard.

He put his hand up to his head, and reflexively, without thought, touched the brim of his cowboy hat, and tipped it. "Howdy."

"What are you doing here?" She looked around, shocked, and he realized that she had gone as white as the snow outside.

He slowly moved from behind the counter, and began to walk toward her. She was the only thing. The only thing. "I might ask you the same question. Because I looked at the books, and your name is not on them."

"I don't check into hotels under my real name," she said.

"Oh right," he said, "because you're fancy now. Because everybody knows who you are. Everyone knows everything about you, don't they, Tansey?"

"Yes. I know you're trying to be mean, and trying to make it sound like maybe I'm above myself, but it's true."

"It seems there's something else you don't do. You don't look to see who owns the hotel you're staying at."

Her mouth dropped open. "I've been here before. You've *never* been here."

"I just bought it. It's mine. And you're the only guest." He spread his arms wide. "Looks like it's just the two of us."

CHAPTER TWO

RUN.

That was all Tansey could think. She needed to run. Because she'd never, ever wanted to come face-to-face with Flint Carson ever again. Not in her whole life.

But there he was.

Maybe if she closed her eyes, she could be not in this moment. Maybe if she concentrated really hard, he would disappear.

Maybe this was a dream.

The whole drive up here had been a nightmare, and maybe it hadn't even been real. Maybe that was the thing. Maybe the whole drive, with the intense, freezing snow, the white stuff piling up on the road and making it slick and almost impossible to keep her tires on the road, had been part of a nightmare. Maybe the branches falling across the road, the tree that had fallen down after her on the soft ground, and the lack of cell phone service, had all been an elaborate nightmare.

Ending with Flint. Standing right there in the lobby of the hotel.

Like it was *The Shining*. Except, it wasn't a crazy grounds-keeper; it was her way-too-hot-for-anyone's-own-good ex-boyfriend, who had absolutely destroyed her and broken her into tiny pieces.

Ex-boyfriend. He was never your boyfriend. He was a guy who had sex with you. And you were an idiot.

Yes. She had been an idiot. And she'd had grace for that young idiot. That young idiot who had known better, whose mother had told her better, who had purposed to not act out her daddy issues in that way, but had done so because Flint was just so charming. Because she hadn't actually had any experience.

Because she had told herself that she knew getting sexually involved with a man who wasn't going to fall in love with her could hurt her, but she hadn't really understood it. Because she had told herself she could handle a fling, and then she had let herself believe that she had been convinced on some level she could change his mind about it being a fling.

She had been like every other dumb twenty-two-year-old who didn't want to believe that she was, in fact, like all the other girls.

Well, she'd made her peace with that, because she was more than two years past all that, and a heartbreak sure offered a lot of clarity. She didn't waste her time being outraged at that girl.

No. She knew where to put her outrage. It was on him. And there he was.

If this was a nightmare, she could take an umbrella out of the umbrella stand by the door and start whacking him with it.

She pinched her arm. It hurt, even through her heavy coat. But he was still standing there.

"What the hell are you doing?"

"I'm trying to see if I fell asleep on my way up here. Or maybe hit a tree and I'm unconscious in a ditch, so I'm hallucinating the ghosts of back-when-I-was-stupid past."

"Well. If you're hallucinating, then so am I."

"Great." And she had fantasized about running into him before, even though she had never wanted to see him again.

That seemed like a pretty normal thing.

In her fantasies of seeing him again someday, she had imagined herself in a beautiful designer dress—not looking soggy from her tramp through the snow up to the lobby, and being caught off guard.

No. She had always imagined they would run into each other at some soiree, not that Flint would have any reason to be at a soiree, but it was her fantasy.

Realistically, she hadn't thought it would happen, so she could imagine whatever scenario she wanted.

She had imagined that she would be dressed meticulously, looking every inch as wealthy as her music had made her, maybe with a handsome man on her arm—forgetting the fact that she hadn't been on a single date since she and Flint had broken up—and the look of regret that would wash over him would be profound.

But she would be happy. And she would drink champagne, and she would *show him*.

Because the best revenge was living well.

She had written it into the song because he had said it to her. He had said that to her about handling her own father's abandonment. And when she had written the song, she had hoped that he would hear it and appreciate the irony.

And now she found herself horrified by the realization that he had undoubtedly heard it.

Because all the self-protection that she had engaged in when he had broken up with her suddenly didn't matter. Because she had put it all in a song.

She had known that, but knowing it and coming face-to-face with it were two very different things.

And this was in no way what she wanted. This was way too real. She preferred the glossy fantasy.

This was him. And it felt like the first time...

Before

SHE HAD NO idea what the hell she was doing. She didn't do this kind of thing. Didn't go out and have drinks with extraordinarily handsome cowboys. He was extraordinarily handsome. She'd known that, though. Ever since she first started riding with the rodeo two years ago.

She'd gotten into it hoping to see her dad again.

It was so stupid. All of it.

Her little pursuits to try and make a connection with a man who didn't give a shit about her at all. But she'd thought… Their paths would have to cross. Even when he wasn't competing in calf-roping events, he was often doing odd jobs around the rodeo. It was his whole life. Plus, she'd figured… He paid attention to the rodeo circuit; he was bound to see her name.

Those were the two things her dad loved. The rodeo and country music. She was bound and determined that she was going to reach him through one of those ways or the other.

Funny that Flint had mentioned the taillights thing sounded like a country song.

She already knew it. She'd already made it one.

Of course, it wasn't the demo that her manager was shopping. It felt too personal. She hadn't played that song for anyone.

The frothy little love song that she'd recorded a couple of months ago when she'd found somebody who wanted to take a chance on her and push her to the labels was easier for her.

Not that anyone had shown any interest in it. But she did all the open mics that she came across while traveling for the rodeo, and that worked out pretty well for her.

Everything she did had a purpose. She'd joined the rodeo to find her dad, being in the rodeo let her travel, traveling helped her get her music out. That was how she did things.

But this… Having a drink with Flint Carson accomplished nothing. She didn't know why she had kept talking to him.

Didn't know why she had stood there, unable to drag herself away. And she did not know why she'd said yes to this. But when she pulled up to the motel at the same time he did, and got out, crossing the dusty, two-lane Arizona highway to the little dive bar across the street, she stopped questioning it.

He opened the door for her, and she looked up at him, at his chiseled face, square jaw, strong chin. He had dark stubble over that jaw, and it looked rough, and she couldn't deny that she felt her fingers itch slightly with the urge to touch it.

Which was very stupid. She liked to think that she was smarter than that. That her body was smarter than that. Because it knew the memories of what it felt like to be abandoned. Remembered what it was like to crumple down on the ground, on her knees, with the gravel biting into the denim as her father's truck got farther and farther away and she gave in to her anguish. That was embedded into her soul. It was more keen, more real, than any desire to touch a handsome cowboy's stubble could ever be. That moment of it being the last time she ever saw her father would always be more burned into everything she was than…than the dark blue of his eyes. Like worn denim. So compelling and enticing…

She took a deep breath and pressed on into the bar.

The floor was rough wood, and there were neon cactus signs all over the place. And also a pink flamingo. She admired the commitment to tackiness, even if it wasn't totally following a theme.

There were a lot of cowboys and cowgirls already in there, people that she knew. She felt slightly embarrassed to be coming in with Flint, because why would anybody be with him unless they were going to sleep with him? She had never known Flint to hang out with a woman that he wasn't going to hook up with.

Well. Allegedly.

Maybe she had sort of noticed him from across the bar before, and that was what some of the girls she was with had said about him… And maybe she had committed some of that to heart a little bit more than she ought to.

Maybe she had gone back to her room and scribbled down a few song lyrics about unobtainable men who were nothing but bad decisions wrapped in dust and denim.

Maybe.

She was an artist, though. She often wrote about things that she had no desire to experience. She often wrote about things that she would never do. Things she didn't even want to do. She wrote about the human experience. Not necessarily her own.

The love song she'd recorded was a prime example of that.

She'd never been in love.

She thought about the song she'd written about her dad again, and shoved all that to the side.

"What will you have?"

"Uh. Beer?"

She just really wasn't a big drinker.

"Sure. What kind?"

"I don't know."

"Okay. That helps me make a decision."

He went over to the bar, and she sat down at one of the little tables in the corner. He came back a few moments later with two beers, one in each hand.

"How did me not knowing tell you anything?"

"I got you something easy. Something friendly. Since clearly if you don't know what you're drinking, you don't have a lot of experience with the drinking. So…mainstream it is."

"Are you insulting me?" she asked, drawing the glass toward her.

"Not at all. I'm giving you something accessible."

"Out of deference to my inexperience?"

He cleared his throat and took a drink of his beer. And far too late she realized the potential double entendre with that. Of course, he didn't know how inexperienced she was. Anyway, her experience, or lack thereof, when it came to things other than beer was immaterial to this moment and this conversation.

"What exactly are we doing?" she asked, lifting her glass up and taking a sip. Damn him. It was good.

"Having a beer."

"It's just… You have a reputation."

"That I do. Though, you're going to have to tell me which one you mean. Because I have a reputation for being a very good bull rider, as it happens. Maybe you missed it, but I'm in first place right now."

"I didn't miss it. And that isn't the reputation I'm referring to."

"You mean that I like to have a one-night stand. Many, many of the people who travel with the rodeo do."

"Right. Well. I don't."

"Great. Good to know."

"So why are you talking to me?"

"Why are *you* talking to *me*? Because as you said, I have a reputation. You seem to know it…"

"I don't know why I am talking to you. It's just that I wanted to."

"Well, I wanted to talk to you too. I can't say that I know why either." He huffed a laugh and took another drink of his beer. "I'll just tell you, I've known what I was doing for a long damn time. I joined the rodeo when I was eighteen. I knew that I wanted to be the best. I knew I wanted to win. I *have* won it all. Several times. I knew that was my goal. I achieved it. On a smaller scale… I tend to know what I want out of a given day. I knew what I was going to do tonight. I was going to leave the arena, I was going to come to this bar. I was going to go over there," he said, gesturing to the corner where there was a jukebox, and a gaggle of women dressed to the nines, their hair done up, their best push-up bras doing admirable work.

"I was going to strike up a conversation with one of those women, and we would've both known from the very beginning exactly where that conversation was going. We'd have had sex. Sorry. But it's true. I would've said goodbye, and she would've been on her way." He shrugged. "Yeah. I usually know exactly what I'm doing. I have no idea what I'm doing right now. No idea what's happening here. And I guess maybe that's part of why I like it. Why I'm interested. Because you ran into me… And changed the course of my evening. I think I'd have to be a particular kind of fool not to see where that went."

"It won't be bed."

"You've been very clear on that. And I have no interest in pushing."

She sat with that for a minute. Did that mean that he would have liked her that way if she'd said she wanted it? She had never been particularly flattered by the attentions of cowboys. In fact, just the opposite. Her mother had always made it very clear that cowboys had absolutely no standards. *"Darlin',"* she'd said. *"Men will stick it in the hole of a hollow tree. Don't you ever let yourself feel flattered because they want to put it in you."*

She knew that it came from a place of protectiveness. A little rough around the edges though it was. Darlene Martin was rough around the edges. It was part of what Tansey loved about her.

Her mom had taught her how to arm herself, protect herself, where she hadn't been able to do the same. Tansey was appreciative of that. She learned all of her mother's lessons, so she didn't have to learn her own.

If she wasn't careful, a man like Flint Carson could be a very difficult lesson.

But you know better. And this is just a conversation.

"What are your dreams?" he asked, leaning back in his chair. "You want to win it all in the rodeo?"

"I wouldn't be opposed. But… My dad is Huck Jones."

He frowned. "I know that name."

"Yeah. He's done roping and a few other events, plus general setup and teardown work, with the rodeo for a long time. I got into the rodeo to be closer to him. To find him again. Because I was a kid when he left and…"

"Taillights," he said.

"Yeah. And I guess I thought that I was going to change something. Redeem something, fix something by finding him. But you know what? He's never around. Even though I tried coming to him, I haven't ever encountered him. He hasn't been competing. I… I thought at least he would see me, and he would want to get to know me. If I was doing something that interested him. I thought that I would matter. I thought that I would matter more. I really did. I guess I thought maybe the hearth-and-home thing wasn't for him, but if I took myself out on the road…"

"Right. Well. What a prick."

And that made her laugh. "Thanks for that. I think so too."

Except it hurt. It hurt a lot. And there was a reason she didn't go around just talking about this, but it was such a strange thing. To be sitting here like this with him. She had felt like she didn't want to leave his side from the moment she fell against him. This felt natural. And maybe that was why she felt compelled to ask him what it was they were doing. Because it shouldn't feel natural. Not to her, not to him.

They shouldn't just want to sit and talk to each other with no ulterior motives. In this world, in any world, it didn't seem to be a thing as far as she could tell.

And yet.

"What else? You didn't say that your dream was to win big here."

"I enjoy barrel racing. But no. It's not my dream."

"What's your dream?" he asked.

"I… I just recorded a demo. I… I want to be a singer. Well, I'm a songwriter. Really. And if what I end up doing is selling songs, that's fine too. It's okay if I don't actually end up being famous or anything like that." Except she kind of did want to be famous. She kind of did want to show him. She wanted to buy her mom a big house and end up on TV. She wanted to force him to see exactly what he'd walked away from. He acted like she was an anchor. Something that was dragging him down, holding him back.

She wanted to prove that she would've been the thing that got him ahead.

Better than he could do for himself.

Maybe that was bitter and toxic. But she couldn't help herself.

"Well. They do say the best revenge is living well," he said.

That was like balm.

He understood. He got it. She hadn't even had to say any of those dark, ugly things that rolled around inside of her chest. He just knew. He understood.

"Yeah. Well. That would be about the favorite revenge, I have to say. Especially because that version of revenge involves some pretty nice cowgirl boots."

"If you win the overall prize barrel racing this year, I'll buy you some boots."

"I don't need a man to buy my boots," she said. "That's the point."

"I get that. But maybe it would be nice if there was a man who wanted to buy you boots?"

"Sorry. I don't think that's a very good goal either."

"Why is that?"

"My mama raised me to be independent. At the end of the day, the only person you can depend on is...you."

She felt sad for herself just saying it, and she waited for him to look at her with pity. But he didn't. That was the interesting thing about him. He looked her straight in the eye. He looked at her like an equal.

He was a strange sort of man. Not exactly what she'd thought. Though she was wary of him all the same.

"Can't you depend on your mom?"

She hesitated. "Yes. Though she is also an independent woman, so she has her own life. We stand for each other, but we mostly stand alone."

"I see."

"You have a lot of family, don't you?"

He nodded. "Yeah, I'm lousy with brothers." He hesitated for a moment. "And you probably know my sister, Callie. She was barrel racing until pretty recently."

She nodded. "Yeah, I do know her a bit. We're close to the same age."

He winced. "Right."

"You must never be lonely."

He chuckled. "I didn't say that."

"Oh."

"I respect that you want to stand on your own feet," he said, his tone switching abruptly. "But you can't stop me from buying a pair of boots for you to stand in if you win."

"I'd have to win," she pointed out. "And I'm not number one right now. Or did you not notice?"

"I didn't notice. I was too busy catching you when you tripped."

He met her gaze for too long. She looked away.

"Okay. So tell me how to win."

"You have to love nothing more than the moment you're in. Think about nothing more. Care about nothing more. You didn't ask me what my dreams were."

"Okay then... What are your dreams?" she asked.

"I don't have any."

"Oh."

"But that's why I win. Because it's very easy for nothing else to matter to me. Nothing but the moment. Nothing but the ride. Nothing else tugging on my attention. Nothing splintering my focus. There's not a single damn person out there that I care about more than I care about that moment. Not a single thing. Not a truck, not a house. Nothing. That's how I do it."

"You don't... You have a really big family..."

"Yeah. I mean... I love them. I do. But... I'm very good at

putting a wall up over my emotions. In fact, I'm not entirely sure that I could get to them now if I wanted to."

He said it so casually. But she had a feeling that it was true. A deep truth. And one that he probably didn't go around speaking out loud. And he told her because...because they were able to talk to each other. Because it just worked.

If he wasn't going to question it, then neither was she.

"I'm not sure that I can do that. I care about too many things. Sometimes I feel like I care about... Everything," she said.

"You just have to learn to shut it off. Don't burn so bright with passion that you let it smoke you out." He snapped his finger. "You have to remember it can work for you. It can get you where you're at right now. But don't let it sabotage you either."

"Thanks."

She finished her beer. And the two of them stood.

They left together, and she was keenly aware of the fact that people were watching them. She made a show of putting a lot of distance between their bodies as they walked through the parking lot, and across the street.

"Bye," she said, waving.

"See you at the next stop."

"Yeah. See you then."

After

"SO WE'RE THE only two people here?" she asked.

"That's about the size of it. And I don't know what's going on, if a tower got knocked out or something, but there's no cell service. We've got a landline, as long as that holds."

"Are you letting me know how easy it would be for you to kill me and bury me in a snowbank?"

His lips quirked up on the side. "I wouldn't do that. You're famous. Too many people would miss you."

It was the edge to him that surprised her, though.

Does it? If he's heard the song... You know him. You know how private he is, how protected.

Yes. And on some level, she knew that if he ever did hear the song, he would probably view it as a betrayal. And maybe part of her wanted that. Had wanted to pour out her own pain and anguish, to make everybody understand the intimacy of it. What he had taken from her. Not her virginity, it was deeper than that.

She had never slept with another man before, and she hadn't slept with one since, because she had been afraid of being hurt.

That was the part that got her.

That he knew what it had meant to her to give herself to him.

Yeah, she could see how maybe he would be upset that she had advertised that. But hell, people didn't know that it was him. Well. They did know that it was him. There were entire online forums dedicated to analyzing every single part of the song. If her scarf was a metaphor, or if it was real. If she was writing about the bull rider that she had been seen with on the coast that summer she'd gotten famous. Or if it had been a whirlwind affair in the studios with Harry Styles.

She had never met Harry Styles. But somehow, there were rumors about the two of them. Imaginary Tansey had a way more interesting love life than actual Tansey, who had one lover and a broken heart.

Your heart is not broken anymore. You just feel fragile because you are facing down your problematic past.

But yes, there were a lot of rumors. And many of them were true. It had been especially jarring to read a thread about lyrics where somebody had correctly identified the blood was about a miscarriage or a pregnancy scare. And it wasn't like it was subtle; it was just reading people trying to get deep into her words, rather than just applying their own experiences to it. Because to an extent, she had imagined that the song itself and what it could mean to people would be more interesting than what it had meant to her.

But somehow, she herself had become an object of fascination and… And that meant that people had wanted to know what the song meant for *her*.

But she had never said his name out loud. His name hadn't passed her lips once since they had parted that last day.

All that to say, she felt like she didn't fully deserve his rage, but she also couldn't deny that she had known it would be there.

Deep down, she had known, because she knew *him*. If he hadn't thought she would write a song about it, then he had never really known her. Hadn't been paying attention. Not even when she had played him the song about her dad, the first song that had made her famous. The one that he had encouraged her to record. He had been an audience of one the first time she had ever played a song that had come so deep from her heart like that. And he had been the one who had said it was the key to her fame.

He'd been right.

As famous as the song about her dad had made her, the one about her heartbreak had taken things into the stratosphere.

That forced her to think about why she was here, and she'd rather not do that. So she focused instead on the blazing blue of his eyes.

She'd seen those eyes look a lot of ways.

But never angry. Not like this.

"Well. Good for me then. Because yeah, it would be kind of a bad idea for this to be the last place that I was headed, with you being the owner and all. That is a totally traceable murder. I wouldn't attempt it."

"Lucky for you, I'd rather have the notoriety of having you have stayed here, than I would getting rid of you."

His voice was hard, and it was like some of the anger was slowly beginning to subside. There was something flat there. Something unreadable. Except… She didn't trust it.

"What?"

"You're going to make sure that everybody knows that you stayed here. Wrote a song here or some shit."

"Right. So I'm going to tell everybody that I stayed at my ex... Sorry. Is it better if I just keep your name out of everything? Because we can go ahead and address the number-one hit in the room if you want."

"I don't want to talk about that shit. Except to say that you and I both know that whether you ever confirmed it or not, people know it's about me. I'm the one that gets yelled at by crazy fans walking down the street. You can deny it, you can refuse to address it, but the best thing you could do is show everybody that we're fine."

But they weren't fine. Nothing in her was fine. She felt utterly and absolutely rattled. And this was her retreat...

And it was never going to be again after this. Because he owned it now. She could never come here again.

If this was fate, fate was a bitch.

Or maybe this was all balancing the cost of what she'd been given. Maybe poor country girls didn't get to have fame and money if they weren't also given heartbreak and exes they couldn't forget.

"You know, that's quite the weird, blackmail-sounding thing that you can't make me do, but I think I would rather just leave."

"You're welcome to try. But the weather has picked up. Everybody else was smart and didn't come up. All my staff left. Because it was the smart thing to do. You were the only fool that decided to make the trek up."

"And I can make the trek back down." She turned around and started to head for the door. She pushed it open, and the wind just about blew it back. She shoved it, and headed back out into the night. Fuck all this, and him too. Him *specifically*.

Maybe there was a song in this.

That was the real problem. She couldn't think of a song. And she didn't want anyone to know that. She was completely dried up. She had written the greatest breakup album of all time. With a song that had reached into people's souls and taken hold of them. Had taken on a life of its own. She had done the same writing the song about her dad. She knew how to grab on to pain. She knew how to grab on to pain and turn it into something real and relatable.

And now she was famous and successful and…

And she was still sad. Because it had given her money. It had let her buy a house for her mom. But it hadn't given her a relationship with her dad.

And she was alone. And she couldn't figure out how to trust people any more than she could before.

Hell, it was even worse. Because the only person she had ever trusted was Flint. The only person that she had ever hoped might be more than he seemed was Flint.

And he had proved that he wasn't. And then she had gotten famous. And her ability to trust people had become even more compromised because people could actually get things from her. They actually wanted things from her, and that? That made everything feel fraught. It made everything feel impossible.

And now it felt like there were no more songs. Because all she had was old, lingering pain that she didn't want to keep writing about, and the thrill of a success story that she couldn't quite access. It made her feel ungrateful. It made her feel small and sad. To be standing in the spotlight and still feeling like she was shrouded in darkness. She was beginning to feel terrified that it would all go away. Because the only thing worse than the idea of staying in the spotlight, bombarded with all the fame, was what would happen if it went away.

Because one thing was sure. It was exposing to write a song like she had about her and Flint. But it gave her a way to expel some of that pain. It gave her a way to talk about it. She didn't have anyone in her life that she could talk about it honestly. The only person had been… Flint. And then it had ended. So she had written songs about him instead. And talked to the world about how he had let her down. There was a catharsis in that.

She battled the wind and walked down to her truck, forced the door open. All of her bags were still inside. The door to the hotel opened, and she saw Flint, up the stairs, looking down at her, backlit by the lights from the inside.

And he came down the stairs, heading out after her, the wind whipping the T-shirt he was wearing, tightening it over what she knew was a very firm body. And she did not need to be looking at him right now; she was trying to run away from him.

"What the hell do you think you're doing?" he shouted. "You were lucky to make it up here okay—you are not driving back down in this."

"You lost any right to have an opinion on what I do," she yelled back.

"Did I lose it, or did we agree to dissolve it?"

Well. There was the rub. With the wind and the snow blowing between them, and ferocity and fear burning in his blue eyes.

"I was protecting myself. If you were worried about anything other than your own feelings in that moment, you would've known that."

"You should've said it all to *me*," he said.

The song. That was what he meant. That she should have said all those things to him, and not the world.

It hurt, because it wasn't unfair.

"What would it have changed?" she asked.

She was breathing hard, and so was he.

"Nothing," he said, his voice rough.

It was hard to hear. For one moment she'd forgotten. For one moment she'd hoped. But this was the reality of it, of them.

"Okay then. Don't lecture me. Don't lecture me on what I should've done. Don't lecture me on what the right thing to do would have been when I told you that I might be having your baby and you looked back at me and said you didn't want it."

"If you had…"

"You never even texted me back."

"Because you said that you weren't."

"I wasn't. Or maybe I was. But I lost it either way. I never took a test."

"I'm sorry. If you had been…"

"Is this what you do? Tell yourself if I'd been pregnant you would have handled it well? You didn't handle anything about it well. What makes you think you would have been better if there was a baby? You're rewriting the story."

"We all get to write our own stories, Tansey, you of all people should know."

The words hit hard, and he stood there, blue eyes blazing.

"I'm leaving."

"*Don't*," he bit out. "It's too fucking dangerous. You're not leaving just because you don't like me."

"I have to leave."

She just had to. She couldn't stay, not with him. It was too much, too real.

Nothing had been real like this since him.

And she couldn't stand it.

CHAPTER THREE

SHE GOT INTO the truck and started the engine, and he stood there in front of the vehicle, the headlights pouring over his body. She found some joyful irony in that. That she was the one driving away. When she had written a whole hit about the taillights on her father's truck, and watching him leave.

This should be a triumph. As soon as she started back down the winding road to the main highway, she regretted trying to leave.

There was snow all over the road, and her tires were slick. She had four-wheel drive, but this was solid ice. The temperature had dropped with the passing of time, and the movement of the storm.

Her truck was slipping and sliding, and her heart was pounding. She tried to drive slow, tried not to put herself in a position where she would have to brake suddenly, which would cause her to slide right off the road and over the edge of the embankment. Her palms were slick. She rounded the corner, and had to slam on her brakes, because there was a giant tree down in the middle of the road. Stretching from end to end. Her breathing was ragged, and she could barely hear it over the sound of the wind whipping against the side of her truck.

Shit. What was she going to do? She couldn't even turn

around. The road was too narrow. And she would have to...to walk back up and...

There was a pounding on the door of the truck. She jumped, and turned toward the passenger side, and saw Flint standing there looking in the window. "Come back to the hotel," he shouted.

He was shouting because of the roar of the wind; she knew that, except he still sounded angry.

"No, thanks."

"Fucking hell, Tansey, don't be suicidal because you don't want to see me."

He didn't understand. It felt like suicide to see him. To be sharing air with him. To be sharing the same space with him. Because the problem was, he was still beautiful. And no matter how she had rewritten him into the perfect storybook villain, no matter how she tried to make herself remember only that terrible moment when he had shut all of his emotions off, and had been a blank wall she couldn't see through, couldn't reach through, couldn't get through, when she saw him, she had to remember that he was a whole human being. A man. Flesh and blood.

A man who had kissed her, touched her, given her pleasure.

A man who had held her, and cared for her, and given her things that no one else ever had before. And then taken them away from her.

Yeah. It was easier to remember him as the collection of truths she had put into that song. Because every line had been true. But he was right. It had been a story. Carefully chosen details designed to create a neat narrative. One that highlighted the things that had been so good they were painful, the things that had cost her. The risks she had taken. But none of his.

She hadn't put in all the ways he'd helped her, respected her, listened to her...

Hadn't put any of his risk, any of his vulnerability into it. Because even though he'd never opened up to her, not all the way, even though he'd never told her why he was the way he was, she'd seen how he was. That being with her scared him sometimes.

All the fear, the vulnerability in her song… It had all been hers. And so in the end it had been about her pain, because she hadn't given any credit to the idea that he might have had any.

But looking at him now, she knew the man. The whole man. Not just the one from the song.

And it made her ache.

It was why her little fantasy about running into him and coolly walking away could never actually happen. Because it wasn't really Flint in that fantasy. Just a hollow stand-in that looked like him. Not one that embodied his heat, his life. Everything he was.

"Come on," he said.

"I can't turn around," she said.

"I know," he said. "If you get in the ditch right now, you're never getting back out of it. And it's too slick to try. So just get out of the truck and leave it here. No one else is getting past that tree either. We are going to have to get a chainsaw out and cut it into pieces to move it. And we could do it now, but to what end? There's just going to be more obstacles down the road. There's a hotel a quarter of a mile back that way."

"We have to…walk back?"

"Yes. We both have to walk back. Because you were playing the part of idiot in a horror movie. Congratulations."

"You're being such an asshole," she said.

"You too."

And it was only then that she realized they were literally shouting at each other over the howl of the wind and through the window of her truck. And her own voice was ringing sharply around her, and she didn't like it.

Reluctantly, she got out of the truck.

"Where are your bags?" he said, his voice hard.

"Just behind the seat…"

He reached back there and grabbed her duffel bag, and her guitar, slamming the door shut with his elbow.

"You don't have to carry…"

"If I were you, I would give it a rest. You can stop telling me what I can and can't do, and what I should and shouldn't do, because people who run off into blizzards don't get to make proclamations."

He wasn't wearing a coat. He had come after her in only that T-shirt, and she was so aware of how the wind was biting at him, but he just put his head down and kept walking forward.

It made her feel small, and strange. She was walking directly behind him, and she realized that she was using his body to help shield her from the wind.

And that was sort of a humbling realization. She couldn't say she cared for it.

She was freezing, and she was wearing a coat. His arms were bare.

And this was the problem with Flint. There were these moments. Because this was exactly who she'd begun to believe that he was. The man that would shield her from everything. The man that would carry it all on his shoulders. And that was more, and different, than the sharp heartbreak she had been carrying around all this time. It was a deeper, more fully realized regret.

All that she didn't have because of what she had wanted him to become.

Because she hadn't been wrong about everything. Because that was the problem with a heartbreak anthem. It didn't give credit to the good things. And it was the good things that made losing love sad.

It was the fact that he was the man who would chase her down in a snowstorm, block the wind and carry her bags, while he was wearing only a T-shirt.

There was good in him, that was the issue. When things were wonderful, they were just amazing. But when he shut down, it was like he was a blizzard all by himself.

She couldn't reach him.

When he was cruel, it cut deep.

There was something in him that made him like this and she didn't know what it was. Didn't understand what had shaped him into this man who was so perfect in so many ways, until he wasn't.

Of course, the fact that she didn't know what his issues were was his fault. He could have shared with her. He could give her something. He could tell her more about himself. But he had never wanted to. He had told her what he couldn't give, but he hadn't told her why.

Maybe there was no *why*.

Except, she had one. Her reasons for not being able to trust were specific, and ample. And he'd added another layer to it. It was neat, explainable. Easily written into songs, and easily folded into stories.

Him? He hadn't given her those pieces. But she knew enough about people to know they must be there. And to know that he wasn't sharing for a very specific reason.

But she didn't actually want to feel charitable toward him. And even though he had just saved her from a storm, he had also been the reason that she had run out into the storm. Because he hadn't even bothered to not be a jackass to her.

He did ask you to stay.

Fine. He had. But it was much too little, too late, and it wasn't when she had wanted him to ask her to stay.

The walk was icy and cold, and her boots were not equipped for the task. She slipped as she tried to get up the hill, and a squeak came out of her mouth, and he whipped around, dropping her duffel bag and grabbing her arm, keeping her from falling. She looked up at him, and their eyes met. And she was brought right back to that first time they'd met each other.

When she'd stumbled coming out of the gate.

And everything in her went still.

The terrible thing was looking up at him and knowing exactly what she'd seen in him. Knowing exactly what she'd been thinking. And knowing that if she had been put in that exact same position all over again, she would've made the same mistakes. Over and over again.

Because there was something about him. Something about him that was her own personal brand of favorite mistake.

It was horrifying.

"I'm fine," she said, pulling herself out of his hold.

"Right."

Words bubbled up inside of her. Ones she shouldn't speak. But… They had been apart for two years, and there were endless wells of unspoken words between them.

Why should she give him the benefit of leaving it all unspoken anymore?

"It might make you happy to know I don't need my mom to warn me about cowboys anymore. I have my own warnings."

"Good. Listen to them," he said. "Because God knew mine weren't enough."

"Excuse me?"

"It's not like I didn't tell you." He picked up the duffel bag.

"We were…whatever we were for how many months? You gave me warnings, but you never gave me reasons."

"Why do I have the feeling that's going into a song?"

"It already is," she said.

"Wow. Quoting your own song lyrics at me. That's something."

She growled, and went ahead of him. She didn't need him to shield her from the wind. She didn't need him to shield her from anything. She didn't need anything from him.

"You don't know your way around here as well as I do," he said.

"You don't even know how many times I've been here," she said.

Three. But she didn't need to tell him that.

"Yeah. But I've actually been staying up here for the last

couple of weeks," he said. "Making sure the transition went smoothly. There are some changes that I'm going to make."

"What are you…? What are you doing, anyway? You never expressed any interest in owning hotels."

"Yeah. Well. My brother and his fiancée bought a hotel in Lone Rock. He's more of a silent investor, but I found the whole thing really interesting. So I started looking around for properties. And this came up. I thought it was perfect. But I'm also looking at a hotel in downtown Portland. And considering something in Nashville."

"Right. Why Nashville?"

He shrugged. "Music city. Exciting."

"You know you don't have to tell me that."

"I do know," he said, his voice heavy with irony.

"Why would you buy something in a place where you might actually be in proximity to me? Since you hate me so much. Apparently."

"Why do you sing about the end of our relationship every single day?"

Ouch.

"Because it makes me a lot of money." He didn't say anything after that. Neither of them did. Finally, the lights of the hotel came into view.

"I'm surprised there's still power," she said.

"There's a backup generator, and some backup solar as well, with energy stored that we can feed off of. Because this is so rural, these kinds of things are a problem, even when the weather isn't this bad."

She huffed, and pushed through the lobby door. It wasn't a huge hotel, but it probably had about one hundred rooms. All in a big, gleaming log-cabin-style structure. The furniture was made of rough-hewn wood, with big geometric-patterned rugs over every surface.

She had always found the place restful. And had also found that nobody here was overly impressed with celebrity even if they did realize who she was, so she enjoyed the peace that came with it.

There was no peace now, though. There was Flint.

"What brought you to Oregon? Because you know this is where I am."

"Weirdly, Flint, I didn't think of you at all." She had enjoyed staying in Oregon when she had come with him, and they'd done quite a bit of traveling around the state with the rodeo. The Pendleton Round-Up and the big event in Sisters were both huge, and she had enjoyed being there every time.

That was all. She didn't necessarily think of Flint when she thought of the state.

Liar.

"Right. Fair. So maybe I didn't think of you when I thought of Tennessee."

"Except you sorta said you did."

"Maybe it was because a certain song came on the radio. Tough to say."

"Which room am I in?"

"Well. You can take your pick," he said. "The one we have you down for is the suite, though, and I imagine, given how fancy you are these days, that's what you want."

She scoffed. "What do you mean how fancy I am?"

"Don't tell me those aren't six-hundred-dollar jeans."

She blushed. Because yes. Her jeans were expensive. She had never imagined she would become that person. It was the weirdest thing. The way her money meter had adjusted. How she had gone from spending thirty dollars on a pair of jeans to one hundred, to more. And each incremental increase, as her income had gone up, hadn't really seemed like much of anything at all.

And to think, she'd once been so disdainful of people she thought of as excessive. But she hadn't done much to keep herself from enjoying certain kinds of excess that had come with her success.

She didn't drink, she didn't do drugs and there had been absolutely no sex since parting from Flint, so surely expensive clothes and a new truck were reasonable. Also a new house. And a house for her mother. *Of course* a house for her mother. That had been the most important.

"There's no reason for me to not take the suite," she said.

"Full-service. I'll walk you there."

"You don't need to," she said, holding her hands out for her bag and her guitar. "I'm going to go get settled in."

"All right. Do you want some dinner?"

Her stomach growled. And she really wished it hadn't, because she would like to say that she didn't need dinner, but she had been planning on eating here. The food was wonderful; she remembered that from her last visit. Except...

"Where is the food going to come from?"

"There was a certain amount preprepared by the chef in anticipation of the weather."

"Great. I'll have some of that after I get settled in."

"Well, let me get you your key."

He went behind the counter, the counter that he had been behind when she had first walked in, when he had stood up and nearly given her a heart attack. He took out a key card, and ran it through the device that programmed it before handing it to her.

"Thanks," she said, but his fingertips brushed hers, and she hadn't expected it. And all of the air in her lungs felt like it had been removed. Evaporated.

They just stood there for a moment. And memories swirled through her head. Memories she'd rather not have.

She took a step back. Decisively.

She needed a shower. She needed to get her head on straight. This was all unexpected, and a little bit too much.

She walked up the big, curved staircase—made of the same sort of log as the rest of the big lobby area—and headed down the hall toward the room she had stayed in before.

She unlocked the door, and let herself in. There was a large four-poster bed at the center of the room, done with plush bedding. There was a window seat, which she had spent a lot of time in last time. And a desk in the corner. She set her things down, and opened up her bag. She found her writing notebook, well-worn, but not used recently, and set it on the desk. Then she took her pen out, and...

She pulled out a little neon cactus key chain. It didn't light up anymore—the batteries were dead, and she hadn't been able to bring herself to replace the batteries, because that would be admitting that it mattered to her.

She ran her fingers over it, staring. And then she set it down next to the notebook.

This was the situation she was in. So she might as well embrace it. Might as well live in it.

What else could she do?

CHAPTER FOUR

HE WAITED AN HOUR, and then he went into the kitchen and dug around for one of those preprepared meals. There were strict instructions on how to reheat the steak without overcooking it, and how to plate the meal and all of that. He ignored a good portion of them, because he didn't care about whether or not it looked fancy. But for some reason, he did feel compelled to serve her something that tasted good. Hell, if he was too petty, she'd write a song called "Overcooked Steak" and he'd never hear the end of it.

He stopped for a second, and simply stood there. Tansey was here.

Tansey Martin. The only woman who had ever gotten under his skin.

The woman he had told himself he was outraged at for the last two years.

Outraged because she reminded him of all of the things in himself he hated.

And she was still beautiful.

Hell, it was no mystery why he'd gotten involved with her. *Remember when you didn't think she was your type?*

Yeah. He remembered it vividly. He also remembered the

first time he had tried to hook up after he and Tansey had parted ways. And hadn't been able to muster up even the tiniest bit of interest in the beauty queen he was chatting up. He had ended up going home alone. As he had every night since then.

Two years. It was a hell of a dry spell.

But he was too filled up with demons to want sex. That was the problem.

What you need is an exorcism.

He tried not to think about her, or how beautiful she was, or the fact that they were alone here, and it was pretty much prime time for the sort of exorcism that he was thinking of.

No way. Never again. Not her.

He already knew how that ended.

But you can only ever have relationships that end. So why not?

The carrots finished reheating and he put them on the plate, not caring at all how they were arranged, and then he covered the plate with a big domed lid, and started up the stairs.

He knocked on the door, and a few moments later, she opened it.

Her hair was wet, and she was wearing a white plush bathrobe. It covered everything. From the base of her throat down to her ankles. It was huge on her. But he was so very aware of the fact that she had just been in the shower. He could remember showering with her.

His hands moving over her slick curves… "Dinner," he bit out.

"Oh. I didn't realize it was room service," she said.

"Yeah. This is a fancy ass establishment, Tansey. I figured you knew that. Since you're the resident expert on the place."

He walked in, and looked around, then he saw that the desk had space. But he stopped when he got over there, because her notebook was sitting there, and beside it…

Beside it was the cactus.

Before

HE DIDN'T KNOW what possessed him to buy a little neon cactus, didn't know what possessed him to stick it in the cab of her truck before they departed for the next stop. But he did.

And when she came to find him when they got to Sedona, with the little light hanging from her finger, and a strange expression on her face, he felt something expand inside of him. "What's that?"

"A reminder," he said. "A talisman. Stay prickly. And remember to put a wall up when you get on that horse. Don't think about anything but the ride."

"What does a cactus have to do with a wall, Ace?"

"Because we were in the Cactus when we talked about it," he said.

"Okay. Your symbolism sucks. But I'll hang on to it."

He watched her ride that night; she won. He went to find her after, and gave her a high five. "It was the cactus," he said.

She rolled her eyes. "It was not the cactus."

"It was the damn cactus. You can't prove that it wasn't."

That was how he found himself asking her out for a drink again. This time, they had two beers. Not just the one.

And she didn't put quite so much space between the two of them when they left.

They had three nights in Sedona. She won every single one. On the last night, it was three beers.

"Okay. So now I'm in the second position. But that doesn't mean you're going to buy me boots," she said.

"The hell I won't," he said, jamming his finger on the table. "Have you not figured out that I don't let anyone tell me what to do?"

"I don't know. I haven't really pondered you all that much."

"Liar," he said. It was a little bit more flirtatious than he had been with her.

She wasn't his type.

That was the thing.

But she was awfully damn pretty in the bar light. And just after she finished her ride, even with those fluorescent lights shining down on her. She was pretty in every light—that was the thing.

But not his type.

"I never lie," she said. "Not ever."

"Because your daddy was a liar?"

"I assume he still is. He's not dead, and his mouth is still moving."

"Fair."

"What about you, Flint?" She rarely called him by his name. She usually called him Ace. He didn't know why. He liked it, though. "Are you a liar?"

"I try not to be."

"That's not very definitive."

"How about this. I don't know if I'm a liar or not. Because I don't get close enough to anyone to need to lie."

"I'm not sure I follow."

"You lie to protect yourself, right? You lie to make people think better of you, mostly. I've never needed to do that, because I've never cared enough to do it."

"Well," she said, and suddenly, the bar seemed quieter. "I guess that's about as honest as a person can be."

"Like I said. I try."

He downed the last of his beer and they both got up, walking out the door. This time, it was a little bit farther of a walk to the motel, but they'd decided to walk so they could drink. They took the walk back kind of slow.

For some reason, he stopped. But she seemed to have the same idea he did. He turned to her. The sky above was lit up only with stars, and he could see them reflected in her eyes.

He couldn't remember the last time he'd wanted to kiss a woman. Just kiss. That was what he wanted to do then. He wanted to reach out and cradle her cheek in his hand and feel how soft her skin was. He wanted to lean in and press his mouth to hers, but slowly.

He just wanted to kiss her.

He didn't want to take her back to his motel room. He didn't want... He didn't want anything but to kiss her. She hadn't said that he couldn't kiss her.

"Ace," she whispered. "Please don't."

He took a step back. "Okay."

They started walking again.

"Did you only stop because...because I asked you to stop? Were you going to...?"

"Yeah. To both."

She nodded. And then they reached the motel parking lot. And she beat a hasty retreat toward her room, which was at the opposite end of the complex. And he wondered if he had ruined whatever this was. And for some reason he felt...torn up with regret over that.

He didn't want to lose her.

He knew that much. So he wouldn't let himself be that stupid again.

After

"You still have this," he said.

Tansey looked at him in horror. She hadn't meant to leave that there. But then, she hadn't known that he was going to come here. She hadn't realized that he was actually going to come to her room to bring her dinner. And she felt exposed. She felt unmasked in some strange way.

"Everybody needs a good-luck charm," she said, her heart pounding hard.

"I would've thought that this wasn't a good-luck charm to you anymore."

"Well. That's the thing. You don't know me. Maybe you never really did."

"I think I did," he said, his voice rough.

"Well. Well." She took the lid off the food. "I'm actually not... The thing is, Flint. That was the first relationship that I ever had. You know that. Because I told you a lot of things about myself. It was the first relationship that I ever had, and the first heartbreak that I ever had. Of course I wrote about it. I'm..." She was trying to decide if she was going to outright lie to him or not. "I'm sorry. I didn't consider how it would make you feel when I released the song." That was partly true. Because if she had considered it at all, she'd hoped that it would make him *see*. She'd hoped that it would upset him.

She had hoped that it would show him.

She'd hoped that it would hurt him.

"I only thought about how I felt." What she had felt had been the only thing that mattered. "And I'm not actually invested in people yelling at you on streets. I've never asked anyone to do that, and I've never confirmed that the song is about you for that reason. I don't like any of that. I never asked anyone for it."

She sat down, and took a bite of her steak. "Do you want to have dinner?"

"What?" he asked.

"Let's just have dinner together." She didn't know why she felt compelled to do this. Except...here they were. Thrown together for a reason.

There had to be a reason, right? Fate, or Christmas magic or something.

She did still have the cactus. She needed...something. She needed something to jar her inspiration loose. Being with him these past couple hours she'd had more complicated feelings than she'd had in the past two years.

She felt more alive.

And she might be angry, that was for damn sure, but at least she felt something.

That feeling of wistfulness that she'd had when she'd been

watching him walk in front of her—the feeling he might be a better man than he'd been when they'd broken up, but the man that she had always imagined he *might* be—was the beginning of a song. Was the beginning of something.

It was what she was here for.

And anyway, she knew better now. She wasn't in love with him anymore. Yes, she was still kind of angry. Yes, the hurt was still there. And yes, he was still beautiful. But she knew better now. Intensely, and wholly.

"We can eat downstairs," she said.

She resolutely picked her plate up. "Come on."

"Do you want to get dressed?" he asked.

She suddenly realized she was still in her robe.

"Oh. Yes. I do." She set her plate down. "I'll meet you downstairs?"

"Yeah," he said.

By the time she'd gotten her sweats on, she was resolved. Determined. She was going to use this to find a new angle on their relationship. She was going to use this as a way to heal.

And maybe it would also heal whatever was happening with her music.

Because she needed that. Otherwise that would really mean that the most exciting and wonderful part of her life was over. She had fallen in love and lost it. She had success and it was slipping away...

She pushed those thoughts away.

There was more for her. There was.

Flint Carson was not the end of her road.

But he might be the key to her reclaiming some of her creativity. And she was going to run with that.

Except thinking like that forced her to think back, and the whole time she headed down the stairs, she was thinking about him. And about how tonight paralleled another moment he'd come to her rescue.

Before

SHE FELT LIKE a coward leaving the motel as early as she did, a coward for avoiding Flint. But he'd been about to kiss her. Or he'd at least been *considering* kissing her.

And she'd…she'd panicked. Because she wanted to kiss him. She wanted to kiss him so much it consumed her every waking moment. She couldn't do that. Because…

He's not just a cowboy, though. He's Flint.

He's your friend.

Yes. He had become her friend over these last few days. It seemed improbable and strange. But she liked him. He was the highlight of every day. She…

She was headed down the highway when her truck started to overheat. Persistently.

"Shit," she shouted. She hit the steering wheel with the palm of her hand. "Shit."

Smoke started to pour out the top of the engine and she pulled to the side of the road.

She sat there. And she looked at her phone. No service. No damn service. What the hell was she supposed to do? It was Arizona, and it was hot.

She squinted and looked up ahead. There was a call box, blessed be. She got out of the truck, panic making her move quickly. It was hot, and she had Cinderella in the trailer, and she needed to get gone.

She was halfway between her truck and the call box when she heard the sound of another engine. She stopped and looked behind her. It was a sleek, shiny Chevy pickup, and it pulled sharply off the road behind her.

She ran back toward her truck, ran back… And realized exactly who it was.

"Flint," she said, not knowing if she sounded scared or relieved… Relieved. Overly relieved.

"What happened?"

"I overheated. It's this…this shitty truck. I need a new truck. It's fine."

"Well, if you win…"

"Do not offer to buy me a truck, Flint Carson," she said.

She stuck her finger out toward him, and he grabbed it, and shook it, the contact of his skin against hers making her tremble. She pulled it away, and took a step back.

"Okay, I won't offer," he said.

"Flint…"

"I have an idea. I'll unhitch your trailer, we'll get it hooked up to my truck, and we'll call someone and have them get yours. Then we'll get on the road together so you and your steed aren't sitting here in the heat. How does that sound?"

There was no way to argue with this. She'd tried to avoid him, she'd broken down. He was the one who'd found her.

Maybe it was fate.

"Thank you."

About half an hour later, they were driving down the highway in Flint's truck, with his superior air-conditioning keeping them both cool.

"Lucky I happened down the road when I did."

She could argue. She could say that it wasn't lucky, because there was a call box, and while it would've been a whole thing, she could've handled getting out of there herself. But this was better. And not just because she had been rescued sooner. Because she was with him.

"Yeah. I was lucky. Look, I… I'm sorry." She wanted to fix what happened last night. The way that she had freaked out and overreacted.

"You don't need to apologize to me for anything."

"I was weird about last night. And I was avoiding you. It's why I tried to leave really early today. But apparently we both had the same idea. And thank God," she said.

"It was my mistake. You made yourself clear. I was trying to give myself a loophole. You know, a kiss isn't a one-night stand."

"Now that's a song title," she said.

"It would be a good one."

There was nothing but the sound of the tires on the road. "You really just wanted to kiss me?"

"Right in that moment, yeah. Now, what I would've wanted thirty seconds after that..."

She leaned across the cabin and pushed his shoulder. He was solid and warm, and she could smell soap and his skin, and she regretted all that a little bit.

The touching. It was dangerous.

Why?

She shoved that to the side. She shoved that ridiculous question right to the side, because she knew that it was dangerous. She wanted to be friends with him. He had helped her; their friendship was valuable to her. She enjoyed talking to him, and he had given her the cactus, which now—against her will—seemed to function as a good-luck token.

He had rescued her from the side of the road.

It didn't have to be dangerous, this thing. It didn't have to be wrong or bad. It could be good. But she had to be... It had to be *not* kissing. It had to be friendship.

"I really like you," she said. And she felt so stupid with those words coming out of her mouth. He was a man. A man who had one-night stands. A man who probably didn't have silly girls saying that they liked him.

And when she had said it, she hadn't meant to be confessing that she *liked* him. It had started out as a speech about how he was a really good friend. But the truth was...she liked him. In all the middle school glory that it implied.

It was just that she wanted to be his friend more.

"You're the only real friend that I've made on the circuit," she said. "You're the only friend I've had in a long time."

"Same," he said, his voice sounding rough.

"It just matters a lot to me. This."

And he didn't say anything for at least an hour of the drive.

CHAPTER FIVE

After

WHEN SHE CAME down the stairs, he had his own dinner ready, and had sat down at one of the tables in the dining room. He was still wearing jeans and a short-sleeve shirt, and she was in sweats, no makeup on her face.

He wondered what her adoring fans would think of her now.

They would probably love her for this. Classic Tansey. So down-to-earth.

If he happened to look at the things that people said about her, well. He was only human. He didn't have an endless amount of resistance and restraint where she was concerned. But then, he never had. It had always been… It had always been fraught. She had always been someone that he couldn't look away from. No matter how he couldn't explain it.

"Why exactly did you want to have dinner together?" he asked.

"Because this is ridiculous. Because…because you were an important part of my life, Flint. And now we don't even talk."

"As far as I know, that's how breakups go. Admittedly, I'm not an expert."

"Oh. So you admit that it was a breakup?"

"Yes," he said, his voice rough.

There was no point denying it. Because there was no point denying that they had been entangled in each other in a way he wished they fucking hadn't been. In a way they *shouldn't* have been. In a way he never had been with anyone else, and never would be again.

But here they were, and somehow it was like something entirely different and something altogether the same. Because he hadn't been charming for a single moment since she'd walked into his hotel, and he had no intention of being charming.

He didn't put up the performance for her.

But then, he never had.

She'd never believed it. She didn't buy into the facade that he had put up to interact with the world.

What he knew about himself was that he was a bigger bastard than most people realized.

Boone knew.

Boone knew better than anybody else, and seemed to forgive him for it, but that was kind of what younger brothers were for, he supposed. They had to see you better than you saw yourself. They had to see you better than anybody else did.

Didn't mean that *he* should.

Because Boone knew the truth, and he was still the brother that Flint was closest to.

And Tansey knew the truth.

Without even knowing any of the details of his life, she knew the truth.

Because he had shown her. He had shown her what he did when the chips were down.

Even with all that discomfort, there was something...undeniable about it. His connection to her. The same way there always had been.

Because he was himself when he was with her. Unvarnished and raw and not even bothering with the face he tended to show the world. And it was true now too.

Except she took that and she wrote a song about it. And she might do it again.

"I want... Do you want royalties from the song?" she said, as if she read his mind.

Everything in him rejected that. Everything in him was disgusted by the offer. Outraged by it. "No, I don't want to make any money on that shit," he said. "I don't want to make any money off of the things that you told everybody about us."

There they were, eating really good steak, and not getting along at all, and he had a feeling that wasn't at all what she had expected out of having dinner with him. Or what she had wanted. But here they were. And he was committed to the lack of facade. Because why couldn't they just be honest? Because he had been telling his brothers for two years now that the song wasn't about him. He'd been telling anyone who asked that it wasn't about him.

Part of him had told *himself* that it wasn't.

That she'd made it up. Because she hadn't fought him. She hadn't said any of those things *to* him. So maybe there *had* been another man.

Except he knew he was the first. Except he knew that he was the one.

And he knew that he had her scarf.

He had it here.

Just like she had the cactus. So whatever other stories they told, whatever they had told each other the moment that it had all ended, there were lies buried in there. And that much he knew. Even if he didn't know himself well enough to know what the hell all the lies were. Or what he was supposed to do about them. Because he hadn't known what to do then, and he knew even less of what he was supposed to do now.

Except his feelings were carefully kept behind the wall in his chest that he normally kept them behind. She was here and he was angry. She was here and he thought she was beautiful.

She was here, and they were having dinner in this fancy dining room, with her in sweats and him in his mud-covered boots, and they were fighting.

Whatever it was…it was real, and it was them.

So he was just going with it.

"Is that how you feel? That it was wrong for me to make money off of it?" she asked.

"Yeah. I fucking do. Because it was…"

"You told me it was nothing, Flint."

"And you told me it was fine. So are we going to be angry with each other now for a lack of honesty?"

"That was never why I was angry with you."

"Why *are* you angry with me then?" he asked.

"Because you ended it. I didn't want it to end. And you know what, I was too afraid to tell you that. Because I knew it wouldn't make a difference, and I knew that it would just… expose me. But now here I am sitting with you, and you might be mad at me about the song, but I'm kind of mad at myself about it too, because now you *know*. All the things that I didn't say, all the things that I couldn't say, you know what they are now. The song is the truth."

"The song is *part* of the truth," he said.

She winced. "The song is *my* truth. My feelings. It isn't yours. Only you could write that song."

"Good thing I'm tone-deaf."

"Can I at least do what you…demanded, asked, me to do first? I'll promote the hotel. I'll tell everybody how much I loved it, and that it's under new ownership and… I can make a big song and dance about the fact that I was here during the snowstorm and it was wonderful."

He shrugged. "Yeah, because I might as well get something out of it. And maybe if people know that you were here with me, they'll stop yelling at me on streets."

"Yes. Fine. That seems fair." Silence lapsed between them, and she stabbed the carrot with her fork and took a bite of it. "You're going to quit riding rodeo, aren't you?"

"What makes you say that?" he asked.

"Because of what you told me. About focus. About goals. About how you couldn't want anything else as long as you were trying to win. So this is what you want now? This is what you're trying to win?"

"Yes. You know, I have a trust fund. But I wanted to make sure I didn't use it for this. I don't want my dad's success. I want my own. And inescapably, my success is going to be built on some of that. I can't erase the advantages I got from him. Because my winnings that come from the rodeo... I was in the rodeo because of him."

"But you won because of you."

He didn't know quite what to do with that. With that kind word from her, because it was as real as any of the mean ones, but he wasn't sure why she had bothered to give it to him.

"I didn't really choose it, though. So now I decided to have something that I chose. I decided to make sure that it could be something that I wanted. That I was..." He was going to say that he was proud of. He wasn't sure that he was proud of a damn thing. Because what everything came back to was... This was something he *could* do.

He was fine enough at doing things.

It was why he'd worked for his family all those years. Because he could.

Feeling? Being there for someone emotionally? That was beyond him.

Something had broken inside of him a long time ago, and he didn't even have the desire to fix it. If something could have, it would've been Tansey.

But he hadn't wanted her to fix it then any more than he wanted it fixed now.

So maybe proud was a bridge too far for anything that he was going to do.

"I wanted something that was mine," he said.

And that much was true.

Because a man had to have land. His own. And his own achievements to stand on.

She nodded. "I understand that. You know...you know that I joined the rodeo to show my dad. And you know that I... I wanted to be successful and famous to show him. He doesn't care, Flint." She swallowed hard, and looked away. "He asked me for money. He found me, of course, not when I was barrel racing, no, nothing like that. He found me when I was really successful. When I might have something to give him. And you know... I couldn't figure out what I wanted to do. If I wanted to hold the fact that I had money and he didn't over his head and deny him. Or give it to him so that he would need me." She wasn't looking at him. She was looking past him. "Neither reason was very good motivation. Both make me...kind of a terrible person."

"What did you do?"

She swallowed hard. "I gave it to him. But not so I can hold it over his head. I gave it to him because... I just wanted it to not mean anything. And for him to not matter. If I withheld it, it was admitting I was angry. There was no way for me to really win. So I gave him money. Payment for the emotional scarring that produced the music, except I didn't say that. I didn't want to give him any credit for it. He never mentioned it. I think if he had known that the song was actually about him, like if he had known that it was autobiographical, he wouldn't have asked for money."

"He knew you were famous, but he's never listened to your music."

"No."

"Well. He's a special kind of asshole. Even I listened to my expert takedown."

"You thought *he* deserved it, at least that's what you said when you heard the song."

"I didn't say I *didn't* deserve it, Tansey," he said. "I said I didn't like it."

And that was the truth. It was a strange thing, this conversation. These honesty pitfalls. The fact that he remembered too keenly how much he had liked her.

It was easy to let all the pain that had come after that erase the friendship. His genuine affection for her. It was easy to tell himself it had all been some kind of sexual fever dream, followed by an immature tantrum on her part.

That was a lie.

He'd been in too deep with her. And it had not been his imagination. He couldn't deny it. Not now.

It was way too easy to remember the good times. To remember that friendship as the foundation, and the way that had shifted. The way it had shifted under his feet without him making the decision to let it.

Because he knew better. That was the thing. He had never in his life let himself get drawn into a relationship with a woman because he knew he didn't have the capacity to give a woman what she needed. He had always known that marriage and children weren't for him. He had known that since he was fourteen years old. And he had never, ever crossed those lines; he had never done anything that he was ashamed of with a woman. Not until her.

But he knew why it happened.

Because of her. Because there was something about her. And in the end, he supposed it wasn't all that surprising that she'd ended up famous. If he couldn't look away from her, it stood to reason the whole world couldn't look away from her.

He gritted his teeth. And he tried not to remember. He really did try to not remember.

Before

IT TURNED OUT that her truck was effectively blown up, and while she absolutely refused to let him buy her a new one, she did concede to the fact that while she sorted it all out, she was going to need a ride. And he offered to be that ride. They would be driving from Utah to Nevada over the next few days, and they'd be taking the road trip together. All that would be fine if he didn't still want to kiss her. And if she hadn't been very clear that it wasn't going to happen.

I really like you.

He couldn't remember the last time a woman had said that to him.

I want you, sure.

But not *I really like you.*

He liked her too.

It was a hell of a thing.

He took his position back behind the gates to watch her event, and his heart was pounding harder than it did when it was his turn to ride.

When she rode, she rode spectacular, and it put her right up in the number-one spot.

When she got off, and came out of the gate, he pulled her in for a hug, lifting her up off the ground.

"Easy there, Ace," she said, her arms wrapped around his neck. He put her down, and kept holding on to her. She kept holding on to him.

"Tansey…"

She looked around, then stretched up on her toes, and kissed his cheek.

It was so innocent. A butterfly kiss. A whisper.

And it made him hard as a rock, instantly.

She was not his type.

He would do well to remember that.

She turned beet red, then ducked her head and extricated herself from his hold.

This time, when she went back to put her horse away, he did help with her tack, and he didn't accept any argument. He was driving her back to the motel. Because they were riding together. And once they were safely ensconced in the truck cab, all the tension that bloomed between them felt like too much to handle.

What was this? He had no idea what the hell it meant. No idea what the hell was happening. He wasn't...

Did he have a *crush* on this woman?

That was the weirdest damn thing.

He couldn't accept that.

They pulled into the motel parking lot and he put the truck in Park, then turned the keys off and pulled them out of the ignition.

"Wait."

Tansey put her hand on his. He froze. And looked at her.

She scooted across the distance of the truck cab, and put her hand on his cheek.

He just sat. Perfectly still. And he let her decide what to do next. He let her choose.

She leaned across the space, and she pressed her mouth to his. Tentative. Soft.

He sat completely still. And waited. She lifted her other hand, held the other side of his face and pressed more firmly against him, and that was when he wrapped his arms around her waist, pulling her closer to him, angling his head and deepening the kiss.

She made a muffled sound, wrapping her arms around his neck.

She kissed him back, all enthusiasm, no skill. He slid his tongue between her lips, and she returned fire, kissing him like she would die if she didn't.

It was all he could do to keep his hands still. To just keep holding her, rather than letting his palms move over her curves, not pushing his fingertips up beneath her shirt.

It was a temptation. It was a real damn temptation.

But there was something beautiful about letting the kiss just...be a kiss.

He thought he might drown in it. Thought he might die. He had no idea how long it went on. Just kissing her. Holding her. Lust was a drumbeat through his whole body. But the moment...

The *moment*.

He lifted his head. "You don't happen to have that cactus on you, do you?"

She laughed. The press of her breasts against his chest as she giggled making him groan.

"Why did you ask about the cactus?"

"Because nothing mattered but the moment."

She let out a long, slow breath. Her eyes looked a little unfocused, her lips swollen. And they were very close to his motel room. Normally, that would be the assumption. He didn't kiss a woman just to kiss her.

But he had to let the kiss with Tansey just be a kiss. Because it needed to be. It just did.

"You did good tonight," he said. "The barrel racing. I'm not grading you here. But that was good too."

She laughed and lowered her head. "Thank you."

He leaned in and kissed her. Shorter this time. "I need to tell you good night," he said.

"Why?"

He gave her a meaningful look. "Because I need to. I'm trying to be good."

"Oh," she breathed.

"I'll see you tomorrow."

And he didn't know how any of this had happened. How they had gone from friendship to this.

They might be... Hell. He might be dating her.

He didn't know what he thought about that.

But he also knew that he wasn't willing to let her go. And that told him quite a bit.

After

YEAH. THAT WAS the problem. He had known. He had known that he was getting in too deep. He had known that he was walking into something he had no right to walk into.

And there was no excuse for him. There was no getting older and wiser. Because it was about him. It was about what he had to give.

And sitting across from her now, he could feel the echo of unfinished business inside of him. Except it wasn't. They'd drawn a line under it because that was what they'd had to do.

Maybe that had always been one of the issues with the song. Maybe one of the issues with the song had always been that it showed him the line hadn't actually been drawn where he thought.

Because he'd been convinced that he got out of it before he devastated her. And it was a lie; he knew that. But that was part of the problem. He thought that he had a pretty good handle on who he was. But it turned out he wasn't as strong as he thought when it came to his resolve. And he'd been convinced that he just knew himself. That his resolve was what had kept him from those relationships, when in fact his resolve had had nothing to do with it. There had never been a woman that compelled him. And the minute she'd been there…he turned away from everything he knew. Everything he knew that he had to do to keep someone safe from him.

Maybe the real issue was that as much as she hated him, it had made him hate himself even more.

"I keep waiting," she said. "To feel triumphant. I keep waiting. I had pretty great revenge on you, you have to admit that."

"I thought you said you didn't think about how I would feel."

"I did. I wanted to hurt you. I wanted to find a way to hurt you, because I looked at you in the face and… I didn't hurt you. I couldn't hurt you. And I hated that. I wanted to."

"That's the problem," he said. "You can't get to me like that."

"That's what I don't understand. I don't understand why."

"Let's just call it a night," he said, pushing his plate back to the center of the table.

"Why?"

"Because the point of this wasn't to rehash what we were. I thought the point of it was to find some common ground now."

"Yes. I guess so. But I… I gave you everything, you know that. I gave you everything. And…" She swallowed hard. "I guess it just doesn't matter, does it? But part of me wanted to hurt you. To take even half of what you took from me away from you."

"If you want the fucking scarf, you can have the scarf."

"I don't care about the scarf," she said. "It was never about the scarf."

"Are you going to tell me the scarf is a metaphor, because I *literally* have your scarf, so I think you know it isn't."

"No, the scarf doesn't matter. It's just part of a lie that you told. That I didn't matter, because if you do have it, if you can really give it back to me, then why? Why do you have it at all?"

Rage welled up inside him. And other emotions he didn't want to examine.

Couldn't.

"I have it," he ground out. "Because the idea of getting rid of it feels like cutting my arm off. Are you happy about that? Is that what you want to hear?"

She sat back, and he just stared. He didn't know why the hell he'd said any of that.

"I will go get you your scarf."

He pushed the chair back, and stepped away, and he didn't look back at her.

CHAPTER SIX

Before

SHE HELD HER breath while she watched him ride. She always did. But he was always perfect. But last night she'd kissed him, and somehow things felt…really tangled up now. But that kiss had been…everything she'd ever imagined a kiss might be. No, she had never kissed anyone before that night. Before him.

She hadn't wanted to.

Was that really all she was going to do? *Really?* Was she *really* just going to…kiss him?

She couldn't afford to be distracted. Not right now. She couldn't afford to be derailed.

Maybe she was even on the verge of something with her music. And the last thing she needed was…

All the dire consequences her mother had ever told her about what happened when you got with men who were far too pretty for their own good rolled through her.

She knew better. She did. They opened the chute, and the bull with Flint on his back tore out of there.

She held her breath, but he didn't make it eight seconds. It was only four. And he was on the ground.

"Oh shit," she said, her hand going up over her mouth.

Sure, he got another chance. Another ride.

But she'd never seen him fall.

He got up and shook it off, went back and got back on. The gate opened again, and out he went. This time he stayed on, but only barely. And his score was... It wasn't good.

It hadn't been a clean ride.

She greeted him at the back of the gates, right when he came through. "What happened?" she asked.

"I was thinking about something else," he said.

And everything in her went still.

They just stood there and looked at each other. There was space between them, but it felt filled. With something. Something big. Bigger than maybe the two of them.

"Oh," was all she could say.

"You better win," he said. "One of us has to."

She did win.

It didn't really matter that much. And maybe that was the thing. It didn't matter; he did.

They ended up in his truck again, kissing like they might die if they didn't.

This time, his hands moved. Rough, up under her shirt, moving along the line of her spine. She arched against him, and when he pushed his fingertips beneath the band of her bra, she stopped. "Flint... I have to... I haven't done this before."

He froze. "You haven't done what?"

"I haven't had sex. I'm not... I'm not ready."

He slowly released his hold on her. "Okay," he said slowly. "I didn't... I didn't realize that."

"I know. Because I didn't tell you. Can we still kiss?"

"Yes," he said. "Definitely can."

"Okay. I don't... Just not yet."

She just needed to be more sure. Of her feelings. Of his. Of everything. She was just afraid.

"My dad really hurt me," she said. "And yes. I get that I'm a cliché. I get that it's like…a whole lot of daddy issues. But I'm aware of them. I'm trying to not…"

"Okay. It's okay."

But they didn't kiss again. Not that night. Instead, he walked her to the door of her room, gave her hand a squeeze before he left her there.

But the following night, they were right back in his truck, and just before his mouth met hers, she tried to lighten it. "No sex yet, Ace."

"Noted."

But the kissing was hotter this time. Longer. A wildfire that seemed like it was on the verge of burning out of control.

She wasn't aware of when she had pulled his shirt off of him, but at some point she did, and was moving her hands over his chest, down his back, and that was how she found herself laid across the bench seat in the pickup truck, her legs parting easily for him to settle between, and she could feel the hard ridge of his arousal up against her. She rocked herself against him, and then shook her head. "I'm not… I'm not ready for…"

"Okay," he said, breathing hard. "It's okay."

"I'm sorry," she said, terror warring with need. She wanted him so much, but she already cared about him far more than she was able to deal with or admit. If she actually let him inside of her body…

She just had to be sure she knew what she was doing. Sure she knew how she was…arranging all this inside herself.

And what if…?

What if she got pregnant? That was what happened to her mother.

It had just been an endless stream of heartbreak not only for her, but for Tansey as well.

There were consequences to this, and for the very first time, she felt somewhat sympathetic toward her mother, and her place in all of this, because apparently, charming cowboys were a lot harder to resist than she could have ever imagined. She had thought that *knowing* was enough.

But knowing *about* cowboys was different than knowing Flint.

"Do you want to come?"

It took her a second to realize what he was asking. His voice was hard like gravel, and she was desperate. Sensitized all over.

"Do I want to…? Oh. But I can't… Flint, I'd… You…"

"Not about me. I want to make you feel good. But only if you want me to. We don't have to have sex. But do you want to come?"

"Yes," she said.

"Can I?" He put his hand on the button of her jeans.

She shivered. "Yes."

He undid the button, then the zipper, and moved his hand slowly beneath the waistband of her panties. She wiggled as his rough fingertips made contact with her very, very slick flesh. She moaned as his skin made contact with hers. As white-hot desire rolled through her. He began to stroke her. Her hips moved in time with his fingers, and she let her head fall back. "You're so pretty," he said.

And that was it. It sent her straight over the edge. She cried out as her climax slammed into her. She found herself immobilized by it, as wave after wave pulsed through her.

She was left spent and breathless in the aftermath.

He buttoned her jeans, zipped them back up. And then moved away from her, straightened up, there in front of the steering wheel, and put his face in his hands.

"Flint…"

"Just a second." He let out a slow breath. "You might kill me," he said.

"I don't want to kill you."

"I don't think you're going to have to try." She pushed herself into a sitting position. "Are you okay?"

"I'm great. I'm…" Her voice came out unsteady. She felt like she was going to cry. But she was good. She felt good. Well. Her body felt good. She felt like she needed to go lie down on the floor and curl up in a ball and wail about all these emotions that she didn't fully understand. That was what she felt like.

"I've never had sex with a virgin. I mean… Not saying that's what… I just don't want to do anything you don't want. I don't want to push you."

"You didn't push me. You didn't push me at all. You… I wanted it."

And she felt weird about it. And like she should've maybe offered him something. Except she knew that if she did, he would get irritated. It would sound like a transaction. She knew that he didn't want that.

"I'll walk you to the door."

They got out of the truck, and her legs still felt like Jell-O. She still felt unsteady.

And so she turned to him, and just pressed her body against his. He wrapped his arms around her, and just held her steady. And she had never felt quite so safe in all her life.

And she pushed against the emotion that was rising up inside of her.

"What is this?" she asked.

He shook his head. "I'm not really sure."

"We should call it something."

"Wilbur?"

"Oh, shut up."

She punched him in the shoulder.

"What did you have in mind?"

"A fling," she said, her heart pounding.

"I'm not sure you can have a fling without sex," he pointed out.

"Well…well, I'm not saying we won't. But maybe we should agree that it…that it will run its course and when it does, we're both okay with it. You said you don't… And I mean, I have all those goals."

"And you don't want to depend on a man," he reminded her.

"No, I don't," she said.

"Then it's a fling."

She nodded.

"Good night," she whispered.

"Good night."

After

SHE JUST SAT at the table, immobile. Frozen. Her mind caught in a cascade of memories from the past. When things had been easy with him. When things had been beautiful with him. When they had kissed like it was inevitable, and she had hoped.

But he had her scarf.

It doesn't matter. None of it matters. Because you know where this ends.

Yeah. And she was beginning to feel like one of her favorite genres of country song. The one where you felt tempted to sleep with an ex that you shouldn't touch. But...

Yeah. It was tempting.

Not that he'd made any kind of gesture that indicated he was interested in doing that. She had to make sure not to confuse the intensity of the feelings that she felt around him, and the way that it picked at her creativity with actual desires.

She was smarter than that. She knew better than that. She was not the same girl that she'd been the first time she met him.

She heard footsteps and looked up. He was standing in the doorway of the dining room, and he was holding it in his hands. And it was the weirdest thing. Because she had actually forgotten what the scarf looked like.

Because it didn't really matter.

It wasn't the point. It had been literal, but it had been a metaphor.

It was the one thing she had put in the song that held hope.

She'd hoped he'd kept it. That he hadn't just thrown it out.

That it was everything he'd said. That he hadn't been able to throw it away because it had felt like finishing something.

Ending it.

And yes, they had ended it.

But it wasn't over for her. Not really. And she wondered if it wasn't really over for him either.

"Here," he said. He extended his hand and she stood up, walking over to him. Her footsteps were somehow muted and loud at the same time. And she reached out and took hold of the edge, but he didn't release his hold on it easily. Or quickly.

Until he did.

"Feels better to give it back to you than to get rid of it."

She studied this man, and tried to figure out…who he really was. Because he claimed he didn't do emotions or connections. And he claimed he wasn't sentimental. And God knew she had experienced the destruction of what it was like when he was finished with the relationship.

Yes.

She had been destroyed by that.

But this man… The one standing there holding on to her scarf like it meant something. The man who had it with him on… He didn't live here. He had packed it to come here. For this day. For this business trip.

And you have the cactus he gave you.

Yes. And everything else.

She wondered how many women he'd had. How many women he'd kissed since he'd last kissed her.

There hadn't been anyone for her.

Suddenly, it was far too easy to remember all those old feelings. Far too easy to feel them. Far too easy to simply exist in them. Like no time had passed at all. Like he was still her lover, and not the man who had broken her.

She had tried so hard to turn it into a kind of complicated destiny. That if she hadn't been with him, she wouldn't have the song. She had turned it into an integral step in her life.

But it didn't feel like that here. It just felt like regret.

And like unfinished business.

Except maybe that was the story she was telling herself now because he was there and he was beautiful. And she still wanted him, no matter how much she tried to tell herself she didn't. It was painful. It immobilized her. She suddenly ached with it. Was on fire with it. And thought that it might burn her alive.

But it wasn't the kind of heat that they'd experienced when it had been new. When she'd been terrified and trembling, but so in need of it.

She knew. And she wanted it anyway.

Wanted *him* anyway.

So she took a step back, clinging to the scarf. "Thank you. For this." She wanted to forget everything. Everything that she knew.

About him. About heartbreak. About pain. She wanted to forget all of it. And jump into something she knew she shouldn't.

But she kept remembering all those times back then. When he'd made it very clear when she brought up sex that he wasn't offering.

Except he had wanted it.

No. Don't go there.

"I'm tired," she said. "I'll go... I'll go to my room now."

"Yes. See you tomorrow."

"See you tomorrow."

CHAPTER SEVEN

HE COULDN'T SLEEP. He couldn't sleep because all he could do was think of her. He couldn't sleep because everything kept rolling through him like a thunderstorm. Memories, things from the past, and need from now.

He got out of bed quickly, and went over to the window, looking out at the snow falling below. It was coming down thicker and harder now, and the wind was unforgiving.

They could be stuck up here for days. And he...he didn't know what the hell he was supposed to do with that.

He didn't know why he'd shown her the scarf, except... Maybe it was the penance that he needed to make. Because he could see that he hurt her.

Not that he didn't know that. He'd known that ever since the song had come out.

You knew it before.

But the fact was, this was another of those moments. Where he could turn back, or he could take a step forward, a step into something he knew wasn't a good idea.

Just like he'd done back then.

Before

THEY DID A little more talking than kissing after that. It was a good thing. Because she needed to take it slow, and he understood that. He still wasn't quite sure what was happening between them. Not really. What the point of it was. Where it was going.

He didn't want to think about it. He was good at that. *Not* thinking about it. He hadn't lied to her when he'd said he was very good at putting up walls.

He was so good at it, he didn't quite know how to take them down. And he figured that was all right.

They both ended up winning top spot in their events for the season.

And he bought her the boots. Before they ever left the final event in Vegas.

"I told you not to do that," she said.

"Yeah. Well, I did."

"What are you going to do now?" she asked.

"I'm headed out to the coast for a few days." He always went and stayed in one of his parents' properties when the season was out. A little time to breathe between going and working the ranch and all the hard traveling and riding that happened all season long. "You should come with me."

He didn't know why he asked her to do that any more than he knew the why of anything from the past couple of months. Why he was making out with this girl who wasn't his type. Talking to her for hours every night. Thinking about her all the time.

"Yeah, all right. But I'm still not having sex with you, Ace."

"Didn't ask you to." A smile tugged at the corner of his mouth. He wasn't even upset about it. He was a little physically frustrated, but he wasn't mad. Not even a little.

Because like everything else with her, the fling was unpredictable.

And he liked that best of all.

After

SHE COULDN'T SLEEP. She paced around the room, and then for some reason, opened the door. She crept down the hall. It was silent. The building was huge. She didn't even know where he was sleeping. And the odds were, it wasn't anywhere near her.

It was strange to be in such a big place like this with nobody in it.

Nobody but him. And somehow she felt his presence looming large as if they were staying in a tiny house.

She huffed. And continued down the stairs, into the lobby. The lights were off.

She looked around, up at the tall, arched ceiling with beams extending across it. The dim chandelier. And then she continued on toward the large windows that faced out over what she knew was a beautiful view in the daylight.

She could hardly see anything, it was so dark. But she could make out the swirling of snowflakes coming down.

She touched the window, and felt that it was freezing cold.

They had never been in snow together. They had spent the summer together. A summer that had been full of heat and longing.

A summer full of lies that she had told herself. But the truth was, he'd never lied to her.

She'd broken her own heart.

Even after two years she couldn't quite figure out how to make it beat normally again.

She sat down on the couch by the window, holding her notebook in her lap. And she started to write.

A prayer, really, more than a song. For what she wished could have been. For who she wished he could be, and who she wished she could be for him.

Somebody, someday would be enough to tear down the walls in his heart. She was only sorry that it wasn't her.

A tear slipped down her cheek. She had really thought that she was done crying over Flint Carson.

She'd thought that it had scabbed over.

That she had come to a place of reconciliation with it.

But he was here. And the problem was finding out that her feelings weren't anywhere near as different now from then as she would like them to be.

She closed her eyes, and she let herself remember. Because maybe that would jolt her back to reality. Maybe that would remind her.

It was so easy to remember that summer. To remember the beginning. To remember the end.

CHAPTER EIGHT

Before

THE HOUSE WAS BEAUTIFUL. They had driven separately, so that they could go their separate ways after, because it made the most sense, after all. They still weren't claiming to be a couple or anything like that. They were friends who kissed a lot.

And she was still trying to sort through her feelings for him. Or rather, trying desperately to come up with something to call him that wasn't as terrifying as the word that seemed to echo inside of her whenever she thought of him.

She'd brought her guitar, and she was looking forward to spending a little bit of time working on her music. They'd reached pretty much a dead end with her demo, but she knew that was just how it went. They had gotten a couple of completely unknown internet radio stations to play her songs, but nothing big. And definitely no interest from labels.

She wasn't used to being on the coast. She got out of her truck and looked around: there were big, tall pines surrounding the house, and it was up on the edge of a sheer rock face, overlooking the great, pounding sea. The roar of it was intense, beautiful.

The front door to the house opened, and Flint stepped outside. Barefoot. She didn't know why that was notable. Only that it was. It felt intimate. She was wearing her boots. The ones he had bought her. She hadn't been able to help herself. But at least she hadn't let him buy her a new truck. She just fixed the old one. That was reasonable.

"Glad you're here."

She smiled. "Me too."

Her room was on the second floor, and had a breathtaking view of the ocean. It was also not his room. Which was fair. Because she had told him that she wasn't having sex with him. So of course he'd given her a separate room.

But she was starting to feel like holding on to her virginity was more of a habit than anything she actually wanted.

She wanted him.

And it was so difficult to figure out how much of that was weakness or giving in to something, or being just like all the people who didn't know better. When she was supposed to know better.

Know better than what?

He was a good man. He'd been nothing but a good man to her. He hadn't pressured her into anything. Quite the opposite. He was being so respectful it was… It wasn't like anything she'd ever been warned about; that was for sure. Her mother had told her that men only wanted one thing. But Flint seemed to want to talk to her, buy her cacti and boots and kiss her. Let her stay in a beautiful beach house. Share meals with her. Share drinks with her. Flint seemed to want a lot of things from her. And he gave a lot of things to her.

There was no map for this. Not in her experience. And maybe not in her mother's experience either. It was okay that her mother would be wary. Upset about this. There were reasons she hadn't told her mother that she was here. Reasons that she had never mentioned Flint to Darlene Martin.

But she had never known a man like Flint. Tansey never had before either. She couldn't compare him to dire warnings that had nothing to do with him. He wasn't just a cowboy. He was Flint Carson.

And he was everything.

But he couldn't be what she stood on, what she leaned against. That didn't mean he couldn't be everything for right now.

For their fling.

She wanted to laugh and cry.

By the time she finished putting her things away and came downstairs, he had set a beautiful dinner out on the terrace. Right over the ocean waves.

"Did you cook?"

"My parents had this house for a long time, and knowing what to do with fresh seafood is awfully helpful. So yes. I did. But doing a crab boil is pretty basic."

"This does not seem basic. This is extremely fancy."

He poured her a glass of wine, and she felt like this was a life she had never even dreamed of. She wanted to know more about him, though. He was very good at asking her questions about herself. And he certainly alluded to certain things about him. But he didn't open up all that easily.

"So you won," she said. "Does that mean you'll be back again next year, or...?"

"Most likely. I don't really have anything else to do. What about you?"

"Well. Since nobody was all that interested in my demo song, and it certainly isn't going to pay the bills, I guess I'll keep riding for another couple of years." She shrugged. "It's okay. Wanting to get into the music industry is... It's very unlikely. I don't have any connections or anything like that. So... I don't see it as something that would be terribly easy. And definitely not something that's just going to happen."

"I've never even heard you sing."

She didn't want him to turn it around on her. Not just yet. "How come you're so good at hiding your emotions, Flint?"

"Practice?"

"But why? I guess what I don't get is… You don't really tell me that much. I mean, you're vague. You like to ask me questions, and you let me talk about myself, which is… It's nice. Sort of like therapy. But with a really good-looking man. But what about you?"

He lifted his wineglass and looked out at the ocean. It was strange to see him like this. The sun setting out on the sea, at a family home. They weren't in a cheesy motel or a bar. Or the cab of his truck. There was no one around. It was just different. And she felt different.

"What about me?"

"You never talk about yourself."

"There's not much to say," he said, and there was something in that smile that seemed false. It seemed very clear now, that the man she had met that first night, and the man she was looking at now, was a character. She had seen real pieces of Flint in the time since then. But this…this was a put-on.

The whole charming thing he did. The whole devil-may-care thing. She had seen moments of real emotion in him, but they weren't accompanied by revelations. The way that he gave her advice, that was real. The way that he listened to her, the way that he cared for her.

The care that he showed by respecting her boundaries, all of that was real.

But it also kept them protected and safe.

She wanted to find a way to get through those walls. But she was at a loss as to how.

Because here they were, theoretically temporary, so why should she be able to get through those walls? Why should he give her anything? She didn't know the answer to that.

And she didn't know if wanting to break them down was particularly fair.

She had plenty of her own defenses, so she understood that. She might not do such a great job of repressing her emotions, but the whole thing with him… Not sleeping with him… Holding herself back from him... Well, that definitely had to do with her dad.

With being afraid.

Because they'd said it was a fling, but now things felt different for her, and she wanted to be blasé and sophisticated and basically the most okay with the fact that this would have an end, but she didn't know if she could be.

It didn't make her want to leave, though.

She wanted to do something, give him something. To find a way to make him open up to her the way she had him. She wanted to know him. Know him like he knew her. But she didn't know what to do. So she just sat with him. There was a firepit out on the deck, and he started it up, and they sat on the couch there, and just sat together.

Not speaking.

They did that a few nights, things getting fairly hot and heavy in front of the fire more often than not.

It was harder and harder to not just join him in bed every night.

But she just wanted to be sure.

Do you? Or are you just scared?

Well. She didn't really have an answer for that. Because she was scared. She did know that. She just didn't know if that fear was smart, or if it was holding her back.

She got out her guitar that night when they sat by the fire, and started to pluck the strings.

"Play me a song."

And she knew exactly which one she wanted to play. The one she had never played for anyone.

"All right. This is some... This one's called 'Taillights.'"

The thing I remember most of all is the taillights on your truck
When you drove away from me and Mom, you said we weren't enough

I remember the taillights most of all
If you were ever there on birthdays, it doesn't matter now
If you ever sang me to sleep, I really can't recall
It's the taillights, from when you drove away

Her heart ached as she sang the song. As she poured every-thing of herself into the phrasing. Because when she'd written those words, she'd bled for them.

It was the very end that flipped it.

Someday, I hope you're sitting in a crowded bar, and you look out the window
And you'll see my taillights
In a car that's way fancier than anything you could ever afford
And you'll think of all those times
Of those missed birthdays, and when you should've said good night
Every time you see taillights, you'll think of me.
And I won't think of you at all

She stopped, and wiped a tear off of her cheek.

"You need to record that," he said.

"I don't have anything I'd…"

"No. Just like that. Just you and the guitar. Send that to your manager. And have them share that. It's amazing, Tansey."

"I don't know about that…"

"No. It really is. You should do it while you're here. We've got another week."

"Okay. I'll do it."

She did that night, and uploaded the file for her manager to grab. It wasn't professional, there weren't other instruments, it wasn't as good production-wise as the other song they had sent out, so she really didn't expect anything to come of it. And it wasn't what she was focused on right now anyway.

The next day they went to the local coffee shop, and as they walked down the street, he held her hand. And that was when she knew. It was when she really knew. That it was right. That she was ready. Because it wasn't just kissing, or fraught moments in the cab of his truck. It was holding hands. On the street. For anyone to see, and yeah, neither of them lived here, and no one knew who they were, but it was the principle of the thing.

It was the gesture that was just about touching. Just about being linked. Not about anything else. And she loved it.

Because she loved him.

It terrified her to think that. It broke the rules to feel it.

And she was willing to throw every last bit of caution that she had held in her chest into that coastal wind, and let it fly out into the sea. Because the world could keep all that, as long as she could keep him.

They had dinner out on the deck like they had done every night, kissed by the fire, and then he excused himself to go to bed. And she sat there.

For one breath. Two. Three.

And then she went after him. She took a deep breath and opened the door to his room, crossed the space and got into bed beside him. He sat up, looking at her. And she curved her arm around his neck and leaned in, kissing him on the mouth.

"Tansey," he said. "I am all about not pushing you to do anything. I am very committed to not pressuring you... Getting into my bed is maybe a bridge too far."

"I'm actually here for sex, Ace," she said, pressure and need building in her chest until she thought she might die of it.

"Well, that's something," he said.

She kissed him, his mouth that was so familiar now, but it was like falling. Knowing that it wasn't going to stop here. Knowing that it was going to keep on. That every desire inside of her would be answered tonight. That he would be inside of her tonight. It made her shiver, shake. He was already wearing nothing but boxer shorts, and he drew her up against his body, taking her shirt and stripping it up over her head. He made quick work of her bra, and he had already touched her between her legs once, so she wasn't really embarrassed.

And...why should she be?

They cared about each other. They had built to this. This wasn't a one-night stand with a stranger; this man had sat and talked with her.

He knew her.

She couldn't feel embarrassment in front of him. Not when he was...he was the one.

It made her feel jittery and strung out to even think such a thing, to believe in something she had told herself she didn't. Except maybe the problem was, maybe the issue all along was that she had always imagined that she would be one and done. That when she felt comfortable enough with a man to be with him this way, it would be love.

And that losing it would be devastation.

Would be something she would never be able to recover from.

He moved his thumbs over her nipples, and she gasped, arching her back, pressing her bare breasts to his chest. Oh, his chest. And suddenly, a surge of excitement went through her, because she had been thinking about being naked in front of him, and processing whether or not she was going to be embarrassed. But she hadn't thought about seeing him naked.

And that...

She hooked her thumbs in the waistband of his boxer shorts, and pulled them down. Throwing the covers back, and exposing his body to her gaze.

"Well, holy shit," she said.

"That's not exactly a song lyric," he said, his voice gruff.

"You're really hot," she said.

"Glad you approve."

She reached out tentatively, and wrapped her fingers around his thick arousal. He was glorious. Beautiful.

She squeezed him.

"Fuck," he said.

"See, it is a song. Just one only we're ever going to listen to."

He chuckled, and pulled her against him. He kissed her neck, down her collarbone, taking one nipple into his mouth and sucking hard. And it was better than just putting her fingertips on his cheek so that she could feel his stubble; his whiskers burned all over the tender skin of her chest.

It was intimate. Real and intense in a way she had never imagined this could be.

She felt like all her desires were somewhat childish. Or something she didn't quite understand. She got it now. She didn't know why the Tansey before this moment had been afraid. That girl hadn't understood. How right it would feel. How perfect.

She hadn't known just how wonderful it could be. She hadn't understood.

How easy, how right it was, when it was the person. The one.

But he knew her. The dark and ugly things. Her petty little heart and how much she wanted revenge on her father, how profoundly she'd been hurt by him.

How afraid she was. He knew those things. He knew those things and he seemed to just like her anyway. The way that she was.

And when he took the rest of her clothes off, and put his hand between her thighs, she cried out, not just because of the pleasure, but because of the overwhelming sensation of the emotion that was flooding her body.

Because it was deeper than desire. More than arousal.

He pushed a finger inside of her and she flexed her hips, trying to acclimate to the unfamiliar sensation. She liked it; it was just not…not something she'd experienced before.

He put a second finger in and began to thrust in and out of her gently, allowing her body to get used to him.

And then, very suddenly, she felt pleasure break over her like a wave, her internal muscles pulsing around him. She cried out, and he withdrew from her, then put his fingers in his mouth, sucking on them, slow and leisurely, like he was savoring the taste of her. And she shivered. "I have been waiting for this," he said.

He moved down her body and grabbed hold of her thighs, then he pushed them out wide, lowering his head to her center and tasting her deep. Long. She clung to him, forking her fingers through his hair and holding him there. Arching her body against him as she writhed with need. He pushed his fingers back inside her again as he teased her with his lips, his tongue. She couldn't breathe. Couldn't think. Couldn't do a damn thing but submit to the onslaught of pleasure.

She lost herself. In the absolute wave of need. In the wildness of her desire. And as she lay there spent, he moved away from her, going into the adjoining bathroom for a moment and returning with a box of condoms.

She was torn between...indignation, a lot of questions and relief.

"I'm an optimist," he said, by way of explanation. "And anyway, it's better safe than sorry."

"Well. I guess that is true."

He chuckled, tearing the box open, and then taking a strip out, tearing an individual condom from the strip. And then opening it quickly. He took care of the necessities, and then joined her back on the bed. He pressed his forehead to hers, and kissed her, deep and long. "Ready?"

She nodded, words deserting her entirely. He pressed himself inside of her, inch by inch, filling her. And the emotion that swamped her was almost too much to bear. It was beautiful. Wonderful. And so much more. This wasn't just about pleasure. Not just about satisfaction. Flint was inside of her. And she felt like something more than she'd ever been before. Complete in a way. In touch with parts of herself that she had never given a whole lot of thought to.

She had been right to be afraid of this. It was too much. It was transformative. She had been right to be afraid of it, but now, she embraced it. Wholly. Completely. With all that she was.

He began to move, deep, decisive thrusts, and she clung to him, until she began to feel the rhythm, find it. Arching her hips against his each and every time he moved against her.

She surrendered to it. To him. And when her climax hit, she could scarcely breathe. It was too much. And not enough all at once. Overwhelming, leaving her storm-tossed and just right where she needed to be.

With him. She was wild, and fractured, but safe all at once, because she was in his arms, and she knew that she could trust him.

And when his own climax hit, when his control fractured, his movements becoming hard and erratic, a growl rising up inside of him, she thought it might almost be better than her own pleasure. This man's pleasure. This man coming apart because of her.

Because he might be her first, but he'd had any number of women. And that he could still fall apart over her mattered.

And she didn't think of her mother's dire warnings then. Because it was different. He was different.

And they were different together. Maybe different than anyone had ever been.

The euphoria of it all carried her off to sleep. And she just let him hold her.

And she felt…like she was home.

SHE WAS STILL in a euphoric haze the next day when her manager called and said that a major radio station had picked her song up for airplay as part of an indie artist showcase. She wasn't really going for being an indie artist, but if it got her radio airplay… Well, it was more than anything else had ever done.

It felt exposing, that song. And yet… It was what she wanted her dad to hear, wasn't it? What he had done to her.

"It's going to be on a radio station," she said to Flint.

"That's amazing," he said. "And fast."

"I guess… When they know, they know. I just kind of can't believe that… Something I just kind of threw together like that…"

"The song was from your heart. It didn't need anything other than your voice."

And she held that close. That confidence. That simple belief in her.

Her manager decided to distribute the song online, which she hadn't done before, mostly because she didn't see why anybody would want to hear the song if none of the radio stations wanted to play it, but he was adamant that they get it out there before it played so that people could look it up after. Which was a good idea.

So within two days, the song was published onto various streaming platforms. And then something very unexpected happened.

The song got picked up on a popular app when a viral "daddy issues" challenge happened, and people played the song in the background while listing terrible things their fathers had done. Making light of it, and using dark humor, but it pushed the sound around, which pushed it up various streaming charts in a way that no one expected.

Least of all Tansey.

"It's number one on the country streaming chart now," she said, shaking as she walked down the stairs into the living room.

Flint stood up and picked her up and swung her in a circle. "Does that mean I get to buy you a truck now?"

"You can't buy me a truck."

"Well, you won *something*, surely."

"You did," she said. "You're the one that told me I had to record that song."

"I think you gotta go with your feelings."

That was when she got a call that a morning show wanted to

interview her, because she had gone from unknown to number one streaming thanks to the viral nature of the hit.

And she really had no idea how to process the fact that all of this had happened in a couple of weeks. The nature of the internet, she guessed, but it was just so far outside her comfort zone, and she was dealing with the fact that she was in love for the first time in her life, and having sex.

The morning show bit was short, and they didn't fly her out or anything; she just did an on-camera interview over the computer.

And when she asked the local bar that night if she could play, it was a resounding yes, and what she couldn't believe was how the place packed out. For her.

And Flint sat in the front row, watching her, the pride on his face doing something to her insides.

When they got back to the house, he kissed her. Rough and intense, and she let herself get caught up in it. Let him hold her close. Tear her clothes off of her. He lowered her down onto the bed, and their need for each other was a whole tornado. He was inside of her before she could think, and even though it was fast and furious, she came twice, dizzy in the aftermath.

He kissed her throat, her jaw. "You're amazing," he said.

And she just felt it. Welling up inside of her. The need to say it. The need to think it. To really get it out there. "I love you."

His withdrawal was immediate, and she felt horrified. How had she said that; how would she even let herself feel it? That wasn't what this was supposed to be. And she knew it.

It was a fling. It was supposed to be a fling. And yes, she had started to fantasize about it being more. Of course she had. But... But she wasn't going to tell him like this. She was going to... She was going to feel out how long he could see this going. She was going to do it differently. That was all.

"Forget I said anything," she said.

"Tansey, I'm not sure that I can."

He looked grave. He sounded even graver.

"You have to," she said. "I know… I know that's not what this is."

"Do you?" he asked seriously.

"Yes," she said. "Yes, I…"

"Because if you can't…"

"I'm not done yet," she said. "Are you?"

"No." He shook his head. "I'm not done."

"Good. Then we don't have to talk about this. You can forget I said it. It was… You know. Post-sex euphoria, or whatever."

"I need you to listen to me. I can't give you that. I can't give it to anybody. Don't take it personally."

"No, I know. I… I listened to you. I did."

But she couldn't ignore the fluttering of her heart. The vague hope there.

She just felt like… She felt like maybe there wouldn't be grand declarations or anything like that, but like they might settle into something that was a little bit more long-term. That was all she wanted. Just a little longer.

She didn't need for him to love her.

And she didn't need to say anything like that again.

She didn't.

She just wasn't ready for it to end.

And she would do whatever she had to do to keep him with her. For now. She would do whatever she needed to for now.

A WEEK LATER, she realized that her period hadn't started when it should have. And she had no idea what to do. She was usually pretty regular, and she knew full well that they'd had unprotected sex the night of the open mic.

She wasn't stupid. If you spent your whole life not having sex, and having regular periods, then you started having sex and the period didn't come…

She knew what that meant.

She was terrified. Trembling. But she couldn't risk going out and buying a pregnancy test. People were already starting to take pictures of them. There were weird rumors online, a lot of speculation about her personal life. People treated her like she was a fictional character. There were so many stories about who her dad was, and what he had done, and it was like what she shared about herself had taken on a life of its own.

And if anybody took a picture of her buying a pregnancy test... How did actually famous people handle that? She had one song, and was having some kind of a moment on the internet. She didn't know how anybody stood this for years on end.

But before she did any of that, she would tell him. Tell him what she suspected. Because she wanted to have a deeper conversation with him about...about the fact that this wasn't a fling anymore. That much was clear. It had become something so much deeper. So much more serious. They actually talked. They shared things. And really, it had always been wrong to call it a fling.

They had been friends first. And it mattered.

A baby.

She wasn't ready for this. And she was afraid. What if he rejected her? What if he rejected the baby?

This is why you can't depend on anyone else.

No. Because she was shaking. Because it felt like he held her life, her future in his hands.

It was horrible.

She walked downstairs, into the kitchen, where he was preparing dinner. It felt domestic. They felt domestic. They felt like something special and perfect.

Except for... Except for all the walls. He had told her about those walls from the beginning.

To see what he says, you have to tell him. You can't keep it a secret.

"I need to talk to you."

"We talk all the time," he said. "Does it require an announcement."

"This might," she said. "I'm late."

She looked at him, full of meaning. And waited for him to get it. She watched as about ten emotions cycled over his face. More than she had maybe ever seen him express in their time together.

"Well... You need to find out."

"I'm just... I don't know how. I'm afraid of what will happen if I go to a store here. Because people know that we are here. You saw that stuff pop up online. It's... It's a little bit unnerving."

"You need to find out," he said, his voice hard.

"I know," she said. "I will, Flint. I promise... And..."

"I don't want a baby," he said.

She blinked. "Well... I don't know that I was really planning on..."

"No. We said this was a fling. That was it. I told you, I am not up for this."

"I..."

Everything in her started to shut down. She didn't know how to handle this. Because he looked like a stranger. His eyes had gone deadly flat, his body language so distant... So...

"Are you saying that you would want me to get rid of it?" she asked.

He shook his head, decisively. "No. I'm not gonna tell you what to do. I just..."

"So you would just not have anything to do with it?"

"I didn't say that either," he said, his voice hard. "I said I didn't want a kid. And I don't. But I would be responsible. I would make sure that you had everything you needed. I'd be there. Physically. But I don't have anything to give, Tansey. Not emotionally. This... This was nothing. We hung out, we ate, we talked. We fucked. It wasn't real life. It wasn't really me. It was... It was something different. It's not my life. It's not who I am."

"So you... What? You would be in your child's life, begrudgingly?"

"Like a kid is going to know the difference."

"I… I can't have this conversation. I can't…"

"This has to end," he said. "Whatever the outcome. It can't keep going on like this. It's already too much."

"What?"

She didn't know how she had gone from telling him that she might be pregnant, to him talking about how he didn't want a child but he would be there in the child's life, to him wanting to end things.

"We've been careless, and this was supposed to be short-term. If you're not pregnant…"

"Right," she said, everything inside of her dissolving, breaking apart. And she could see herself, the little girl that she'd once been, collapsed on the gravel driveway, watching her father drive away. And if he had looked at his rearview mirror even once, he would've seen how badly she was devastated.

She wouldn't let Flint see it. She pushed the rising dread, the awful pain down. She cut it off; she didn't let herself feel it. She didn't let herself show it. She couldn't. She couldn't give him that. Because she would be different this time. She would push it down.

She would handle it.

She would stand upright, because she knew who she was.

"I should go," she said.

"Right now?"

"Yes. If it's done, then it should be done. I… I'll let you know. I'll let you know what happens."

"I don't want you to leave until…"

"You said it was finished. And you're right. Of course you're right. It was getting to be too much. And this is just… It's proof. I promise I'll tell you."

She packed up her things, and everything was numb. It wasn't until she left, until she drove all the way to a roadside motel six hours away that she let her chest break open entirely. That she let everything dissolve within her.

She cried until she thought she would be sick with it.

Curled up in a ball in the middle of the bed, weeping.

She didn't find a pregnancy test. She didn't know whether or not to pray that she was or pray that she wasn't.

Five days later, she started bleeding. And she was angry at herself, because now she would never even know if it had been a fluke, or if she had one of those early miscarriages that were far too common. Maybe it was better. Except nothing felt better.

She texted him.

Not pregnant.

He didn't respond. And she tried to heal. She tried to write music. She tried to move on. But the only lyrics she could write were about him.

And finally, during one session, she gave in to that. All the anger, all the pain. All the brokenness. The most scathing, personal lyrics that had ever come from her.

She couldn't stop them.

"It's perfect," said her manager. "It's the best song you've written."

"I don't know if I can put it out," she said.

"It's your pain," he said. "You can do whatever you want with it."

She held on to that. It was her pain. He was the one that had said they needed to be finished, and she hadn't fought him, because what would the point have been? She didn't want to show him that she cared more than he did. She refused to show him that.

And it had to go somewhere. She had to put it somewhere. It was her pain; her manager was right. Didn't she deserve to get something from what they had?

"Yeah," she said. "You're right. Let's...let's make that the next single."

CHAPTER NINE

After

HE DIDN'T KNOW what had drawn him downstairs. And he didn't expect to see her sitting there, her face in her hands, and notebook in her lap, and her elbows resting there.

Her shoulders were shaking, and he found that no matter what, he wanted to walk to her. He wanted to go and pull her in his arms, even though he had no right to do that. Even though he had no right at all, because it would just be more promises he couldn't keep.

"Tansey?"

She looked up at him, her eyes wide, tears streaming down her cheeks.

"I didn't expect you down here, I'm sorry. I'm just…"

"What's wrong?"

"I was just remembering," she said, her voice watery. She swallowed hard. "And maybe…maybe it's okay that I'm letting you see it. Because I didn't let you see it then. And I told myself that I didn't feel it anymore. And that's why it's been easier to snipe at you. But that's how it was in the beginning too, wasn't it? I was mean to you because I wanted to push you away."

"You were never all that mean," he said, something sore blooming at the center of his chest.

"Don't tell me that. That ruins my street cred. I was really trying to be mean."

"No, the thing was, I just liked it," he said, taking a step closer to her. It was dark, and he wanted to give her this. A little bit of honesty. Because the truth was, they hadn't spoken with honesty about what had been happening between them at the time. She had called it a fling, and he'd let her do it, because he needed to put those parameters around it in order to deal with it. He needed that border so that he could allow himself to do it.

And he hadn't given her or himself any honesty about that.

"Why did you like it?"

"Because you didn't act charmed by me. And I found that fascinating. You were not my type."

"I wasn't your type?"

"No. I didn't like squeaky-clean, fresh-faced virgins. I liked women who knew what they're doing."

"That is actually really insulting. I'm not sure why you thought that you would come in here while I was crying and…"

"Because you got to me. You got to me and I couldn't explain why." The words were rough and tortured. His voice didn't even sound like his own. "And I kept telling myself that it wasn't anything. That I wasn't attracted to you, because I couldn't be. Because you weren't a rodeo queen, and you didn't have a single rhinestone on. Because you were too young for me. Because even before you told me that you were a virgin, I knew that you were more innocent than anyone that I should be… talking to at all."

He took a breath, and his chest hurt. "But yeah, I loved that attitude. From the beginning. It was why I couldn't stay away from you. And I couldn't stay away from you, you remember that, right?"

"I try not to. And actually, most of the time I remember my version of events. I remember the breakup. But I forget… I forget that I stood there and hid everything that I felt, and that I told you that I agreed. I mean, I know I did, but I forget...that you couldn't see inside me to how I hurt."

"I knew," he said. "I knew because I hated it too. You don't... You don't know, Tansey. I had feelings for you. In a way that I never had for anybody else."

He swore he could hear the snowflakes falling outside it went so quiet between them. It was like his heart barely dared beat.

He had never admitted that out loud. He had barely admitted it to himself in coherently formed sentences in his own mind. He had allowed himself to act on feeling only, and call it nothing.

Making excuses about what he couldn't feel and what he couldn't do. But the problem was—and he knew it—that his feelings were there; they were just erratic. Uncontrolled. And he couldn't handle them.

He'd never wanted to inflict them on another human being. He had trained himself in that brutal art a long time ago. Built a wall up around himself. Toughened himself up. Because he had never ever wanted to feel...

"You know, I feel too much. And sometimes I feel nothing at all. And sometimes when I feel too much, it turns into anger. And it's bullshit no matter what scenario it is. Believe me when I tell you that. I didn't want to admit to myself that I had feelings for you. I didn't want to admit that you telling me you might be pregnant scared the hell out of me. Really, the hell."

"It scared me too. It scared me too and then it... I felt like I was dying. When I started bleeding. Because I wanted it. I *wanted* it. Even though I didn't want it. And it was such a mess. It was a horrible mess. And you were the only person that I wanted to talk to about it, and I texted you and you never texted me back." She was breathing hard now, crying again, and he felt like this was what he deserved. This conversation.

"I didn't know what to say," he said. "I didn't know what to say, because part of me wanted you to be pregnant. So that I could keep you anyway, even though I knew it was a bad idea.

I'm… I'm toxic, Tansey, and I tried my best not to be toxic with you. I did. But I froze you out instead, and it wasn't better."

"So you know that about yourself and, what, you just sit in it?"

"Yes," he said.

"Why?"

"Because I don't want to fix it. I didn't want to care about you. I didn't want it. I wanted to *possess* you. I wanted to keep you. And hell, the contortions I would've gone through to do that if the whole pregnancy scare hadn't happened… I would still be torturing you. I can't even imagine. Not letting you go, not really, and not giving you what you wanted. Because I can't let myself care that deeply about someone. But it doesn't mean I don't want you. With absolutely every part of myself. It doesn't mean you're not the only woman I dream about."

"You…you do?"

"How many women do you think I've been with since you?"

She looked away from him. "I don't want to have this conversation."

"None," he said. "I haven't been with anybody. I haven't even wanted to. It's just you. You're the reason that I wake up at night hard. You're the reason I wake up in a cold sweat. You are what I want. You are everything that I want."

"Please don't," she said. "Please don't. Because if you can't give me one more piece of you, if you can't give me one more piece of who you are and why you're this way, then why are we having the conversation at all?"

"Do you want to know why? Do you want to know why I'm like this?" He swallowed hard. "My sister died. When I was fourteen. And I was…fucking destroyed. And it just… Everybody around me fell apart. They were so sad. And I was just so angry. So angry. At the universe, at God, at my parents, at the doctors. And at everybody for just crying all the time. Because it killed me."

"Flint," she whispered. "I didn't… I'm so sorry."

"I didn't want you to know. I didn't want to have the conversation with you, because I didn't want you to look at me like that. Like I was an object of pity that you could fix, because you can't fucking fix it, Tansey. Nobody can. That's what death is. It ends something, and you can't fix it. You can't get it back. It broke something in me. And I had to... I had to find a way to get rid of that anger..."

"What did you do?"

"I put a wall up..."

"No," she said softly. "What did you do? Because you are not acting this way because of a feeling you had. You must've done something."

"Yeah," he said, shame burning over his skin. "I did. You know my brother Boone? One time... We shared a room all the time when we were on the road. Right? When we were on the road with the rodeo. And one night he was crying. He was twelve. And he was crying and crying and he wouldn't stop. He just said how much he missed her. I told him to stop. I told him he had to stop. Because it was like... Every time he cried, it was like I was being stabbed in the damn chest. I couldn't handle it. I couldn't listen to it. Because everything that came out as sadness for him stoked the fire of rage inside of me. Because what was tragic to him was just so desperately unfair to me. I told him to stop crying and he didn't. He couldn't. So I punched him in his face. I punched him in his face and I told him he'd better not cry like a little girl anymore. Because it wouldn't bring her back. Because it didn't do anything. It didn't mean anything."

He watched her face, watched to see if she was shocked, because it still shocked him. He still hated it. And he still hated himself for it. "I still remember what that felt like. That anger. It was so pure. It was probably the most real thing I've ever felt in my life. I hated him. And I hated his feelings and what they did to me..."

"That was grief," she said. "That was grief. And I know that I've never experienced grief like that, but I know what it's like to feel angry. I know what it's like to feel like you would rather just be a toxic awful person than the bigger person. Because everything is terrible so why should you have to be anything but terrible."

"You know, my brother still loves me. A lot. He still loves me, because that's what younger brothers have to do. And we're still family. But you… You're not stuck with me. My brother needed me and I failed him. And that's all I know how to do."

"And you don't want a relationship because of what you'll…"

"Because if something happens, that's who I'm going to be. Because in sickness, that's who I would be. Because for poorer, that's who I would be. Because the dark side of those vows would show the dark side in me. And I have never wanted to submit anyone to that. Or a child. I can't imagine that. I would be such a bad father."

"Why do you think that? Because of a reaction you had when you were fourteen? To something hideously traumatizing. Flint, you can't live your entire life based on…"

She faltered. And anger ignited in his gut.

Didn't she understand? He was protecting her. From him. She'd seen a little bit of what he could be like when he was cornered, when someone got too close.

Didn't she understand this was for her?

"Isn't that what you've done? Lived your whole life in response to a few things that hurt you? Turned them into the biggest thing about you?"

"That's not fair. That's not fair at all."

"Why? Anyway, who said I had to be fair. You wanted to know. You wanted to know why. And that is why. So now you know."

"I'm sorry," she said again. "I'm sorry I… But I want to fix it. I want…"

He didn't know why it hurt so much to talk about, still. It just did. And it probably always would. And it was the pain that he hated so much. That pain that wouldn't go away.

That pain that felt like it defined him.

"And that's why I didn't want to tell you. Because I don't want you to try to fix me. You need to understand that I'm broken, and I know that. I know it. The mistake was getting involved with you at all. And maybe not explaining it then. But I didn't want it to be... I was pretending. I was pretending that I could be something I wasn't. I was pretending that it wouldn't matter. That it could just be for a little while, and I wouldn't hurt you. I really didn't want to hurt you."

He moved toward her, and he put his hand on her cheek. But that was a mistake.

Because he felt it right then. All the anger and pain rising up inside of him, mixing with a desperation that twined around them both.

"Flint," she whispered.

And that was when he leaned in and tasted her lips for the first time in two years.

CHAPTER TEN

SHE WAS LIVING in a riot of pain. Of grief. And she knew that she should turn away from him. She knew that she should stop this. She knew that it was insane. He had just told her...everything. He had bared his soul to her. He had told her what he was, who he was. And it was... It was so painful. It was still spinning around inside of her, and she was trying to grapple with it, and failing.

He had lost his sister.

He and his brother...

And he felt like somehow that made him wrong. Made him beyond redemption.

Made him broken.

But it didn't. She knew that it didn't. And she knew she shouldn't kiss him. But his mouth was on hers, and she couldn't deny it, not any more now than she had been able to back then. Because he tasted like everything she wanted. Everything she had always wanted. And there was a reason it had been him. Only him.

And there hadn't been anyone else for him, not since her.

She had been so certain that he had broken her. But maybe they had broken each other a little bit.

"Flint," she whispered. "I haven't… There hasn't been any-one else."

He growled, his large hand cupping the back of her head as he deepened the kiss.

She knew that this was a mistake, for a variety of reasons. They should probably keep talking. They should probably keep talking instead of this. Because this was always there. And it was too easy. And it was maybe going to cut her open. But she couldn't stop. Because it was everything she wanted. Because it was maybe the language he spoke.

Or maybe it was just pure, unsquashed hope inside of her; no matter how much she wanted to believe she was immune, no matter how much she wanted to believe she knew better, she just didn't, never did, never would. Not when it came to him.

And so she kissed him. And kissed him. And there they were in an empty hotel, and there was nobody to walk in on them. Nobody to see.

"I need you," she said. "Please. Please."

Except, he didn't keep her on the couch; he lifted her up into his arms, and began to walk her through the lobby, up the stairs. He carried her away from the direction of her room, down the hall to where she hadn't been to before. He pushed a door open, and her eyes went wide.

It was amazing. A larger, much more masculine bed was in the center of the room, the large windows open. And she knew where they faced. The mountains. So even with them open, even with the lights on, and the darkness outside, nobody would be able to see them.

He set her down at the center of the bed, and pulled his T-shirt up over his head. His body…

It was so perfect. As perfect as it had ever been. His mus-cles well-defined and cut, every movement making them rip-ple and shift.

She began to desperately tear at her own clothes. She didn't have a bra on, thankfully, so it was just a sweatshirt, and the pants. And she wasn't embarrassed. Not to be with him. But she never had been. It was right. It felt right. It always did, and it made her want to weep. Because whatever happened, whatever happened when the sun rose, whatever happened when this was all said and done, she was going to be with him again now. And she wanted it. She needed it. Was desperate for it.

"I'm on the pill," she said, her lips feeling numb as she got up on her knees and went to the edge of the bed, putting her hand on his bare chest, her breath hissing through her teeth as she touched him. "I... After I..."

He put his hand over hers, pressed it more deeply against him. "I get it," he said. "Because...because I hurt you. Because I changed things for you. Because I... Fuck," he said. "I'm sorry I said that to you. About being defined by those things. I just hate that I did it. I hate that I did that to you."

"Well, don't hate it right now. Because you probably don't have any condoms, do you?"

He shook his head, a rusty laugh escaping his mouth. "I sure as hell don't. Because there hasn't been anyone. Not even a temptation, and I definitely didn't plan on meeting anyone up here. Least of all you." He touched her face, skimming the edge of his thumb over her cheekbone. "Least of all you. But then... I never counted on you. Not ever."

She laughed, the sound almost a sob as she wrapped her arms around his neck and kissed him, pressing her naked body against his bare chest.

He growled, moving his hands down her back, to her hips, to her thighs. Then he lifted her up, wrapping her legs around his waist as he carried them both to the center of the bed. He was still wearing his jeans, and she arched against him, his erection, covered in denim, hard still against her body. Rough.

She moaned, rolling her hips against him.

She was so desperate for him. So filled with need, but it wasn't just physical. She felt like she had been alone for two years. While this person, the one person that had ever got to her in this way, was just out there, away from her. Gone from her. And it had been hell.

Singing about it... All the time. Hearing it over and over again, her own pain, unfiltered and raw, playing in her ears all the time...

It was hell, and this wasn't heaven. Because it had a time limit on it, like it always did. Like it always would. And it made her want to hide from truth, from reality, from the intensity of what was rioting through her, but she wanted it too much to hide from it. And that, in the end, was the hardest thing. To know that you were running square into the thing that had mortally wounded you before, and to accept that you were making the choice anyway.

That's what she was doing. She would never know better when it was him. Or maybe she did. Maybe she did, and it would never matter as much as being touched by him.

Maybe it would always be worth the burn to play with his brand of fire. She would despair of it in the morning. Maybe. She would despair of it for years. She knew that already, because she already had.

But now... Now she had him. Now she was with him. And it was everything, and so was he. She skimmed her hands over his chest, down his back. Up to his face again. And she cupped his cheek, and whispered against his mouth, "I want you. I want you so much."

"Tell me," he growled, flexing his hips against her again, her internal muscles pulsing as his hardness hit her right where she needed him most, unerringly.

"I'm wet for you," she said. "Only for you. Only ever for you. I can have anyone. I'm rich and famous. I basically have groupies. Men, women, I could have anyone I want, but I just want you. I just want you. You fucking broke my heart. And look at me, I'm desperate for you. You, Flint Carson."

He growled, and undid the buckle on his belt. Stripped his jeans off, and her breath caught when she saw him, totally naked. Glorious. Beautiful. She needed him. Needed this. More than anything.

"Take me," she said. "Make me yours again. Please. Please." And maybe she said other things, but they were incoherent. Other things, but she didn't understand them. She didn't understand anything except him. He was like a map to herself. This desire a guiding star, bringing her home.

And maybe it would never, ever make sense to anyone else, but she didn't need it to.

She only needed him. Only ever him.

"Take me," she whispered, and he thrust home.

She gasped, tears forming in her eyes, because it felt so right. To have him in her. So deep, she couldn't tell where he ended and she began. And she didn't want to. She wanted this. This feeling of being one. This feeling of being his.

And he began to move, and it was like an ignited spark within her soul. She clung to his shoulders, and she kept her eyes open, because she didn't want to look away.

His name was her every heartbeat.

Flint.

Because whatever happened after this, he was here now. Whatever happened after this, he was hers now.

Whatever happened after this, she would be okay. She had to be okay. Because this had to be worth the risk. This had to be more than a sad country song about being drunk and lonely and missing the one you shouldn't.

Because they had to be more than that. More than a country song. More than a few verses, a chorus and a bridge.

More than her anger. More than her hurt. More than his grief.

Right then, she felt like it might be true. Like they weren't just Tansey and Flint, but all the stars and everything else. Like they weren't just the bad things, but a whole universe of possibility.

She didn't want the moment to pass, because once it did, there would be reality to contend with.

And she didn't want it.

She just wanted him.

That was the scariest thing. After all this time, after all of this.

Knowing better. Knowing he was the cowboy her mother had warned her about...

She just wanted him.

As orgasm crashed over her like a wave, she let herself get taken under.

His heart was still beating so hard he could barely breathe.

He was back in bed with her. With Tansey. And he could pretend that sex was all the same. That he had been the one with experience, so he was the one who was armed against this kind of thing. The one who knew what it was. Whatever that meant. Because there was no defining what this was. Not easily. It wasn't that simple, and it never could be.

It was something different, though. It was something he'd never experienced before, and it was why he hadn't been able to touch anyone since.

She shifted beside him, and he rolled onto his side and looked at her.

And there was something still about it. Something peaceful.

A feeling that he hadn't let himself feel in more years than he could count.

"I'm not really sad that I'm stuck up here anymore."

"Good to know."

"You haven't been with anybody... Why?" She frowned. "Why haven't you?"

"Well. I could go into a whole monologue about broken trust. And another one about being famous. And how it affects the way that people see you. How it affects the way that you interact with people in all of that. But the simple truth is... I didn't want to be."

He shook his head. "Me either." He wasn't good with feelings;

he wasn't good with words. And it wasn't just that he didn't like sharing his feelings; at this point, it was like a language that he had lost. He had feelings—he could acknowledge that. But he had done such a good job of pushing them behind a wall, of suppressing them, that the truth was, he didn't quite know how to translate them. Within his own self, to his own self.

"There was something different about being with you. The idea of letting somebody else put their hands where you'd put them… It was like cursing in a church. Walking on top of sacred ground, when you're supposed to leave it be. I don't know."

She rolled onto her back and looked up at the ceiling. "I don't think I can claim to have felt like it was sacred ground. I just couldn't imagine… I just couldn't imagine. And maybe we needed this. Maybe we needed something more finished. Something not quite so painful." She turned to her side again and put her hand on his chest. He closed his eyes. There was a goodbye in those words. He knew that. Goodbye had always been the only option. Because he couldn't do forever. Which meant goodbye was inevitable, which meant he couldn't rail against what she was saying. Not without changing everything, the entire landscape that he had built up inside of his chest.

The map to who he was.

He remembered vaguely thinking that she was a map to somewhere else, but… He wasn't sure he could follow it.

He wasn't sure he wanted to.

And that meant accepting the silent goodbye.

But for now, they were here. For now, there was no leaving here.

"You changed me," he said finally. "Everything that I'm doing… It's because of you."

"Well, because you were angry at me," she said.

"Does it matter? It was still a change."

"I guess not. Because I guess the same could be said for me."

"What are your plans for Christmas?" he asked. His own

family would have their big rowdy get-together, and he would pretend he didn't hate it.

"I'm going to visit my mother. In Palm Springs. That's where her house is. She wanted to be warm. She wanted palm trees." He saw a tear slide down her cheek. "I'm always so afraid that I might lose this. You know, the money is a big deal. My mother raised me in a trailer, never knowing if we were going to have enough to make rent, to keep the lights from being shut off. I found that in the end, revenge wasn't the important piece so much as love. Giving back for the love my mother showed me. She's a tough woman. But she loves me. I know that having me made her life harder, but she never acted like I was a burden. She always said that I was a gift. I like giving her things. I like paying her back… I like…"

"You bought your mother a house," he said. "And on top of all of that, you're her daughter. I don't think you'd lose her if something happened with your career."

"Maybe not. But she's the only person that stayed in my life always. The only person who was there at every step, and I finally got to give back to her, and what if someday it isn't enough?"

Unspoken was the idea that she clearly felt like she hadn't been enough for her father.

"Do you think you weren't enough for me?"

The words scraping his throat raw, it was dancing close to things that he didn't want to talk about. Things that he didn't want to admit.

"What else is a woman supposed to think? If I had been enough…"

He reached out and put his hand on her cheek. "No. If you learn one thing from what I told you, if you take one thing away from it, then take this. If there was anything that could fix me, it would've been you. It was never fair for me to touch you. Because when I tell you my problems are mine, and when I tell you they are built into the deepest part of who I am, I need you to believe that."

She didn't say anything. "Like I said. I think we needed this. I think this is important."

He nodded slowly. Except he didn't really like that conclusion for some reason. He'd always been like this with her. He wanted it both ways. To have her. To stay safe. He already knew he couln't do both.

"I might not be able to fix all the things inside of me, but maybe I can fix what I did to you," he said.

"I don't need you to fix me, Flint. That's actually been part of the conclusion that I've come to. Yeah, I was angry at you. I was. But I was afraid too, because if I hadn't been, I wouldn't have saved all of that for a song. I would have said it to you. Yes, I was hurt by what happened. You know that. I was devastated. I let myself believe that what you said about yourself was wrong. I let myself believe that because things changed for me they would change for you too. But I wasn't trying to spare you by holding back, I was trying to spare myself."

"That's all any of us are trying to do," he said, the words coming from somewhere deep inside of him, and he hadn't realized how true they were until he'd said them.

But he made a concerted effort to shut off any realizations that might come as a result.

"My family always does a big Christmas thing," he said finally. "And I pretend that I like it. But I don't. I pretend that I like it, because you have to do that with your family. You have to do that for your family. Especially when… You know, I feel like they've all moved on without me. Like they've all reached some kind of healing that I just can't find. Some of my brothers have lagged behind a little bit. But now three of them are getting married." He laughed. "Well. Not all of them. My brother Buck… Something happened a long time ago, and he left. There was an accident and he… He wasn't the same after. I know that eats at my parents. Because even though he didn't die, they lost another child. He was never himself, and then he went away. He's the only one that didn't stay. The only one that didn't stay on the ranch, the only one that didn't stay in the rodeo. I'm angry at him, you know. I'm angry at him for leaving. For not doing what I do."

"And what's that?"

"I don't feel any of it either. I don't feel healed. I don't feel happy to be there. I can't handle the emotions of it. I can't handle the way my mom wants to talk about my sister and share memories. I can't handle sitting around and telling stories, like there could ever be happy memories of somebody that you'll just miss for the rest of your life. But I do it. And if I want to rage, I do it on the inside. Because I did what I had to do to deal with myself so that I could be there for my family. So honestly, fuck him."

He watched a series of complicated emotions flit across Tansey's face. And of course, he saw pity among them.

"I never wanted you to feel sorry for me," he said.

"Only a jerk wouldn't feel sorry for you. Are you sorry for me that my dad left?"

"Well, yeah..."

"I'm sorry for you. Because this is hard, and terrible. Because it's more than anyone should have had to deal with. Because it's difficult and sad. Because..."

"What?"

"Because it's not fair. All the things that happened to us that break our hearts before we can ever make choices. You don't choose your family. And I had a terrible father. You have a great family, but it still came with tragedy, and I... I just don't think it's fair."

"No. It's not." An idea turned over in his head. "But you know, I was going to take the opportunity to decorate the hotel while it was empty."

"You were going to decorate."

He shrugged. "I told you. That's the thing I'm good at doing.

And I figured I would do it myself. Get the Christmas decorations up before the guests start coming to spend their holidays here. There's a lot of people planning to spend Christmas Day right here. We got a big Christmas dinner and...there's a big tree out on the back porch that I haven't brought in yet, and decorations ready to go in one of the back offices."

"Let's do it," she said. "Let's decorate."

"You want to decorate?"

She nodded. "We had a tiny tinsel tree in the mobile home, and then... We don't really do Christmas every year. Because sometimes I'm busy, and we're not always in the same place. We always call. But if I'm by myself, there's no reason to put up decorations and..."

"Well. If you're interested."

And he didn't say what he knew. That they were both maybe trying to make the night last longer. Because who knew what would happen come morning. When trees could be moved and roads could be plowed, and the temperatures would get above freezing and everything would start melting.

Yeah, he didn't know what would happen after that.

CHAPTER ELEVEN

SHE WAITED, wrapped in just the robe again, while Flint went and got boxes of ornaments from where they'd been stored back in the manager's office.

He was shirtless, and in her mind, she knew this would always be Christmas. This man, wearing nothing but jeans low riding on his lean hips, carrying big boxes of decorations.

And it made her a little bit sad, because it was another thing that would belong to Flint Carson forever.

You have to figure that out.

She did. Because she hadn't slept with him again to break her own heart again. She had wanted to say goodbye.

Not because anything he'd told her about himself horrified her. No. He wasn't the monster that he thought he was, and she knew that. It was simply that she also knew who she was.

And they had tried this before.

And now she needed to listen when he told her who he was.

And what he wanted.

She pushed off the sadness, and watched as he went toward the back of the major lobby area, throwing open the doors at the back.

They had the whole place lit up, and she wondered if anyone could see that, at 2:00 a.m., this giant building was a beacon of light on the hill. If anyone could see the outline of his body as he stood there, backlit in the doorway. Snowflakes whipped in around him, and she just sat and stared.

"What are you doing?"

"Christmas tree," he said. "It is a huge ass tree."

He had already placed a stand at the center of the room, and he disappeared a moment later, and then came back. The tree was huge. It must weigh hundreds of pounds, and he had it hefted over his shoulders, like one of those guys at the gym that did all the major weight lifting like it was just a fun thing people did on a Saturday morning.

"You need help?"

"Oh come on," he said, a grin curving his lips.

So she just sat there, and watched as he positioned the tree in the stand. It was massive.

But she didn't really care about the tree. Mostly, she was watching him. How beautiful he was. How perfect.

There was just no other man that made her feel this way. No other man that captured every facet of her attention. But she didn't think there was a more beautiful man in the entire world. How could there be? And she sat there, living in the feeling she'd had when they had walked up from her truck. When she had let those broad shoulders—so perfectly defined and glorious, revealed to her now—shield her from the wind.

And she realized, it was the man he was.

Not the man he could be.

Because she listened to him talk about his family.

It wasn't that he didn't do that, all the time. Shoulder other people's burdens, protect them.

He used his strength all the time, every family gathering, every Christmas. He denied himself, and his own comfort, for the people he cared for.

The issue was, he just didn't have the capacity to extend it to her too.

It was a painful realization, but one she could accept. How

could she not accept the fact that he gave everything to a family that loved him so much?

Family was supposed to be who you did that for.

Her father had never done it for her, and look at the way it had broken things.

His older brother was gone, and that, she knew, put more pressure on him. It was why he was angry.

Because he was already at capacity.

She couldn't ask him to do any more.

It would make her love a burden.

It wasn't a flaw in him. It was actually because he was just so...

"All right," he said. "Let's get some decorations on this thing. Well, let's start with a fire, because now I'm freezing."

"That's the hazard of going outside half naked in this weather." She grinned. "Not that I'm complaining." She didn't want to slide into morose thinking. She didn't want to think about when the sun would rise. She didn't want to think about anything but this moment.

Because this would be the moment that sustained her. The moment that moved her on. That moved her into a place of acceptance about what they'd had, and what was possible. Because that was the issue; that was why she was so hurt. It was believing they could have had more if only... If only he could change. And she realized that he couldn't. That he needed to be who he was to survive, and to be there for his family.

It wasn't a deficiency in him.

It was almost sadder than if he just wasn't good at all.

But only almost.

And this was their moment. So she was going to take it.

He built a fire, big and warm, almost enough to take her robe off. But she felt like maybe decorating the Christmas tree naked was a bridge too far.

They took strings of sparkling white lights out of boxes, and he put up a ladder so that the lights could get wrapped all the way around, all the way to the top.

There were large sparkling red globes, and gold stars, and when they were finished, she had never seen anything more beautiful.

A Christmas tree that was theirs. That had nothing to do with her mother's stress with the season, or her childhood guilt over making her mother put any extra effort into anything, because she already worked so hard, and she definitely didn't deserve to feel guilty over the presents that she couldn't buy Tansey.

Just something that belonged to them. And even in this moment it was absent the sadness that had been inside of her ever since…

Ever since she had met this man, and then had to figure out how to live a life that didn't have him anymore.

Ever since they'd lived one summer that had defined so much of who they were. Because even he had admitted that it had changed him.

And maybe that was the real thing that she needed to understand. That it had been fate, even if it had been a bruised and bloody fate, one that they'd had to fight to find the meaning of.

Maybe she had to accept that sometimes she had to go through hard things, terrible things, to become who she was supposed to be.

Wasn't that every highbrow Hollywood movie? The complicated happy ending, rather than the traditional one.

She had certainly never seen that sort of happy ending in real life.

In real life, her mother was having a happy ending by herself, in Palm Springs with other people her age, laughing and drinking and enjoying life by the pool. Reaping the benefits of having been a good mother, a hard worker, and not having to do it anymore.

She didn't have a man. She didn't need a man. The lesson of her heartbreak had been that she didn't need one to be happy.

Tansey had needed her heartbreak for her fame, and she needed this bittersweet moment to find the next phase.

Flint was important to her. But that didn't mean he was her forever, not in a way that meant he would be in her life always.

He was forever in terms of how he'd changed her, though.

And maybe that was the most real way for a relationship to last.

"Hang on just a second."

He went behind the reception desk, and bent down for a moment, and then music filled the room. Old-fashioned Christmas carols. And she looked around the glittering space, looked at the way his body was in the firelight and the way the tree sparkled.

It was the sweetest, sexiest moment of her whole life. And she didn't know how those two things combined to become one thing, but they had. Did.

He reached his hand out. "Want to dance?"

"I don't know how," she said.

"Me either. But I want to."

She took his hand, and he lifted her up off the couch, and twirled her in time with the music, her robe spinning out around her, exposing her legs, and maybe more, but there was no embarrassment with him. She laughed, and he brought her back to him, and they swayed back and forth, and whether or not it could be called dancing was up for debate.

But it was perfect. This moment, was perfect. Even if she couldn't see past it.

And with the music swirling around them, and the firelight glowing, she stretched up on her toes, and she kissed him.

HIS HEART WAS pounding so hard he thought it might burst through his chest.

He had never liked Christmas. He had never liked any of the symbolism associated with it. But for him, he knew that this would always be Christmas. Every time he had to sit through an endless family present-opening session, every time they

went down to the fanciest restaurant in Lone Rock for their an-
nual Christmas Eve dinner, he would think of this. He would
think of her.

The only person he'd ever wanted to do a romantic thing
for. The only person who had ever made him wish that he was
someone else.

He didn't waste time regretting the things that had happened.
He didn't waste time railing against the universe anymore for
taking his sister away from them. Because it didn't do any good.
It only reopened old wounds.

But this made him want to do that. She had always made
him want to do that, and maybe that was the biggest reason he
had let her go. Because she made him wish that things could be
different. And he knew that that was an endless trap that you
could fall into and never get out of.

But right now, he just wanted the moment. He wanted to surrender to it. To her.

And so he did. He kissed her, with every ounce of desire in
his soul. He held her against him, relishing the feel of her curves
against his body as he did.

He kissed her. Kissed her like he might die if he didn't, and
he wondered if part of him had. All these years when he'd been
without her. All these years when he'd told himself that he didn't
need her. That he had done the right thing. *How can anything
but this be right?*

He cradled her face in his hands, kissed her deep, kissed
down the elegant column of her throat, sliding his tongue over
the line of her collarbone. At the same time, his hands found
the belt on her robe, and undid it slowly, pushing it away from
her body. Letting it fall to the ground. She was beautiful. And
it was like unwrapping a Christmas present. The only one he'd
ever cared about. The only one he could remember ever wanting.

She was famous now. A woman the whole world wanted a
piece of.

But she was a woman that he had. A woman whose body

he knew better than his own, even though before tonight it had been two years since he'd seen her. Two years since he'd touched her.

Mine.

The word welled up inside of him. He couldn't remember the last time he'd wanted anyone or anything this badly.

Maybe he never had. Because he hadn't let himself.

Because wanting... Wanting like this, it was almost a curse. But he couldn't turn away from it. Not now. Not when it was like this. So desperate. Her hands went to his belt buckle, undid it slowly, then to his jeans.

And he let himself feel what he hadn't that first time. The all of it. That she had never let anyone else inside of her, except for him. And he had done what with that?

Why had he taken it if he had known that he couldn't honor it? Why had he taken her if he had known he couldn't give her what she deserved?

Maybe because he wasn't as strong as he liked to think. He was weak. For her. It had always been that way. From moment one.

And right now he just needed her. He hadn't needed sex in two years. It wasn't just about that. Wasn't just about a simple dry spell, because if so, he would have done something about it. If so, he would have found someone else. That was just sex. For him, it was about her.

And he wanted to show that to her.

He laid her down slowly on the thick rug in front of the fireplace, kissed her mouth, kissed her breasts.

Her body was a brilliant gift, something rich and lovely in the firelight. Something that nothing and no one would ever be able to overshadow.

She was his summer. And now she was his winter too.

Or maybe he'd made his own winter these past two years, but she was the reason why. The reason why it felt so dark. The reason why everything in him had changed.

Because it had been an eclipse on anything good when he let her walk out of his life.

He wanted to show her that.

He wanted to give her everything.

He kissed his way down the softness of her body, kissed her inner thigh, then licked a line to her center. She gasped. And he fed off of her. Off of her pleasure. Off of her arousal. Her need.

He let himself disappear into the moment. Into the glory of pleasuring her. The responsibility of it. The honor of it.

To be allowed to taste her like this. To be allowed to touch her like this. Who was he? He was just some dumbass. And she had always been special. Always been singular. And the men in her life, him included, had made her feel like she was second. Had made her feel like she wasn't good enough. Made her feel like she was a burden. How dare they? And how dare he?

He didn't deserve this moment. He didn't deserve her.

But he was taking her. Because he needed it. Because he needed her to know.

He licked her, took her essence as an offering, a gift. Even as it fed his soul.

The taste of her. The sound of her cries. Her desperate arousal, the way that she clawed at his shoulders, the way that she cried out her need when he pushed two fingers inside of her and took her to the heights.

He waited for her to come down, and then he kissed her hip bone, her stomach, back up to her mouth, where he let her taste the evidence of her own desire on his lips.

"You," he said, "are like no one else. You are like nothing else. You are air. And I hadn't realized that I'd been suffocating all this time."

"Flint…"

The way that she said his name, all sweet and tender and questioning, it did something to him.

The way that she looked at him, like he might be something amazing. Something great.

He wanted to be.

He wanted to be more than he'd been. He wanted to be something better. Something right for her.

He wanted that.

He kissed her, deep and long, lost himself in her.

But it was what she did next that he couldn't handle. It was what she did next that broke him.

She pushed against his chest, reversing their positions, and once he was stripped naked, she knelt down before him, and took him into her mouth. She looked up at him, her beautiful green eyes piercing him through the soul while she racked his body with torturous pleasure.

Fuck.

He pushed his hands into her hair, held her there, bucking his hips, desperate for release and desperate for it to go on forever.

He could remember when a blowjob had been entertainment. When it had meant nothing to him. When it had touched nothing but his cock. And now... It was like it was all of him. He couldn't take pleasure anymore unless it was her. He couldn't take pleasure with her without involving everything. His whole body. All that he was. His soul.

She sucked him deep, and he growled. "No. I need to be in you."

It was her turn to kiss him. Her turn to let him taste what she'd done to him.

And then she straddled his hips, angling herself so that the head of him was pressed against the slick entrance to her body. He gritted his teeth as she lowered herself onto him, allowing him in, inch by torturous inch.

She was so tight, so perfect.

And he had never done this before her. Taking a woman without a latex barrier. That was the kind of thing reserved for trust.

Trust.

She had trusted him so much back then and he had broken it.

He didn't deserve it now. But he needed it.

Needed her.

Needed all these things that he had no call to want. Dammit all, he did.

With his whole soul.

His heart was raging, as she began to move. She began to ride him like she was made for it. And hell, she had to be. Had to be made for this, for him. Because God knew he thought he might be made for her.

In another life maybe. One where he hadn't lost so much. One where he hadn't hurt so damn much.

That realization almost stopped him, but then, he was overcome, seeing her body as she rose over him like that, feeling the clasp of her around him, watching the pleasure on her face as she began to chase her own climax.

He wasn't a man who had the ability to do what she did. To take feelings and turn them into song lyrics. Hell, he couldn't even take feelings and turn them into words.

He couldn't take feelings and turn them into much of anything.

But he wanted to. For her.

He wanted to do more, to be more. To be better.

For her.

He wished that he could erase his past. His loss. His pain. Because it had broken him.

And he never wished that. He never wished it because there was no point. Just like there was no point in tears. No point in regret.

But she had come to him untouched, and not without pain, and he had come to her broken beyond repair.

He wished he could be different.

And he gave himself up to that. To the need to be more than he ever had been for her.

Because who had been there for her?

Here she was, worrying about what she could give her mother… Who worried about what they could give to her?

She thought she wasn't enough.

And he had been part of that.

"You're beautiful," he said, gripping her hips and guiding her up and down on his cock. "The most beautiful woman I've ever seen. You deserve everything. You deserve the world."

Hands braced on his chest, he could see her eyes begin to glitter. See tears welling there, and it just made him want to give her even more.

"You deserve everything you've got. You deserve all the money from that song. You are absolutely perfect. In every way."

She closed her eyes, and began to shake, and he could feel the tenuous grip he had on his control beginning to slip. "You're a star," he said. "And you're more than enough."

And then she dissolved, and he went right along with it, his climax like a vicious beast, grabbing him around the throat and shaking him hard.

"I love you," she said. "I love you."

And just like that, very deep inside of her, with her words echoing inside of him, it was like a sledgehammer had been taken to the walls all around his soul. The gates that held back his emotions demolished with three simple words.

And he felt like he had been dragged out into the middle of an open field, naked. Exposed and vulnerable to every attack.

It was as if blinders he had put up intentionally had dissolved. As if everything that he had put up between them had vanished.

Everything.

I love you.

And it was too much. Too much. It reminded him of the moment when he had hit Boone. Because it was like something sharp and vicious was cutting open his insides. Like his heart was going to explode. It wasn't that he felt nothing. It was that he felt everything, and he had no idea how to combat that. No idea what to do about it. There was nothing, he realized. Because the problem was knowing it was the truth. Knowing that what he had been protecting himself all along from was the intensity of it.

The desperation of it.

And he couldn't un-know it now.

He felt terrified. Utterly terrified. Because she loved him, and he felt more than any one person should. Because she loved him, and he felt like he might break apart. Because she loved him, and it truly felt like hell. Because she loved him, and he was faced with the realization that she was so fragile. So beautiful. And life had come along and taken that from him. It had already taken so much.

The more you cared, the more you could lose.

And he realized...

That was all this was. It was all it had ever been. All he had ever been truly afraid of. It was losing someone he loved again. It was caring so much he could be in that position where he felt too much. Where he wanted too much.

He had punched Boone, because Boone had felt all of the things that lived inside of him. All of the things he wanted to turn away from. All of the things he wanted to deny.

But he was still holding her, and he was still in her, and he couldn't help himself. "I love you too."

He lay back on the floor, feeling like he had just lost a war.

One he had been fighting for the better part of his life. One he hadn't even realized he'd been on the slow path to losing from the minute he had first seen her.

Every bit of his resolve. Every bit of everything, it was broken. Demolished. And so was he.

He knew why he had been fighting it all this time. Knew why he had been fighting her.

He damn well did.

Because this was terrifying. He was happy to throw himself on the back of an angry bull; he was happy to work until his body ached and his hands bled.

It was the feeling. That was what he didn't want to do. Not

what he couldn't do. It was the thing that scared him. Believing so much in something, hoping so much. Loving someone so much, and losing them anyway. Losing everything anyway.

"You love me?"

He sat up, staring straight at the Christmas tree that they had just decorated together.

Staring straight at the Christmas that could be his if...

"Shit," he said.

"What?"

"I..."

He was suddenly choked. By the memories. The memories of that night that they had broken up. The memory of the night that he had lost her.

That he had let her walk away.

She had thought that she might be pregnant with his baby and he'd said he didn't want it. Of course he wanted it. He wanted everything with her. He wanted a whole life. A baby and everything, but facing down that possibility, that little bit of hope... It had been too much for him. He hadn't been able to claim it. He hadn't been able to admit it.

And now... He felt swamped with it. With the loss of it. The loss of that potential future. The baby, her.

All the things that he hadn't been able to say then. And he wanted to say them now.

So he looked up at her, and he tried. "I don't know if I'll be a good dad," he said. "I don't know if I'll be able to be a good husband. I have lived in absolute fear for so long, Tansey. For so long. Because when I was a kid, I knew my sister was sick. Of course I did. We spent all that time in hospitals, all that time around doctors, and it wasn't like my parents didn't try to prepare us. But you don't understand *dead* when you're fourteen years old. And you can't. It's just the most absurd thing. I had a sister. And she was wonderful. The cutest kid. The sweetest... And why? *Why?* It never made any sense. That I could never... I couldn't live with what it made me feel. I had to figure out some way to stop it. I couldn't help Boone with what he felt because it was killing me. As if my own pain wasn't enough, I had to watch it torture him too. I had to watch it torture everybody, and that was what broke me. It absolutely broke me into pieces. And that was the man that met you."

He sat there, his words so heavy. Everything so heavy. "I have told myself that I did not have it in me to give anybody the support they needed if they were going through a hard time. That I didn't have it in me, because of the way I reacted to Boone. But when you said that... When you said you loved me just now... It was like you shone a light on all those dark places inside of me, and I can't pretend I don't know what it really is."

"What is it?" she asked.

"Fear. I'm afraid. I'm a coward. Because you're a gift. A beautiful, lovely gift. Too perfect to be real almost. And more what I want than I ever wanted to admit. More than I ever wanted to want. And suddenly it terrifies me. Like the sky might cave in and take you away from me." He cleared his throat. "When you told me that you thought you might be pregnant... It was the ferocity of what I felt that shut me down. Because it was like...hope, with teeth. It's the best way I can describe it."

"I know all about that. About hope with teeth. Every time I've ever looked at you, Flint. And wanted to believe that we could be something that we were never meant to be. Because you were that cowboy, the one that I was supposed to stay away from. The one that I was never supposed to love. You were that cowboy. And I knew better. But something in me didn't want to know better. Because it just wanted you. What I really wanted was you."

"I don't know what to do with this. I don't know. But I know that I can't walk away from you. Not again. Not ever again."

"I can't walk away from you either. I need you too much. I need us."

"I... I don't know if I can. I don't know... But I want it. I want to do whatever I have to do to figure this out. To fix myself. So that I can be what you need."

"Flint..."

"But you were always enough," he said. "It was me. It was always me. I was the one who couldn't cope. I was the one who flinched. You were always enough. What your father couldn't do was fix himself. I want to. For you. For us. For the future. I'm glad you wrote that song. I'm glad you told the truth about what I did to you. Because I needed to know. I needed to really know."

"But what about you?"

"It ruined me. Broke me. And now... You put me back together. I'm still not quite in perfect condition. But I'm trying. I want... I want forever. Please."

"Are you serious?"

"I am dead serious. I know that I don't deserve that level of trust. I know that I don't deserve for you to give that to me... But damn, I want you. More than I've ever wanted anyone or anything. And I want you more than I want to be the kind of safe I've been all these years. Because it was too late. The minute I caught you outside that gate, the minute that happened, it was too late. Too late for me to keep doing what I was doing. Too late for me to hang on to all the ugly stuff. All the broken stuff. I tried. And I nearly broke us both. So now I just want to surrender to it."

"I had accepted... I had accepted the idea that there was no way for us to have a happy ending. That I was going to have to accept that it was going to be another kind of happy. You know, the kind when you walk away, but at least you learned something."

"It's the easy way," he said. "This... What I want with you... It's going to be the hard way. Because I'm not perfect. And I am certainly not perfectly healed all of a sudden just because I want to be. This might be hard. Deciding to be together instead of just deciding to walk away wounded. I know that. I get that.

But I think it's worth it. You and me. I think it damn well will be. Those endings… Those endings where people are apart, it's not better. It's not deeper. It's just easier. Because it's easier to walk around with your own shit and never have to deal with it. It is so much harder to have to take someone else's on, and I got to ask you to take on mine."

Her face went soft. "Well, you're gonna have to take on mine too. I'm not exactly in perfect working order myself. I couldn't tell you what I wanted then."

"Tell me what you want now. I will do my damnedest to give it to you, because I love you. Because you are worth it to me. Because you are everything. You are everything and none of it matters. Because there is no protection worth having, there is no piece of my soul worth preserving, if you are out there in the world and I'm not with you."

Tears started to fall down her cheeks. "I want to spend the rest of my life with you. I don't want this to end. I want you to be the father of my children. I want you to be everything. I fell in love with you, Flint, even knowing that I shouldn't. I fell in love with you even though it wasn't what I wanted. I was afraid, but I knew that loving you was worth the risk. I just did somehow. These last two years I questioned it, and I tried so hard to call it something important. To call it something worthy. I tried to tell myself that I didn't need that fairy-tale happy ending. But I wanted it with you. It was never enough to not have you. When you sent me away, I was devastated." She wiped tears away from her cheek. "I waited until I got to a motel six hours down the road, and then I cried. For days. And then…"

"Do you think you were pregnant?"

She nodded slowly. "Probably. Even if we would've stayed together, I think I would have lost it."

"But I could've been there for you," he said. Everything in him felt wrong. Sad. Angry at himself for the choices that he'd made. For the ways in which he hadn't protected her. The ways in which he had protected himself instead. "I wish that

I would've been there for you. Because if there's one thing I know, it's that I cannot promise you a life without pain. It's something I'm coming to accept. The fact that I can't escape it no matter how much I might want to. But I can promise to be there for you. And I can promise to help try to carry the burden if it's too heavy. And to carry you if I have to."

"Yes," she whispered, closing her eyes. "But I need you to do something." She put her hand on his chest. "I need you to forgive yourself. Because our relationship shouldn't be a penance that you're paying. Our love isn't you making up for the past. You did the best you could then. I just want you to do the best you can do now."

"I promise you that," he said, his heart about ready to pound through his chest. "I promise."

He felt raw, and exposed. He felt fundamentally changed. His whole world felt like it had been tilted a bit. Or maybe like it had been put right. It was a lot, to recognize that he was afraid, and had been all this time.

And he was going to take a long time to sort through it; he knew that. But he knew one thing now. And he knew it well.

"I love you."

CHAPTER TWELVE

OF ALL THE things Tansey had thought she would hear from him as the sun was just beginning to rise over the tops of the mountains...that was not it. The night had not turned out the way she had expected. Because she had been certain they would be parting from each other in the morning, again.

She had even been ready for it.

But she kept thinking about what he said. About how redemption, change, was the hardest thing.

She knew it was true.

Forgiveness, and the choice. The choice to just love.

To believe that it wasn't her that was broken, but her father. To believe that she was enough all on her own.

But that she really wanted to be with Flint all the same.

She had accepted that she might say she loved him, and not have a life with him.

She had never imagined this. The chance to have a life with him.

And suddenly, none of it mattered. If she ever wrote another song—but she was pretty sure she would. It just all felt like... there was more now. More than striving. More than trying to show people that she was worth something.

More than trying to be the best. It was the strangest thing, but loving him, being in this moment, it made her feel like she might be able to live for herself for the first time.

And living that way with him...

It was a happy ending that was somehow beyond anything she had ever fantasized about.

"I love you too," she said.

"Marry me. The whole thing. Everything. The forever thing."

"Just like that? Just like that you aren't scared anymore?"

"I'm terrified. Fucking shaking in my boots. It's just that now I know it doesn't matter. I would rather love you, and live every day with some kind of fear that I might lose you, than not have you in my life. I would rather feel everything. Be damn near overflowing with it, than live comfortable and empty without you."

"You make it sound awful."

"No." He smiled. "It's wonderful."

And she thought what she had concluded earlier. That they were some kind of fate. Even if it was a bloody, hard-won fate. And she knew that it was even more than that. Because they had the chance to be the kind of fate that she had imagined briefly earlier tonight. The kind that was bittersweet and sad.

But they were choosing to be more. The kind of fate that was more. The kind of fate that was everything. She realized that this kind of fate involved a whole lot of choosing. Because you could fall right into a man's arms, but unless you chose each other, you might not end up together. Unless you decided to let go, of all kinds of things, of hurt, of fear, and embrace hope...

Hope with teeth.

She knew exactly what he meant by that. And she would risk getting savaged by hope every time, if it meant getting to be with him.

But as she looked at him, as she went willingly into his arms, she realized, it wasn't hope with teeth. Not anymore.

This was hope with strong arms, with a steady smile and the truest heart she knew.

"This is a song," she said.
"I can't wait to hear it," he said.
She grinned at him. "I can't wait to live it."

CHAPTER THIRTEEN

HE DECIDED TO go home for Christmas with Tansey. She called her mother and invited her to come from Palm Springs, and she had agreed to make the trek, which had surprised Tansey, since her mom was pretty wedded to her warm weather and palm trees.

But it also pleased her.

He would've done whatever he had to do to make sure they could do Christmas in both places, or maybe he would've had to disappoint his family.

He was willing to do that.

Because he was done performing. Done trying to do things to make up for what he thought he lacked.

But there was one thing he needed to do. And it was the thing that made Christmas so special this year.

Not just because he was going to be introducing Tansey as his fiancée, but he was pretty excited about that.

First, he had to give her the ring.

Which he intended to do at midnight on Christmas Eve. Then on Christmas morning she could wear it and show his family.

Yeah. He was looking forward to that.

But first, during a family board game, he sneaked into the kitchen to find his mother. "Hi, Mom," he said.

She turned to him, smiling. "What is it, honey?"

He reached out and pulled her into his arms, hugging her. "I just wanted to tell you that I love you. And that I'm sorry. It's been hard for me to say things like this. But... Things are changing for me. I'm going to try to change. I'm going to try to be different."

His mother put her hand on his forearm, and patted it. "Flint, honey. You never needed to change."

"I did. I think... I think in time you'll see the difference."

"Well, I love you all the same."

He nodded, and walked out of the kitchen. The next person he needed to talk to was Boone. When he walked out into the hall, Tansey was there. "Are you okay?" she asked.

"Yeah. I'm just... You know. I'm doing what we talked about."

"Yeah. It's going to be fine."

"I know it will be. Because I have you."

"Good luck." She squeezed him, and he went outside, where he knew his brother was, down at the barn.

Boone was facing away from him, on the phone. "Yeah, well, if you're going to go on a bender on Christmas Eve, you might want to fucking call your wife and let her know where you're at... No idea... She texted me, because she was looking for you. And I think you should be ashamed that your wife has an easier time getting a hold of me than she does you... Yeah. Well. Get over yourself. You're drunk. And it's not even 5:00 p.m., and your wife and your two kids are... Seriously. Whatever. I'm not going to lie for you. I'm going to tell her that you're drunk. It's your problem to sort out, Daniel." He hung the phone up and turned around. "Oh. How long have you been standing there?"

"That Daniel Stevens?"

"Yeah. Fucker." He rubbed his hand over his face. "It's... You know, it's Christmas Eve and he's not home and Wendy texted me looking for him and... I can't lie for him. And I'm not going to. She's way too good for him. He's such a dick."

The ferocity on Boone's face told a whole story. But Flint had a feeling his brother wasn't in the space to tell it. Daniel was another rodeo rider, and a friend of Boone's, and he'd gotten married ten years ago. Flint had met his wife on a few occasions. She was very pretty. He had to wonder if his brother thought so too.

"Well. Sounds like you should do the opposite of lying for him. You should probably tell on him."

"Yeah. I have half a mind to."

"Boone…" He cleared his throat. "This is going to seem like it's coming out of the blue for you. But… You know I brought Tansey home."

"Yeah. And the song was about you."

"The song was about me. And she and I had a lot to work out. In regard to that. We had to address why I broke up with her in the first place. And I told her about…about the thing I am most ashamed of."

"What's that?"

He looked at his brother, and he could see that Boone genuinely didn't know.

"When you were crying about Sophia. And I hit you. And I told you not to cry anymore."

Boone looked away. "Hey. That's not a big deal. We were kids. You were a kid."

"Yeah. I was. But there was still… I was afraid. I was afraid of everything, and most of all, I was afraid of that pain never going away. Never ending. And your pain made mine worse. So I lashed out. And then… I have carried the guilt for that, and I use that guilt as an excuse. I used it to tell myself that I didn't deserve to have relationships because I wouldn't be able to be there for someone, because look at what I did to you when you needed me most." He shook his head. "But that wasn't it. I was just afraid of how much I felt. And I took it out on you. And I used it as an excuse my whole life."

"There's no guidebook on how to handle stuff like that,"

said Boone. "And I'm not gonna claim I'm any less messed up than you."

"Yeah. But some of the messed up you are might be my fault."

"No," said Boone. "Hell no. You were always there for me. And yeah, you're kind of a stoic bastard. But you're a good man, Flint, and you have been the whole time. Not saying you haven't made mistakes. I've heard the song."

"Well. She forgives me. I'm going to marry her."

"Good," said Boone. "You should. And hell, if she can forgive you, I certainly can. Even if I don't feel like there's much to forgive."

"Thank you," he said, and he meant it. Because whether Boone was willing to admit it or not, Flint knew that he needed that forgiveness.

And then he did something he knew his brother would be allergic to. He reached out and hugged him. Clapped him on the back. "I'm going to ask her to marry me," he said. "Well. I already did. But I'm going to get down on one knee and give her a ring and everything."

Boone looked at him long and hard. "Good for you."

"Do you think you're ever going to do that?"

He chuckled. And it sounded kind of bitter. "I have a barrier to that. It isn't the same thing you have. But it's...an issue."

And yet again, he wondered about the phone call he just overheard.

"Well. If you want to talk about it, I'm here. And newly in touch with my feelings."

"Wow. I'm going to pass on that."

"Okay. Love you."

And he'd said it. And he meant it. Boone flipped him off, and that felt about perfect.

At midnight, he and Tansey were in his room, and that was when he did it.

"I have something for you." He got down on one knee in front of her. "Tansey Martin...will you marry me? For real. Forever?"

Tears sparkled in her eyes as she nodded, and he took the ring out of the box and slid it onto her finger. "I know you can buy yourself any piece of jewelry that you want."

"But I want this one. Because it's from you." She smiled. "I have a song that I want to play for you."

"Well. Then I want to hear it."

She sat down on the edge of the bed, holding her guitar, and this one was different. A little more upbeat than the songs she usually played.

And this song was about love. Choosing it, hanging on to it.

Love is cactuses
Good-luck charms and bad-luck nights
Sunny days and colder weather
Letting go and holding on
And I've heard the best revenge is living well
But the best is letting go
So you can just love
In the end, it's all that matters
In the end, it's the greatest

And he knew it was true. The real story of them. Good and bad and the two years in between, when they didn't have each other at all. And he was grateful. So grateful, that she had decided to let go of all the anger she had every right to have, so that they could love each other instead.

She had apologized to him recently, for the song. For the fact that some people would never accept they were back together, because they were still holding on to that story she'd told so well.

"It's part of our story," he'd said. "And I wouldn't trade it. Because it had to happen for us to end up here."

It was true. He'd had to break again to know that he wanted to be whole.

"You know," he said. "I was wrong, about winning. I said that you couldn't love anything. That you couldn't care about anything more. But loving you, that is winning. And everything else… Everything else is just noise."

She kissed him. "I love you. And it's winning for me too."

"It was the cactus."

She laughed. "You can't prove that."

And he smiled against her mouth. "You can't prove that it wasn't."

* * * * *

Part Time Cowboy

To Haven. I've dedicated a lot of books to you, but in truth, you deserve them all. You're the reason I get anything done, and the reason I believe in love and happily-ever-afters. I'm so grateful that I've got you.

CHAPTER ONE

WHOEVER SAID YOU couldn't go home again had clearly never been to Copper Ridge. The place hadn't changed. Not in the ten years before Sadie Miller had left town, and not in the ten years since. It probably wouldn't have changed much in another ten years.

Well, it would change a little bit now. The population sign would increase by one, adding back the resident she'd taken away when she'd left town at eighteen. And it would also contain at least one more bed-and-breakfast.

So, in an unchanging landscape, she would be responsible for two changes in a very short amount of time.

She deserved a medal of some kind. Though she doubted anyone in this town would ever give her a medal. She was just the wild child from the wrong side of the tracks. Not many would be welcoming her with open arms.

But that was fine with her. She wasn't here for them. She was here for her.

She looked across the highway, at the ocean, barely visible through the trees on her left. She could remember walking there as a kid. A long hike in the sand, through gorse and other pricklies, around the lake and across the road.

A walk she and her friends had always made without their

parents. Because the main perk of getting out for an afternoon was getting away from their parents, after all. At least it had been for her.

It was strange to see something familiar. She'd spent so many years moving on to the next new place. She never went back anywhere. Ever. She went somewhere new.

This was the first time she'd ever been somewhere old. And she wasn't sure how she felt about it.

She looked at the gas gauge on her car and sighed. The little yellow light was reminding her that she hadn't made a pit stop since she'd gone through Medford, nearly three hundred miles ago. She was going to have to stop somewhere in town before she went out to the ranch. She wasn't exactly sure where the Garrett ranch was, just that it was on the outskirts of Copper Ridge.

She'd never been invited onto the property before.

The fact that she was leasing a business on it now would have been funny if she didn't just feel horrible, stomach-cramping nervousness.

But then, she figured facing past demons was supposed to be scary. She wouldn't know for sure since she'd spent years avoiding them. Six months ago, that had changed.

Working with people dealing with grief and loss was always impacting—there was no way around it. But one very grumpy older woman who'd lost the house she'd been in since the 1940s had forced her to think about things she'd always avoided.

"Home is wherever you are," Sadie had told her.

Maryann, whose every decade on earth was marked clearly in her snow-white hair and the deep lines etched in her face, had scowled at her. "Home is where I raised my children. Where my husband breathed his last breath. I don't know who I am outside those walls."

"You're still you. I've spent a lot of my life moving from place to place, and I take my essence, my soul, or whatever you want to call it, with me wherever I go."

The other woman had waved her hand in dismissal. "You can't know, then. You're a vagrant in your own life. If nothing matters to you, how can you sit there and tell me that something I poured the past sixty years of my life into is meaningless?"

And that was when she'd realized...as a crisis counselor she'd helped so many people deal with loss. Either the loss of a loved one, the loss of a marriage or, very often, the loss of a home, and she'd realized that all that advice had been thin. Rootless, because she was.

Because nothing was permanent in her life. Because not one thing had the kind of deep resonance and meaning for her that Maryann's home had for her.

She'd never before been quite so conscious of the transient nature of her life. But in one blunt sentence her patient had reduced the past ten years to a tumbleweed in her mind's eye, while Maryann's own past had risen up like a redwood. Towering, significant. Rooted.

After that she'd felt so aware of how alone she was. That she'd let every friendship she'd left behind wither on the vine and die, that she'd done a crap job of making new friends since she'd moved to San Diego. That her last boyfriend, Marcus, hadn't been missed from the day she'd rolled him out of bed and out the door for the last time.

Those revelations had led to online perusals of Copper Ridge. Which had led to an ad she hadn't been able to get out of her head.

Long-term lease. Perfect for a private residence or bed-and-breakfast.

From there, she'd examined her savings, done estimated profit and loss based on exhaustive research of similar businesses, and before she'd quite realized what she was getting herself into...she'd committed. Committed to leaving the career she'd spent more time in school for than she'd spent actually practicing.

For the first time in ten years, she'd agreed to an extended time frame in one location. And for the first time in ten years, she was headed back to the one place she'd ever called home.

Of course, now she felt like she was approaching doom. Which she didn't think was at all dramatic. Since she was never dramatic.

Except for when she was dramatic.

From the backseat, she heard Tobias, more commonly known as Toby, let out a plaintive meow. The entire road trip had been endured with growing indignation by her cat. But then, she paid the rent, so he had to deal.

"Sorry, bud," she said. "I have the thumbs, I man the can opener. That means you have to stick with me. And if that means moving up the coast, it means moving up the coast. At least I didn't fly and throw you into cargo." Which, during their many moves together, had been a necessity on occasion. Toby wasn't a fan of air travel.

The cat didn't respond to her attempts at mollifying him. Which didn't really surprise her. In many ways, she was much more dependent on him than he was on her.

Sadie looked out at the expanse of evergreen trees that lined the road, a rich, velvet green that she hadn't found anywhere outside of Oregon. California was sun and palm trees, deep blue ocean and heat. It was beautiful, but in a different way.

Copper Ridge was all majestic mountains, shades of green and steel-gray sea. Not the kind of beach you hung out on in a bikini unless you were a local. The wind was cold and blew the sand up hard and fast, the grains biting into skin like little teeth.

It was its own kind of beauty, that was for sure. She'd been all over the United States. From the Deep South to the East Coast and back west again, and nothing had ever been quite like this. She'd never thought she'd be back.

But she was. And the dread was ever encroaching.

Suddenly, the car engine started to growl, and she pushed down the gas pedal, hoping to feel it rev again, only to be disappointed.

"Oh, frickety frick," she muttered as she pulled to the side of the road and the engine went totally silent.

Gas had apparently been needed sooner than expected.

She leaned forward, pressing her head against the steering wheel. "I knew it was doomed. I knew I was doomed!" She straightened up and looked backward at Toby. "Don't start. Don't get judgey."

Toby did nothing but stare at her with green eyes that were extremely judgmental despite her command. "You suck, cat," she said, reaching down and digging for her purse, then feeling around for her phone.

She pulled it out and saw one bar of service. Oh, right. Because that's what you got for moving away from civilization and settling in the absolute sticks.

She tapped her fingernails against the side of the phone and contemplated who to call. She didn't really know anyone in town anymore. Her own parents had moved away ages ago, and she wouldn't call them even if they hadn't.

Thankfully, she could get roadside assistance, but what a freaking pain.

She pulled up the browser on the phone and typed *tow trucks* into the search engine, then grimaced as she watched the little wheel up in the top left-hand corner of the phone spin, and spin and spin while it tried to grab hold of a satellite signal for long enough to pull up some results.

"Oh, Copper Ridge, you've bested me before, you aren't allowed to do it again." She kept her eyes on the phone and then growled at it, setting it on the passenger seat while she leaned over and pulled a stack of papers out of the glove box. She had to have a number for her insurance on hand at least.

Somewhere. It had to be somewhere.

A loud rap on the glass behind her shot a shock wave through her and she whipped around, releasing her hold on the stack of papers, sending them flying through the car, where they settled in both the front and backseats.

She looked around at the mess, then at the knocker. On the other side of the glass was a man in a tan uniform, a gold star on his chest, sunglasses over his eyes. What she could see of him was…well, hot. Which was the last thing she expected, because she'd been living in San Diego for a few years, the land of the beautiful, and rarely, if ever, was she so overcome by a man's face that all she could think was "hot." But maybe that had to do with the recent startle. She was just a little dazed, that was all.

He pointed downward, an authoritative gesture that took her a minute to attach meaning to, mainly because something was pulling at the back of her brain. A memory that was attempting to come to the forefront.

She blinked and tried to get herself together, tried to get herself back into the present. She pushed the button on the door and the window slid down, removing the barrier between herself and Officer Hottie.

"Hi," she said. "I'm out of gas. But I have roadside assistance so… I mean, I'm okay. Except I don't have very good cell service. So I was looking for… Well, anyway, did you stop for a reason?"

"To check on you," he said, the expression on his face strange. He looked like he had a memory tugging on his brain, too, and that made her own memory pull even harder.

"Yes…because…distressed motorist." She looked around at all of the scattered papers. "Right. But I'm not really distressed. I'm fine."

Wow, but he really was hot. Chiseled jaw, short dark hair. He created a response, low and deep in her body, that felt familiar in a very disquieting way.

He bent down in front of the window and she caught the name on his badge.

E. Garrett.

Oh, no. No no no no. There were not enough swearwords in the English language to express all of the bad in this situation. She was stranded on the side of the road, and she'd just encountered one of the chief demons from her past. In a uniform. The welcome committee from hell. Not that she'd imagined she'd be able to avoid him forever, considering her B and B was situated on his family's ranch, but she'd imagined she might avoid him for at least ten minutes after hitting the city limits.

She was not in the mood to deal with him. She was revising his nickname. Not Officer Hottie. Officer Stick-Up-the-Ass. That's who he was.

Not only that, he was a reminder of a whole host of things she would rather just forget.

And then his expression changed, and she knew he was catching up.

"Sadie Miller," he said.

"Well, damn." She smiled at him as best she could, but her palms were starting to sweat. Authority figures did that to her in general, and authority figures who had once fingerprinted her were an even bigger issue. "You do have a good memory."

"You never forget the first woman you put in handcuffs," he said, his voice low and firm, giving zero impression of a double entendre, and yet, it hit her that way.

Hit her and ricocheted around to parts inside of her that had gone ignored for a long time.

She cleared her throat and straightened her shoulders, trying to look arch and serious, and everything she'd spent the past ten years turning her life into.

Eli Garrett wasn't allowed to make her feel like a scroungy teenage girl, because she was not a scroungy teenage girl anymore. Similarly, he was not allowed to make her feel hot and bothered like he'd done back then, either, because…well, because she wasn't the same person she'd been then.

"Indeed," she said.

"What brings you back into town?"

He didn't know? She looked at him, studied him. He didn't know. Well, that was just peachy. Connor Garrett had neglected to tell his brother that he'd offered her the lease on the house.

She had a feeling that was going to go down with Eli like a live leech in his breakfast cereal.

"Am I, um…am I being detained?" she asked, fidgeting in her seat.

"No," he said.

"Then am I free to go?"

"Where? You're out of gas."

Point to Officer Garrett. "Yes. I am. Maybe…maybe you could help me with that?"

His lips, which were far more interesting than they should be, didn't smile, didn't lessen their tension. They simply remained in a flat line. Uncompromising. Unfriendly. Like the man himself. "Just a second." He turned and walked back toward his squad car and she started picking up the papers she'd strewn all over the car.

Her heart was beating so hard she thought she might have a medical event. What were the odds that he was the first person she saw when she came back to Copper Ridge? It was a bad omen. A very bad omen.

Of course, her first thought, still, was that he was hot. She'd thought that at seventeen. But then, to a rebellious kid with an affinity for underage drinking, a man who was part of the sheriff's department was sort of the ultimate fascination. The ultimate no-go. So of course, even when she'd resented his presence, she'd gotten a little kick out of checking him out.

She let out a long breath. She'd sort of hoped that he'd gone on to law enforcement in another town. Or that maybe he'd given up wearing a uniform altogether and discovered a passion for pottery…maybe in the south of France.

But no. Eli Garrett had done what most people from Copper Ridge seemed to do. He'd found his place in the little community and stayed in his carved-out niche.

You should judge. Since you're back and all.

Yes, she was back.

At this point in the game, Copper Ridge had seemed as good a place as any to give her demons the big middle finger.

And hey, she was facing one of them a little bit early. But, considering he had a gun strapped to his lean hips, she thought maybe giving him the finger wasn't the best idea.

"I put a call in for you," he said from over her shoulder.

"Gah!" She startled. "Could you not sneak up on me like that?"

"Do I make you nervous?"

"No. Why would you make me nervous?"

"Criminals *do* seem to get nervous around the badge."

She frowned. "I am not a criminal. I am a licensed therapist in eight…no, *nine* states."

"With a criminal record."

"I was a minor."

"No arrests since then?" he asked.

"I ask again, am I being detained?"

"No."

"Then… I'm free to go."

"Except that you're out of gas," he pointed out. Again.

"Well, *you're* free to go, then."

He lifted a shoulder. "Yeah, I could. But I feel like it's my mission to make sure you don't get into any trouble. Or light anything on fire."

"Okay, look, I didn't light anything on fire on purpose. I knocked over a lantern."

"Which is why arson wasn't on the list of things you were arrested for."

"Do you forget anything?" she asked.

"Public drunkenness. Disturbing the peace, resisting arrest. Not arson, though. And that's not even mentioning the number of times we had to come and ask you and your friends to leave a store, or stop loitering where you didn't belong."

"Good lord, what a sad small life you must lead to remember my rap sheet. *I* barely even remember it."

"As I said, you don't forget your first."

She screwed up her face. "That sounds possibly more sexual than I think you mean it to."

"How does it sound sexual?"

She squinted. "Really?"

She waited for a full four seconds while it registered. She could see when it did because his humorless, impassive face had a slight shift before going back to being total granite. He still had his sunglasses on, so she couldn't see his eyes, only her own reflection. Which looked flushed and flustered. And not from heat, that was for sure.

"Why are you here?" he asked.

"I didn't say," she said.

"I know. I tend to remember conversations that happened less than five minutes ago."

"Yeah, well, I don't see how that's any of your business, since I'm not being detained for questioning."

"For someone who hasn't been arrested more than just the once, you have the lingo down perfectly."

"I'm a therapist. I work with some troubled souls. I've seen more than one arrest."

"Hmm," he said. A noise halfway between a word and a grunt.

"What?"

"I'm surprised you became a therapist, is all."

"Why?"

"Because."

She knew what that because meant. *Because you're such a mess.* That was what it meant. And she was not a mess. She wasn't perfect, but she wasn't a disaster, either. Anyway, thankfully, having your crap together was not a requirement for being able to help others get their crap together. So there. She didn't say that last part, though. Because…well, gun. Badge. Handcuffs.

"I like to fix things," she said. That was honest. "To fix people, actually. I don't just arrest them and throw away the key. I try to make an impact on people's lives."

"Well, it takes both types, I guess," he said.

"Yeah. So anyway, don't you have some teenage miscreants to harass? I seem to recall that being your MO."

As soon as she said it, an old red pickup truck eased into the space in front of her and an old man, one who looked familiar, got out, holding a gas can the same color as the truck.

"Well," the other man said, a smile on his face, "if it isn't Ms. Sadie Miller."

Apparently she was wrong about not having anyone in town who still knew her. It was like these people had nothing better to do than remember every single soul who was born in this burg. For all eternity.

In fairness, though, she remembered Bud, too. She had no idea what his real name was. Or if he had one. Hell, that could be it. There was more than one Bubba in town, and they went by it completely un-ironically, so there really was no telling.

"Yes," she said. "Yes, it's me."

"What brings you back to town?" he asked. "Your parents aren't back, are they?"

"No," she said. "They're still down in Coos Bay." Not that she spoke to them. For all she knew they could be somewhere else entirely by now, but she didn't care. Not anymore.

She couldn't watch their dynamic, not now that she had a choice. She'd moved away from her father's rages. She wasn't going to expose herself to them again.

And her mother wouldn't leave. No matter how many times Sadie begged, her mother wouldn't leave.

"I see. Well, it's good to have you back." He put his hand on the bill of his ball cap and tugged it down sharply before heading to the back of her car and opening up the gas tank.

Just like that. Like her presence mattered. Not like she was some hooligan who'd accidentally started a little barn fire and gotten herself arrested. Not like she was the child of a wife-beater or a disturber of the peace.

Like he was happy she was there.

Darn. She felt a little emotional now.

She unbuckled and got out, standing next to the car and watching Bud, bent at the waist and pouring gas into her car. "Hey, whatever I owe you, I'll bring it by the gas station. I don't have cash, but…"

Bud straightened. "Don't you worry about it," he said. "Consider it a welcome home."

She couldn't fathom why he was being so nice. She'd barely had any interaction with him. Back when she'd been a kid she would often go into the store that was adjacent to the station, after she and some friends had gone swimming in the river, and buy candy bars for fifty cents. Shivering in wet bathing suits in the cold, air-conditioned building.

But she hadn't really thought of him as someone who would know her. Or…care. "I appreciate that." But she would still be going down to the gas station to pay him back as soon as she could.

Maybe even before she went to the Garrett ranch.

"Thank you. Both." She wasn't going to let Eli Garrett get to her. She wasn't going to let this stand as some sort of sign of how the rest of her venture here was going to be.

Nope. Just because it began with a vehicular disaster and Eli Garrett did not mean it would continue on that way.

Her eyes clashed with Eli's and she looked down at the ground before realizing that was more awkward than just looking at him like he was a normal person. And not like he was a very handsome person who had once handcuffed her.

Even though he was.

She cleared her throat. "I'm going to go now. I have…places to be." Eli would find out what those places were eventually, but hopefully that didn't mean they would have to actually see each other.

She got back in the car and shut the door, and saw in her rearview mirror that Eli had done the same. Good.

She took a deep breath and started the engine, then put the car into gear. She was on to new things, reclaiming an old past and stealing its power.

And a little run-in with Eli Garrett wasn't going to change that.

CHAPTER TWO

THE CATALOG HOUSE was even more beautiful than advertised. Rough around the edges, yes, but Sadie had been warned about that.

The lawn needed replanting. Or sod. But she wasn't sure she had the budget to lay down a grass carpet. Which meant she might be stuck with seeding, and patience. She hated being patient. She didn't like sitting around. And she had never waited for the grass to grow.

She leaned back against her car and studied the house. From the rocks that went halfway up the facade, to the solid, original wood paneling and the cut-glass windows, it was something that spoke of a different time.

It was hardly a rough-hewn cabin. It was almost too elegant to be out here, buried in the trees at the base of the mountains. But she knew, from what Connor had sent in his email, that the house was one his great-great-grandfather had ordered for his wife from a Sears and Roebuck catalog around 1914. Something to make the wilderness of Oregon seem a little less wild, compared to their old home in Boston.

Sadie imagined that, in a land of log cabins, this had been the most modern dwelling in the area.

Not so much now, but it had charm. And really, that was what a bed-and-breakfast needed. Connor had said renovations would be up to her, but she had permission to do what she wanted to the place, so long as she paid for it and—per her lease—left it in better condition than when she came. Which meant, according to him, "no stupid shit like shag carpet."

She took in a deep breath, let the smell wrap itself around her. The sharp tang of salt from the sea, wood that was heated by the sun, and pine all lingered in the air.

It was familiar, but different, too. She'd been away from this air for a long time, and when she'd left, there was nothing about Copper Ridge that had felt special to her. She hadn't been able to see the beauty anymore. It had all shrunk down to a little house on the wrong side of the highway, and the smell of dirt, blood and booze.

There hadn't been a lot of moments where she'd stopped and smelled the forest. If she'd ever gone into the forest it had been to hide out, in a little alcove not far from the Garrett ranch, and smoke a cigarette. Which sort of negated the fresh clean air aspect of it all.

It struck her then that she was within walking distance of the place. That if she wanted to, she could leave her half-unpacked boxes and see the haven she'd gone to with her friends all those years ago.

A strange ache filled her chest, a feeling of longing and homesickness that was unfamiliar to her. There was weight in that clearing. Roots. And, she strongly suspected, a high probability of ghosts of bad decisions past.

She and her friends had been nothing more than children then, angry at life. Determined to do whatever they could to take back some control. Which had taken the form of drugs, alcohol and sex. Because those little rebellions felt like an achievement.

But she was an adult now. And she had the control. The life she made here would be hers. More than just a reaction to what was happening in her family home.

She didn't need to see the clearing. And there were no ghosts.

With that final thought, she picked up Toby's pet carrier and strode up the front porch and lifted the lid on the mail slot by the door. Connor had said he'd put a key in there for her. She had the impression he intended to interact with her as little as possible.

Which suited her just fine. She had the money she needed to do the remodeling on the house, and she was sort of looking forward to spending a few weeks in relative solitude handling all of it before she got things up and running.

Maybe then she'd look up her old friends. Or not. That would be…well, it would be too close to revisiting times that hadn't been fun for anyone. Maybe she would meet a guy. Go on a date.

Lately she'd been out of the habit of both dating and making friends.

The moves made it hard. And if she was honest, starting fresh was her preference. She didn't like bringing old places with her into the new ones. Not that there weren't friends and boyfriends she had cared for. She had cared. She did. It was just that she liked them as happy memories. She didn't like letting a relationship stretch on to the point it started to show wear and tear.

She pulled the brass key out of the box and put it in the matching lock, turning it hard before it gave. "All right, Toby," she said. "Welcome home, whether we like it or not, because we can't back out of the lease, and after I remodel this place, we'll officially be broke."

She walked them both inside and looked around. It was dark, but it was clean. The wood floors were definitely in need of polishing, but nothing was seriously wrong with them. There were some threadbare rugs that needed replacing, light fixtures that needed updating. But it didn't smell like mold or anything, so that was a bonus.

"It really does have to work out," she said, setting Toby's carrier up on the kitchen table. "Because otherwise you'll be reduced to standing on a street corner and offering kitty head scritches for money. And none of us want to see you stoop that low."

She opened up his cage and he wandered out, looking around and sniffing the air, his tail twitching. She ran her hand over his gray striped fur, then scratched him behind his ears. "Really, though, you could charge for this service," she said. "You give me instant Zen."

Toby just looked at her, as though to say he would be much more Zen if they were back in their bright, white apartment in sunny San Diego.

But then, Toby was used to following her around at this point, so she knew his indignation would be brief.

First order of business was to get Toby's litter box out of the car. The second was to start making this place habitable.

Like it or not, ready or not, she'd made a five-year commitment, and she had to see it through.

"All right, Toby," she said. "It's time to do this thing."

"THERE WAS A car over at the Catalog House. I saw it when I pulled in," Eli said.

"Yeah."

Eli glanced at his brother, who was at the kitchen table looking more sullen and antisocial than usual. Which was saying something.

"And there was a light on," Eli continued, pushing for an explanation.

"Yeah."

"You don't sound surprised."

"No shit. I thought you were the law enforcement around here. You'd think you could put two and two together."

Eli was tempted to hit Connor over the head with something, but it was June. And June was a bad month for Connor, since it was his anniversary month. But then, March was a bad month for Connor, too, because it was Jessie's birthday. And April was a bad month because it was the month she'd died three years ago. August was when they'd started dating, ten years ago. December was when they'd gotten engaged.

So basically, there were a lot of bad months for Connor. And Eli got it, and he hurt on his behalf. But it didn't mean he didn't want to hit his brother for his obnoxious surliness sometimes.

"Would you care to explain?"

"Sure. We need some more revenue. I leased the house. Long-term."

"What? Don't you think we should have talked about this?" he asked.

"No," Connor said. "Because while I respect that this ranch is yours, too, you have to respect that it's more essential to me. It's my only job, Eli. You and Kate have work outside this place, but I don't, because someone has to run it full-time."

"I know that, but you didn't think about telling me you were going to lease out a house on our property?"

"I did think about it. I decided against it. Because I thought, at the end of the day, it was my damned decision."

"Dammit, Connor, I say this with love, please get drunk and pass out. You're impossible when you're like this."

"I'm always like this," Connor said.

"Yeah, and you're always impossible."

"Why are you all growling in here?" Kate, the youngest of the Garrett clan, walked into the kitchen, her dark hair in a low ponytail. She looked like she'd been working hard all day, and it was probably because she had been.

"Because Connor's in the room," Eli told her.

Kate smiled and crossed to Connor, planting a kiss on his cheek. Connor grunted.

"I love you, too," she said. "Did anyone make dinner?"

"No one made dinner," Eli said. "We all have jobs. But I did bring a pizza, just in case." Eli turned and put the box of pizza on the granite countertop. Kate started getting plates out of the cupboard.

This was Connor's house, the main house on the property, which he'd shared with Jessie during their years as a married couple. He stayed because this was the family ranch, going back generations. Because he was the one who worked the land, and the one least likely to leave. This was his rightful place.

But Eli often got the feeling he hated it.

"I will take a beer now," Connor said.

"Get it yourself," Kate suggested. "I'm already dishing up your dinner, and I am not a waitress."

"You wouldn't get a tip if you were one," Connor grumbled, getting up from his spot at the table and wandering to the fridge, jerking it open.

Eli noticed that there wasn't much in it beyond beer and cheese. He wasn't sure he liked what that said about his brother's mental state. Or maybe it was just that Connor hadn't had time to go shopping recently. That could be it.

"You should get a housekeeper," Eli said.

Connor grunted, which was something he seemed to do a lot lately. "I don't want a stranger rifling around in my stuff."

"Then hire someone you know."

"No."

Eli took a piece of pizza out of the box and set it on a plate, doing his best to ignore Kate, who wasn't using her plate, but was standing, arched over the bar, dripping sauce onto the otherwise clean surface.

Eli didn't like that. He liked things in their place. He liked things clean. He'd spent too many years putting things in order to let them slide now.

When they'd been kids, cleanliness hadn't just been a preference, it had been survival. Connor keeping things going on the ranch and Eli making it appear that there was a functional adult managing the household had been the only way to keep Child Protective Services away.

Order had been the only thing keeping them all together.

"So, Connor was just telling me about our new tenant."

"We have a tenant?" Kate asked, her mouth full.

"Yes, we do."

"Get me a beer, Connor," Kate said.

"Do I look like a damned waitress, Katie? Do I?" he growled, while he stalked back to the fridge and got out two beers, handing one to each of his siblings.

"Guess so," Kate said, taking the bottle and popping the top on the counter.

Sometimes Eli wondered if Kate had suffered a bit for having nothing but men in her life. But if he mentioned that to Kate she would probably spit on him. Which just proved his point.

"So," Eli said, leaning against the counter. "The tenant."

Anything to get his mind off the events from earlier today. Sadie Miller. He remembered her as a little blonde ball of trouble. Dressed in all black, ripped jeans, she'd been a stereotype of social rebellion. His least favorite kind of brat to deal with. She'd also been feisty as hell. Resisting arrest was putting it mildly. It had been his first summer with the sheriff's department, and they'd broken up a big party in an empty barn. Drunk, freaked-out teenagers had made the whole thing a nightmare. Basically, all hell had broken loose.

And he had ended up handcuffing and booking seventeen-year-old Sadie, making her the first person he'd ever arrested. Though ultimately she wasn't charged, as he'd said, with ill-advised word choices today, you never forgot your first.

"I drew up a long-term lease so that the Catalog House could be used as a bed-and-breakfast," Connor said.

"A what?" he and Kate asked the question in unison.

"You heard me. With the renovation of Old Town, and the fireworks show on the ocean getting bigger every year, tourism is a big deal. And I want in on that industry."

"How is your going behind our backs us being 'in on the industry'?"

"Income from the lease, and a small percentage of profits. And like I already told you," he said, directing his words at Eli, "some of us only get money from the ranch, so the more profitable I can make it, the better."

"And you're sure that your lessee isn't going to destroy the place?"

"She's a local. Or at least, she was."

The hair on the back of Eli's neck stood on end. "Is she?"

"Yeah. Younger than us, older than Kate, so I don't think any of us would have known her in school."

He would have laughed if there were anything remotely funny about it. "I have a good guess about who it might be," he said, setting his beer on the counter. "Sadie Miller?"

"Yeah. How do you know her?"

"I arrested her once."

Connor's eyebrows shot up.

"Well, damn, I didn't know she was a criminal."

Eli let out an exasperated breath. "She's not a criminal. At least, I don't think she's a career criminal. Granted, she committed a crime, that's why I arrested her, but she's not going to make a skin suit out of anyone."

"Bleah." Kate stuck out her tongue.

"I'm just saying. I arrested her for being drunk and disorderly about ten years ago. It wasn't exactly organized crime. And before that she was the kind of kid you'd see wearing too much eyeliner, smoking cigarettes and looking angry at the world. A bigger danger to healthy lungs than to society at large."

"Well, that's comforting," Connor said.

"I take it you didn't do a background check?" Eli asked.

"I did. But apparently not a thorough one. Credit check, though. Because her rental history reads like an epic novel. I needed to make sure she wasn't dodging. But she wasn't. She just likes to move."

"Well, I can't have any of this interfering with my campaign," Eli said.

He'd thrown his hat in the ring to run for the position, with the blessing of the current sheriff, who was now retiring. And since he'd decided to do it, it had become more and more important daily. Especially after he'd won a top two spot in the primary, his lead over the other man running substantial enough that a win in November looked almost certain. But that didn't mean he was resting on his laurels. No.

There were spreadsheets. Lots of spreadsheets. Because he couldn't help himself. Anything worth doing was absolutely worth doing right.

"It's not going to mess with your campaign. She's going to run her business, and you'll take care of your business. While I increase some of my profits."

"So how long do you think she'll stay here?" Eli asked, hoping the answer was "not long." She disturbed his sense of order. All of this did, but the fact that Sadie Miller was involved only made it more disturbing. And he did not need disturbing. Not right now. Not ever, really.

"She signed for five years."

"Five years?" he and Kate spoke together again.

"Will you stop repeating my answers back to me in question form? Yes, five years. It's going to take time to get a business going. There's some updating that needs to be done on the house. She's agreed to pay for it, and orchestrate it all."

"You're crazy. You're going to let someone else, a stranger, live on our property for five years without even…meeting her first?" Eli asked.

"It's over. It's signed. I'm not discussing it any further," Connor said.

Eli leaned back against the counter and took a long drink of his beer.

Kate shrugged. "It might be nice to have a woman around again."

"She's not going to be around," Eli said. "She's running a bed-and-breakfast, apparently. There's a difference between that and her being around. This is a big property."

"I was just saying. And maybe I'll go visit her," Kate mused.

"Eli's right, Katie," Connor said. "Everything is going to be kept separate."

"That's fine." Kate picked at the top of her pizza. "But I do think it would be nice to bring her something. A housewarming something. Foodstuffs. Small-town hospitality in action and all."

"Feel free to deliver foodstuffs," Connor told her. "I don't give a sh—"

"Yeah, yeah, I know," Kate said. "You don't. About anything. I get it. You're a grumpy codger and you aren't going to be sociable. Ever. Again. I won't make you."

"Good," he said.

Kate turned to Eli, her brown eyes wide.

Eli put his hands up. "Don't look at me," he said. "I'm not joining your small-town welcoming committee."

"Fine. I'll be the representative for this family. And try to prove we weren't—" she took a bite of her pizza and spoke around a mouthful of cheese "—raised by fucking wolves."

"Well, we'll leave that up to you," Eli said. "I have faith in you."

"Gee, thanks."

"I'm going to head home," Eli said. "I'll leave the pizza."

That earned him a thanks from Kate and a grunt—no surprise—from Connor.

"I've got the afternoon off tomorrow," Eli added, "so that means I'll be by to help out. Do you have anything big going?"

"Not a lot. We have to tag the calves this weekend, though. Are you free?"

"Yeah," he said. "I'll be around for that."

He was in law enforcement by choice, but he was a rancher by blood. He, Connor and Kate all did some local rodeo events now and then, too, though Kate was by far the most successful and was looking to turn pro when she got the chance.

Of course, the fact that he was either working for the county or working on the ranch was a big part of why he had no social life. But he didn't really miss it. Unless he was horny. Then he kind of missed it.

"Great," Connor said. "See you tomorrow, then."

"See ya." He turned and walked out of the kitchen, through the entryway and onto the porch. He stood for a minute and looked out at the property, and at the light in the distance. The light that was coming from the Catalog House.

Sadie Miller was in there. On a five-year lease. Damn it all, it didn't get much more disrupting to his sense of order than that. Of course, the past couple of years had been one big, giant disruption for their family.

They all felt the loss of Jessie. And they all felt the hole that her death had carved into Connor. He wasn't the same. He never would be.

But then, that was the way this place was. Or at least, that seemed to be the way love was for their family. You got it, you lost it.

It had started with the first generation of Garretts on this land. His great-great-grandfather had ordered that house and had it built. His great-great-grandmother had lived in it for only two years before getting pneumonia and dying.

Then there were his great-grandparents. His great-grandmother had died in childbirth, leaving her husband a shell of a man, barely capable of keeping the land going, and not entirely managing to keep track of his children. His grandfather had run off with a woman from town, leaving his grandmother to raise her kids alone. And then there were his parents.

Their mother had gone when Kate was a toddler. Off to God knew where. Somewhere warmer and sunnier. Somewhere with men in suits instead of spurs.

A place without needy kids and the smell of cows.

But it had left her husband to sink into a mire of alcoholism and despair.

It had left Connor to grow up at fifteen. And for Eli to follow right along with him.

And all that pain had started in the house that now sheltered Sadie Miller. It seemed fitting in some ways. Since she was a pain in his butt.

He walked down the steps to the driveway, then headed down the path that took him the back way to his house.

Sadie Miller wouldn't be a problem, because he wouldn't let her become one.

He was the law around here, after all.

CHAPTER THREE

SADIE WOULD VENTURE down into town today at some point. Grab some supplies. After she'd taken inventory, of course. She knew there were some tools in the shed, per the typed-up—and very brief—note Connor had left on the kitchen counter.

But until she had some clue about what sort of work she might need to do, the tools were fairly useless. She had some basic information on the minor flaws in the house, but there were other things she wanted to tackle.

Most of the place had the original wood paneling. Wainscoting that went halfway up the walls, which were painted a deep cream. The wooden detail was echoed on the ceiling, crossbeams forming a checkerboard over the plaster ceiling.

It looked like the crown molding in a few of the rooms had been replaced at some point, and it didn't match. Which meant she was going to need to take it down, and then mount some new stuff.

That wasn't a part of her original plan, but she had a little cushion for some surprises. And money set aside for some major projects, like the addition of a back deck. And since structural issues were Connor's problem, she didn't anticipate running into anything that would absolutely kill her budget.

Some people might call her a flake, but she was a well-educated flake with a basic understanding of money management.

She walked into the kitchen, and to the walk-in pantry that was larger than some bedrooms she'd had in her years of apartments. The solid wood shelves had a fine layer of dust over them. A mop and broom standing in the corner were the only residents, except for a few daddy longlegs hanging on the ceiling.

She made a mental note to take care of those guys later and walked back out into the kitchen, opening up cabinets that were mainly empty. There was one cabinet filled with mismatched teacups, and she counted that as a good find.

A quirky touch to add to the place. As inspiration went, it was a good place to start.

She wandered back through the dining room, which was nearly dominated by a large wooden table that was scarred from years of use. Refinishing that would go on her list of to-dos, but not for a while. She'd throw a tablecloth on it for now.

Out in the hall, the old wooden floor squeaked under her feet. Weirdly, she liked the sound. Liked the reminder of the age of the house.

The boards on the stairs were the same, her fingertips leaving a light trail on the banister as they cut through the thin film of dust. The house had obviously been cleaned when the previous tenant had left; it had just been a couple of years since anyone had been back inside.

She walked down the hall and pushed open the doors to each of the four bedrooms. They all had gorgeous four-poster beds. They would need all-new linens and drapes, but she'd been expecting that. The two bedrooms on the backside of the house faced the thick, undeveloped forest, and the other two provided views of a bright green field, dotted with cows.

All the rooms needed blinds to block the light so guests could sleep as late as they liked, and do whatever they wanted with no privacy concerns.

Two rooms had private bathrooms, while two others had to share one in the hall—not ideal, but given the age of the house, that it was as well-appointed as it was was sort of a miracle.

All it would take was a bit of scrubbing, polishing and the addition of matching molding. Also, some knickknacks, new furniture and a carload of linens.

The shopping would be the fun part. She would try to keep it local so that the finished product reflected Copper Ridge. She was really getting into this whole concept of community.

For now, she was going to go and hunt for those tools Connor said were in the shed. What she would do with them was up for debate, but she had a kind of driving need to do whatever she could.

Sadie tromped down the steps and into the yard, the bark-laden ground soft beneath her tennis shoes, dew from the weeds flinging up onto her pant legs and sending a chill through her.

It wasn't warm yet this morning, but the wind was still, the trees around her seeming to close in tight, sheltering her and her new house from the outside world.

She whistled, the sound echoing off the canopy of trees, adding to the feeling of isolation. She liked it. And even more than that, her guests would like it.

Well, they'd better, anyway, since she was committed to five years here. Claustrophobia's icy fingers wound their way around her neck when the thought hit. Five years. In one place. In Copper Ridge, no less, the keeper of her hang-ups and other issues.

You're confronting your past. It's what you'd tell a patient to do.

Her inner voice was right. But her inner voice could go to hell. She wasn't in the mood to confront things. She was just... trying to feel a little less wrong. A little less restless.

A little less like she was a rolling tumbleweed. Or a running-at-full-tilt tumbleweed.

She'd given so much advice that she'd never once followed. Facing fears, facing the old things that held power over a person. Going back to a point of trauma and seeing that it held no magical properties.

Well, she was following it now.

She zipped up her hoodie, fortifying herself against the general dampness that clung to the air, and walked down the path that should lead her to the shed.

An engine roar disturbed her silence, and she turned to see a black truck barreling down the long, secluded drive that led to her house.

She stopped and watched, trying to catch a glimpse of the driver. She failed, but she figured it was too grand an entrance for someone who wanted to Freddy Krueger her, so she was probably good.

She shoved her hands into the pockets of her hoodie and headed back to where the truck had parked. "Hello?"

"Hi."

The feminine voice that greeted her wasn't what she'd been expecting. Neither was the petite brunette who dropped down from the driver's side, wearing a flannel shirt and a pair of Carhartts. Her braid flipped down over her shoulder as her boots hit the ground, and she looked up and smiled.

Sadie vaguely remembered that there was a female Garrett, but she'd never known her. Unsurprising, really, since this girl looked wholesome and shiny, and all the things Sadie had never been.

"Kate," she said, extending her hand. "Kate Garrett. The sister."

"Nice to meet you," Sadie said, shaking the other woman's hand.

"I didn't want to drop by last night because I thought it would be rude, but I thought I'd stop in today just to say hi. And to ask what all your plans are."

There was something wide-eyed and sweet about Kate, something that stood in contrast to her firm handshake and confident manner. She was strength, and openness, and for a moment, Sadie envied that. The bravery it must take.

"Well, I have plans to turn the house into a B and B that will hopefully be ready for guests in about a month and a half." She put her hands on her hips and let out a long breath. "Enough time to get things arranged, and to settle in, hopefully."

"If you need any help, or anything, I'm happy to give it. I work at the Farm and Garden, and I know a lot about plants, animals, general repair stuff."

It stunned her, yet again, how nice people had been to her—exception being Eli—since she'd shown up. She'd imagined... she didn't know. She'd turned Copper Ridge into such a dark place in her mind that she'd been sure people would all but greet her with torches and pitchforks. And yet, no one had.

Facing your demons, and finding out there aren't quite as many as you thought?

"That's really nice, but I don't want to take any of your time," Sadie said.

"Really, I don't have a whole lot happening right now. Just work. And it's very male around here, so it's nice to have a more feminine influence."

It occurred to her then that it was time to stop resisting connections. *Five years, remember?*

"If I need something, I'll take you up on that," she said. "You'll be better company than a random hired hand."

Kate laughed. "I try. What are you after today?"

"Trim. Light fixtures. I might look at new hardware for the cabinets."

Kate wrinkled her nose, then looked at the house, and at Sadie's car. "If you have renovation stuff to buy, you aren't fitting it in there. Ten pounds of potatoes, five-pound sack. But if you want, you can come in with me and use my truck to make deliveries back to the property. You just need to be able to pick me up at closing time."

Sadie hadn't had a firm plan for the day, but she couldn't

deny that the use of a truck had a very high chance of coming in handy.

Her immediate gut response was to say no. Because accepting help meant the possibility of needing to pay someone back. Sadie was fine giving help, and expecting nothing in return. But she'd always been afraid of leaving town owing a debt.

But you're staying here. At least for a while.

"Thank you, Kate," she said. "That's so nice of you. I would really appreciate your help."

"WELL, SHIT," CONNOR SAID, looking around the field. "I think we missed a calf."

Eli straightened and wiped the sweat off his forehead. It hadn't seemed too hot earlier, but now the sun was high in the sky, beating down on them. The middle of the field provided no shade, and the work they'd been doing wasn't easy.

"You think?" he asked, looking around the field and spotting a red angus, one of the few reds who had ever popped up in their herd, who he knew full well had been ready to birth a while back. "Oh, yeah. She calved already."

"And I don't see baby. Which means she's got him hidden somewhere, or he's dead."

"Dammit." Eli tugged his T-shirt up over his head and mopped the sweat off his chest before chucking the shirt on the ground and getting up onto his horse. "Let's go find him."

Eli spurred his horse on. "Got her number?" he asked, meaning the identification number on the mother cow's ear.

"Yeah, I know it."

"I'm going to guess he's under the trees somewhere." Eli gestured to the back of the field that led toward the houses. It was still heavily wooded, providing the herd with a place to escape the weather.

Connor followed him, the horses' hoofbeats the only sound as they galloped across the field. Eli kept an eye out for a carcass in the grass, but the absence of crows and buzzards had him feeling optimistic.

Death was a part of ranch life, but it wasn't one he enjoyed.

Sure, they raised cattle for beef, but they took care of them. They had value to his family that ran deep. It was hard to explain to someone outside of the ranching community, but those in it understood the connection without him having to voice it.

Hell, with a job this demanding, you had to love all the elements of it, or you'd never choose to do it. It was really why he chose to do it only part-time. Maybe that made him a fair-weather cowboy, but he was okay with that.

He still got his job done. Both his jobs, in fact.

He tugged his horse's reins and slowed her down when they got to the edge of the trees and Connor dismounted.

"Oh, great," he said, looking back. "We got mama's attention. But then, I guess that means we're close."

But the last thing they wanted was to be on a twelve-hundred-pound mother cow's radar while they tried to run down her three-day-old calf and give him a piercing.

Eli got off his own horse and followed Connor under the trees. "Okay, Con," he said, "make this fast because I don't want to deal with mom cow's attitude, all right?"

Then he saw it, spindly and wobbly, under the trees. Black as night, obviously not inheriting his mother's coloring.

"Okay..." Eli said. "Let's do this thing."

Connor crossed his arms over his broad chest. "Get in there, part-time cowboy. You're on shift." He handed Eli the applicator, which was already clean and ready.

Eli took it, then flipped Connor his middle finger before wading into the foliage.

He looked over his shoulder. The mother cow was jogging now, heading toward them, not happy to see them getting closer to her baby. And they couldn't blame her. But he needed to get the baby's tag on so they could match him up with his mother later. Easy enough to figure it out now, but harder later in a field of black calves.

"Hurry up, man!" Connor called.

"Right," Eli said, tossing the word over his shoulder as he battled through the brush, sticks breaking beneath his boots as he headed toward the calf, who was attempting a getaway. "I'll just speed this along."

"I don't want you to get your ass trampled."

"Well, neither do I," Eli growled.

Eli lunged for the calf, and as he did, the mother started to charge in their direction.

"Hell!" Connor dodged to the side and the mom nudged at him with her head, bellowing and generally trying to intimidate him. He sidestepped her next attempt at butting him.

Eli turned his focus back to the calf and grabbed him, fitting the applicator to his ear and punching as hard and secure as he could, holding the animal's neck and head still with one arm while he finished the job with the other.

"Got him!" He released the little black calf, who now had a yellow tag on his ear and seemed none the worse for wear.

"Then haul ass," Connor said, moving through the trees and back to his horse. Eli did the same, and fortunately the cow was now just focused on her baby, who was making a low bawling sound.

"He's playing it up now." Connor wiped his forearm over his brow. "Trying to make his mom even madder."

"I don't think she could possibly get much madder," Eli said, trying to catch his breath.

"Probably not. I'm going to ride back out for a minute," Connor told him. "Just to check everything over. You want to meet me back at the barn?"

"Yeah, sure."

Eli mounted his horse again and rode back toward the barn. One of the ranch hands, a high school kid Connor had hired to help with menial stuff, looked up from mucking stalls as he entered.

"Hey, Mike," Eli said. "Mind taking care of Sable for me?" He got off the horse and patted her neck.

"Got her," Mike said.

"Great, thanks." Eli walked around the barn, Connor's most prized acquisition. They'd poured all the money from their father's life insurance settlement into it.

Eli braced one hand on the solid wood wall, arching backward. Damn. He had a hitch in his back. He was too young to get old.

And he had to work a shift for the force in the morning, which meant he didn't have time to be sore. Double duty was a bitch. But he couldn't ever give up either job.

Connor lived and breathed the ranch, but Eli appreciated the break.

Because, when it came right down to it, he'd rather chase bad guys than be chased by a damned cow.

Though, being sheriff potentially meant doing a lot more paper pushing, and a bit less bad-guy chasing. But it also meant the chance to effect some good change in the county. Sure, some of it was down to the fact that he was a control freak, and the chance to take total control of the filing system was almost irresistible, and some of it was even ambition, but mainly he wanted to be sheriff because he loved Copper Ridge and the surrounding areas. And serving in law enforcement was the best way he could think of to show that love.

He heard a loud crash, followed by several more crashes and a shrill curse word. He started toward the noise without even thinking, because that was what he did. If there was something wrong, he went toward it, not away from it.

He walked down the path toward the din. Toward the Catalog House. And he already knew that whatever he was going to find there was going to make him very, very grumpy.

When he came through the trees he saw her, across the driveway in front of Kate's truck. Sadie was standing at the end of it, holding a bundle of crown molding or trim of some kind that had to be ten feet long at least. And in front of the tailgate, down by her feet, were various pieces of hardware and what had probably been a light fixture before it had met an untimely demise on the gravel driveway.

And here was the distraction he just didn't need.

"What are you doing?" he asked.

"Oh." Her head whipped up, her blue eyes wide for a moment, before they narrowed, her expression turning into a scowl. "You have to stop sneaking up on me. I've been in town less than twenty-four hours and I think you've scared a grand total of twenty-five minutes off my life."

"Somehow I think you'll be fine without them."

"Says you. That's an entire sitcom's worth of life you just cost me. Now my plans of watching one final episode of *Friends* before I go to meet my maker are completely dashed."

"Do you need help?" he asked patiently.

"Do you ever laugh? Because that was funny."

"Rarely. Not as rarely as my brother. But rarely."

"Maybe it's a male Garrett thing. Your sister is more fun than you are."

"So much fun that you stole her truck? Are you already adding to your list of felonies?" Eli asked, making his way over to the truck and surveying the small disaster around Sadie's feet.

"You of all people should know I was never charged with a felony, Deputy Pedantic, so let's not be dramatic."

"Just looking out for my sister." And he meant it. Because Kate was too sweet. Too trusting. And Sadie was someone he couldn't predict. The combination made him nervous.

"Kate stopped by and offered her pickup truck. Because she's very, very nice."

"Too nice," he said, still looking over the items that had spilled out onto the ground. "And you figured you'd unload this all by yourself?"

"Well, the trim isn't heavy. It's just unwieldy. But I didn't realize the guys had packed my bags up against the gate, and they had one tangled in the trim and… Anyway, I had a momentary disaster, and I have a broken pendant light. But it will be okay."

"I could help."

"Helping me wouldn't make you burst into flame?" she asked.

"Depends. Are you planning on lighting something else on fire?"

She let out a growl. "I told you. I did not light anything on fire. I knocked a lantern over. There is a difference."

"You started a fire. It was an accident, but you did, in fact, light an entire barn on fire."

"I feel like intent should matter here."

"All right, then, I intend to help you. Maybe you could stop trying to make everything so difficult and let me get to it."

SADIE WATCHED, AND tried not to let her mouth hang open, as Eli came closer, shirtless and muscular and just im-damned-possible not to stare at. He had dirt on his chest. His hairy, masculine, muscular chest.

He'd looked so clean in that uniform of his. Like he ironed it directly onto his body so that it would form straight to his physique and never wrinkle. And he looked good in it.

But never had she imagined that there was something so raw and manly underneath it all. He was downright…rough and uncivilized beneath all that law and order.

She suddenly realized she was staring. Pretty much at his nipples. It didn't get more horrifying than that.

She cleared her throat and looked back up at him. Met his brown eyes, which was the socially acceptable thing to do.

"Thank you," she said.

And all her good intentions fell like a Jenga tower when he grabbed the middle of the trim and crown molding bundle she was holding and lifted it up, out of her hands, to hoist it over his shoulder.

"Where do you want it?" he asked.

Her brain was taking in too much stimulus to compute the exact question. He was standing there, every muscle outlined to perfection by the stance and the weight of the items he was holding. He just looked so damned capable. Standing there and holding things that had been almost impossible for her to manage, like they weren't anything at all.

Actually, that part was really freaking annoying.

But it looked great. And she couldn't refrain from letting herself have a little moment. One where she admired the strength in his chest, the sharp, defined lines in his stomach. And down beneath those abs, a perfectly flat plane with deep grooves on either side of it that disappeared beneath the low-slung waistband of his jeans.

She almost had to bite her own fist to keep from whimpering.

What the hell was wrong with her? She didn't lust after guys she didn't like. Anymore. Sure, she'd lusted after him—mildly, until he'd arrested her. But she'd grown up since then.

She liked it simple, she liked it happy. She liked nice men who wanted a sweet, easy relationship, and when that wasn't easily available, she did without.

She'd been without for a while, so she was clearly just having a weak moment on the physical desire front. And hey, that happened. But that didn't mean she was going to do anything about it. Most especially not with Eli Garrett. No, thank you.

She wasn't a fling girl anyway. Mainly because the idea of getting naked with a total stranger was not at all appealing. She always got to know a guy before she hopped into bed with him. And getting to know the guy made it not a fling, but a relationship.

And if relationships were not, at present, a happening thing, flings weren't a happening thing ever. Ergo, sex was not a happening thing for her.

Ergo his abs had just killed 65 percent of her brain cells.

"Just...the porch is good," she said, walking backward, her

eyes still trained on him. She grabbed one of the plastic bags, which was lying, tipped and spilled, on the tailgate, and bent, her eyes still on Eli as he turned and started walking toward the house.

His butt.

Oh, my.

Yep. She'd just crossed over into shameless ogling and she didn't even care. Didn't mind even a little bit that she didn't even like the guy.

Why not look at him for a minute? The fact was, thrills were few and far between for her. Connor might be just as hot. She might ogle him next.

But he wasn't here. So for now she would just take a moment to note the way the denim cupped Eli's muscular, rounded...

"So...you gonna nail this up or what?"

It took her a full second to realize "nail this up" wasn't a euphemism for a sex act.

"The molding?"

"Yes," he said, setting it down across the porch.

She scrambled to pick everything up, avoiding the broken pendant light and gathering the rest of her odds and ends. "That was the plan. There's a nail gun in the shed. At least, I think Connor had that on the list. He left me a list."

"Decent of him."

"He's been sort of the invisible man since I arrived. He left instructions, but I haven't seen him."

"Yeah, well, he's like that. Actually—" he bent down to straighten up one of the trim pieces and she cocked her head to the side and watched the muscles on his back shift and bunch "—he didn't tell me anyone was coming to rent the place." He straightened. "Let alone signing a long-term lease and spending the next five years running a bed-and-breakfast on my damn property."

"It's sort of a shared property. If you want to be technical." She scurried up toward the porch, her bag in hand.

"Right. So how is it you're going to install all this? And why are you installing all this?"

"I want the trim to match. Obviously over the years some things were replaced at different times and some of it doesn't match. The wood in here is beautiful and I don't want anything detracting from it."

"But even the replacement molding is older than…we are. It might as well be original."

"Well, no, it might as well not be, because if it were, it would match. It gets accolades for age but I'm still replacing it."

"So you're going to put this cheap-ass stuff in there?"

"It is not cheap-ass! Look at how much of my budget is devoted to this and you will see just how not cheap-ass it is. It's very nice, actually. And if all you're going to do is insult my molding, then…get off my porch."

He crossed his arms and leaned against the railing. "I don't think I will. It's my porch. You're just leasing it."

"I have rights!"

"It's a bed-and-breakfast. What if I want to make a reservation?"

"It's not open yet."

"It could open faster if you didn't want to replace perfectly good molding."

She sputtered, her comebacks all jumbled around because… biceps. And forearms. And things. Why was he so distracting even while he was annoying? Why did it seem like the annoying only made it all more interesting?

She had no idea what was wrong with her. She needed some wine. A bottle of wine. And for him to go away. She was done with her thrills. She was on thrill overload. She was clearly giddy with the thrills and had crossed over into crazy town.

"What else do you have in the bag?" he asked.

"Things," she said.

His dark eyes narrowed. "What kinds of things?"

"Things of a home-improvement nature. Which I will use to improve this home."

"What the hell does it need improving for?"

She huffed and stalked to the front door, fishing the key out of her purse before pushing the door open. "Come in and see for yourself."

She walked in ahead of him, trying not to be overly conscious of just how big and masculine and *there* he was.

"Look," she said. "And by that I mean really look, like someone who's never seen this place before, and not like someone who loves it because it's sentimental."

"Who said it was sentimental?"

"Obviously it's sentimental. You're attached to molding."

"I just don't like change," he said, the words coming out stilted.

"Oh, really?"

"There's an order to things," he muttered. "It's easier to keep track of them that way."

She waved a hand. "Well, I love change. It's what makes life interesting."

"Which begs the question why you're back here. Committed to five long years…"

"Because there's no place like home. I've been all over the country and I've never been anywhere that felt like Copper Ridge."

He paused, studying her far too intently for her liking. "How long did it take you to get that response down so perfectly?"

Anger sparked through her. Because he had her number. "Are you saying my response seems rehearsed?"

"Yes. Very. Why are you really here?"

Oh, damn him. "Because. It was time. Because… I was tired of feeling like I was running away."

"From?"

She lifted a shoulder. "Things."

"Same things you got in that bag?"

"Yep. Nuts, bolts and other assorted crap."

Toby chose that moment to come padding down the stairs and into the kitchen.

"You have a cat," he said, "in the house."

"Yes," she said. "Where else am I going to keep my cat?"

"The barn."

"You don't keep a friend in the barn. Well, maybe *you* keep your friends in the barn. That could be why you don't have any friends."

"I have friends."

"I haven't seen any."

"You've seen me at work and at home."

"And I've seen nary a friend. Are they in the barn now?" She made her eyes round and looked at him in mock horror.

"None of my friends shed. And they don't leave dead animals on your carpet."

"Neither does Toby. I don't think he'd kill a mouse. He's too civilized for that."

"A cat that won't kill mice? That just sounds worthless to me."

She shot him a dirty look and scooped Toby up from his position by the table. "You can't have it two ways. Either it's bad for him to leave dead animals lying around, or it's bad for him to not kill things."

"I like it when cats kill things. Outside."

"Then have your cats the way you want them. I'll have mine the way I want him. And I will have matching molding. We're just going to have to disagree on the fundamentals of life. Big surprise there, right?"

"Good point."

"Well. Good. Glad we've come to that...conclusion." She set Toby on the table. "So...now I need to get back to work."

"You honestly think you're going to do all this alone?"

"Yes. I am. I'm a hard worker and I'm not afraid to get my hands dirty."

"I thought you were a therapist."

"Was."

"Didn't you listen to people for a living?"

She blew out an exasperated breath. "Listening is hard work, I'll have you know. It's why so few people do it. And anyway, I have the desire to finish all this work, and one thing you should know about me is that when I set out to do something, I get it done, okay?"

"Well, I'll look forward to seeing you get this done."

"Yeah, well, I look forward to you putting a shirt on," she said.

The words hung between them and she tried not to pull a face and reveal just how embarrassing they were to her. Because, damn it all, she was trying to pretend that she hadn't noticed. And she was pretty sure she'd been managing to hide the whole I'm-helplessly-checking-you-out thing from him, too. Except now she'd gone and shown she was disturbed by it.

Bah.

He cocked his head to the side. "This bothers you?"

"No."

"Then why did you say…?"

"Because. Because this is a place of business."

"I thought you weren't open."

"I'm not, but…still."

He leaned in and she caught his scent—sweat and skin. Man. And the want, the need, grabbed her around the throat and shook hard, unwilling to let her go. She should move. She should stop breathing him in.

But she couldn't think about what might come next. Because her brain was totally blank.

All she could do was stare. At his lips. At the square cut of his jaw. It was dusted with stubble now, not clean like it had been yesterday. Yes, today he looked more out of order in every way, and she had to admit, it was interesting. Fascinating. Dangerous.

Something crackled between them, and he seemed to feel

it, too. Because his expression wasn't granite like usual. There was heat there. Even fire. It flickered, quick and hot, in his dark eyes, and then it was gone.

"I think I've imposed on you a little too long," he said. "I have my own work to do."

"Right," she said. "Go on, then."

"If you need anything…"

"I'll call Kate."

"Call Kate." His words came at the same time hers did.

"Right," she said. "I'll do that. I'm picking her up…soon, actually. So. Okay, then."

He ran his hand over his hair, and she felt a little zip of attraction hit her low as the motion highlighted his biceps. Yet again. There was something wrong with her. It must be all this fresh air.

"I think we'll be okay, Sadie," he said, his voice rougher than it had been a moment ago.

"You…do?"

"Just stay out of my way, and I'll stay out of yours. And try not to change too many things."

CHAPTER FOUR

SADIE MILLER, IT turned out, was incapable of following orders. She'd done nothing but change things in the two days since she'd breezed onto the Garrett family ranch, and she showed no sign at all of stopping.

First of all, she'd had a crew there reconditioning the wood, stripping paint. Then she'd followed behind, repainting trim. She was like a little blonde windup toy, and every time Eli drove on the road to Connor's house or the main part of the ranch, he caught glimpses of her working outside the house. He could always resolve to hole up on his end of the property. The road to his own house ran the opposite direction, but that would mean no visiting with his family, and no ranch work. And he wasn't that desperate to avoid her.

Still, he didn't want to catch glimpses of her. He didn't want her there. And dammit, even he knew that verged on curmudgeonly. But he couldn't be bothered to care. He had things happening in his life. Important things. And he didn't need her wandering around the place like a breeze-blown hippie.

Shit, he was uptight. But even so, he hated the feeling of an interloper on Garrett land, and yeah, dammit, he was totally a curmudgeon. There was no denying it. But it just felt...invasive.

He didn't like change. He didn't like people crowding. It was a habit from childhood. They didn't have friends over, well, friends other than Jack Monaghan, and they didn't invite company in past the front porch. They didn't let them see what was inside. They didn't let anyone know the extent to which things had fallen apart.

It was a habit that died hard. Or not at all.

Eli pulled his car past the Catalog House, determined not to look again. Determined not to care. He'd promised Connor and Jack an evening of poker and beer and he planned to deliver. Connor would probably be happy as hell if they canceled, which was one reason he was determined not to.

He parked in front of the porch and looked up at the house. When Jessie had lived there, it had looked nicer than it ever had in Eli's memory. And everything had slipped since losing her.

Connor's muddy boots and other random castaways from a day's work were spread out on the wooden deck, which was in bad need of staining. The windows, vast and prominent, were spotted with water drops and splattered with dirt. Even the door had dirty handprints. Like a very large child lived here. A man child who'd crawled down into a bottle of whiskey the day his wife had been put in the ground.

A man who echoed their father a little too much. Not that Eli had a right to judge, considering that he'd never loved anyone. Not the way Connor had loved Jessie.

He'd never lost like that as a result, either, and he planned to keep it that way.

He got out of the car and noticed Jack's F-150 was already parked in the muddy driveway—which badly needed to be graveled, Eli would handle that—and he walked up the steps, knocking his boots against the top stair to get some of the mud off before pushing the front door open.

He could hear Jack's voice already—animated, loud, the same as he'd been since they were a bunch of skinny preteen boys. Jack was a year younger than Eli, but had always been close to both Connor and himself. If Eli had gotten in trouble as a kid, Jack was the reason. As much as Eli liked order, Jack liked disrupting it. Eli couldn't help but foster a strange admiration for Jack's total disregard for rules.

He couldn't partake, but he could admire. From a distance.

"The police are here," Eli said drily, walking through the entryway and into the dining room, where Connor and Jack were already seated, a stack of cards and poker chips in the middle of the table.

"Sadly," Jack said, "we haven't had the chance to do anything illegal yet."

Connor just sat there looking long-suffering. It was painfully obvious they were trying to pull him out of the pit he was in, and as always, he was so damned aware of it that he'd dug his heels in and was clinging to rock bottom for all he was worth. Stubborn ass.

"And now you won't get a chance. Are we ready to play? And drink? Thankfully, I'm within walking distance so sobriety is not a necessity."

"Public drunkenness?" Jack asked.

"Private property."

"Fair enough."

"Liss is coming," Connor said.

"Then why isn't she here?" Eli asked.

"I invited her," he ground out. "But she's not off work yet."

"So now we have to wait, I take it?"

"She's bringing the good alcohol," Connor said.

"Well, in that case," Jack said, relenting.

"Where's Kate?" Eli asked.

"Home, I expect," Connor told him.

Kate lived in another house on the property. It was small, and designed for two people at most, but it was perfect for her.

"Does she know Liss is coming? She might want to see her." Liss was one of Connor's best friends, and had been a very close friend of his and Jessie's, both before and during their marriage. And Kate seemed starved for female companionship, as evidenced by her obvious desire to wrap Sadie Miller up in a blanket like a little stray kitten. But he was not having that. There would be no adopting of Sadie Miller.

He grabbed a beer from the center of the table, out of the bucket of ice emblazoned with the Oregon Ducks O on the side, and popped the top off.

"We don't really need Katie hanging out and listening to us talk," Jack said.

"Don't call her Katie," Connor said. "She hates that."

"You call her that exclusively," Eli reminded him.

"Yeah. I'm her older brother. I can." He jabbed a finger in Jack's direction. "He can't, though."

"Oh, for God's sake, Connor. Isn't it hard work being this unpleasant all the time?" Jack asked.

"You're still here," Connor said. "The door is open. There are plenty of other men for you to play cards and drink with. Though they'll never satisfy you the way I do."

Eli almost choked on his beer. "You have to warn people before you break out random acts of humor, Connor. It's unexpected."

"I hate to be predictable."

"Yeah," Jack said. "You also hate puppies, rainbows, and I'm pretty sure if compound bow season ever opened on unicorns you'd be first in line."

Eli heard the front door open, and the sound of feminine shoes on the hardwood floor. Which meant it wasn't Kate, because she wore boots, just like the rest of them.

"I'm here!"

It was Liss. She breezed into the room, tugging her auburn hair from its bun and shaking her head. "Gah. Nightmare of a day. Going through financial records for…a place. Confidentiality, sorry."

"Yeah, I know something about that," Eli said.

"I'm sure you do. But accountant work doesn't show up on

a police scanner." She set a brown bag on the table. "I come bearing Jack. Daniel's, that is."

"Then you can sit down," Connor said, already reaching for the bag.

Liss frowned.

"Stop it," he said. "Don't give me the sad eyes." He looked around. "This isn't an intervention, is it?"

"Does it need to be?" Eli asked.

"No. I'm fine. Let's play cards."

"Strip poker," Jack said. "Because Liss is here."

Liss looked him over, then looked at Connor and Eli. "I'd win that game, Jack. No matter how you cut it."

"No strip poker," Eli said.

"You're just still mad because the last time I talked you into taking your clothes off, when we were about twelve, I think, we ended up getting caught skinny-dipping by that group of high school girls," Jack said.

"And that was the day I quit listening to you."

"Less talking. More betting," Liss said, pounding the table.

"Fine. Fine."

There was a knock at the door that sounded borderline frantic. And Eli knew that Kate wouldn't knock.

Connor got up. "Just a sec."

He walked out of the room and they all watched after him, listening. "Oh! Thank God you're home." A woman's voice.

"I'm always home," Connor said, his flat tone carrying into the dining room.

Connor. Full of charm as always.

"I'm having a slight disaster." Oh, no.

"Come in." Damn.

More footsteps, then Sadie Miller walked into his brother's dining room.

She was a mess. Her hair was wet and hanging in twisted, yarn-like strands over her face and down her shoulders. She wore a baggy gray sweatshirt that had damp spots spreading wherever her hair touched the fabric. "I'm having a problem," she said a little bit sheepishly, looking around the table at everyone.

Jack and Liss both looked confused.

"This is Sadie Miller," Eli said. "Our new tenant in the Catalog House."

Liss's eyes darted from Connor back to Sadie. "Oh. Hi. You're the one doing the B and B?" For some reason, her friendliness sounded forced. And of course Liss knew about the bed-and-breakfast. In fact, Eli had a feeling she'd been involved somehow.

"Yes," Sadie said. "That would be me. Though, right now the B and B is doing me. So to speak."

"What happened?" Connor asked, crossing his arms over his chest.

"Pipes. Burst. And I was trying to—" she brushed wet hair out of her face "—stop it. To a degree. But I couldn't. So I...uh... wrapped the pipes as best I could and changed and came here. I'm not sure where this falls under our tenant agreement. Technically this had nothing to do with my renovation and everything to do with me trying to shower in the upstairs bathroom."

Connor's brows locked together. "Well...hell if I know. I didn't really anticipate having to be involved."

Sadie blinked. "Well, we signed a whole...agreement. And there are certain things...as the...the landlord...and..."

Eli sighed. "Would you like me to go and take a look, Connor?"

Connor nodded once. "If you don't mind."

I mind. I mothereffing mind. "Nope," Eli said, sliding his beer toward the center of the table and pushing his chair back to stand.

Sadie was eyeing him warily. "Thank you," she said, and he could tell she minded about as much as he did. But she had no place to be irked in all this. She was the one who'd chosen to rent a place on his family property.

She was the one with really quite nice breasts, thank you very much, that were causing him some problems currently.

Getting laid in a small town was problematic. Which made breasts that were actually probably no better than average more noticeable than they should be.

She didn't look hot right now. She looked like a wet hen. He should remember that. He sent a meaningful message below his belt, but he had a feeling it was going to get lost in translation.

Mainly because his body never seemed to want to translate those kinds of messages. But then, what guy's did?

Especially not when the only company said body had enjoyed for the past six months was that of his right hand.

"All right," he said, "let's go check out your disaster. I'll sit this round out," he told Jack.

Jack swept the deck of cards to the edge of the table and leaned back, shuffling expertly. "All right, kids, get ready to lose your hard-earned money."

"Sorry," Sadie said, as they walked out of the room. "Obviously I'm interrupting."

"It's not a big deal. It's a thing that happens a lot. Poker. I'm not going to miss one game. And the sad fact is, Jack's right. We're all going to lose our hard-earned money to him. And he'll continue the grand tradition of having non…hard-earned money."

"I bet there's a story there," she said.

"Isn't there always?" he asked.

She nodded. "Yeah, in my experience, there is. Speaking of—" she pushed the front door open and he followed her onto the porch "—what's Connor's story?" The end of the sentence was hushed.

He closed the door, feeling a little uncomfortable having a stranger digging for information. Mainly because he was so used to family junk staying in the family. Because it was still ingrained in him. To keep the exterior looking shiny, no matter how bad the inside was.

But Connor's deal wasn't really a secret. A cursory visit to Copper Ridge's cemetery would tell his story in full.

"I don't know if you remember Jessie Collins."

"Vaguely. I might. Did she work at the Crow's Nest?"

"I think so," he said, trying not to picture his sister-in-law too clearly. Because it was too sad, even for him.

"Well, she was Jessie Garrett for about eight years. But, uh… she was killed in an accident."

It was a night Eli would rather forget. He could remember the scene clearly. A dark two-lane highway, and a car wrapped around a tree. He'd known it was too late for whoever was inside. That it had been from the moment of impact. He'd seen too many accidents like that, and not enough miracles.

The car had been so messed up he hadn't recognized the make or model. Hadn't realized it was Jessie's until one of the volunteer firefighters, who'd been first on the scene, had come charging back from the car yelling at him not to come closer.

They'd been trying to spare him because of who it was. But in the end, he'd looked. Because he had to be sure.

And then he'd been the one to officially notify his brother. And nothing in all of his life, in all of his training, had prepared him to stand on the front porch in his uniform and tell his older brother that his beautiful wife wasn't coming home. Not that night, not any night after.

Damn trees. Damn road. Two people they'd loved lost that way.

Though in their dad's case, he'd been at clear fault. Alcohol had caused his crash. Jessie had probably swerved to miss a deer, but they'd never know for sure.

"Oh," Sadie said, her voice muted.

"So he comes by his attitude honestly," Eli said, walking down the stairs to the driveway. "You want to ride in the patrol car?"

She looked at him, a brow raised. "It's a short walk. Anyway, I don't want to have any flashbacks."

"Emotionally traumatized?"

"Completely."

"Good. I probably kept your ass out of trouble."

"Ugh," she said. "Do not act like you did me any favors. What helped was getting the hell out of this town."

"Is that what helped?"

"Yeah. There's not enough options here. And there's way too much free time. I badly needed to escape."

"So why are you back?"

She sighed loudly. "Can I get away with repeating what I told you earlier?"

"No."

"Well, fine. That is just a damn good question." She took a big step and her foot landed in a pile of sticks that crunched loudly beneath her boot, before she shifted, her other foot making contact with soft dirt as she continued on toward the Catalog House.

"And you don't have the answer?"

"You know…you have to live somewhere. And I've had a hard time finding a place that didn't…suck. So I'm back here. Because—" she turned partway and offered him a shrug and a sheepish smile, the setting sun igniting a pink halo around her pale hair "—well, I am. And currently, all I've achieved is drowned-rat status."

"Don't go near the barn. Connor has rat traps."

"And cats, I hear," she said, tromping through the tree line and into the driveway of her…his…house. He followed, frowning involuntarily as he caught a glimpse of the bare flower beds. Sure, all that had been in them before was overgrown weeds, but she had them completely stripped now.

"Those are the rat traps I was talking about."

"Don't talk about cats that way in front of Toby. He's sensitive."

"He's probably been talking to you about his feelings too much."

"Was that a therapist joke?" she asked, moving ahead of him and up the stairs to open the front door.

"Yeah, it was. Excuse me, I'm out of practice with jokes."

"Obviously."

Her cat was there, on the kitchen table, looking at him pointedly. As if he sensed that Eli had absolutely no use for him, and he was greatly offended by it. Except Eli knew that wasn't it because it was a cat, and cats had no higher consciousness, as evidenced by their reaction to string.

He stared back at the cat.

"He is unimpressed with you," she said.

"The feeling is mutual. Now hang on a second while I try to figure out where the water shutoff is."

"That would be helpful," she said. "Water shutoff valves would be helpful."

"Connor should have left you a list of that stuff. Where it all is. Fuse boxes and water mains. Though I'm betting he doesn't even know where it is here."

"How long has it been since anyone's lived here?"

"A couple of years. An older lady rented it for about ten years, until she died."

"This place is kind of full of sad history," Sadie said.

"Yeah. Welcome to the Garrett Ranch, where the motto is, if it doesn't kill you…just wait."

"That is distasteful. I'm sure."

"Completely, but also the story of our lives. Now, I'm willing to bet your shutoff is somewhere inconvenient, like…maybe the shed outside?"

"I haven't looked."

"All right, come on. If we find it, I can show you how to shut it off."

"Maybe I know how to shut it off," she said, following him back out the door and down the stairs. "Maybe I'm a water-valve expert."

"But you aren't," he said, opening the door to the shed.

"Fine. I'm not. But I usually have nearby landlords who… do this for me. Which is sort of what's happening now, except you're involving me. Although, I have to say, I have never had a pipe just…explode all over me before. Not a euphemism."

"How could that be…?"

Her eyes widened and she looked at him meaningfully. "Pipes…burst…liquid all over the… Oh, wow. Think about it. Please don't make me say it. And I'm going to stop talking now. Please shut my water off."

Suddenly, he got it. Heat shot from his face down to his groin. This was what happened when he spent six—okay, honestly, it was closer to seven—months without sex. His mind was completely void of anything that went beyond boobs and the innuendo that had just popped up. So to speak. It was enough to… well, as she'd put it, *explode his pipe*.

He did not have time for this. He didn't have the patience for it, either.

"Fine," he growled, stalking to the pipe that was sticking out of the ground in the back of the old building, wrapped in a thick swath of insulation. He reached down and pushed the valve up. "So now your water's off. Direct me to your flood and I can see if there's a quick fix that won't require you to go without water all night."

"It's in the upstairs bathroom. So…back to the house. And I hope you're enjoying this tour of…things that are not finished in the yard," she said, leading them both back to the house.

"What are you doing with the flower bed?" he asked, looking at the bare dirt.

"I don't know… Something. I was hoping someone could tell me which plants you…plant here this time of year. I don't know anything about flowers or grass or… I'm going to do some investigating tomorrow."

"Haven't you planted flowers before?"

She shrugged. "There's never been any point. I leave before anything grows. Or…when I was in San Diego I had an apartment and I had, like, a little pineapple plant in a pot. But some asshole stole it off the balcony. So I figured unless I wanted chains on my potted plants I'd just forget it. This is nice. I don't have to chain things to the porch." She opened the front door and walked in, then paused at the base of the stairs. "Up that way. The one off the master bedroom."

He sighed and walked upward, toward his watery doom. Or something like that.

He could hear her following behind, her footsteps softer and off rhythm to his own.

He walked into the bedroom and saw a few damp footprints on the wood floor, then he looked into the bathroom, where there was a sizable puddle by the sink.

He sighed heavily and got down on his knees, the water seeping through his uniform pants, then he opened the cabinet doors. "What the...hell?"

"I had to improvise," she said, her voice small.

He leaned in and examined the makeshift stopper she'd wrapped around the pipes. A shirt, a pair of sweatpants and...a black lace bra winding it all together.

"I was about to get in the shower, so I was already naked, and then there was water and so I had to stop it, and then I had to...tie it off. With something. I think that bra is toast."

He cleared his throat. "Probably." He reached out and started unwinding the bra, and tried not to think about how this was the first time he'd touched a woman's underwear in seven—okay, maybe it was more like eight—months.

It was Sadie Miller's bra. He should focus on that. On the fact that he remembered what a gangly, hissing little miscreant she'd been back when she was a teenager. All long limbs and blond shaggy hair, smelling like booze and cigarette smoke as she kicked at him while he'd tried to put her in handcuffs without breaking her slender wrists.

Sadie Miller's bra should hold no interest for him. And neither should her breasts. Or her innuendos.

ELI UNWOUND THE strap a little bit more and the rest sprang free, spraying his face with water.

Sadie bit her fist to keep from whimpering as she watched Eli Garrett, on his hands and knees, fiddling with her bra. She was so mortified she wanted to flush herself down the toilet. It would be preferable to this nightmare.

She was just one giant explosion of embarrassment after the other tonight. The whole pipe euphemism? What was her problem? Why did she say things like that around him? Good gravy.

She was good at talking to people. She did it for a living. Spoke with calm authority and with self-control, and with carefully chosen words.

And here she was pointing out every innuendo and dying a million tiny deaths—not in the good French way—like some extra awkward high school geek she'd never been.

What was it about Eli that caused regression? It was a mystery to her. He made her feel flaily. And kind of...horny. And that was just stupid. Cracking lady-wood over a cop said nothing good about her deep emotional issues. She was a therapist. She really should have a better handle on this.

Though she wasn't really a therapist at the moment. She was a bed-and-breakfast owner who was sinking her life savings into a place with leaky pipes, populated by grumpy, muscular men. Who said she didn't make good life choices?

He unwound all of her clothing—thank God she hadn't used her panties. She was just really, really thankful. Then he stood up, the sodden garments in his very large hand, his dark brows drawn together. "This isn't a quick fix. You will need a plumber. Which my brother will pay for."

"He said he wasn't sure where all that fell in the agreement." She reached out and took the ball of clothes, water dripping onto the floor.

"But I am," he said, his voice hard. "It's BS to act like he won't pay for a burst pipe. Obviously that had nothing to do with your improvements. My brother is just being a lame landlord. Trust me, he's not doing it on purpose. He's just…non-functional right now."

Sadie's heart squeezed tight. "I'm sorry about his wife. I… If he ever needs to talk…"

"He would rather shove barbed wire under his fingernails. And I'm being literal."

"Okay, then, so maybe vouchers for my services wouldn't go over well in exchange for this debacle."

"Connor isn't a talker," Eli said.

"Well, big surprise," she retorted, dumping the wet clothes into the sink and walking out of the space that really was way too small to be sharing with a man of his stature.

"What is that supposed to mean?"

"It just seems like it runs in the family, that's all."

"Meaning?" he asked.

"You're a little uptight," she said, walking near the bed and feeling a sudden surge of heat and self-consciousness. Dear Lord, it was like she wasn't even an adult anymore. Internally jittering because she was standing near both a man and a bed and they were alone.

"If by uptight you mean responsible for a shit-ton of stuff, sure," he bit out, "I'm uptight. Do you need water?"

"I have some," she said. "All over my floor."

"That isn't what I meant," he said, his civility clearly almost at an end. "You're going to need…coffee in the morning at least, I assume, and you need to shower."

She lifted a shoulder. "It wouldn't hurt."

"Either Connor will get his ass in gear and try to fix this tomorrow, or we'll want to call out a plumber. Either way you don't have water tonight, because the main has to stay shut off since the pipes are so old. And it means you don't have water until midmorning tomorrow. So, would you like to come to my place and shower and get a couple gallons of water?"

She blinked. "I…uh…"

"It's a simple question."

"I just didn't expect you to extend me hospitality," she said.

"I'm not a complete asshole."

"Oh. Okay."

"You say that like you don't believe me."

She shrugged. "I don't know, Eli, but whenever you're around I get a tension headache. Or I end up in handcuffs. So, suffice it to say, I'm not entirely convinced that you aren't a total asshole. Sorry."

And she also wasn't convinced she wanted to go to his house and get naked when he was in a nearby room. And run her hands all over her wet, slick skin, which would inevitably feel really good. And with his image so very large in her mind...

Yeah, well, again, she regressed in the company of this man. What grown woman worried about this stuff? It was...prurient. And juvenile. And things.

She needed both a shower and some water and the man was offering. So she should stop sweating, and stop insulting him, and just go with it.

"That would be great, actually," she said. "And I'm sorry about the asshole thing."

He put his hands on his lean hips and she took a moment to admire him. His uniform conformed to every muscle in his body; the tan shirt and dark brown tie, along with the gold-star-shaped badge honest-to-coffee did things to her insides that were unseemly.

Obviously she needed to buy batteries for her long-neglected vibrator. Dammit, how sad was it that her *vibrator* was neglected. A sex life, sure. People had crap to do. Who had time to go around hooking up and sweating and making walks of shame? She certainly didn't.

But she barely took the time to orgasm anymore. And when she did, she had to kick Toby out of the room, because it was awkward, and then it sort of felt like she was announcing her masturbatory intentions to her cat, which felt even weirder. There was something unspeakably sad about the whole thing.

But that was the reason Eli's presence had her so shaken. That was her story, and she was sticking to it.

"Whatever," he said. "Come with me."

He certainly didn't make a big song and dance about graciousness. He almost seemed burdened by inescapable chivalry, which was sort of hilarious, or would be if she wasn't so busy marinating in her embarrassment.

"Let me get some clothes," she said. "You can wait downstairs." Because she would probably fizzle into an ash ball and blow away in the wind if he watched her pull a new bra out of a drawer.

"Fine," he said, walking out of the bedroom and swinging the door partway closed. She waited until she heard his footsteps on the stairs before rummaging for new clothes. She pulled out a long-sleeved thermal shirt and a pair of black yoga pants, and a new bra and panties. And then she got a duffel bag to conceal it all in.

She stuffed the clothes inside and walked downstairs to where Eli was waiting, standing there staring at Toby, who was still on the table, looking defiant.

"I'm ready," she said. "Do you have jugs at your place?"

"Yes," he said. "We always save a bunch for target practice, so that won't be a problem."

Holy hell, she really wasn't in San Diego anymore. She was in Oregon, no question at all. "I should have guessed."

"What's that supposed to mean?" he asked, holding the door for her.

"Nothing. I just forgot the kinds of things you good ol' boys get up to in your spare time. I've been living in a city, if you recall."

"You've been gone for how long?" he asked, walking down the front porch steps. She followed him closely, clutching her bag to her chest. Looking at his dark brown pants, which seemed to be giving his butt a hug while shouting, "Look at it! Look at it!"

"Ten years."

"And where have you been in those ten years?"

"Polite conversation?" she asked.

"Why don't we try it?"

"I'm game if you are. Okay, I went to three different schools in four years. I started in Tampa, because, parties and the beach. Which is nothing like the beach here. Turns out, I hate college parties and breathing in Florida is like inhaling soup. So I lasted a year there. I basically toured the South." She increased her pace to keep up with Eli's long strides, following him down the darkened driveway. He pulled a flashlight off his belt and used it to light up the bark-laden ground. "Louisiana, North Carolina, and after I graduated I went to Texas, which you really don't want to mess with, just ask the locals."

"After that you went to California?" he asked.

"Nope. After that there was New York, Chicago and Branson."

"Branson?"

"Missouri. It's Las Vegas for families, Eli. Incidentally, I also lived in Vegas, but not for long. Then I went to the Bay Area and quickly discovered I couldn't afford to live there unless I wanted to donate a kidney to science, and then I went to San Diego. And now I'm back...here."

He stopped walking, the flashlight beam still directed at the ground. "I can't imagine picking up and moving that much."

"No?"

"I've got too much to pack up and bring with me. You know, Connor, Kate, all their stuff. The cows. Plus, there's this land. Our family land."

"Yeah, well, it's just me and Toby. We travel light."

He started walking again, continuing on straight down the drive. "I'll regret asking this, because... I shouldn't care. But what the hell did you expect to find moving from place to place?"

She lifted a shoulder. "I don't know. Everywhere is so different. I managed to trick myself into thinking that I'd find a place that made me different. And to a degree, it's true. Every place changes you a little. When I was doing therapy, I was a crisis counselor, so I always dealt with people going through the worst things possible. Every patient I spoke to changed me in some way. Every home I lived in, every restaurant I ate at… But…the one thing I've never done is go back to a place. I've only ever gone somewhere new. I thought I would see what it was like."

"And?"

"No magic yet. But I do think I've finally realized that it doesn't really matter where I live. I'm not going to find a perfect place that makes me perfect. So I figured I'd come back here and wrestle demons."

"What kind of demons are you wrestling?" he asked.

It was said drily. Insincere. And yet she found she wanted to answer. She found she wanted to talk to him about the demon she'd met head-on the night he'd arrested her. The night she'd nearly been killed.

She didn't blame him for that. Not really. She knew dimly that some people might. But she'd never put her father's actions onto Eli Garrett's shoulders. Because it had started long before then. Because she had a feeling that night was inevitable. Regardless of what date it fell on, regardless of what triggered it.

And it had been the reason she'd gotten into her car and driven away. And never once looked back. Until now.

"This way," Eli said, pointing his light toward a cluster of pine trees off to the left. "We can cut through here. It's faster."

She followed him through the trees and into a clearing. There was a house up the hill, surrounded by trees, the porch light on as if someone inside the two-story wooden cabin was waiting for them. Wide steps led up to a wraparound deck with a glass door, and large windows dominated the front of the place, making the most of the location, set deep into the trees and far away from any roads.

"No wonder you've never left," she said.

"Well," he said, "not much point when you have a house ready and waiting for you, is there?"

"Sure there is," she said. "If my parents had given me their house I still would have run. Happily for me, they never offered. I think the house ended up with the bank when they went to Coos Bay." She felt like the statement was a little more revealing than she might have liked, but oh well.

"Well," he said, obviously uncomfortable. And obviously unwilling to say more, even though the *well* held a wealth of meaning. He was really, at his heart, a decent man, even if he was reluctant in his decency.

"Well," she said, matching his tone, "my parents' house was essentially the crap cherry on top of a landfill, so for that reason alone I wouldn't want it. Thank you for being too nice to say that." She hopped over a tire rut that was filled with muddy water and continued following him down the road.

"I wasn't thinking it."

"Bull, and ten points if you can guess the word that follows."

"I wasn't, Sadie. I've been to a lot of houses like that. I've seen a lot of things. People have hard circumstances. And I don't like to think of their living situations that way."

"Why not?" she asked. "They do. Trust me. I mean…we do. We know."

"I don't judge people based on where they live."

"Is that honestly how you feel? Or are you just throwing out some…good-guy line?" she asked, as they came to the end of the road, where it narrowed and led up to his house.

"Honestly?" he asked, turning to face her. "I care about this place. I care about Copper Ridge. And I care about Logan County. This is my home. And the people here are my responsibility. It's not my job to look down my nose at anyone. It's my job to protect the people here." He continued walking, turning away from her again, his broad back filling her vision.

Her heart jammed up against her sternum. Anger mixed with

a strange kind of longing that she didn't want to apply to him. That she didn't want to apply to anything or anyone, really.

"And you do a damn fine job, I'm sure," she said, following him up the steps and waiting for him to unlock his door. The man locked his door. In Copper Ridge. Dear Lord.

"I know," he said. "I haven't exactly been hanging out for the past ten years so my first arrest could tell me that, but now that you have, it's sort of nice and circular. I could use it for my campaign."

"Hold up," she said. "Campaign?"

"Yes. I'm running for sheriff." He bit the words out as if sharing them with her was a monumental task.

"Oh, really?" she said, eyes widening. She couldn't help but be…intrigued by that. Maybe *intrigued* was the right word. Because Eli Garrett seemed to be a few things to her, and none of them were overly diplomatic. And it seemed to her, not that she was an expert, that a person running for any sort of elected position needed to behave, at least some of the time, like he didn't have a stick lodged in his rear.

But that was just her take on it.

"Yes," he said. "Really."

"Well, color me intrigued. What all does this entail?"

"Right now? I was the top finisher in the primary, and the final election is in November. My lead was pretty strong, but I still need to keep campaigning. Make more signs. I have a few months to prepare for a community Q & A," he said, pushing the door open. "This is the house." He swept his hand in a broad gesture across the living space. It was open, and neat, very different from his brother's place, which had an air of sad neglect about it, every bit of dust and dirt a fingerprint of grief. Eli's home had no fingerprints at all. Which, in and of itself, she found fascinating.

"Wow. Connor should hire you," she said.

"Because I'm not at all busy," he said. "I mean, obviously

I'm not. I'm here getting water for you and letting you use my shower."

"Because you care for the members of the community," she said. "Which I am, at this moment, grateful for. Much more so than that time you cared for the community by handcuffing me and putting me in the back of your patrol car."

"That seems to come up a lot."

"It's our cute meet, meet cute, whatever they call it. It's part of our story," she said, watching the tension between his brows intensify with each word. There was no doubt, she disturbed him. And he was growing even more disturbed having her in his house.

"Right. So, the bathroom is upstairs. Feel free to take as long as you need in the shower. I'll get the water ready for you to take back."

She cleared her throat, annoyed with herself for finding sincerity so hard. She was a basket case. Why anyone took her advice on anything was a mystery to her, particularly when she acted like this. "Thank you. Honestly. I know that I've sort of crashed into your life sans finesse here, and I appreciate you... well, I'm glad you haven't found a reason to arrest me again and I'm very grateful for the chance to shower."

He nodded slowly. "You're welcome."

"I'm going to go and...shower now." And she was going to hope that she could do it without thinking too much about his proximity. Or without thinking about him at all. Yes, not thinking about Eli Garrett at all—in the shower or out—would be the ideal thing.

If only she could manage it.

CHAPTER FIVE

ELI GRITTED HIS teeth and hunched his shoulders, trying to ignore the sound of the running water. Trying to ignore any and all thoughts of Sadie in the shower.

It was hard, no pun intended, because there hadn't been a woman in his house, in his shower, in…possibly ever. It had been so long since he'd had an actual relationship, he couldn't remember. Longer still since a relationship had mattered, since every actual girlfriend he'd had sort of faded into the distant past like a soft hazy dream.

The kind he had no desire to revisit. Because girlfriends were a whole level of responsibility he didn't want or need. At this point, with Kate still unsettled and Connor deep in his grief, Eli couldn't fathom taking on much more.

Which is why it's obviously the best time to increase your workload.

He pinched the bridge of his nose and took a deep breath, before dropping his hands back to his sides and stalking to the fridge. He was going to drink a beer. And he wasn't even going to bother to go back for the poker game. They'd all do fine without him.

He pulled a cold bottle out from the back and popped the top off with the magnet opener he kept stuck to the freezer.

Yeah, it was a terrible time to take on more. Connor needed help on the ranch, and he always would. It was their legacy, and Eli had to take part in it. Then there was the emotional aspect of dealing with his family.

On top of that, Sadie being in residence was adding another layer to his to-do list that he did not need. Because for all Connor said he was going to handle it, here *Eli* was, freaking handling it.

Not a huge surprise and not much he could do about it, either. Five years. Five years of Sadie and foibles that would undoubtedly be similar in nature to this. Sometimes he wondered if he'd been an ax murderer in a past life and he was destined to spend this one atoning.

But then he remembered reincarnation was bullshit and took another drink of his beer.

And reincarnation was not the only thing that was bullshit. That there was a naked, wet woman in his house whom he could not and would not touch was also bullshit.

He'd had a permanent frown etched into his face since Sadie had shown up. He didn't even feel like trying to fix his attitude. It was just one more thing to add to his list of things to worry about. One more thing that he had to add to an increasing, unwieldy pile of Things For Eli to Manage.

Things he knew without a doubt wouldn't get taken care of if he didn't do it. Because that was life. It was his life.

Which he was normally not so bitter about. But something about the addition of a woman whom he wasn't allowed to touch, a woman he shouldn't even want to touch, naked in his house was like jamming an injured thumb into the center of a lemon. Grabbing two empty gallon jugs from under the sink, he began to fill them for the woman he was trying not to picture naked.

He heard soft footsteps on the stairs and turned to see bare feet come into view. Bare feet with shocking pink nails. Followed by baggy black pants and a very soft-looking shirt,

molded to breasts that he should not stare at—but did anyway—and then the rest of Sadie appeared.

Her blond hair was wet and piled on top of her head, tendrils
falling down the sides of her face, her cheeks flushed from the
hot water. Her makeup was gone. Lashes that had looked dark
and heavy were now spiky and pale.

She looked damp and warm and he had no business wondering about her body temperature, or her level of dryness.

"Thank you," she said, her feet hitting the floor. She walked
to the kitchen counter and slung her bag, and her shoes, onto
the granite surface. "I feel more like a human and less like a
mole person, so that's always good." She was smiling now, ef-
fortless, friendly.

As if she hadn't been pissy and sulky with him only a few
minutes ago. As if they had no history between them whatso-
ever.

Fine, it didn't matter to him. She was just a problem to check
off his list. He was not going to waste time overthinking her.
He didn't have the time to waste.

"Shoes," he said, the muscles in his back tensing from his
belt line to his shoulders.

"What?"

"Take your shoes off my counter, please."

"Sorry," she said, pulling them from the surface that would
now have to be disinfected.

"Yep," he said. "I'll grab your jugs for you."

Her blue eyes rounded. "Oh, really?"

"What?"

"You're going to…grab my jugs for me… I don't… You've
had sex before, right?"

Heat assaulted him, starting in his face and burning a line
straight down his chest to his cock. "Yes. What does that have
to do with anything?"

"You seem to be operating on a frequency wherein sexual
innuendo doesn't exist."

Jugs. Suddenly an image of him putting his hands over her breasts and, well…grabbing them…flashed through his mind. "Because I'm not a fourteen-year-old boy," he shot back. "And I don't call women's breasts jugs." He said the last part through gritted teeth, trying to figure out how in the hell he'd gotten into a conversation about breasts with the woman whose breasts had been tormenting him from the moment she'd crashed back into town like a blonde tornado.

"Well, that's mature of you. I don't typically call them jugs, either. I prefer 'the girls' or 'sweater bunnies,' but even I went there."

He about choked on the sip of beer he was trying to take. "Don't you have work to do back at your place?"

"Nothing pressing," she said.

He gritted his teeth. "Do you want a beer?" He didn't want her to stay for a beer. Why was he so compulsively appropriate? Especially when she was standing there talking about *sweater bunnies.*

"Thank you," she said, "that would be good."

He laughed, even though he found nothing about any of this funny, and turned back to the fridge, tugging another bottle out, and opening it before sliding it across the counter toward her.

In spite of himself, he found he was curious about her plans for the Catalog House. Because maybe if he knew about the changes, they wouldn't feel quite so invasive. A long shot, but worth a try.

And anything was better than talking about her breasts.

"What's next on your list for the place?" he asked.

"I have to make the downstairs back bedroom livable. That's going to be my room. It's small, and part of an addition. So it's a little damp and chilly, but with caulking and some oil heaters I won't die. And since we're headed into summer it won't be bad at all. Then obviously I need to make sure the plumbing is better than it is. Flower beds are a priority, and linens and blinds. And after that, barring menu creation, I should be good to start advertising and getting special events scheduled."

"Wait…special events?"

"Yes! I thought it would be fun. Ranch tours. Picnics. And I'm thinking on Independence Day a community party would be great."

"People. Here?"

"Yes, people. I'm opening a bed-and-breakfast, for people and not, despite what you may have thought, cats. And if I want to attract people, it seems like bringing visibility to the place is the way to do it."

"What's the point of attracting locals?"

"Uh, locals go away on romantic weekend getaways to local places. And also, their family members come and visit. And people from surrounding areas might come to the parties and think of me. And honestly, maybe they'll think of Garrett specifically when they go to buy beef."

"How do you know about what we do on the ranch?"

"I Googled it. Because I am interested in helping you. And me. It's all…symbiotic helpfulness. And what's wrong with that?"

He felt like he was losing control. Like she had come along, grabbed his control and was running around holding it over her head, laughing maniacally as he tried to reclaim it.

"What's wrong with that is you're proposing to turn this place—*my* place—into a fun fair. We live here. We work here. This isn't a carnival."

"I never said it was! But what's wrong with a few special events? It's not like I have to take over the barns. I mean, I would, but I can keep it contained."

"Have you run any of this past Connor?"

She shrugged. "Not…specifically, but he did agree to let me bring a certain amount of the public onto the property when I initially sent over my business plan, so I didn't see why this would be a problem."

"You didn't see why it would be a problem?" he asked.

"No. I didn't." She took a drink of her beer. "I'm running a business, and it benefits Connor, benefits Kate and you. I have a five-year lease agreement, and it seems to me that we should all be into ideas that will make things more successful. Right?"

"Not ideas that include my ranch crawling with a bunch of random people. I don't like that kind of disorder."

"You are the singularly most frustrating, uptight, obtuse... No one makes me mad, Eli. No one. I am not an angry person. I like to smile. And every time I'm around you, no matter how cheerful I determine to be, I end up irritated."

"That's funny, Sadie, because I feel like I end up irritated every time I'm around you."

"I just think your irritation is contagious," she said.

"Maybe you're so irritating you irritate yourself."

"Oh! Bah! What are you, twelve?"

"I thought you were the one acting like an adolescent boy, not me."

"No, I am the one acting like I have a sense of humor. Because I do. And you," she said, drawing her beer against her chest, "are ridiculous. And humorless."

"If you think that barb is going to wound me, you obviously don't know me very well."

"I don't know you very well. And I'm content with that. I think I will spend the next five years not knowing you very well." She grabbed her shoes from the stool and plopped onto it, bending over and fidgeting while she put them on her feet. She straightened, a clump of wet hair falling out of her bun. "I'm going to go now. And I'm taking the beer. And the water. Thank you. Again. I'll try not to bother you anymore."

He snorted. "Good luck."

"Oh, I don't need it. I don't mind bothering you. You are clearly the one who is bothered by being bothered. So...you're the one who needs the luck, not me."

She stood up, collected her bag and managed to grab the

water jugs as well, then turned on her heel and stormed out toward the entryway, out the front door, slamming it shut with her foot and rattling the windows.

She had no right to be angry. He was the one who had every righteous reason to be pissed. She was a tenant, not a part owner. She had no right to be making decisions that affected his life and his business.

Tomorrow, he was going to talk to Connor about her. And very definitive boundaries. After he was done with work anyway. He groaned and shoved his beer back. It was officially getting too late for him to stay up and drink. Sadie Miller had ruined his entire evening, and now he was going to have to go shower in a shower still wet with water that had been on her body. And then he was going to have to sleep with visions of sweater bunnies and strangers doing the hoedown on his porch dancing in his head.

Which meant he was better served getting on the computer and working on campaign plans. At least planning would help make him feel like he had some control.

Yes, tomorrow, he would talk to Connor about what needed to be done.

And tonight? Tonight he would just have to deal with his annoyance. At least annoyance was better than sexual frustration.

ELI TOOK A sip of his coffee and walked out of Copper Ridge's coffee shop, The Grind, and onto the main street. Connor gave him endless grief about the fact that he cut his coffee with steamed milk. And that he ordered lattes. But he wasn't a fan of the black sludge his brother poured down his throat all day.

Eli needed caffeine, and he would get it in the way he found most palatable, even if his older brother called it Bitch Coffee.

Besides, he needed his coffee extra bad today because of his encounter with Sadie last night.

He'd been so annoyed that he'd barely been able to sleep, thanks to the images of his property being overrun with civilians. And he knew that it shouldn't bother him. But he also knew that if it really did happen, he would be putting caution tape all around his portion of the property and shouting, "Get off my lawn!" to anyone who got too close.

Old habits died hard, and things like that.

Anyway, that kind of behavior wouldn't be good for his campaign. And he had to think about that kind of thing now.

He let out a breath and headed toward the crosswalk. He waited for the signal to change, then started to cross, heading back toward his patrol car. A breeze came in off the waves. Salt, brine and moisture filled his lungs.

He needed to get his head on straight and stop worrying about Sadie. Though if there was a magic way for him to just stop worrying he would have found it a long time ago. But it seemed like the day his mother had walked out the door, she'd taken his stability and shoved a knot of anxiety straight into his chest that he'd never been able to get rid of.

He put his uniform on every morning and took it off at night, and the worry didn't go on and off with it. It was in him. Part of him. He'd more or less accepted it. And accepted that the only way to really deal with it was to make sure things were taken care of.

"Deputy Garrett!"

He looked to his left and saw Lydia Carpenter signaling him. He really didn't have time to field any issues from the Chamber of Commerce today. Lydia always had something to talk to him about. From obtaining proper licensing for an event, to dealing with complaints from home owners about "noise pollution" during one of her carefully planned summer concerts.

Everything in him screamed, *Not my problem*, but on the outside he just smiled and nodded. Because, most especially, when someone was hoping to gain the good favor of the voting public, one had to be pleasant.

"Ms. Carpenter," he said, "nice to see you. I'm on patrol so this has to be quick."

"Oh, fine, fine, fine," she said, tucking a strand of dark hair behind her ear, spitting the words out rapid-fire. "It will be. I just wanted to tell you I had a chance to meet with Sadie Miller today."

"You what?" he asked.

"Sadie came by the Chamber with a list of ideas for community events hosted on the ranch."

"She did what?" he asked, the words coming out a bit terse.

Lydia didn't shrink under his terseness. She didn't react at all. Her petite frame was unshaken, her smile firmly in place. She was young to be in the position she was in, possibly a bit younger than he was. And when he thought about it, he had to concede that the woman must be almost entirely composed of efficiency and stubbornness to achieve what she had, even in a town so small.

Her smile broadened, which he would have thought was impossible. And he had to admit that she was actually very pretty. But it didn't make this less annoying.

"She stopped by and we had a lovely chat, Eli." Suddenly he was Eli and not Deputy Garrett. "Her ideas for the Independence Day community barbecue are so good. She's talking about canvassing all of Logan County with flyers. I suggested we get it listed on the nightly news Community Chalkboard and on the Chamber's website. I think it's the kind of thing that could really benefit Copper Ridge. The coastal fireworks on the Fourth are already such a big draw, adding events that extend tourists' stays will only be good for everyone."

He was afraid, honest to God, that a blood vessel in his eye was going to burst. Sadie'd circumvented him and Connor, and now he was effectively roped around the balls by the president of the Chamber of Commerce.

If he tugged too far the other way, he could find himself neutered. And if not anything half that dramatic, he could at least find himself out of the running for sheriff.

"Thank you, Eli, so much for allowing this to happen on the

ranch. I can't think of a better place, or a better man to host. All things considered, I mean. I'd love to help with anything I can," she said, looking at him with large eyes. "I can help plan games. I could come by your place and look at different areas that might be of use for the event."

He cleared his throat, hoping it would help dislodge the rage ball that was blocking his ability to breathe. "I'll get in touch with you, Ms. Carpenter," he said, very purposefully not using her first name, because for some reason he just had a feeling that was asking for trouble. "Now, if you'll excuse me, I need to get on with my day."

He turned around to face his patrol car, which was parked against the curb, to see Sadie two blocks down, exiting one of the little shops on the corner, a small paper bag in one hand and a coffee in the other.

Before he could even think through his next move, his feet were propelling him toward her. And he was pissed.

She lifted her head and froze when she saw him walking toward her, her eyes widening, before she schooled her expression into an easy smile. "Why, hello, Officer Garrett," she said.

"Deputy," he bit out. "And do not give me that overly innocent face, Sadie. I know what you did."

"Do you?"

"Yes, I spoke to Lydia just now," he said.

"Ah," she said, nodding. "Yes. Lydia. She was so excited about the ideas that I had. And very keen to come over and help me get everything in order. And very, very excited to talk to you about it."

"What does that have to do with anything? What does it have to do with the fact that you have, yet again, overstepped?"

"Nothing. I was just making an observation that you have a big fan there."

"What?"

"She likes you," Sadie said, taking a sip of her coffee. "A lot. And I'm not really sure why, but I sort of assumed you have to possess something that looks like a personality when you're not around me, or you wouldn't have half the people in your life that you do. Which leads me to the conclusion that you just don't like me. But back to Lydia... Yeah, she likes you."

"What the hell do you mean she *likes* me? Who says that anymore?"

"Fine. She wants your body. Do you approve of that assessment?"

"No," he said, frowning. "No, I don't. She's just friendly because she's president of the Chamber of Commerce, and it's her job to be friendly."

Tourism was an emerging industry in Copper Ridge, and it was quickly becoming the heart and soul of the town, which was, in his opinion, the jewel of this section of Oregon coastline. The coastal Old Town section had been totally revamped half a decade earlier, and what had once been dilapidated was now made charming.

With that had come vacation rentals, small motels and a smattering of bed-and-breakfasts, similar to Sadie's.

In addition there were now candy stores, boutiques and shops specializing in crap made of salvaged flotsam that were destined to collect dust on mantelpieces up and down the West Coast.

The rest was mill and timber towns, run-down fishing communities, all banded together under the header Logan County, so named for its surplus of loganberries that lined the highways and tangled around the trees in the forest. All his responsibility. A responsibility that was starting to feel a little more burdensome just at the moment.

"Sure. I'm not going to argue the point with you," Sadie said. "But...you're a little oblivious."

"I find that ironic coming from a woman who seems oblivious to the fact that I don't want to host a community barbecue... picnic...pie eating contest or whatever the hell it is you're—"

"Oh! Pie eating! That would be great!"

"Sadie," he said, his tone warning.

"What? You're being a stubborn cuss," she said. "I am working hard to establish my B and B as something special. Yes, there are several in town, but they're just that—*in town*. Which, I grant you, provides the ocean view, but if you want solitude, a chance to be surrounded by the mountains. To just…be on a ranch? Well, that's what I provide. I want people to come and see it. I want people to *want* to be there."

"And you're going to accomplish that with pie eating."

"Argh! I genuinely don't understand what your issue is."

"Because I didn't tell you what it is," he said. And he didn't plan on it. The bottom line was, he was uncomfortable opening the ranch up to the public, and that was all she needed to know.

"Well, maybe you should."

"Do you want me to talk about my fucking feelings?" he asked, the language, in this context and while in uniform, not something he would normally use. But the woman was standing on his last nerve and grinding it beneath the heel of her impractical sandals—and yes, he'd noticed them, since the top of her head was now just above his shoulders, rather than at the middle of his chest. "Because we're not in your office, and I would not pay for that level of torture."

"I would refer you to someone else," she said. "A specialist of some kind. And anyway, I'm not practicing here. I'm just opening a bed-and-breakfast and trying to bring cheer—and pie—to the community." Her pale brows locked together, a slight crease forming between them. "Do you hate pie and cheer?"

"I like both, in the appropriate place, at the appropriate time. I assume you still haven't run any of this by Connor."

"Not as of yet."

"Well, his *hell no* will be even more emphatic than mine."

"What about Kate?" she asked.

"If you use my sister against me I am throwing your cat out into the barn with the rest of the rat traps," he said.

"Okay, then, note to self, speak to Kate about this, because she will clearly side with me."

"I have work to do," he said. "Work that does not include playing house on someone else's property. We'll have to resume this at another time."

"Okay," she said, lifting her chin in the air, "we will."

SADIE WATCHED ELI'S retreating back and fought the urge to throw her coffee at him. She imagined it, though. Imagined the cup landing smack in between his broad shoulders and spraying that uniform with dark brown liquid.

She would mourn the loss of such a gorgeous, well-fitted garment, but it would be a small price to pay for how satisfying it would be in terms of venting her frustration.

No, she hadn't talked to Connor yet, but when they'd discussed the agreement—granted, over email—and come to an understanding about the percentage of her income he would be entitled to, they'd also discussed taking steps to ensure that it was a very profitable venture.

Connor wasn't the friendliest guy, even via email, but one thing he had talked about was the ranch, and why he was interesting in leasing the house. Ranching was hard and increased restrictions made it even harder. Selling their product wasn't as simple as it had been when the ranch had first started, and the cost of getting cattle to official USDA stations wasn't negligible.

One thing she'd picked up about Connor was that the ranch was the most important thing to him. And she felt like he would be on board with her plans when he saw the merit in expanding what they used their property for.

Of course, the chance remained that he was as unreasonable as his younger brother.

She huffed and headed down the street, the opposite direction from Eli, toward the Farm and Garden, where Kate Garrett was currently working her shift. And no, Sadie was not above using the youngest Garrett in a bid to get her way.

She pushed the door open, a bell tied to a string resting above the entryway signaling her presence with a soft, pleasant sound.

Being back in a small town was jarring and strange, but comforting in a million little ways she hadn't let herself imagine it might be. From gas station attendants who knew your name—and pumped your gas for you, welcome to Oregon—to little bells in doorways.

"Hi, Sadie, what brings you in today?"

Sadie smiled at Kate, who was behind the counter, her dark hair in a simple braid, her figure disguised by a plaid flannel shirt that was tucked into a pair of tan Carhartts.

The urge to strangle your brother is what compels me today, thank you very much.

"Flowers, actually. I need to get the front flower beds in order and I know absolutely nothing about anything leafy or petally."

"Well," Kate said, coming out from behind the counter, "you've come to the right place. Because I know a lot of things about plants."

"Good. So...you sort of know where I'm talking about, right?"

"Just the boxes in front of the porch?"

"Yeah, um...what can I plant there?"

Kate laughed. "I'll help you out. Just come out to the back with me."

Sadie tucked a strand of hair behind her ear, adjusting the paper bag she was holding as she did so, then took a sip of coffee as she followed Kate out through double, automatic glass doors to the back patio. Plants were hanging from metal scaffolding overhead and more pots were on pallets raised up from the ground. Flats of flowers were stacked into racks, and against the chain-link fence in the back rested bags of potting soil and fertilizer.

"I'm going to have to have you load up a cart for me, because I don't know what I'm looking at," Sadie said, surveying the plant life.

"I'm more than willing to do that. And I will even give you

my employee discount." Kate looked around, her expression shifty. "Just don't tell."

"Don't do it if you'll get in trouble. Otherwise, please and thank you, because I'm not *that* well-off."

"It'll be fine. It's for Garrett land, after all." She grabbed the handle of a flat metal cart and turned it, then stuck a flat of dark purple flowers onto it. "This will get you started. And…" She started hunting through the displays.

"So," Sadie said, feeling ridiculously adolescent for what she was about to say, but unable to stop herself from saying it, "what is your brother's deal?"

"Which one?" Kate asked.

She could always deflect now, and say it was about Connor, which should in no way make her feel less awkward, but it did. Probably because, as handsome as he was, in that grieving, several-weeks-old-beard kind of way, she just didn't want to look at Connor's butt. Eli's, on the other hand…

"Eli," she said, grimacing at her honesty and thankful that Kate was still eyeballing plants.

"Uh…" Kate straightened and flipped her braid over her shoulder. "I'm not sure he has a deal."

"He doesn't seem that happy to have me around. Furthermore, he got a little…testy when I suggested we might have some events on the ranch."

"Oh, well…he's private. I guess. I mean, I never really thought about it, but it's not like we have parties or anything at the ranch. Birthday stuff we do at Pappy's Pizza, and for stuff they don't include me in they go to Ace's. So…yeah, maybe that's it. Maybe he just doesn't like to have people out. I never do, but that's not really a choice. More of a happenstance. Because…you know, this town is really small and everyone knows I have a brother with the power to arrest them. And one who would probably shoot and bury someone with no blip of conscience." She frowned. "Anyway, I'm sorry about Eli. Usually it's Connor we all have to apologize for."

"No, don't…apologize for him. But…is there, like, a plant I could get him?" she asked. Maybe a peace offering was the way to go. Right now she seemed to just be going the Purposefully Ruffle His Feathers Route, which was honestly really stupid and wasn't going to solve anything.

"Well, sure…you could get him an azalea," Kate said.

"An azalea?"

"Yeah, it's a flower, but they grow native here so it's less… groomed and more…manly. A manly flower."

"Okay," Sadie said. "A manly flower. I'm down with that. I'll get him an apology azalea. And then maybe we can try to talk again. Like adults instead of sniping children."

Kate winced. "Was it that bad?"

"I don't know. But some of it was my fault. We just…rub each other the wrong way." And she had a feeling that a lot of her annoyance boiled down to the strange tightening in her stomach whenever he was around.

Of course, putting it like that made it seem like she didn't know what that was, when she knew full well what it was. It was just…unusual in this context.

Usually she felt that level of excitement, that sort of low, giddy tug, when she was about to have sex. A brief little flash of anticipation. If she remembered right. It *had* been an awfully long time.

She was not used to it in regards to a man she wasn't interested in. Was not used to it being connected to a man she didn't like, much less a man she wasn't in a relationship with.

She was something of a serial monogamist. She'd meet a guy, they'd go on a few dates and they'd have fun while it lasted. And when things got…un-fun, they'd stop. There was no second-guessing, or yelling at each other. There were no question marks. She liked it straightforward and simple.

Her most recent ex, Marcus, was a classic example of that. They'd met at her gym. He was hot. He was fun. They'd gone on some dates, and then slipped easily into a physical relationship. And then, he'd gone and screwed it up by asking for a drawer. The man had never spent the night, and he wanted a *drawer in her dresser.*

It had been, to Sadie at least, a clear sign that they wanted two different things. And while her instinct had been to placate him or string him along, she knew that it wouldn't benefit either of them. And a lovely time in their lives would only be remembered for the discord in the end. She said a big no-thank-you to that.

It was always better to let someone go too soon than to hold on too long.

She liked it clear. And she liked it *simple.*

There was nothing simple about the way Eli made her feel. And there was nowhere for it to go. So, it could just stop.

But then, even when she'd been a teenage miscreant, loath to deal with his presence, she'd found him hot. So, if she knew anything about herself, it was that her body was die-hard stupid for Eli.

"Well, Eli really is a decent guy," Kate said, adding a plant with fuchsia flowers to the cart. "So I'm sure once you get on the same page he'll be reasonable."

"You think?"

"I don't know. But I'm just his sister. So often he's not reasonable with me, but I tend to think that's genetics at work."

"Right. Well, I'm an only child, so I'm not really up on the dynamic."

"That must have been lonely," Kate said.

For some reason, her words hit a sore spot. "Uh..." Sadie cleared her throat. "I had a lot of friends." Friends she hadn't spoken to in a decade. Were they here? Were they gone? She had no idea.

She didn't hold on. It wasn't healthy. And she was a bastion of positive mental health and good feelings. And stuff.

"Well, that's nice. I have...minimal friends, actually," Kate said. "But you know, the ones I have are good. People who love horses as much as I do."

"Hey, that's important. And it's better than lots of crappy friends anyway." Her friends hadn't really been crappy. Sure, they'd been terrible influences on each other, but they'd all had sucky lives. Smoking in the woods, drinking beer and making out were the best they could do since their homes were in such a sorry state.

"Yeah, I'm sure that's true," Kate said, putting a few leafy greens onto the cart. "Do you want some basil or mint or anything?"

"Oh, yeah!" she said. "Any. All. Can I put those in the windowsill in the kitchen?"

"Yep. I'll grab herbs on our way back inside and you can wait for me at the counter."

"Thank you," she said. "For your help and the discount and… not hating me."

"Eli doesn't hate you," Kate said, shoving the cart in through the door, her petite frame obviously a lot more muscled than it appeared at first glance. "He doesn't hate anyone. He's really very decent down to his core."

Sadie went to the front of the counter and set her coffee on the rough-hewn wooden top, digging in her back pocket for her credit card. "He seems like he is."

"He took care of me for most of my life. Our mom left when I was little. You probably knew that. Everyone knows that." She reached around and tugged on her braid, the gesture so childlike and sad it made Sadie ache a little bit. "Anyway…" She flipped her hair over her shoulder and went about grabbing the scanner and checking the plants. "Our dad… Things were hard for him after that and someone had to take care of the ranch— that was Connor. And someone had to take care of me and the house. And… Eli did that."

Sadie cleared her throat, strange, aching emotion pressing in and making it feel tight. "Well, then it's a good thing I plan on extending an olive branch. Apology azalea. Whatever. I mean, since he's such a good guy."

The total flashed up on the screen, and Kate tapped away on the ten key, bringing the amount down by almost half, and Sadie sighed in relief. "Really. Really, thank you."

"Really, no problem. Maybe…maybe we could hang out sometime?"

"Yeah, maybe. I think… I probably won't get to plant these until tomorrow. But if you're around, maybe we could work on it together?"

Kate brightened. "Sure! And actually, if you don't need them now, if you want I could put them in the bed of my truck and bring them home tonight. Then you wouldn't get dirt in your car."

Kate's offer gave Sadie serious feelings in the region of her heart. She wasn't sure she deserved the other woman's friendliness. But she wanted it. She wanted a friend, darn it. "Thanks. I'll take the apology azalea, though, since I need to talk to Eli and I'm not doing it without reinforcement."

Kate grabbed the largish potted plant from the cart and handed it to Sadie. "Here you go."

Sadie wrapped her arms around it, holding both her coffee and the bag of knickknacks she'd purchased earlier. "Great. Well. See you later." She turned and headed toward the door, pausing when she realized she had no available hands.

"Sorry!" She heard Kate scurry around the counter, rushing to hold the door for her.

"No problem," Sadie said. "I'll see you."

She walked out into the warm afternoon, wind kicking up from the ocean, blowing her hair across her face and into her mouth as she walked back up the sidewalk toward where she'd parked her car. She did a little cursory scan for Eli's patrol car but didn't see it.

And she tried not to think too much about the sinking, vague sense of disappointment she felt over that.

CHAPTER SIX

BY THE TIME Eli clocked out, he was ready to sink onto the couch and zone out. Maybe watch whatever sport was on. He wasn't picky. Hell, he'd take tennis at this point. Just something that didn't require thought.

But when he pulled his car into the dirt drive that led up to his house, it didn't take long for him to see that was not going to be in his future. There was a shiny black sedan in his space. Which meant there was a person here. Which meant he had to be on still. Which had him cursing internally in a variety of interesting combinations.

He groaned and pulled his car to the side, so that whoever owned the sedan could easily get out again once their business with him was done.

He put the car in Park and killed the engine, unbuckling and getting out, letting out a long-suffering breath as he did.

He took a few steps toward the house and saw the back of a dark-haired woman, long hair, shiny and curly, swinging down to a slim waist. She was facing...well, off into the vague distance as far as he could see.

He frowned and moved closer, then he noticed that there was another woman kneeling down in the dirt, her face partly blocked by a curtain of blond, straggly hair. He could see one pale, dirt-splattered arm. And for some reason, the sight of the bedraggled woman on her hands and knees gave him a jolt that the back of the glossy brunette hadn't.

Then the brunette turned, and revealed both her identity and that of the blonde. And suddenly everything, including his reaction, made very irritating sense.

Because Lydia Carpenter belonged to the glossy dark hair, and the gritty mess in his dirt was, of course, Sadie Miller. Of. Course.

He and his dick needed to have a very serious conversation about appropriate reactions to women who were very annoying.

"What's going on here?" he asked, realizing, in some dim part of his brain, that this was not a socially acceptable way to greet people.

"Eli!" Lydia said, smiling broadly, taking a few steps toward him, her tan legs on display in a very short summer dress she had not been wearing earlier. She was also wearing red lipstick, which he didn't remember from earlier, either.

Sadie looked decidedly less happy to see him from her position on the ground. She looked up, squinting against the sun, offering an approximation of a smile that looked a little bit like she was baring her teeth at him.

"Hi. Did we have a…meeting I forgot about?" he asked, looking from Lydia to Sadie.

Lydia's smile suddenly went a little snarly. "Uh. No. Great minds, I guess. Though I feel like I should have brought a plant."

"What?" He took that moment to look a little more specifically at what Sadie was doing.

There was a mound of fresh dirt around an azalea plant, bright pink buds mocking him with their cheeriness on the ends of the branches.

"Surprise!" Sadie said weakly.

"Uh…" And he had nothing to say after that, so he just let it hang there.

"Eli," Lydia said, and he wondered, yet again, how they'd

gotten all first-name basis all of a sudden, "I wanted to let you know that I ran the barbecue idea past everyone on the board and the response was massive. We're so thankful to have someone running for Logan County Sheriff who has such a vested interest in the well-being of Copper Ridge's economy."

Oh, dammit. This was like his worst nightmare come true. He was being railroaded. By two petite, smiling, *evil* women.

"Well... I... Of course I care," he said, and Lydia's expression changed to something else entirely. Something that he couldn't quite identify, but that terrified him down to his soul.

"I knew you did," she said, walking toward him and putting her hand over his. "And it's so greatly appreciated. By me. And...of course, the whole town. And county."

"Of course," he said, drawing back slowly. He looked down at Sadie, who seemed frozen, her eyes wide with a combination of amusement and horror.

"Well, I have to go," Lydia said, "but we should discuss this further. Over coffee." She reached into her purse and dug a card out, pressing it into his hand.

"Okay," he said, curling his fingers around it.

Lydia turned and smiled at Sadie, and again, he had a feeling it was a smile meant to convey something other than happiness. There was a lot of strange emotional subtlety happening here, and he basically needed to be bludgeoned over the head with feelings to have any idea of what was going on, so he resigned himself to confusion, and relief when Lydia walked back to her car and started the engine.

He turned back to Sadie, who was still on the ground. "What is happening here?"

"I brought you an azalea."

"Why?"

"To apologize," she said, blinking as if she was suddenly realizing that her idea might not have been the best. "And to extend...goodwill."

"Some people just say they're sorry. They don't go planting unsolicited shrubbery in front of someone else's house."

"Yeah, well, some people lack imagination." She straightened and brushed her hands off on her jeans, leaving a trail of light dust streaked over the dark denim.

"Or have a greater grasp of social boundaries."

She made an indignant sound in the back of her throat. "That's also a possibility. I mean, maybe. But your sister assured me this was a manly plant. And also didn't seem to think it was a terrible idea."

"It has pink flowers."

"Honestly, the whole gendered colors thing is extremely ridiculous to me. Colors are colors. How can one be masculine and one be feminine?"

"I'm going to skip over this part of the conversation if it's all the same to you."

"It is."

"Great. What was Lydia doing here? Was she part of the plant installation?"

"No. Our missions were separate and coincidentally intertwined with each other."

"She's really into your barbecue idea. Congratulations on your evil plan working, by the way."

"I don't think it's the barbecue she's into."

"Are you still gnawing on that bone?"

"You don't need to whip out that much leg to talk community barbecue. Also, she was a little chilly to me."

"Why?"

Sadie rolled her eyes and crossed her arms. "She's threatened by me. Me and my azalea."

"She has no reason to be," he said.

"You like her that much?"

"I like you and your azalea that little."

"Dammit, Sheriff, right in my soft white underbelly. I'm trying to be nice to you."

"You've put me in a position I don't want to be in. Now I'm going to have to advocate for your little circus."

"Why?"

"Because. You heard her. The whole Chamber of Commerce is really excited, and it's an indicator of my commitment to the community. And my votes are riding on this stupid crap that I don't want to do."

"Oh. Ouch. Public opinion is a new concern for you, isn't it?" She didn't look at all sorry. She looked downright gleeful.

"Not exactly," he said.

"You have to join forces with me," she said. "Assimilate or die."

"You don't have to enjoy this so much."

"But I do!" she crowed. "I really do. And anyway, it's not going to be that bad. No one's going to make you participate or smile."

"I need boundaries," he said. "And a plan. If it's going to happen, I'm going to oversee it."

"Control freak much?"

"Yes," he said. "Much. And I'm fine with it. Now, if you're going to do something on my property you have to be okay with it, too. You don't have to like it, but the bottom line is, you will do as I say, or it doesn't happen at all."

"Oh, really? I thought you acknowledged that I had you over a barrel." She tucked a strand of blond hair behind her ear and arched her brow as if to say, *Gotcha.*

No. Way.

"Oh, no, baby," he said, not sure where the endearment had come from or why it had rolled off his tongue, but he didn't stop to try to figure it out. "You may have me in a position where I have to be willing to consider your idea, but make no mistake, it's you who has the most to lose. I don't *have* to do a damn thing, and I'm the one with his name on the title for this chunk of earth. So if you want to play, you'll play my way."

SADIE FELT AN unfamiliar surge of raw, unmitigated anger course through her veins. This was not her style. It was not her game. She didn't do toe-to-toe shouting matches. Not with men, not with anyone. No. She did yoga. She meditated. She had a pottery wheel somewhere. That she never used, but still, she had outlets. Outlets that were not screaming like a child. Or hitting people with your fists until the anger beast cooled in your chest.

She didn't believe in giving free rein to negative emotions. It was healthy to acknowledge feelings, yes, and to talk about them in a safe space. But to let them explode out of your mouth and through your chest and let them take over all of everything? Which was what was happening right now, whether she wanted it to be happening or not.

She was…seething. And it was overflowing. Onto her, onto him, onto everything. And sure, maybe planting the azalea had been a step too far. But Lydia had shown up when she was dropping it off. And something about the other woman made her feel…competitive. Which was annoying.

But somehow she'd told Lydia that she was supposed to be there. Planting the azalea. And Lydia had lingered. Her mere presence a challenge. So plant it Sadie had.

And he was rejecting it. Honestly, even if her gesture was weird, it was nice. And he was being an ass.

"I bought you a motherfucking azalea!" she said, the words shooting out hard and short, intense like gunfire.

"And I didn't want it," he said, taking a step toward her. "I don't want it here. I don't want you here."

"Why?" she asked, moving nearer to him, compelled forward by the kind of deep, negative emotion she hadn't even known she possessed. "Because I'm getting my dirty, been-arrested, other-side-of-the-tracks, poor-girl filth all over your hallowed Garrett walkways?"

"Because," he said, "you are a mess. And I spent most of my life managing a giant-ass mess, and I don't see any reason why I should willingly subject myself to another one. I have things just the way I want them." He moved closer, a muscle in his square jaw ticking, the cords on his neck standing out. "And I do not need you coming in and ruining anything."

"Oh, really?" She moved nearer to him, so close she could feel the heat of his breath on her face. "I guess you are awfully neat and tidy," she said, her gaze flickering over his uniform, so perfectly pressed and…sexy, in spite of everything that was going on between them. "It would be a shame if I got my mess on you." And before she could police herself, she'd reached out and grabbed his tie, her dirt-encrusted hands sliding over the fabric, leaving a pale dust streak and tugging his face down closer to hers.

Her heart was pounding so hard it was making her light-headed. Her blood pumped to parts…more southerly. She had no idea what was happening to her. This was no sexual attraction as she knew it. It wasn't anything as she knew it. She was angrier than she'd been in recent memory, and a hell of a lot more turned on, and she genuinely didn't know how to process the two together.

She also didn't know how to process that she was inches from his face, his tie clutched tight in her hand, as his dark eyes blazed rage into hers. Rage and something else. Something hotter. Something that looked a lot like the fire burning in her belly felt.

And then…and then he dipped his head, his lips crashing into hers. And that's what it was. A collision. It wasn't a testing, or a tasting, or anything tentative at all. It wasn't nice, or fun, or easy. It was gasoline on a lit match. An instant conflagration that had gone from spark to out of control at the moment of contact.

She had no idea what was happening, only that she didn't want it to stop.

She tugged tighter on his tie and angled her head, parting his lips beneath hers and slipping her tongue into his mouth.

He groaned, rough and raw and not anything like the good guy he seemed to want the world to think he was.

He locked one arm around her waist, drawing her tightly against his hard body. His lips were firm and sure. And everything about him, about this, was so much more intense than she'd imagined it could be.

She released her hold on his tie and cupped the back of his neck with her hands, holding him to her. She shifted, breaking some of the contact, and he growled—an honestly feral growl—and bit her lip, drawing her back in close.

Pleasure rocketed through her, her nipples tightening into hard points, desire settling low in her stomach, an iron fist gripping her inside and tugging hard, sending a shock wave of need straight down to her core.

She wanted... She wanted it to go on forever. This need that wrapped her up in a cocoon and held her to him. That blocked out everything. All the worry, all the anxiety, all the anger, and turned it into something... *Good* seemed too insipid a word. And she wasn't sure if this was good at all.

But it was necessary.

Suddenly, it was so very necessary.

She arched her hips against his and felt the very hard, irrefutable evidence of his own investment in this explosion of need. She wanted everything all at once with an intensity that defied anything she'd ever experienced. And she wanted it with all of herself.

Her heart seized tight, a painful spasm, and suddenly she felt herself move away from him, jumping back like a startled cat.

She was shaking. Her hands, her knees and everywhere in between. And kisses did not make her shake. And she didn't kiss men she didn't like. She didn't kiss men in uniforms who had a fetish for order and cleanliness.

She didn't yell at people, either, but right now the yelling was lower on her list of sins than the kissing.

"What did you... I don't even... I'm going to go." She turned, her shoulders stiff, her heart hammering in her ears.

"If I'd known a kiss would have gotten rid of you, I would have kissed you the moment I saw your car sitting on the side of the road."

Oh. That. Did it.

She whirled back around, anger gaining traction in her again. "Well, sure, your kiss got rid of me. Congratulations. Now who's going to help you get rid of the hard-on it gave you? Your right hand?"

He lifted a shoulder, his expression stone, the dull red color on his cheekbones the only indicator that he was affected at all. That the casual manner was a lie. "My right hand suits me just fine. And it's a hell of a lot quieter than you."

"Oh, sure, the masturbation reference you get. You must spend a lot of time alone."

A muscle in his jaw ticked, the color in his face deepening. Embarrassment or anger? For some reason, she felt compelled to find out.

"No comment on that?" she asked. "Hugely shocking to me that women aren't flocking to you." But honestly, his body was stupid sexy and there were, in fact, women who seemed to flock to him. Or at least, one woman. That she'd seen. But, whatever, she was trying to make him mad, so truth didn't have to come into it. Petty meanness was the only thing that mattered. "I mean, you're a jerk. And you don't like anyone in or around your house. You don't even like flowers."

He crossed his arms over his broad chest, and she had to fight to keep herself from looking below his thick utility belt down to where she was sure she would be able to see evidence of his arousal. She was so, so tempted. Because she'd felt it, and it had felt so good. And she was curious beyond reason about how it looked. How he would feel in her palm...

No. Stop it.

"I'm not fighting with you," he said. "But I'm not changing my stance. My way, or no way. It's up to you."

So he wasn't even going to acknowledge the kiss? He wasn't going to fight back and feed her anger and make her feel justified and...and... That bastard.

"Fine," she bit out. "I'll work with you. But if you kiss me again, I'll bite your tongue off."

"Don't worry," he said. "I don't think I'll be tempted again."

That stung. And she had no idea why. Because they shouldn't kiss again. They shouldn't have kissed once. So that meant there was no reason for her to feel upset about him not wanting to kiss her again.

But she was.

"We'll discuss this more tomorrow," she said, straightening her shoulders, trying to maintain dignity she knew she no longer had. "And if I come back tomorrow and my azalea is maimed, uprooted or otherwise denigrated I will vandalize something on your porch."

Then she turned and walked away, trying to calm her pulse, trying to calm the racing of her heart.

She just needed to go back to her place, calm down, and—now that the plumber had been in—get herself a cold shower to help recalibrate her stupid body.

And then everything would be fine. Tomorrow morning, she would be over this thing that had flared up inside her, and she and Eli could get on with planning the community barbecue.

Yeah, that was a very nice lie. And it was one she was going to keep on telling herself until she couldn't anymore.

"THAT WOMAN IS a menace," Eli said, pacing the length of his brother's living room, all the blood in his body still heated to boiling since he'd gone and done the most stupid thing imaginable and kissed Sadie Miller like she was oxygen and he was suffocating.

"I don't know, she hasn't caused much trouble other than

244 PART TIME COWBOY

bursting the pipes, but even with paying for that, her rent is bringing in enough that we're still coming out ahead on the agreement this month."

"Assuming she doesn't cause any more disasters," he said.

"Well, sure, assuming that," Connor conceded, sinking deeper into the couch, his legs sprawled out in front of him, his arms spread out across the back.

"Which is a big assumption, all things considered."

"Untwist your panties," Connor said. "You're just still pissed because I did this without consulting you. And you don't like change. And you don't like feeling out of control."

Well, dammit, was he that obvious?

"This isn't about me. It's about her."

"Sure," Connor said, resting his head on the back of the couch and drawing his hat down over his eyes.

"Will you stop that?" Eli asked.

"What?"

"Stop being so damned disengaged all the time."

Connor straightened, pushing his hat back. "Sure, Eli. You going to arrange to have my wife returned to me?"

Eli's chest seized up, his heart squeezed tight like it was locked in a vise. "You know I can't."

"Then maybe fuck off and stop commenting on how disengaged I am."

It was rare for Connor to acknowledge that he was still grieving Jessie. But then, it was rare for Eli to call Connor on his bullshit in a serious way.

"Fair enough," Eli said, his voice coming out tight.

"Now, I believe you were ranting about our tenant." Typical of Connor. Get really pissed, then pretend it hadn't happened.

"I was. She has plans. And dammit, Connor, I sort of have to side with her on them."

Now Connor's body registered some tension. "What kind of plans?"

"Community barbecue plans," he said.

"And how does this concern me?"

"Because she wants to host things here," he said. "Particularly, she's planning on having a county-wide Independence Day celebration here on our ranch."

Connor had the decency to look perturbed about that. "Here? On the ranch? I won't have to do anything, will I?"

Eli let the implosion happen internally. He hadn't imagined his brother would actually propose that he help out with things, but then, it would have been nice if everything that wasn't cows didn't fall to him.

Which was maybe really unfair of him, but at the moment he didn't care.

"We'll have to clear things with you and your schedule. And I would guess base some things around what fields you want your cows in at a given time. Also, if any barns are going to be used, that needs to be cleared with you."

"Right. Fine. Just…when plans get more advanced, run dates and things by me and I'll see what I can do."

The fact that it made Connor look so damn tired brought Eli back from annoyance to pity. "Great. Sounds like a plan."

Connor frowned. "What happened to your tie…and…all of you?"

"What?" Eli looked down and saw the streak of dirt on his tie. It screamed *feminine handprint* to him, but he was pretty sure that to the unknowing observer it looked like a streak of dirt. Still, it made him feel a lot more like a kid caught with his hand in the cookie jar than he would like. And it made him think about what had happened between him and Sadie, which, in all honesty, he hadn't stopped thinking about since he stepped onto Connor's porch, but now he just felt like his face was projecting the words so Connor could read them easily.

He tried to remind himself that Connor wasn't that perceptive. And then he wondered what was wrong with him because any normal man would feel some sense of pride over kissing a woman as pretty as Sadie.

But then again…what they'd shared wasn't exactly a kiss so much as an explosion that happened to be detonated by the meeting of their lips.

"You look like you rubbed up against the side of a barn."

Eli looked at the rest of his uniform, heat making his face sting. He could see where every inch of her had been pressed against every inch of him. "Something like that," he said.

Connor narrowed his eyes. "Something like that?"

"I wasn't paying attention."

"You pay attention to everything. Which means…you paid extra close attention to whatever happened to your uniform, because obviously you're lying."

"Why the hell have you chosen to get engaged with what's happening right this moment?"

Connor raised a brow. "I think this is the first time I've ever caught you doing something you weren't supposed to do."

"I'm an adult. As long as it's inside the law there's nothing I'm not supposed to do."

"But let's be honest, Eli, the laundry list of things you think you can't do is longer than your arm."

"You don't know everything I do."

"No, but I know everything you don't do. We live too close to keep secrets."

"Fine. I brushed up against the barn."

"Giving it a hug because you were so happy to see it?" Connor asked.

"Okay, you caught me," Eli said, keeping his tone dry. "I found two women mud-wrestling just outside town and when I went to make sure they had a permit for it, they couldn't keep their hands off me."

"Now I believe you hugging a barn before I believe that."

"Well, pick one. Because they're the only two stories you're going to get. Now, if you'll excuse me, I have to go and start organizing this disaster of a party, because frankly, I just didn't have enough to do."

"You know you don't have to do everything, Eli. There's a certain freedom in just giving the world the middle finger."

"Yeah, but since you do it so expertly, someone has to get in there and care." Eli turned and walked out the front door, feeling like a total ass.

Grab a woman who hates you and kiss her? Big fat check next to that box. Insult your grieving brother? Check.

He was on a roll today. There was no denying it.

He sort of wished the mud-wrestling story was true. That would have been fun at least. There was nothing fun about what had passed between him and Sadie. Hot, yes. But not fun. And certainly nothing he could strut around feeling proud of.

When she'd pulled away from him...*appalled* wasn't a strong enough word for the look on her face. She'd looked completely horrified that they'd touched. And he'd just wanted to grab her again. And kiss her more.

What the hell was wrong with him?

When he had...affairs, relationships...whatever you wanted to call them, he was careful about his selection. He found women out of town. He found women who weren't needy or close in proximity. He found women who wanted sex and some easy, occasional companionship.

With the notable exception of Brandy, the last woman he'd been seeing, they were all very casual and very nonintense. Brandy had turned out to be something of a secret badge bunny and about the time he found her naked in the back of his patrol car begging him to put her in handcuffs, he'd known that relationship had to end.

And one thing was certain—he didn't pursue women who didn't want him. Sex was easy. Attraction was easy. It wasn't... whatever this was.

And now he was officially too wound up to enjoy his downtime. Now he was on the verge of an extreme hard-on that would have to go unsatisfied. And now he was officially way past rest and relaxation, he realized during his walk through the property.

What he needed to do was focus on Sadie's event plans. Yes, that was what he needed. He needed the control. Which, when he thought about it, was probably what the kiss was about. Some unevolved part of himself was trying to seize control through sex.

It had nothing to do with reality. Or with Sadie. Or with him genuinely wanting to shove her top up and her bra down so he could get a look at her breasts.

No, that had nothing to do with it. It was the power struggle. But there was another way. He changed direction abruptly, heading toward the Catalog House as quickly as he could, determination making each step hit the ground harder than was strictly necessary.

He took the steps up the porch two at a time and then knocked on the door.

SADIE CHECKED THE reheating quiche in the oven and smiled. She'd put it in just before getting in the shower. It was looking perfect. And it had taken her only a few tries over the past few mornings.

She'd done it before, but she usually used a premade crust and she'd decided that wasn't going to cut it at Chez Sadie once she had guests. She took her oven mitts off the cabinet door and opened the oven, pulling the quiche out and putting it on the stove top.

Yes, it looked like heaven. And she was self-satisfied to a ridiculous degree. There was something she liked about all this. Building a business from scratch. Building...quiche from scratch. It was awesome any way.

There was a sudden, impatient pounding on the door that nearly made her jump out of her skin. But almost immediately, she knew who it had to be, without even looking. Because no one else seemed to have emotions strong enough to merit knocks that were quite that intense.

Unless someone had been involved in a terrible wood-chopping accident and was knocking on her door with what remained of their arm. In which case, she should hurry and answer it.

She felt bad for hoping it was someone with a bloody stump, but it seemed oh so infinitely preferable to Eli.

"Coming!" she shouted, pinning her damp hair back and reaching for the door handle, feeling her expression contort to one of horror when she saw who was behind it. "Oh, it's you."

"Who did you think it was?" he asked, his dark eyes intense and far too interesting for her own good.

"I was sort of hoping it was someone who'd been gravely injured and was in need of help."

"Sorry to tell you, it's just me."

"Are you in grave danger? Missing any appendages?"

"All body parts present, accounted for and attached," he said, his tone dry.

And now all she could think of was the body part that had most certainly been present and accounted for during their kiss. And she needed to think of anything else. "Well, damn."

He leaned in and for one moment, she had the fleeting thought that he was going to burst through that door, throw her onto the table and finish what they'd started earlier in the garden.

Which was ridiculous because she didn't want him to do that. And because she was not the kind of person who had crazy, throw-down-on-the-table sex. Because that required a certain amount of insanity that was just not a part of her physical relationships.

She was into relationships where you kept your head on straight and had sex at the end of a nice meal. She was well-adjusted about things. She wasn't an animal.

"I have to work for the next few days, so I don't have time to entertain you, or help you plan your little barbecue. But the minute that I'm off for the week? You and I have some talking to do."

So, he was not here to ravish her. Which was good. It really was. She was relieved. Almost as relieved as she would have been to see someone with a severe wound at the door.

"You make it sound like I'm in big trouble," she said, the words sounding a little softer and a whole lot more flirtatious than she intended.

Her body, it seemed, hadn't realized what her mind had—which was that the ravishment was off the table, so to speak—and had gone into Mae West mode accordingly.

She tried to tell her inner hussy that he could *not* come up and see her sometime, but her heart was still beating at hyperspeed.

"That all depends on your definition of trouble, Miss Miller," he said.

Oh, Lord, why did the way he said those words make a shiver of something rattle through her bones? *Why?* Why did she sort of wish she could go back to being in trouble with him?

She needed another shower. A colder one this time.

"Not really," she said, her words terse. "It kind of depends on yours since you have legal backing."

"I just want to give you a tour of the place. And discuss what is reasonable for the barbecue, and what isn't."

"Okay," she said, feeling a little blindsided by his darn reasonableness. "But I'm not really sure what inspired you to play nice."

"Must have been the azalea. And if you'll excuse me, it's my time off, and I'm going to go unwind."

She really wished she could stop herself from imagining what all him unwinding might entail. She remembered the presumptively thick erection from earlier and imagined him settling down and unzipping his pants...

No. Bad Sadie!

"Well, you go...do that," she said, forcing herself not to look down. Forcing herself to look only at his eyes and nowhere else, which, frankly, she felt she deserved a freaking medal for. His hardness had been pressed right up against her today and never—not once—had she given in to the urge to visually explore it.

"I will. And I'll be here on Thursday morning. Very early. Be ready."

"Bring coffee."

He arched a brow. "All right. I will."

And for some reason, that easy agreement before he walked down off the porch and into the fading light made her more nervous than any fight ever could have.

CHAPTER SEVEN

THE LAST TIME someone knocked on her door this emphatically, it wasn't because of an ax wound, and she had a terrible feeling it wasn't this morning, either.

Sadie wiped her hands on her apron and then untied it, draping it over a chair as she walked to the door. "Coming!"

She smoothed her hair, then jerked the door open with a smile pasted onto her face.

And there was the man himself, the cause of the past four sleepless nights, looking awake and far too sexy for a man in a simple pair of jeans and a black T-shirt. And far too tempting.

She looked down at the mug of coffee in his hand. "So thoughtful of you," she said, reaching out and snagging the bright blue-and-white-spotted tin mug and lifting it to her lips. "Mmm."

"That was mine," he said, pushing past her, "and are you going to invite me in?"

"You're in," she said, feeling warmed both by the coffee and by the implication that his lips had been on it. Which was juvenile in the extreme. She'd kissed him. What was the point of getting warm and sweaty over her lips touching a mug his lips had touched?

"So I am."

She took another sip of coffee, fully aware of the awkwardness that was building as they stood in the doorway, making eye contact and with her drinking his drink. Her nipples prickled and she shifted, the motion seeming to draw his eye right down to the place that was currently feeling quite perky and obvious.

"Do you want to come sit at the table?" she asked. "I actually have more coffee. Lucky thing, since you didn't bring any extra as instructed. And happily for you, my quiche of the day is ready."

"You have coffee and you took mine?"

"It's rude to turn down gifts, Eli. Didn't you ever hear not to look a gift azalea in the mouth? Oh, no...you must not have heard that."

"And gift quiche?"

"Same. It's spinach. And salmon."

He lifted a shoulder. "Well, I might be able to have some."

They moved into the kitchen and she fought to breathe right. She went to the counter and got a knife, slicing a generous piece of quiche for Eli, before getting him coffee, and delivering both to his seat.

"You're my guinea pig," she said, watching him expectantly.

"You're staring," he said, looking at the food, then at her.

"Yeah, I want to see if you like it."

"That's...disconcerting."

"Sorry. I'll look the other way." And she did. Obediently. Until he made a borderline orgasmic sound that sent a thrill straight down through to her midsection and...beyond. She looked back and watched his jaw working while he chewed. So weird, but she found the motion sexy. What the hell was wrong with her?

She wanted to make an excuse about needing to change her top or something since she'd been cooking. Just so she didn't have to sit and eat with him. And stare at his weirdly sexy mouth motions. But that felt self-conscious. If she ran off before he was done, she would look like she was doing it because she was uncomfortable around him—which she was.

Oh, to hell with pride.

She stood up. "I'll be right back. I have to... I got flour on my top and I'm gonna...change."

She turned and scurried out of the kitchen, moving to the back room, where she'd just gotten all of her things organized last night.

It was part of an addition made to the house in more recent years. By which she meant the 1940s or so. The room was skinny and rectangular, set slightly lower than the rest of the house, matching the incline of the property, with windows covering the entire back wall and a slanted, wooden ceiling that had been painted white at some point.

It was weird, and quirky, and she was sure guests wouldn't like it very much. But it suited her just fine.

She opened the top drawer of her dresser and retrieved a new top. She tugged it over her head quickly, then hovered by the vanity, wondering if she should put makeup on. No, she shouldn't put makeup on. That was stupid. It was why she hadn't applied any after her shower this morning. They were just going out on the ranch, after all. And putting makeup on implied she cared about how she looked. And she totally didn't. At all.

While she was thinking, she picked up a blush brush and dashed it through the pink powder before swirling it over the apples of her cheeks. There. She looked awake now anyway.

She frowned and picked up her tube of mascara, brushing some over her lashes quickly. There. In the interest of looking awake.

She slicked some pink gloss over her lips next. That wasn't vain. That was just...upkeep.

She grabbed a rubber band from the little porcelain hand statue on top of the bright yellow vanity and restrained her hair as best she could.

Okay. So that was done. And not to impress Eli but just because…it was basic hygiene. Right. She didn't care what he thought. At all.

She walked out of the bedroom and into the kitchen again, waiting to see the look on his face when he registered the change to her appearance. And…nothing. He just sat there drinking his coffee. She'd put makeup on and *nothing*.

Which was fine, because she didn't care. But…she'd expected a little better than that. From the guy who'd hate-kissed her once.

Okay, nothing about Eli and her attraction to him, her preoccupation with him, made sense. So maybe she should just stop trying to excuse the weird things she seemed to do in his presence.

She tried, for a second, to figure out what she would say to a patient in this situation, and couldn't find any readily available wisdom. Because when it came to attraction, her philosophy was simple. Pursue it and, if there was no returned interest, release it. If there was, continue on with it until it was no longer mutually satisfying.

But there was nothing about that philosophy that applied to this situation.

She didn't like him. She didn't want to be attracted to him. And he clearly didn't want to be attracted to her. If he even was.

Well, she knew he was, because boner.

But was that actual attraction or just some testosterone-fueled rage thing? And if it was, then why did the idea make her feel hot and twitchy and not angry?

Nothing about this man, or her response to him, made sense.

"So, what's the plan, then?" she asked, leaning against the door frame and staring down at him, where he had made himself very at home in one of her kitchen chairs.

"I'm going to show you around. We're going to talk about your ideas, and I'm going to tell you which parts of those ideas are absolutely impossible."

"Or, to make it not sound dire and negative…you're going to tell me what will work?"

"Honestly, I have a feeling we'll be talking a lot more about what won't work."

"You are a ray of freaking sunshine, Eli. Has anyone ever told you that before?"

He looked over his mug and arched a dark brow. "No."

"Well, that's just shocking."

"You don't sound shocked."

She smiled. "That's because I'm not."

She reclaimed her coffee cup, but didn't rejoin him at the table. She hovered back, taking her caffeine hit before putting the mug back on the table. "Did you want to run this to your house or car or…?"

"I'll pick it up later." He tilted his cup back and finished his coffee in one deep drink before setting it back down and pushing himself into a standing position.

"Great. Then let's go tour." She turned and walked back out into the entryway and out the door, pausing just outside. "We're not taking the patrol car?"

"No," he said, walking past her. "I drive the truck around the ranch. And around town. I only drive the patrol car when I'm on duty. And today, I'm playing the part of cowboy, not the part of lawman."

Both of those things sounded so much hotter than they had a right to.

"Well, yee-haw," she said, following him over to the truck. It wasn't a new truck. It was one of those big, growly monsters with big tires and metal runners to assist in getting inside. It was square and boxy, a dull, faded red with mud splatter fanning out around the tires.

She pushed the button on the door handle and tugged it hard, before heaving herself up and onto the bench seat. There was a blanket over the original upholstery, and it made her wonder just what sort of things the man got up to in here.

She could certainly think of a few things that might be fun...

She was really starting to get concerned for her sanity. The mistake, she feared, was that she hadn't had a lover in...a while. Like, since pre-California, which put her at two years of celibacy and that was crazy.

She hadn't really accounted for needing sex when she'd moved to Copper Ridge, but she most certainly did, and the size of the town was going to make everything much more complicated.

Slow down, tiger.

Of course, she hadn't been worried about it at all until Eli. Now she was hyperworried about it.

She settled into the seat and closed the door, her elbow butting against the armrest, her shoulder against the window, anticipating just how intense it would be when Eli joined her in the enclosed space.

He climbed into the driver's side and, just as she'd feared, the moment he shut the door, she felt like all the oxygen had been sucked out, replaced by a heady mix of hormones and the scent of Eli's skin.

And yes, he most definitely had his own scent, one she was suddenly very keyed in to. It made her think of the kiss. Made her think of how he'd tasted. Salt, skin and man. And she really, really wanted more.

But that was crazy and she knew it.

He started the truck and it growled to life, vibrating beneath her in a way that was sort of perilous considering her current thought process.

"What is the first stop, then?" she asked.

"The largest barn seems like a good place to start," he said, putting his arm across the back of the seat as he put the truck in Reverse and backed out of her driveway, taking them to the main road that ran to the different houses and fields on the property.

"So you raise...?"

"Cows," he said. "And we have a hell of a lot of them. Connor deserves the credit for that. I give him a hard time, but if it weren't for him this place wouldn't exist."

"Why do you give Connor a hard time?" she asked, slipping into the easy, question-asking mode that she'd always used with patients.

"Because he's my older brother," Eli said, rolling his shoulders upward, his grip tightening on the steering wheel. "And it's what we do."

"Well, yes, but the way you said it implied something deeper than the natural brother-to-brother expression of affection via 'busting chops.'"

"Are you charging me for this session?"

"What?" she asked, like she was surprised, even though she was fully aware that she was both distracting herself and distancing herself by becoming Therapist Sadie, rather than being Sadie the bag of flail who was marinating in her own lustypants.

"You know. Don't play innocent. It doesn't suit you."

"Is that a value judgment based on the fact that I have a criminal past, albeit a very uncolorful one?"

"Yeah."

That was it. Just yeah. No apology. No attempt to explain. He didn't even seem at all apologetic for the fact that he was some kind of a relic from a bygone era. With his angry kissing and generally judgmental attitude, who even needed him or his kissing or his judging? She didn't. Well, for anything other than getting this whole community events thing started.

"Well, you know, some people might say that the way you judge other people says a lot more about you than it does about them," she said, sounding annoying to her own ears. Pious, even.

"Yeah," he said. "I'm sure it does. It says that I've spent so much time cleaning up the crap that other people just leave around that I'm short on patience for it. That I've spent my whole life being cleanup crew, which means I know people can do better than they do, because I do better. So yeah, it is about me. And I'm judgmental and I don't care to change it."

"Well," she said, "okay."

She was used to very postmodern men. Men who believed in the exploration and articulation of their feelings. Or men like Marcus, who had liked smoothies and telling her about his day over a light dinner.

She was not used to this kind of Neanderthal he-man thing. Well, scratch that, she was. And she'd walked away from it ten years ago. She wasn't going to willingly put up with it now.

She didn't say anything, though. Instead, she just let the silence grow between them until it filled in all the free spaces in the cab and pushed against her throat until she didn't think she could bear it anymore.

Because she didn't do the walking on eggshells thing now. She didn't take the path of least resistance, because she didn't have to. When people were asses, she walked away. No one got to insert their judgments into her life without her permission.

Not even when the person trying to do so was a badge-carrying, gun-toting deputy. Not. Even. Then.

"Listen, I don't care what you think," she said. "And I'm not going to let you try to put me down because of some kind of moralistic—"

"I know you don't care what I think," he said. "And none of this has anything to do with being moralistic. You know full well you were trying to psychoanalyze me, and then you went and played dumb about it. And now what? You're going to get all pissy because I said you weren't innocent? Because you're going to apply that statement way further than it was ever intended to go? And you're going to try to do it while feeling all self-righteous? Hell no, baby, that's not going to happen."

She sputtered. "I don't… You don't…"

"Tell me I'm wrong, Sadie."

"You're wrong."

"Liar," he said, putting the truck in Park in front of a giant barn that she wouldn't have even guessed was a barn at first glance. It had a dark brown tile roof and honey-colored wood siding, glass-paned windows and sliding doors of varying widths. It was more what she'd associate with a high-end stable, not a cattle ranch.

"I'm not a liar," she said, unbuckling and marveling at the severe…neatness of everything. Sure, it was dusty and there was hay all over the ground, but it was neat and tidy. There was no denying that. It was such a sharp contrast to Connor's house, and the lack of organization there.

"You are. And if you don't think you are, you're at least lying to yourself." He got out and slammed the door behind him. And she sat for a moment before scrambling out after him. "Thing is," he said, looking over his shoulder, "it's not that big of a deal. The original thing I called you on. I think you just like fighting with me."

"I don't like fighting," she said. "With anyone. And I went a very long time without doing it at all before you came back into my life."

"Correction, honey, you came back into mine."

"Call me honey one more time, and I'll dip your fist in honey and shove it in an anthill."

"My point stands."

"Okay, sweetie pie," she said, "the point is that except for you, I never fight with anyone. So I think it's pretty safe to say that you're the damn problem. Not me."

"Is it?" he asked.

"Yeah," she said, crossing her arms beneath her breasts. "It is."

"Or do you just not talk to anyone who dares to disagree with you?"

He strode toward the barn and left a hissing and spitting Sadie standing there, stunned for a full thirty seconds before she took off after him.

"Why don't we get back to business," he continued. "Since I

don't really want to get to know you, and I'm betting you don't want to get to know me."

"Yeah," she said, "fine." She reached behind her head and tugged the end of her ponytail. "I don't want to know you. I want to know your barn."

"Get ready for the excitement," he said, his tone dry. "And I'm assuming *barn* isn't a euphemism for my...for anything."

"How could a barn be euphemistic?"

"I don't know. But you're always accusing me of missing those kinds of things so I figured I'd take preemptive measures."

"Right. Well. No. A barn is just a barn. Though, may I say, this is a particularly fantastic barn. Have you ever had weddings here?"

"No," he said.

"You should. Weddings and parties and—"

"No."

"You are the boringest man."

"I thought we were letting go of personal things and getting on with business?"

"Well, I was, but then you started talking about the possibility of barns being something dirty. Which made me think of your—" *don't say anything dirty* "—exasperating nature."

"Just look at the barn." He walked to the side door and released a wrought-iron latch, pushing it open, muscles in his thighs flexing, his biceps and forearms straining just enough to make everything in her tense up to match.

She stepped inside, the wood floor hollow-sounding beneath her feet, the expansive, empty section cleaner than most of her apartments had ever been. "Wow," she said. "I'm serious, you could host events here. And you could charge lots of money for them."

"It's nothing special. Just a place to keep equipment and hay."

"So...just a place to keep your entire livelihood? Yeah, you're right. It's not that special."

"Well, it's a serviceable barn. And it cost a hell of a lot of money. But the old one was run-down, and after we ended up with moldy hay one winter…it was pretty clear things had to change. After Dad died, we got a good chunk of change from his life insurance, and Kate and I gave our share to Connor to invest."

"Well, he did it in a very serious way," she said.

"Yeah, he did. But this place is our family legacy. Connor's the keeper of it, sure, but when…when there's another generation, I guess they'll all have a part of it. Though I'm sort of skeptical about any of us managing another generation."

"Okay," she said. "You, sure, because… I can see that you're not the open-your-home-up-to-chaos-and-crazy kind of guy. But Connor could find someone else."

"He doesn't want to. He seems to think cracking a smile's some kind of hanging offense."

"And Kate?"

"She's a kid."

"She has to be in her twenties."

"Twenty-one," he said. "She's way too damn young to be thinking about that stuff."

"Well, I agree on one level. A husband and kids? No way. Not at her age. But I assume she's dating and otherwise showing a normal interest in that sort of thing."

"Uh…not so much."

"Oh." Sadie's face heated, embarrassment washing through her. "Sorry, I was making assumptions. I should have said partner."

"What? Why?"

"Oh, just the way you said that I thought maybe I'd made a very broad assumption about her sexuality, is all."

He winced. "Can we please not talk about sexuality and my sister in the same sentence?"

"I just meant, if she's a lesbian I have no problem with that and I would hate for it to seem like I was passing judgm—"

"She's not," he said. "Considering the number of times I

found torn-out magazine pages of…what's his name? Zac Efron?"

Sadie laughed. "Okay, but you realize that's an indication that she does have a sexuality."

"I refuse to have this discussion."

"All I'm saying is, don't give up on the next generation yet. You're such a cliché," she said, shaking her head and laughing.

"Maybe," he said. "But I sort of raised her from the time she was two years old, so I reserve the right to be a little insane."

The admission hit her somewhere around the heart. Which made her very uncomfortable. "Oh. Right. I wasn't…thinking."

"Our mom left before Kate turned two. Dad might as well have left. Someone had to work, someone had to take care of the baby. Connor and I were an old married couple before we could drive."

"Eli…"

"Hey, look, I'm over it." Except he so obviously wasn't. He wore it as sure as he wore his uniform. His need for order. His need for control. "But the thing is… I think that's why this place means so much. And why I'm an overprotective crazy person. Because it was all down to Connor and me. And when you have that much responsibility that early, it becomes a part of you in a way it never would otherwise."

She turned and looked at the barn, at the care that had so clearly gone into it. Evidence of money that could have taken them away from here. That could have taken the Garrett family on to other things. College, maybe. Had any of them gone? Kate was twenty-one and working, so she clearly wasn't in school.

They had given their all for this place. To hold it together. Because it was what they'd done all of their lives and it was what they continued to do.

For a woman who hadn't lived in one place for more than a couple of years, it was a level of commitment that was…hideously daunting. It was sticking something out through thick and thin, rain and shine. Old barns and new.

It was choosing to keep on staying even when there was an out. And suddenly all that history, all that intensity, made it feel as though the walls were closing in.

And you're here for five years.

"Wow," she said, taking a deep breath. "Anyway, this is great. I mean, if we could do tables, lots of tables in and around here, that would be...excellent. Just so very excellent." She started to walk back out, quickly, trying to escape the weird, oppressive weight that had settled onto her stomach.

"I'll have to clear it with Connor. Farmwork getting done is going to be the top priority. But I think we can arrange to have the field just over here cleared for parking, which should make things easy. It'll all have to be roped off and...well, it's going to be a big deal."

"I know," she said. "But the city is willing to kick in for some funds. And I think I might be able to entice some vendors. Local beers, wines, cheese. And you know, if you wanted to kick in some beef, I think it could end up being really great for the business side of the ranch."

"Again, I'll talk to Connor about it. I may need to get him drunk first."

"He doesn't have to hang out if people...bother him."

"Everything bothers him. To be honest, I'm not sure if he'd be any more miserable in a crowded bar than he is alone."

"I'm sad for him. Your brother seems like a nice guy."

"No, he doesn't."

Really, he didn't. But she'd been searching for something to say and the blanket, insincere words had rolled off her tongue easily. "Fine. He doesn't seem that nice. But I'm still sorry for him."

"That makes two of us."

"Anyway, it doesn't sound like the worst idea, does it? We'll get pies donated from the diner. We'll get...fried pickles from Ace's. We'll make it a whole thing!"

"You're really embracing this local spirit. Surprising, all things considered."

"Yeah, no one is more surprised than me. But I was ready for a change, and at this point, putting down roots is kind of the only way to feel like something's changed."

"And change is..."

"Good," she said, getting back into the truck. "Healthy. I mean, people should change things around them every so often. Especially when life isn't gelling the way it should." Practiced lines she'd told herself over and over. "So, why don't you take me to see that other field?"

"You want to see the potential parking lot?"

"Sure. And anyway, I thought you were supposed to tell me why all my harebrained schemes wouldn't work."

"Well, I haven't come up with a single damn reason why what you're asking for won't work," he said, slamming the truck door. "Do you have any idea how annoying that is?"

"I have a fair idea of how annoying that must be for you. It must really suck."

"It does."

But somehow, even he didn't seem unreasonable right now. He seemed...understandable. Here in this vast, wild place, so carefully tamed by the hands of his family, by him and Connor, she could see what a huge job it had been. Two boys who had been essentially alone in the world, with a sister to care for. She could easily see how much grit and strength it would have taken to hold things together. She wondered if that impossible task was what had built the solid man she saw in front of her. The man who was still doing the same thing. Still trying so hard to hold the pieces together.

Dammit. It made her heart all achy, and that was much more disconcerting than being horny.

They didn't get very far up the road before Eli stopped the truck again. "Right there," he said, "we'll move the cows to another pasture and open up the gates."

She looked over to where he was pointing and shaded her eyes as she studied the bright green fields, dotted with glossy black animals, their heads down, the sun casting a ripple of light and shadow over muscle and sleek hair.

Yellow flowers popped like little sunbursts across the grass, standing in sharp contrast to the dark green and fading blue of the mountains beyond.

It took her breath away. It reminded her why this place was home.

Which was so strange, because she couldn't remember ever really feeling like it was before, but sitting in the truck, looking out at all this, she felt it. Not like something new, but even better and more rare for someone like her, it felt familiar.

"Parking lot doesn't really do this justice. Will it be okay to…drive on it?"

"Yeah, it's fine. We cycle the cows through the fields anyway and they're about done here for now."

"I can suddenly see why none of you ever left."

"It's beautiful," he said. "Some days I kind of forget to look at it. But the expression on your face just reminded me."

Something warm shot through her, across her face and down into the pit of her stomach. She swallowed hard, fought against it. It was a good feeling, but weird. Deeper than the kinds of feelings she was used to.

And she wasn't sure she liked it.

"Anyway, I have to get out and help Connor for a while, so I'll drive you back."

"I'm fine walking," she said, suddenly feeling the need to escape again. To feel a little sunshine on her face and some wind in her hair. "I mean, really, I want to walk."

He shrugged. "All right. Suit yourself. See you around."

She climbed out of the truck and tried to ignore the somewhat fuzzy feeling his casual, and not at all hostile, goodbye carved out in the pit of her stomach. Right in the middle of all the warmth.

"Yeah," she said, "see you."

She hopped out of the truck and breathed in deep, the air sweet from the flowers and salty from the nearby sea. She looked up and closed her eyes, letting the sunshine wash over her. And even though she wanted to, she didn't look back at Eli. Not even once.

CHAPTER EIGHT

NEVER HAD ELI been so glad for Jack to draw the short straw. That made him the designated driver for the evening, and it meant that Eli could drink some beers. Because he really, really wanted to drink some beer tonight.

Not that he would drink to the point of public drunkenness, since he had a reputation to uphold. And the legacy of being a worthless drunk's kid. But something to take the edge off the Sadie Miller knife that was digging into his gut would be nice.

Just a little haze. That was all he required.

Jack was still sulking because he had to stay sober, Connor had already gone to the bar to order beer and Eli was leaning back in his chair, enjoying being in town in plainclothes. Enjoying sitting back and watching people do things without feeling like he was on duty at a day care.

The bar was packed, but it was Saturday night and there were a limited amount of activities in town. There were average-quality restaurants, very expensive seafood restaurants, a movie theater with five screens and a local dinner theater. The bar was one of the more popular choices for obvious reasons.

Alcohol, darts and pool being some of the most obvious.

"Don't sulk, Jack," Eli said. "It's not a good look on you."

"Drunk isn't a good look on you," Jack returned, his arms crossed over his chest.

"I haven't been drunk since I was twenty-one. On my birthday. And never again."

"You're such a cliché."

Since this was the second time he'd been accused of this recently, he was starting to wonder if it was true.

"Aren't we all?" he asked. "We're in a bar on Saturday with nothing better to do."

"Looking to get laid," Jack said, turning and taking a Coke out of Connor's hand as he returned to the table with drinks.

"Speak for yourself," Eli said.

"Oh, right, you don't shit in your own yard."

Eli grimaced and took the pale ale Connor was offering him. "Not my favorite way of putting it, but the principle is sound."

"Liss isn't coming?" Jack asked Connor.

"Not tonight. She said something about painting her toenails and watching old movies. And that is where having me as her best friend tends to not pay off."

"You don't want to put the little toe separators in for her and blow on her feet until the polish dries?" Jack took a drink of soda to disguise his smile.

"I thought I'd come here and see if you wanted to throw darts at my balls instead," Connor said, tipping his beer bottle back and taking a long drink.

"If I were drinking, I would absolutely take you up on that," Jack said.

"Remember the time we were hanging out at the house," Connor asked, "and we thought we'd play darts? But there was nothing to hang the board we found...and you, you put the board in your lap? And told me to hit the bull's-eye?"

"I still have a scar on my thigh," Jack said. "So yeah, I remember."

"We did really dumb stuff."

"You two did dumb stuff," Eli corrected. "I mainly watched."

And told no one because there was no one who would have cared. Jack's mom was too exhausted from work to look his direction more than once a week, and the Garrett patriarch was usually passed out in his own vomit by 6:00 p.m.

They used to joke that if their parents got married they could be the world's most fucked-up version of the Brady Bunch.

That hadn't happened, because their individual parents had been too busy wallowing in their problems, but Jack basically lived at their house anyway, simply by virtue of the fact that it was bigger and there were more places to find trouble.

Jack liked trouble, and trouble liked him. Typically, female trouble.

He had no issue shitting where he lived, so to speak.

"We were badass," Connor said, a wistful look on his face. He took another sip of beer. "And you," he said, pointing at Eli, "were not blameless. You're the one who thought to build a ramp that went off the hayloft. And ride your bike down it."

"Ah...how did we not die?" Eli asked.

"Hell if I know," Connor said, tapping the side of his beer bottle. "But then, I'm sort of mystified by how those decisions are made." And just like that, the brief light on his face dimmed again.

Dammit. It was way too easy to say the wrong thing when someone had a ghost following them around.

"We all are," Jack said, slapping Connor twice on the back. "And when we're too mystified, we drink and talk crap at the bar."

"Damn straight," Eli agreed, knocking back another drink.

"With friends like you guys... I'll have a hangover in the morning," Connor said, making a weak attempt at a smile.

"You could have been painting Liss's toenails. You're paying for your own awesome choices," Jack told him.

"And you could have had beer," Connor said. "But you drew the short straw."

"It's a stupid tradition. We should just take turns."

"And you'd bail every time it was your turn," Eli said.

Jack smiled and shrugged in the boyish manner that got him out of situations that would have seen lesser men castrated. "Probably."

"And that's why we draw straws. Because one out of three men at this table is a piss-poor friend," Connor said.

"Guilty." Jack looked over Connor's shoulder and frowned. "Isn't that your hot new tenant?"

"What?" Connor asked, turning around completely unsubtly. The motion would have made a bull look graceful.

Eli looked up and saw that it was definitely Sadie, blonde, petite and, yeah, very hot, walking into the room and over to the bar. She leaned in, and he couldn't help but look, really look, at the way her jeans fit her rather fantastic ass.

"She really is hot," Jack said, his eyes getting that keen, focused look that he got when he was on the hunt.

"Not in this lifetime, Monaghan," Eli said, the words coming out a whole lot more threatening than he'd intended them to.

Jack sat back, dark brows shooting up. "Oh, really?"

"Damn straight," Eli said, hooking his hand around his beer and tugging it back, holding it against his chest.

"You're not for real," Jack said. "Sleeping with a woman who lives on your property is almost the same as marriage."

Marriage. That was the last thing he wanted. A little sex on the other hand…

Heat streaked through Eli's gut. He hated that his desire was that transparent, especially when he was still trying to pretend that he wasn't attracted to her at all.

He looked over at Sadie again. "I wasn't even thinking of it."

"Liar."

Connor was noticeably silent during the exchange. Eli managed to tear his eyes away from the view to look at his brother.

Connor looked up, his expression hostile. "What?"

Jack looked at him, too. "You're not commenting."

"Didn't notice she was hot," Connor said. "I was thinking

about it, trying to decide if she was or not. Then I realized my dick is fucking broken."

Hell, maybe Eli's was, too. Because this was a total departure from his usual rules. He hadn't fully realized it until Sadie had pointed out the sheer volume of sexual innuendo he missed on a daily basis when he was with her, but his normal course of action was to just shut his libido down until he was ready to do something about it.

He had great luck with women—when he was pursuing one. Otherwise...otherwise he lived his life with blinders on. And it wasn't by accident.

He kept his life classified in very careful segments. And maybe the problem now was he'd left one segment neglected for too long. And now things were...intertwining that definitely shouldn't be intertwining.

And beyond the intersection of his personal life and his love life, the fact that it was Sadie whom he wanted when she was the most infuriating, irritating woman...well, that just proved that his dry spell had reached Saharan proportions.

"She is hot," Jack said. "But I have a feeling Eli is marking his territory."

"I am not," he said.

"You don't like her," Connor pointed out. "She's a criminal. You arrested her."

"She's not a criminal," Eli said, gritting his teeth. "And it was ten years ago."

"Yeah," Jack said. "Marking his territory."

"Don't say it like that. She's a woman, not territory. And she's definitely not mine. You sound like a jerk."

"I *am* a jerk," Jack said. "It's like you haven't known me since I was twelve."

"As you so eloquently put it, or...as you should have put it, I keep my sex life away from here. Far, far away. I'm not going to pursue a woman who has a five-year contract to live on my property. That's a degree too close to marriage for my taste."

Jack laughed. "Okay, I get that. So does that mean I can…?"

"No," Eli growled. "You can't. Mainly because I don't want to catch sight of your bare ass through any open windows. That is guaranteed to get you shot."

"You're not allowed to shoot my friend, Eli," Connor said. "I only have two of them. I can't afford to lose any."

Eli looked at Sadie and watched as she cocked her head to the side, blond hair spilling over her shoulder, the fluorescent lights from the Mirror Pond Ale sign behind the bar casting a yellow-and-blue glow over the pale strands.

Ace was behind the bar, big and bearded and wearing flannel, which women seemed to be giddy over these days. And Sadie was obviously no exception, with the way she was giggling and smiling and…dammit, touching the guy's forearm with her delicate hands. Hands that were, incidentally, not covered with soil from planting an azalea.

Annoyance coursed through him. She'd just kissed him last week, and now she was in here flirting with Ace.

And so what?

So, it pissed him off. Which made him even angrier. Because he shouldn't care. He wasn't jealous. He was never jealous because jealousy implied that he cared, and he never cared.

Not that he didn't like the women he had relationships with, but he didn't quite care what they did when he wasn't around.

This Sadie thing was messing with his head. Not only was wanting her simply a bad idea, he was sitting here pondering ways to remove Ace's arm.

"Excuse me," he said, getting up and pushing his chair back, leaving his beer on the table. He could feel Connor and Jack staring after him, and he knew that they were probably ready to discuss conspiracy theories about whether or not he'd been brainwashed or body-snatched.

And he didn't really care. Because right now he had Sadie in his sights and he was going to walk over to her and do…something. He would figure it out when he got there.

Hopefully.

His feet hit the wooden floor harder than necessary with each step and he knew that people were looking at him, because he was Eli Garrett, current candidate for county sheriff, walking across a bar like he had sex and murder on his mind.

Both of which were strictly true.

"What brings you into town, Sadie?" he asked, leaning against the bar next to her.

She jumped and turned, blue eyes wide. "What brings you here to talk to me voluntarily, Eli?" she asked, her expression schooled into something casual now, covering up the moment of shock.

Ace looked at them both and turned away from Sadie, pulling a drink from the tap and walking down to the other end of the bar.

"Curiosity," Eli said.

"It's not that weird that I'm at the bar," she said.

"But you're alone."

"Who would I be with? Anyway, I was just stopping by because I wanted to feel out the best local brews and find out if Ace had any contact info for me. For the Fourth of July thing."

"Right," he said. "You're on a first-name basis with Ace?"

"I remember him vaguely from school. Also, I called in earlier."

"Okay," he said, sounding a lot more uptight than he would like.

"Why do you care?" she asked, tilting her head to the side like he'd watched her do earlier.

"Honestly? I don't know," he said. *Honestly?* Why had he been honest? Honesty in this situation was a terrible idea. Because it was ceding the upper hand. It was admitting he was out of his depth and that was not acceptable.

Her expression changed. Not wide-eyed shock or practiced casualness. She lowered her lashes, her lips more relaxed, her gaze falling to his mouth. Each shift almost imperceptible, and quick. And yet, he saw it. Was so painfully aware of it, as if he could hear each change like the cocking of a gun. It was clear, it was intentional. And the only thing he wasn't sure of yet was if she was shooting to kill.

"Is it because you want to kiss me again?" she asked.

She was shooting to kill. This shot had hit square in his gut, radiating down to his groin. He'd only had a half a beer, so he couldn't even blame that.

"It's more because I don't want *him* to kiss you," he said, leaning in, his palm flat on the bar. "I don't want to kiss you. I wish I hadn't kissed you the first time and trust me, Sadie Miller, I sure as hell don't want to do it again." He angled his head and moved in closer, conscious that they were being watched by almost everyone in the bar. Aware that he had to be close enough to make his point, but far enough away that no one would be planning their wedding by tomorrow. "But I'm starting to wonder if I will. If it's inevitable."

She drew back, her breasts pitching sharply with the harsh breath she drew in. "I'm not sure how something like that could be inevitable. I mean, either you want to kiss someone or you don't. If you do, you do. If you don't, you don't."

"I thought it was that simple. Until you. You've completely screwed up my kissing theory." Damn, maybe he *was* drunk.

"That's more than thirty years of kissing theory messed up by one woman," she said, her voice sounding lower, thicker all of a sudden. "That's…a lot of power."

"It is," he said, his own voice following the same path hers had.

"Are you drunk?" she asked.

"I wish."

"Wow. You really, really know how to turn a girl on." Sarcasm tinged her tone, but the huskiness in her voice told him that he actually was turning her on, and he had no idea how to feel about that. "Telling me you don't want to kiss me and you wish you could excuse your being over here with your being drunk."

"That's because I'm not trying to turn you on," he said. And that at least was true.

"I wish I could say it was working."

"Me not turning you on?"

"Yes," she said, looking down at the bar.

"Are we flirting?"

She looked back at him, her pulse beating hard at the base of her throat, hard enough that he could see it. "I don't think so."

"You're probably right. I don't think I know how to flirt."

"You're just trying to keep me from getting flirted with."

"Sounds about right."

Ace came back over to their end of the bar and crossed his arms over his broad chest. "He's not bothering you, is he, Sadie?"

Oh, for God's sake.

Sadie looked at Ace, her lips quirked into a funny smile. "You know he's a deputy sheriff, right?"

"I know who he is," Ace said.

Oh, great, the jackass was in the mood to be tough, and Eli wasn't in the mood to compete for Sadie because he didn't even want Sadie. Or at least, he didn't want to want her.

But there was no way he was going to be able to let it slide. He knew that there was no way because he'd crossed the room to stake a claim on a woman he shouldn't want just because she'd put her hand on another man's arm.

He already knew he was too far gone for common sense. He already knew his head wasn't in charge of this one.

"Then you know that I'm more likely to protect her than drag her off and throw her into my trunk," Eli said.

"What is it they say about cops and the domestic abuse rate?" Ace asked.

"Cute. Did you take an online class?" Eli asked.

Sadie giggled and they both looked at her. "I'm sorry," she said, her smile barely suppressed. "Please go on. I'm enjoying the novelty of two men warring for my affections."

"Outside," Eli said.

"I'm sorry, are you ordering me around? Do you honestly think I'm going to obey like a lapdog? I, sir, am a cat person, and I'll probably just bite your hand."

"Out. Side," he repeated.

She arched a brow but slid away from the bar and started to walk toward the exit. He turned to Ace and shot him a look before he dared glance at Jack and Connor, who were staring at him openly. Connor looking a little annoyed. Jack looking annoyingly impressed.

Bastard.

He turned away from them and followed her out the front door, rounding on her as soon as it swung shut behind them. It was dark outside, the waves crashing against the shore nearby the only sound, the moon glinting on the water like silver fish swimming over the surface. Every pitch of the surf casting white light over Sadie's face.

She was so beautiful it hurt. A real ache that started in his head and pulsed through his teeth, all the way down through his gut and to his cock. Just from a little light across the bridge of her nose. The bridge of her *nose*. He needed his head examined.

But not by Sadie. Because the little therapist was the person causing all of his mental and physical unrest.

"What is going on?" she asked.

"I'm...not sure," he answered, pacing the sidewalk in front of her. "I'm really not sure. I came out to drink and maybe eat some fish-and-chips and definitely not to talk to you, or see you, or think about kissing you."

"Hey, I came down here to talk microbrews, not to deal with you and your chest-beating, rawr rawr, he-man routine!"

"Then why are you dealing with it?" he asked.

"Why are you talking to me?"

"Hell if I know," he said.

"Then consider that *my* answer. Hell if I know!"

He moved toward her and she backed up, the wood-shingled

wall of the bar stopping her. Eli took a breath and pressed his palm flat to the wall, just by her head, his eyes locked with hers, heat arching between them. He couldn't have looked away if he wanted to. And he didn't want to. He wanted to keep looking at her. He wanted to kiss her.

And then some.

He wanted her more than he could remember ever wanting any woman. More even than his first, on a spring night after prom.

Right now he was beyond himself. Beyond control. And Eli Garrett was never beyond control.

Somewhere, in the depths of his thoroughly bent brain, it registered that that was a problem. That he shouldn't have ever let it get this far. That he needed to get a grip on things and stop it before it went further.

Dammit. He didn't want to.

He gritted his teeth against the rising tide of arousal. So intense it just hurt.

He took a breath through his nose and closed his eyes, lowering his head. If he just didn't look at her for a second…he could get a handle on things. On himself.

He breathed in again, slowly, and let it out through his mouth. Then he opened his eyes and looked back up at her. "Here's what we're going to do," he said, his voice almost unrecognizable.

"What?"

"We're going to go back in the bar. And you're going to go back and talk to Ace about local beer. And if he asks you on a date? I think you should go on it."

"What?"

"Yep. I'm going to go back to my table and drink at least two more beers, eat something fried and play darts. And I'm not going to look at you. I'm not going to talk to you. I'm not going to kiss you. We're going to start this night over, like I never walked over to you and opened my mouth."

"Eli…"

"And when we interact on the ranch it's going to be because we have tenant-landlord type business to deal with that Connor's pawning off onto me."

She bit her lip and nodded, a crease appearing between her eyebrows. "I'm even more confused now," she said.

"This ends one of two ways," he said, his throat getting tighter. "Either we keep this up," he said, thinking the *this* in the statement was fairly obvious, "and it goes too far. Or we stop it now. But I have a feeling if we keep it all accidental, then…"

"Right. And what would…be so bad about that?" she asked.

Her simple, nonexplicit words sent a slug of lust through him that was so intense he could hardly breathe around it. "Let me tell you something about me, Sadie. I'm a good man. I pride myself on that. But I'm not a very nice man. And I'm not the kind of man who does relationships. This is my town and I care about the people in it. When I want sex, I go outside the city limits for it because I know before I ever get in a woman's bed how it will end. Quickly. I don't want to bring that here. I don't want to run into old lovers while I'm crossing the street or when I'm making routine stops. And I sure as hell don't want to run into an old lover every time I cross my driveway." The very thought offended his sense of order in every way.

"I see," she said. "But…what makes you think I want any more than a little harmless sex?"

"Because sex is never harmless when it's this complicated. It's like setting fire in a barn instead of a fireplace."

She blinked and nodded. "Great. Fine. Whatever. I don't even see the point of banging a guy who wouldn't know fun if it got on its knees and sucked his…" She looked down, so pointedly that he felt it. "Well, you get the idea. Ace seems like he might be more the type I'm after. So I'll go in before you. I'll talk to him. Maybe I'll leave with him. We'll see."

You will not. His inner he-man, as she'd called it, growled.

"Sounds like a plan," he said instead. Because this was crazy. And it had to be stopped.

She forced a smile, her eyes meeting his quickly, a brief flash of electricity shooting straight through him before she turned away.

He watched Sadie walk back into the bar and waited for the tightness in his stomach to recede, for the ache to go away.

He had a feeling he was going to be waiting for a long time.

CHAPTER NINE

DRIVING INTO COPPER RIDGE the next day, Sadie decided to take a left instead of a right at the last minute. She'd been headed toward the main street of Old Town to visit Rona's Diner and see about pie, and something had pulled her the other way.

A ghost, maybe. The same one she'd been afraid she might find in a clearing. Or maybe just what normal people would call memories. She obviously wasn't normal.

But here she was, driving on the road that led away from the ocean. Away from the picturesque portion of the little town. This was where the other half lived. The poor half. The half who worked in the logging industry and at the mill, or didn't work at all.

The half she came from.

And on this road was her childhood home. Her throat tightened as she shifted her suddenly slick hands on the steering wheel.

She'd never imagined, ever, that she would come back here. In fact, she'd actively intended not to. What the hell was all this? Why was she here?

Who knew why she did anything these days? Coming back here, kissing Eli, almost kissing Eli again last night...

There was no point in thinking about that right now.

She took a deep breath and eased her car to the side of the road as she stopped in front of a blue house with shingle siding.

She took her hands off the wheel and looked out the window. The knot in her stomach eased. It looked different.

It was cleaner. The grass was cut. There was grass. When she'd been there, it had been nothing but a carpet of dandelions punctuated by groups of star thistle.

It was smaller, too. Brighter. She was sure it wasn't actually smaller, but it seemed that way.

A white minivan drove by her car and turned into the driveway of her old house. She watched as it parked and a woman got out. Gently taking her toddler from the backseat, along with a brown grocery bag.

They opened the front door and a small dog ran out to greet them. Sadie hadn't been allowed to have a pet.

Maybe this was what they meant when they said you couldn't go home again. The home that loomed large in her mind, *her* home, didn't exist. It hadn't since the Miller family moved out.

She thought of her patient Maryann, and how much she'd loved her home. How losing it had devastated her, because her memories had sunk into the wood. The love her family shared.

It wasn't like that for Sadie. Not for her family. Nothing of them was still here.

And thank God.

There was no power in this place.

She put her car in Drive and turned back around, shaking her hair out of her face. She felt like maybe things should seem momentous, but instead she just felt deflated.

Whatever she'd thought she might find there, she hadn't. Good or bad, really.

"You're getting weird," she said to herself as she turned onto Old Town's main street and drove to the far end, pulling into the driveway at Rona's Diner before killing the engine.

She didn't have time to be sentimental about a pile of wood, bolts and insulation. She had a pie mission to see to.

Sadie took a deep breath and wrapped her sweater tightly around herself. It was June, but the Oregon Coast had no respect for summer. Even when the sun was shining, the wind had to undermine it with a chill that cut straight through the warmth, and her sweaters, apparently.

She clutched her paper coffee cup a little bit tighter and walked into the diner at the end of the main drag, out near the jetty. She'd been informed that they had the best pies in the county, and she wanted the best for the barbecue.

It was two in the afternoon and the diner wasn't very crowded, the lunch crowd long since dissipated, the dinner crowd not yet arrived. There were some middle-aged men sitting in the corner with cake and pie on plates and coffee all around. Fishermen, Sadie guessed by the look of them.

That was one of the unique things about this place. It was a coastal town, with deep traditions tied to the sea. With fishermen, and crab shacks, seagulls and amazing fish-and-chips. But just inland were the cowboys and ranchers. Sheep, cows and beautiful stables with high-priced horses.

Copper Ridge was the melting pot of everything good in Oregon. Trees and waves, forests and beaches. In that regard, her hometown was a lot more special than she'd realized until she'd been away from it for a decade.

Old Town had changed, too. Where before things had worn a coat of neglect and salt from the sea, they were repainted, revamped and attractive to tourists now. Which was a very good thing for her.

"Can I help you?" a waitress called to her from behind the counter.

There was a glass display case beneath the countertop, laden with the very same pies and cakes the fishermen in the corner were indulging in. There were also doughnuts, giant cinnamon rolls and cupcakes that Sadie was thinking needed to go with her coffee right now.

"I'd like a cupcake. And to talk to whoever does the baked goods."

The woman blinked and something about her expression sent a flash of memory through Sadie. "That's me."

"Oh, well, great."

"What kind of cupcake?"

"Your favorite. I'm not picky."

"I like the chocolate peanut butter."

"Sounds perfect." Sadie watched as the other woman bent to get the cupcake from the bottom of the display case.

Familiarity nagged at Sadie, but she still couldn't quite place her. Obviously she had to be someone she'd known here. Someone from school?

When the waitress rose back up, the motion stiff, a grimace on her face, it hit her. "Alison?" Sadie asked. "Sadie! Sadie Miller. From school. And other things that weren't school-related."

The other woman's eyes widened for a moment and something sad passed through them before there was recognition and then, finally, a small smile. "Oh...oh, Sadie. I didn't recognize you."

"Well, I wear less black eyeliner these days. Clearly, so do you."

She laughed nervously. "Yeah. A bit."

"So, what have you been up to?" Sadie asked, dimly realizing that there was something uniquely wonderful in seeing faces from your past.

"Nothing much, really. Working here. Baking. I got married."

"Congratulations."

"Yeah," she said, forcing another smile that looked distinctly sad.

Alison had been part of her tight-knit crew. They'd caused a bit of trouble together—the barn incident being one of them—and mainly spent time in the woods near the Garrett ranch or on the beach, because for them it had been better than being at home.

They were the misfits of Copper Ridge, and even if no one else had fully realized it, they had. They knew they were different. They knew they were wrong. Broken families, poverty. Abuse.

There was only one elementary school, one junior high and a high school that sat squarely between Copper Ridge and Tolowa, making the most out of the shared student population. That meant they'd spent a lot of years circling each other like wary strays, slowly forming a group. A bond that had been, at the time, thicker and stronger than the bond with their families.

Alison, Damian, Matthew, Kelly, Sarah, Josh and Brooke. A few other people rotated in and out, but that was the core.

And she'd left them behind. She'd never contacted them.

In that moment, she felt ashamed.

"Not married," Sadie said, holding up her bare left hand for emphasis. "I've been...moving a lot. Being a crisis counselor. And now a proprietress at a bed-and-breakfast. So... I still don't make a whole lot of sense."

"Sounds nice to me. You escaped," Alison said.

That was how she'd felt at the time. Now she wasn't so sure.

"I'm back. This place has that way about it. It even called *me* back eventually, and I like moving on a lot more than looking back. Historically speaking."

There was a disconnect happening. Something so fundamentally defeated in Alison's eyes, something so familiar, that it hurt Sadie to look at it. And she couldn't nail down what it was or why. Maybe just fatigue from a long shift.

"Do you ever... Do you talk to anyone else from school?" Sadie asked.

Alison looked down. "Not really. Matt's still here. He fishes. Brooke owns a shop up the road, but we don't... I don't have a lot of time. Everyone else moved like you. Josh went on and made all kinds of money... I'm just still here."

"Oh." She made a mental note to track Brooke down later. "Yeah."

"Well," Sadie said, filling in the silence, which she was professionally good at. "I heard that you had the best baked goods in town. And the thing is I'm organizing a community Independence Day barbecue on the Garrett ranch, which is, not incidentally, where my B and B is. And I wanted to have a dessert booth. Possibly a pie eating contest. So I wanted to talk to you about what you have, what is possible production-wise and if the owner of the diner might be interested in donating a certain number of pies for the contest in exchange for advertising space."

"These are the best pies!" one of the men shouted from the corner. "Alison makes the best everything." There was a round of agreement from the other men at the table and that pulled another smile out of Alison.

Getting a smile out of her, Sadie was coming to realize, was as difficult as pulling Toby out from the back of the lazy Susan cupboard when he was annoyed about the vacuum cleaner.

"There, that's all the validation I need," Sadie said. "So if you're up to it, I'd really like to involve you. And if the diner owner isn't super into it, I'm happy to purchase pies directly from you. Or maybe you'd be interested in manning the dessert booth? You could sell pie by the slice. It'll be a great bit of advertising for you. And hey, since I think you're probably a million times better than me at baking, pies might be a great thing for me to have in the B and B anyway."

Sadie wished she could stop the tumble of words now, because Alison looked wary, and it hit a warning button deep inside Sadie. But the ideas were rolling off her tongue now without her permission. Possibly because of that internal warning signal.

For a therapist she was awfully useless in out-of-office people situations.

"I'll have to check with Jared. If he can spare me for that much time," Alison said.

"The diner owner?"

"My husband," she said, blinking rapidly. "He may not want me getting so involved in something like that. It's already hard with how much I do here."

"Right. Well, I mean, only if you want to. Don't feel an obligation to me or anything."

"I do want to," she said.

"Then I'm sure your husband will be happy for you. It'll be good for you and all."

Alison didn't look so sure and that right there sent Sadie's instincts from warning bells to the desire to maim the guy in the testicular region.

"Right. Yeah. Just the cupcake?" she asked.

"A marionberry pie, too, actually. I'll have it after dinner."

Alison bent and pulled a pie out and put it in a white box before ringing both items up.

"Great," Sadie said. "And now I know where to get my goody fix, and where to see an old friend. So all in all, this was a productive day." Sadie reached into her purse and pulled out a crumpled receipt from the coffee stand she'd gone to earlier, and wrote her cell phone number across the back. "Call me. If you ever need anything, or want to hang out, or have questions about the barbecue."

"Sure," Alison said, taking the receipt. "I will."

Sadie had the feeling the other woman was lying. And again, she couldn't quite place why. But everything seemed wrong. Well, the statement about the husband not wanting her to be gone too much seemed off to Sadie, but then, Sadie knew there might be other factors. Even though her gut response was that it sounded awfully controlling.

"Thanks for the goodies. If I slip into a sugar coma, don't be too surprised." Sadie waved and walked out the door, back down the sidewalk toward where she'd parked her car.

She was happy about the pie, but uneasy about everything else. And this was the problem with coming home. There were so many emotions tied up in things. She didn't like it. Before leaving Copper Ridge she'd had a whole lifetime of heavy. Of bad feelings and worry and outright terrifying crap, and she just didn't like to feel things that were even close to that anymore. It wasn't healthy to dwell, after all.

But Copper Ridge made her dwell, dammit.

And just like that, the magic of returning home was gone.

IT WAS DECK DAY. And Sadie had a bevy of shirtless construction workers off the back of her house, putting down posts and cement blocks in preparation for the building of the massive deck she'd designed for the B and B.

She had big plans for it. Tables. A barbecue. No, a barbecue wouldn't strictly be breakfast, but she could fix other meals.

Her one serious question, though, was whether or not a group of construction workers was a bevy.

Perhaps they were more an assemblage. Or a herd. A pack. That sounded nice and manly. Very sexy. She sipped on her lemonade and watched them from her living room window, privately pleased that she was perving on them rather than the other way around.

"Yeah, baby," she said, tilting her glass back and catching an ice cube between her teeth. "Show me what your mama gave you."

She was determined to get some visual enjoyment out of these guys. It was a way better idea than thinking about Eli and how much she would rather see him shirtless and sweaty.

There was a knock at the front door and she jumped, splashing lemonade onto her hand. She shook her head, walking to the door. She supposed it served her right. Getting caught being a dirty peeping Tom. She still didn't feel guilty, though.

She tugged the door open and saw Kate standing there, schooling her expression into something almost comically casual. "There are a lot of work trucks out here."

"There are indeed," Sadie said. "Because I'm having a deck

built. And the guys are doing it without shirts on if you want to come in and watch."

"That was what I was hoping," Kate said, her cheeks flushing pink.

"Never apologize for being a connoisseur of the male form, Kate. And never blush about it."

Kate blushed deeper and followed Sadie into the living room.

"Dear Lord," she said, and Sadie had the feeling that only the barest hint of decorum was keeping her from pressing her face to the glass like a frustrated window-shopper.

She recalled what Eli had said about feeling protective of Kate, or rather, being content to deny she had a sexuality altogether, and she wondered if Kate ever got to do anything more than window-shop.

"Not bad at all," Sadie said. "Makes me feel like a lady of leisure. Sipping cool beverages and ogling the slick sweaty men. And I'm not sorry about it."

"My female intuition told me that this might be happening over here."

"The force is strong with you. Would you also like a cool beverage? Lady of leisure status could be yours, too."

Kate smiled. "Sure. That sounds great."

Sadie went into the kitchen, humming as she did, and took a glass out of the cabinet before pouring some lemonade from the pitcher on the counter.

She returned a moment later and handed it to Kate. "Get your leisure on."

Kate took a sip and let out a long sigh, her eyes glued to the activities outside. "It's too bad this isn't a transferable skill."

"Not so much a big market for ogling while indulging in cold drinks, no."

"My goal is to make money doing things with horseflesh. Not manflesh."

"Doing what?"

"I barrel race. I'm looking to turn pro, but I haven't quite earned enough points to get my card. I didn't get to compete as much this year because I needed to work more hours at the Farm and Garden. Focus on saving. I won a decent-sized pot a while back, but not much since and I need money if I'm going to travel with the rodeo."

"That's incredible. You really barrel race? Like…you ride horses around barrels and wear sequined jackets and things?"

"I'm light on the sequins, but yeah."

"And you're good enough to go pro."

Kate took another sip of lemonade and smiled broadly. "I think I am. And my winning streak concurs. But it's just getting everything to line up. And feeling like Eli won't implode when I leave."

"Ah. Eli."

"He's a nervous hen."

"I can definitely see that," she said, thinking of him and his do-gooder complex.

I'm a good man but I'm not a nice man.

Oh, no, she didn't need to replay that scene.

Because it made her shivery in…places. Which was silly because that should be off-putting. She liked nice men. She did not like scoundrels. Or men in uniform with hella-bad attitudes and control-freak tendencies.

She could not be controlled or contained. She was the mothereffing wind.

"And he needs me more than he thinks," Kate said.

Sadie had a feeling that was a lot more insightful than Eli would think it was. "Sure," Sadie said slowly. "But you can't live your life for other people, Kate." She knew she was playing therapist again. But she was licensed, so it wasn't really *playing*. She was unsolicited, but she was a professional at least. "It only builds resentment, and in the end it destroys more bonds than honesty will. If you want to go, then you should be free to go."

"You make it sound really simple."

"It is," Sadie said. "It's what I do." She realized dimly that insinuating anyone should do what she had done was edging into bad-advice territory, so she attempted a redirect. "But it isn't as though you'll stay gone. It's just that you may need a bit more independence."

"And more shirtless men in my life that I don't share genetic material with," Kate said. "We're country, but not that country."

Sadie laughed. "Uh, I don't suppose you are."

"But yeah. I need to get away. Small town. Same places. Same jobs. Same guys. Take those guys, for example. I either went to high school with them, and they showed no interest in me. Or they went to high school with my brothers and wouldn't dare touch me."

Sadie figured it was better not to mention she hadn't had that problem with guys in high school. But then, she hadn't given off the salt-of-the-earth vibe Kate did. And she also didn't have two giant older brothers.

There was also the fact she doubted Kate had the knack for finding trouble that Sadie did. Which was probably for the best since Sadie had managed to find serious, life-threatening trouble thanks to the smaller trouble she'd found.

Not that anyone in Kate's family would ever hurt her. She could say that for Eli and Connor. She knew they would never hurt women, or anyone who didn't really deserve it.

And she was thinking about unpleasant things again. Ugh.

This place had a way about it. Good and bad. And both a little more intense than she'd been prepared for.

Though, if she was totally honest, she was never really prepared for intensity.

"That is a problem," Sadie said, keeping an eye on the guys. "Which ones did you go to school with? I feel like they're probably off-limits to me."

"Are you really going to…talk to them?" Kate asked, sounding awed.

She should. She should offer them cold beverages while wearing a bikini top. And get numbers. But she wasn't going to.

And she had a horrible feeling it was stupid Eli's fault.

Why she was still thinking about him in those terms was a mystery to her because he'd made it very clear he didn't want to find her hot. Even though he obviously did find her hot. And he'd turned down her very clumsy, ill-advised, sort-of offer of casual sex, too.

In that moment, if he'd agreed, she really would have hopped into the nearest bush with him and ridden him until she was saddle sore.

Had she ever wanted a man this much?

She didn't think she had, and that made her feel relieved he'd put a stop to it. Well, maybe not relieved. She felt twitchy and annoyed, and super horny.

She scowled and looked more determinedly out the window, trying to decide which guy had the nicest butt, and from there trying to decide if she would enjoy smacking it.

She could not decide. And she did not want to smack *any* of the denim-clad asses, truth be told.

She was broken, and it was Eli Garrett's fault.

There was a knock on the front door, which was still slightly open since she'd let Kate in. "Come in," she shouted.

The door opened and she heard footsteps on the hardwood in the entry, and then in walked the man himself. The new owner of her libido. Who had rendered her mainly useless when it came to ogling. It was all very upsetting.

"Hello, Eli," she said. "Is this your version of avoiding me?"

"Why were you avoiding her?" Kate asked.

"I'm not," Eli said, lying neatly for a man with an honor complex. "I came looking for you."

"How did you know I was here?" Kate asked.

"Your truck is in your driveway, but you weren't, and your horse was in his paddock. You weren't with Connor, so I thought I would see if you were here, and lo…" He looked past them both and out the window. "Are you kidding me?"

"We're learning how to build a deck," Sadie said, arching a

brow and swilling her lemonade, the ice clinking against the glass. "By observation."

Eli looked at Kate.

"The human mind is an amazing thing," she said, on the verge of giggles.

"Just watching all the nailing and screwing," Sadie said. "It's so sweaty." She took the glass and pressed it to her cheek, giving Eli a very meaningful look.

He swallowed visibly and shifted. Well, he'd obviously taken *that* innuendo on board. Good. He deserved to suffer. He deserved to suffer as she was suffering. He deserved to watch beach volleyball and get no joy from the bouncing. Which was mean-spirited, she knew. But she didn't care.

"I was looking for Kate," he said, his words very pointed as he turned back to his sister. "Carl Ames came by and was looking for someone who could possibly board a horse for his daughter. I said we had the space, but the thing is they might need someone to ride him on days they can't make it out. And I didn't want to volunteer you without asking. Of course, you would get the boarding money."

"All of it?" she asked.

"Yeah. I mean, if you took responsibility for the horse, I don't see why you shouldn't get paid."

"Paid to ride a horse. You know I have no problem with that."

"Great. Well, here's his number if you want to call. They'll probably have him by next week." Eli handed her a card and Kate smiled, set her lemonade on the sideboard, then waved at Sadie and dashed out of the house. Obviously construction workers still ran second to horses in Kate's world.

Eli probably loved that.

"That's going to leave a ring," Eli said, indicating the glass Kate had just discarded.

Sadie picked it up. "How did she turn out to be thoughtless of coasters with you in charge?"

"I blame the missing coaster gene on Connor. Anyway, I see

you're being a bad influence on my sister," Eli said, but there was no venom in his words.

"Your sister heard the work trucks a mile away and came running for her chance to gaze upon some prime, Grade A man muscle. Don't blame me for her actions."

"I don't really," he said.

He should leave because there was no reason for him to be there. Not when they were avoiding each other.

"So, you're having a deck built?" he went on.

She nodded. "Yes. Connor approved that plan before I moved in. I'd seen pictures of the place in the online ad and knew I wanted something more than just the front porch."

"Online ad. Liss must have helped him with that."

"Was she the woman who answered the phone call I made?"

Eli lifted a shoulder. "I would guess so."

"His...girlfriend?" Sadie asked, knowing it was nosy but not really caring.

"Friend. You met her at the poker game," Eli said. "She's one of the only people he listens to. Incidentally about the only person who can put up with his bullshit for more than a very short amount of time."

"I see. And who puts up with yours?"

"No one. I put up with everyone else's."

"Right," she said, looking back at the construction workers. "Men and tools are a marvel."

"What about you? Ace putting up with yours?"

She laughed. "Uh...not currently."

"Interesting."

"Why?"

"I'm surprised he didn't ask you out."

Dammit. "He did," she said. "But flannel isn't really my thing. Beards are so...scratchy. You have testosterone, we get it. So much that hair is growing from your face!" She waved her hands, the ice clanking against the glass again. "Just so... obvious."

"You prefer nonobvious men?"

"Just, you know, maybe I don't prefer any man right now. Or any one man. I have a fine assortment right out there. Why would I tie myself down to a date with one bartender, when I could stand here and look at the variety behind the glass, so to speak."

"You're making an awful lot of excuses about turning down a date. To a man you profess not to like."

"I don't like you," she said. "And may I say, you're loitering a lot in the house of a woman that you profess to be avoiding." She looked pointedly at him.

"I guess I am."

"And so…"

"Nothing. I'll go." He turned and she felt instant regret, which was more annoying than anything else. More annoying than not being able to enjoy checking out other guys. More annoying than all the darn emotions this place made her feel.

"I just… I ran into Alison," she said, not really sure why she was prolonging the conversation. He turned back toward her. "Used to be Brown. At the diner. She's the one who makes the baked goods there. I was just wondering if you knew anything about her. Like…if she's okay. I knew her in school and she seems… I don't know. Something felt off."

He nodded slowly, a shadow passing over his face. "Yeah. I know her. From the diner mostly. Her husband, Jared, is a logger. I know him because I've arrested him once or twice for after-work fights with coworkers. And yeah, I think something seems off. But she's never said a thing to me, and I've never seen anything… There's only so much you can do."

Her stomach tightened painfully. The memories from ten years ago were way too close to surfacing. Such familiar words. Familiar regret.

Only so much we can do. If you weren't an adult we could send child services in. But you're eighteen. Your mother is telling a different story. You could always call the police in…

She shook it off. Forcing the memory back into dark, dusty, unused corners of her mind.

She didn't need this. Not any of it.

"Right," Sadie said. "That...sucks. That sucks."

"I'm sorry for her."

Anger built up in her, more familiar now than she would like it to be, and all connected to Eli Freaking Garrett.

"If you were sorry, if you were paying attention, you would do something instead of just apologizing to me."

"What?" he asked.

"That's all people like you do in situations like this. Talk about how it's sad and unfortunate and regrettable—that's when you're not acting like you just don't see it at all." She ignored the guilt that lodged in her chest because that had been the first thing she'd done. Her first instinct. To think she was paranoid, and that it could be other things.

And sure, it still could be. But in the interest of her own comfort she'd been completely dismissive, and she knew the kind of pain that caused. Knew that that attitude could be utterly devastating to the people being shoved into the shadows for the convenience of others.

"The thing is, Sadie, I haven't seen anything. Except that I know the guy is a dick. On the job site and off. But being a dick isn't a crime. Now, when he has committed crimes? It's been handled. But he hasn't recently, and I swear to you I have nothing but supposition about how he treats her."

"But can't you investigate—"

"No," he said. "I can't. Because as much as I would like to sometimes, adults have a right to privacy. If there has not been a crime, then there's nothing I can do. I can't assume someone has committed a crime and go in after them. There are lines, and I can't cross them."

"Whatever. You're a chronic do-gooder. You're all up in your family's life. You feel like you're all up in mine, because here you are in my house again, and you're talking to me about boundaries?"

"I'm sorry, but the girl who runs from everything is going to talk to me about getting involved in people's lives? When was the last time you were involved in anyone's life besides your own, Sadie? When was the last time you took the time to help someone with their problems?"

"I did it for a living, jackass."

"And that helps you sleep at night, doesn't it? It helps you feel like you talk to people and like you've done something, but you never have to stay around, day in and day out and see the same people. See the same struggle. Know that all the help you've offered has meant nothing in the end."

"What are you talking about?" she asked, crossing her arms under her breasts.

Eli turned away from her and stalked toward the entryway and she followed him, her heart raging. "Hey, you just impugned my character, now stick around and explain it," she said.

"People don't change, Sadie. If I've seen one thing in my life, it's that. But to realize it you have to stick around. You got to sit in an office and listen to people talk, for money, but I won't even go too deep into that because, yeah, I take care of this community for money and I don't think a paycheck negates caring. But the thing is, I'm here. Year in, year out. I arrest the same kids over and over again. The same street people, the same addicts. The same abusers. And I wish to God they would get it. That something would reach them, but nine times out of ten, it just doesn't."

"I try, Eli. Even if I don't stay for twenty years, it doesn't mean I don't try," she said, the ball of fury growing hotter, bigger.

"You get to feel superior," he said, "and that's damn convenient. Because you get to judge me for what you think is me refusing to make a difference, and the view from your high horse tells you that you have made one. But it's only because you're all wrapped up in this fuzzy, fake reality blanket you knitted for yourself. You get to say that it's real, that what you do is real, and you get to look around this place that hasn't changed and say that what I do isn't. But it's because you've never bothered to look behind you."

"That is…" she said, searching for words. But it was hard when they were all mired in anger. "That is completely unfair."

"Is it? You're standing here telling me I don't care when, honestly, the thing is, I do. But caring doesn't do a damn thing. You have to act. I act according to the law. I keep things in order, using real rules and guidelines. I don't deal in the subjective, because I can't afford to make irrational mistakes."

"I see. So emotions are irrational."

"Hell yes," he said. "Emotions are damned irrational."

He took a step toward her, the tight space of the entryway growing smaller. "You know what else is irrational?" he asked.

"What?" She shouldn't ask what. Because she shouldn't want to know. Because the answer was going to lead to something stupid, and she knew that better than she knew just about anything at this point.

"Attraction," he said, his voice getting deeper.

Oh, no. That was definitely the wrong topic.

Everything slowed down, except her pulse, which sped up, beating hard in her neck, her wrists and, noticeably, at the apex of her thighs.

"Sure," she said. "Attraction is…you know, not logical, because it originates in your pants and not your brain. Which is not strictly true, actually. Your brain definitely plays a part in attraction…" Which begged the question why her brain and body were conspiring against her.

"It's a nuisance," he said.

"Get off my lawn, sexy feelings," she said, shaking her fist and trying to laugh.

But before she could finish the fake giggle, it was cut off by Eli's mouth over hers, by the fierce strength of his body propelling them both backward until they hit the wall. She dropped her lemonade, hearing it hit the floor, hearing it splash upward and spill the ice. It would be sticky and slippery and she just didn't care right now.

He pushed his pelvis against hers, the hard ridge of his erection evident against her softness. She rolled her hips against him and he groaned, the sound reverberating through her.

She didn't know why anger and lust were all tied into one thing with this man. She didn't know why she couldn't control her emotions or her body around him. She didn't know why she wanted him even when he drove her crazy.

Even when she didn't like him. At least, she was pretty sure she didn't like him.

It was hard to parse the finer feelings just at the moment.

He growled, a kind of deep, low sound. A sound that spoke of both satisfaction and hunger as he moved his hands to her waist to hold her, slid them down to her hips and held her tight.

She wrapped her arms around his neck and pressed herself more firmly against his body, and she found herself backed more tightly against the wall, the kiss intensifying.

She bit his lip and he returned it, his teeth leaving behind a stinging impression that burned all the way down. She was past thinking. She was past anger. She was past caring whether or not they could ever go out to dinner together without fighting.

Because what did that matter when there was this? Nothing else mattered. Not the construction workers outside, not her pride, not anything. Not in comparison with the heat that was burning between them, white-hot and insistent. Perfect.

This was sexual need in its purest form. Undiluted. A straight shot of alcohol that buzzed right through the brain and turned everything on the periphery gauzy. Consequences didn't matter. Eli mattered. While the rest of the world faded, he remained. Sharp and present, perfect. Necessary.

She released her hold on him and ran her hands down his chest, over the thin black T-shirt that seemed to be his out-of-work uniform. She could feel the muscles underneath, the hard ridges, defined peaks and valleys.

And she couldn't stop herself from dragging her fingertips all the way down to the edge of his shirt and pushing her hands beneath the hem. She hissed when her fingers made contact with hot skin and rough hair.

This might kill her. He might kill her.

She didn't know if she had the fortitude for this. Because it was definitely like nothing she'd ever experienced before.

This wasn't a pleasant tightening in her stomach and a bit of slickness between her thighs. It was all-over need. Warmth that bloomed low and spread to all of her extremities, that infiltrated her veins and heated her blood, making it flow hotter, faster, went straight to her heart and sent it into overdrive. Left her shaking and weak and *needy* in a way that should terrify her.

Scratch that, it *did* terrify her. But the arousal drowned out the fear. Mayhem was crashing around her, but it didn't matter because lust was a giant hand holding her head down beneath the waves. Where she was insulated, and at the same time in terrible danger.

But that only made it better. More exciting. More desperate.

She moved her fingertips up over his stomach, over abs that could be played like a washboard in a country band and toward that broad, perfect chest.

"Oh, just take your shirt off," she muttered against his lips, pushing upward while he tugged the end and hauled it over his head.

Her heart stuttered for a second before racing ahead again as she took in the overwhelming hotness that was Eli Garrett. She'd thought of him as Officer Hottie on first sight, but she'd had no. Freaking. Idea.

Tanned and toned with just a smattering of body hair over his chest and down the center of his abs. Like the path on a map, leading to buried treasure. And she could tell, based on the feeling of his hardness against her, that he was packing some serious treasure.

He pushed the straps on her dress down, exposing the thin, peach-colored bra she was wearing. He swore, harsh, breathless, and moved to cup her, sliding his thumbs over her nipples. She leaned her head back, banging it on the wall. And she didn't even care.

He lowered his head, pressing a hot, openmouthed kiss to her cleavage, the desperation in his actions spurring her on, bringing her closer to orgasm with each touch of his lips, his tongue, his teeth on her tender flesh.

Kissing, touching, had never brought her so close. He hadn't even put his hands between her legs—where she was wet and aching for him—and she was still right on the edge, ready to go over with the slightest touch. Another flick of his thumb over her cloth-covered nipple, another calculated slide of his tongue against hers.

He didn't do either. He lifted his head and looked at her, dark eyes meeting hers. His brows were locked together, his lips pressed into a line. He looked like a man trying with everything he had to cling to his control. A man who was losing. The moment jarred her, gave her body just enough of a reprieve that she didn't feel so close to the end.

She moved her hands behind her back, shaking, and unclasped her bra, throwing it onto the ground.

A flame burned hot and dark in his eyes and she could see the moment that all that control snapped. As sexy as it was to see Eli Garrett in full command, seeing him unleashed was even better.

He moved back to her, lowering his head and sliding his tongue around the center of her nipple before sucking it in deep as he moved his hands around her back, slipping them beneath her dress and cupping her butt.

He inched one hand lower, his finger dipping between her thighs. She gritted her teeth in a futile attempt to hold back a hoarse moan as his fingers slipped under her panties, over her wetness, and one pushed deep inside her.

She moved her hands to his back, nails digging in deep as she arched into his touch. Between his hands and his mouth, she was going to lose her ever-loving mind before this was over.

You already have. Might as well enjoy the ride.

That was the truth. But it was hard to regret losing her mind when it had led to the discovery of *this*.

He shifted his attentions to her other breast while he withdrew his finger, then slipped two fingers across her slick folds, over her clit.

She dug her nails into his skin, and she was pretty sure she might be drawing blood, and she didn't even care.

He slipped his fingers back, teasing her entrance with partial penetration before he pushed both inside of her. A ragged curse word escaped her lips as her orgasm crashed through her, as she held tight to him and rode out the storm.

When the waves stopped moving through her, he withdrew, shoving his pants and underwear down his thighs, revealing his body to her.

"Damn," she said, the word tinged with awe.

He smiled for a second, before the expression was replaced with one of total intensity and concentration. Then he bent and grabbed his jeans, fumbling through the pockets for his wallet, and then fumbling through the wallet for a plastic packet that was a more welcome sight than water in the desert.

"I will never mock your sense of responsibility again."

He opened the condom and rolled it onto his beautiful, considerable length, then he closed the distance between them. "Sadie?"

"Yes?"

"Shut up." He bent his head and kissed her, pushing his hand back between her legs and tugging her panties to the side before gripping her thigh with his other hand and tugging her up against him, the thick, blunt head of his cock testing her.

Then he thrust in fully, a raw sound escaping his lips, the sudden, intense invasion leaving her breathless, leaving her on the verge of begging for more. On the verge of coming again, even though she'd just had an orgasm strong enough to render her whole two-year man hiatus forgotten.

She held tight to his shoulders and lifted her other leg up over his hips, her ankles locked behind him as he pushed her back hard against the wall, his hands holding her hips tight as he withdrew and thrust deep inside her.

"Yes," she breathed against his ear, biting his neck gently, then licking it as he pounded into her. Driving her back toward orgasm so much faster than she would have imagined possible.

He captured her mouth again as he thrust in deep and she felt the first ripple of a new climax starting to move through her.

Then he put one hand on her breast again, squeezing gently and flicking his thumb across the tightened bud at the center, and she was consumed by it. Pleasure tore through her, and on its heels was a rough, feral growl from Eli as he lowered his head and gave himself up to his own climax, his erection pulsing inside her as he came.

He collapsed against her and her legs slipped down his lean hips, her feet making contact with the floor, her shaky knees making it impossible to stand straight.

She pressed her shoulder blades against the wall, suddenly very aware that her sundress was tugged down beneath her breasts and pushed partway up her hips, her undies askew. And her lemonade had spilled all over the floor, the ice cubes melting on the hardwood.

So many bad choices made in such a short period of time. And it was hard to regret them when her body was still buzzing, her breath was still MIA and she just felt so thoroughly satisfied that for the first time in her life she didn't feel on the verge of running somewhere else and never returning.

But all of that lasted only a moment.

"Fuck," he said, straightening and pushing off from the wall, walking back and forth for a second, looking down at the condom, which he was still wearing, a crease appearing between his brows.

"The bathroom upstairs," she said. "You can use it without walking by open windows."

He bent gingerly and grabbed his jeans, picking them up and climbing the stairs, and in spite of encroaching regret, she paused to admire his muscular calves, thighs and butt as he made his way to the bathroom.

She was high. On pleasure. On him. And with every step he took away from her, she sank a bit lower. Until her stomach was in her feet.

She wasn't needy after sex. It was not her thing. But she needed something more than this. Something more than a curse and his naked back as he left her.

The bastard. He was post-orgasmically uptight, which was a commitment to crabbiness that seemed almost impossible to maintain.

But Eli was incredible that way.

And in other ways.

The man was built. He'd just proved that the size of the boat had a lot to do with how the motion of the ocean felt, that was for sure.

Under normal circumstances she would feel…triumphant. He was, without a doubt, the single hottest guy she'd ever been with. Not that there had been a lot, but she'd never been too worried about it. It was all casual.

The trade-off with Eli seemed to be that nothing about it felt casual. Amazing, cataclysmic sex, with a side of angst.

Gah, and no thank you.

She preferred no angst to multiple orgasms.

Lie, lie, you lie. That was the best sex of all time. It'd be worth waxing both your eyebrows off in their entirety to experience that again.

Meh. Why did her internal voice have to know her so well?

She heard footsteps on the stairs again about the time she realized she was still standing there half-dressed. She scrambled to get her dress pulled into place, kicking her bra into the corner.

Then she reached beneath her skirt and adjusted her panties and straightened, hoping she looked a little less epically tumbled.

Sadly, she didn't feel less epically tumbled. She was hypersensitive and tingly, and her mouth felt like she'd gotten it too close to a flame.

She turned, and all those feelings got worse. He was walking toward her, down the staircase, jeans low on his hips, very low, no underwear band visible because his underwear was still on the floor and not on his fine body. His chest was bare, his ab muscles rippling with each step.

His mouth was grim. And it still looked kissable. His lips looked extra kissable when they were grim, which was some sort of sick joke her hormones were playing. Because everything in her took it as a challenge. To soften his mouth. To make him relax. To make him groan.

To make him shake and sweat and come.

Bad road. Her mind had gone down a bad road.

"So, that was…fun," she said, clearing her throat.

He shot her a glare that could only be described as evil and bent to get his T-shirt, tugging it over his head, and over her happy fun times ab show.

"I take it *fun* isn't your adjective of choice," she said, knowing she was making it worse, unable to stop herself from warding off the awkward silence with even more awkward words.

He took his underwear off the floor and stuffed them in his pocket. She would have laughed if it wasn't all so horrible. Actually, she might have laughed anyway because anything so singularly hideous had to be a little bit funny.

But she didn't laugh because she didn't want Eli to kill her with those very angry brown eyes of his.

Though, they were starting to make her angry, since it wasn't like she'd assaulted him. He was the one who had kissed her.

He had kissed her and now he was glaring.

And just like that she went from tingly to uncontainable rage.

"Please don't stalk around here like I compromised your maidenly virtue. You kissed me. You pushed me against the wall. You were complicit in the screwing. So get over yourself."

His nostrils flared and a muscle jumped in his jaw. "I am well aware that I'm at fault here."

And that made her bristle, too. "At fault? You make it sound like we had a fender bender. It was sex, Eli. There doesn't have to be a guilty party."

Color slashed over his cheekbones and she knew that he felt... ashamed. Of her. Of wanting her. And that just made her feel like garbage. All the glow was gone. All the good everything. And the anger, too.

It just left her with a sharp sinking sensation, a feeling of aching uncertainty. And just like that, the fear, the knot of terror that seemed to be a constant companion, was back in her chest.

And she wanted to run.

Not just from the room, or the house. But from the town. The state. She just wanted to leave it all so far in the rearview mirror that she couldn't see it. That she wouldn't be able to remember this regret.

"Why don't you just go," she said.

He nodded once and walked out the door, closing it firmly behind him. And she realized they hadn't even locked it. They'd screwed in the entryway of a place that seemed to have revolving doors on every structure and they hadn't even locked up.

"I wish I could go," she said, pressure building in her chest, tears stinging her eyes.

She cried. Of course she did. At the end of books, during commercials for life insurance and movies with intense acts of bravery that were sure to end in death but were performed anyway.

But she didn't cry over real-life things. Because she kept negative space, negative emotion, out of her life. And she didn't feel it. She didn't let it get down beneath the surface when it did run out to confront her.

But Eli had managed to get inside her, and not just in a sexual way. It was…terrible. She leaned against the wall, her heart slowed down to a dull thud that resonated in her ears, her stomach turning, making her feel sick.

Okay, she was not going to wallow. She was *not*. Wallowing didn't solve anything. And repeating the same mistakes twice didn't solve anything, either.

One good thing about growing up with her abusive asshole of a father: she'd learned about human nature in a harsh and real way. Had seen what happened to the optimistic when they believed a bad situation could change with love. With lying to yourself.

She'd come out of that with eyes wide-open. And with a ruptured spleen, but that was another matter entirely.

She sucked in a deep breath and managed to hold back the tears. She wasn't going to cry over Eli. It was a spilled-milk situation. Or rather, spilled lemonade. She just needed to wipe up the mess and carry on.

She heard the soft thump of four paws hitting the kitchen tile, and then Toby wandered into the room, rubbing against her bare legs, his gray tail twitching up above his head.

She bent down and scratched him between his ears. "I messed up," she whispered, because her voice didn't seem to want to function on any other level. "But I guess that's par for the course, right?"

Toby meowed and pushed his head harder against her hand, angling so that she hit a particular spot just behind his left ear.

"How do you put up with me?" she asked, and was met with nothing but a request for more head petting. Which in many ways was just fine. "Kitty before mantitty," she said, moving her hand beneath his chin and scratching.

This was just a onetime thing. A moment of insanity. She should be grateful it had happened. Yes, grateful. Because the intensity brewing between them wasn't healthy. And it had needed some diffusing. That was what today had been. She could draw a line under it and call it good.

What was sex like with Eli? Question answered. What did he look like naked? Question very much answered. There was no more burning curiosity. None.

And that meant the tension between them should be somewhat relieved. So there.

She took another breath, some of the tightness in her chest easing. There was no reason to be upset. They were adults, and they could handle this. Eli would be fine next time she saw him. He'd just been suffering orgasm hangover and hadn't handled things well.

But everything would be fine.

It had to be.

CHAPTER TEN

IT WAS PIZZA night for the Garrett family, and it should have been somewhat enjoyable. Usually, Eli liked the routine of them assembling in the main house for an evening.

Even though there weren't a whole lot of sunnier times for their family to be reminded of, they'd always had each other.

The three of them, and sometimes Jack, against the world.

But tonight he wasn't enjoying it to the degree that he should, and all because of Sadie. Because of Sadie and the fact that, only four hours ago, they'd had sex against a wall, which he'd never, ever done in his life.

Because that spoke of a lack of control he didn't even think he was capable of. Never before had a kiss just turned into sex.

When he had sex with a woman, they both knew it was on the agenda and things followed careful steps. Living room couch to bedroom. And then out the door again because he didn't spend the night, but it was okay, because they didn't expect him to.

It did not just…happen like that. Almost against his will, and certainly against his better judgment. But one minute they'd been shouting at each other, the next they'd been kissing, and then…then he'd been about knocked on his ass by the intensity of his orgasm.

Before he knew it he'd been upstairs in her bathroom, totally naked, pouring cold water down his neck so that he could get back downstairs and out the door again without popping wood when he saw her.

He'd spent the rest of the day riding his horse around the pastures, doing essentially nothing but trying to pound his balls into submission with tight jeans and a punishing day in the saddle.

Unfortunately, he'd just ended up replaying the scene in Sadie's house over and over.

"Why are you scowling?" Connor asked from his position at the counter, where he was sitting on a bar stool and inhaling his pizza. "Scowling is kind of my thing, and I feel like you're edging in on my territory."

"Scowling is your thing? I thought the Robinson Crusoe look was your thing," he said, indicating Connor's beard and hair, which were both starting to get a little long.

"I can have more than one thing."

"What's my thing?" Kate asked, leaning forward on the counter, speaking around a mouthful of cheese.

"Bad table manners and objectifying construction workers, apparently," he said, his words a little testy since, in fairness, it was Kate's fault that he'd gone looking for her in Sadie's house. It was his sister's damn *sex drive* that had put him in this position.

Her cheeks turned pink and she looked down. "Thanks for ratting me out, bastard."

"Objectifying construction workers?" Connor said in mock horror. "That's shocking. Did you whistle at them and say, 'Hey, baby! Why don't you drop that hammer so I can watch the view'?"

"I did not," she said, looking like she was about to fold in on herself.

"Missed opportunity," Connor said.

"Whatever," Kate said, pulling a piece of pepperoni off her pizza and putting it in her mouth. "You would lock me in my room if I ever did that." She stuck her thumb in her mouth and sucked the grease off it loudly.

"Honestly," Connor said, "I don't worry much about you and men."

Kate looked genuinely offended by that. "Why not?"

"I have my reasons," Connor said.

Relationships, or hookups, which was the veiled content of the conversation, were not Eli's favorite topic just now, so he was keeping his mouth shut.

"So what happened the other night?" Connor asked, his focus on Eli now. As if his older-brother sense told him that Eli was clamming up to avoid talking about something.

"Which night?" Eli asked.

"You dragged Sadie out of the bar and returned ten minutes later. She looked like she'd been scolded. You looked like you'd accidentally branded your own ass instead of a calf's. What happened?"

"Why are you choosing this moment to start paying attention to what I do?"

"I always pay attention. It's just you don't usually have anything happening. And I want to know what's happening with Sadie."

He thought about earlier. Soft skin under his hands, her full breasts...what it had been like to take one of those perfect nipples into his mouth. How wet she'd been.

Mind-blowing, cock-busting sex.

"Nothing," he said.

"Yeah, I don't believe you."

"They're avoiding each other," Kate said, looking at him almost apologetically. "Well," she continued defensively when he shot back a mean glare, "it's what she said when you were at the house earlier. When you busted us creeping on those guys."

"I'm avoiding her because she's a pain," he said.

"And yet you told Jack to keep his hands off."

Kate's head whipped around to Connor. "Jack is interested in her?"

"Jack," Connor said, "is interested in tits. Whether they're attached to Sadie or not is immaterial. They are the new breasts in town, and therein lies the attraction."

Kate lowered her head and mumbled something that Eli didn't understand.

"What was that, pumpkin?" Connor asked.

"Gross," she said, a little louder, and a little crisper.

"Men are. Your life lesson for the day," Connor said.

Seemed like it was Eli's lesson for the day, too. Since he'd done a fantastic impersonation of a pig today.

"To be fair, Connor," Kate said. "I appreciate a man's ass in a pair of Wranglers."

Connor looked like Kate had hauled off and slapped him with her meat-greasy fingers. "Sure," he said.

"I just meant Jack's attitude is gross. Sex isn't gross at all." Kate was looking mutinous now, and Eli's blood pressure was rising because he didn't need sex talk just at the moment. And he needed sex talk from Kate never.

"That's enough," Connor said.

"I mean, if a guy wants to look at my tits I'm not going to—"

"Did someone spike your Diet Coke?" Eli asked.

"I'm just sick of this overprotective crap you guys always pull. 'Boys are gross,'" she said, in a bad imitation of Connor's voice. "'You'll get cooties if you touch them.'"

"I *never* said that," Connor said.

"You told me penises had teeth," she said, deadpan.

Eli's head whipped around to face Connor. "Did you really?"

"I don't remember," Connor said.

"You did," Kate said. "I spent the next two years concerned for the health and safety of the inner thighs of every boy I knew."

In spite of his mood, Eli laughed. "I'm sorry, that's just funny."

"Brothers are horrible," she said.

"I know, but we're also the best you have," Eli said. Poor Kate. They were all she had, and they fell short in so many ways it verged on tragic.

"You're good for some things," Kate said. "Not as much for others."

"The same could be said for anything," Connor pointed out. "Badgers. Great for being kickass in the woods. Bad for sharing a shower."

"Connor..." Kate groaned.

"Krazy Glue. Good for sticking things together. Bad for personal lubricant."

Kate scrunched her eyes shut and stuck out her tongue.

"I rest my case," Connor said. "Men are gross."

"*You're* gross," Kate said.

"Your mom is gross."

"My mom's hygiene is open to interpretation because no one has seen her in nineteen years."

"Sorry," Connor said. "Bad joke."

"Sure," Kate said, looking dismissive, "but she's your mom, too."

"Barely," Eli said.

She was the woman who had left them all to drown in chaos. His father slipping away on a wave of alcohol while the kids were left to pull themselves up from the wreckage of glass bottles, unwashed clothes and garbage.

To say that Eli had come out of it a little bit of a neat freak was an understatement. Order and control had become essential to survival, and bleach had been a weapon he'd employed early on.

If Connor had become the man of the house, Eli had become the housewife. No thirteen-year-old boy wanted that job. But they had Kate to worry about. And dammit all, worry didn't even begin to cover it.

But Eli and Connor were both old enough to realize that if

rumors about their dad's drinking got passed around, there was a high likelihood CPS would step in. There had been too much loss for them to be split up. For Kate to be taken away from them. For them to be taken from the ranch.

And so they'd done whatever they'd had to.

School days had been torture for a while. He'd been in hell wondering if his sister was being cared for while he was trapped in a classroom, Kate in a crib while his father drank the day away.

Fortunately, Connor did more with the ranch as a fifteen-year-old than their father had ever done, and they'd earned enough money to put Kate in full-time day care.

So Connor would get up before school and do what needed to be done on the ranch, and Eli would get up and wake Kate. Give her a bath, wash and braid her hair. There was too much to do for him to allow chaos, too much at stake to ever let Kate look like she was less than lovingly cared for.

Connor and Eli had kept up appearances until the old bastard had driven off one of the winding Copper Ridge roads five years ago, drunk as hell, and nobody had been in the dark after that.

In so many ways, it was easier with their dad dead. At least they didn't have to take care of him now, too.

Well, you did a terrible job of taking care of him in the end.

He shook that thought off. What the hell was wrong with him today? Sex against a wall and this stupid stuff.

He didn't like reflecting on the past, and he wasn't really sure why he was doing it now. Maybe just because today sucked like that.

But did it really suck? Because, be honest, you've never had sex that good.

No, he hadn't. And that made it even worse.

Because no matter how bad of an idea he thought it was, he wanted more. The temptation to shove her down onto the floor, hook her legs over his shoulders and have his way with her had

been way too big, which was why he'd stormed out of there as
quickly as he could.

Because he didn't trust himself. He almost didn't know himself, and for a guy like him, that was a terrifying admission.

"Well, genetically," Connor said, "I think we can all agree
that other than in the looks department, we lost the parental
lottery."

Eli almost laughed at that since Connor was currently looking shaggy enough that it would take a very close inspection
to decide whether or not he was good-looking.

"But seriously," Kate said, "brothers are actually good for a
lot of things. So… I've never felt like it was so bad."

Eli cleared his throat. "Dammit, Kate, why'd you have to
get all sincere?"

"You have to warn a guy, Katie," Connor added.

"Call me Katie again, and I won't say anything nice to you for
the foreseeable future." And it was all back to normal already.

Okay, he'd screwed up earlier. No denying that. And things
were going to be weird for a while. And hard for a while, which
was a potential double entendre Sadie would have enjoyed. But
he still had Kate and Connor. And his run for sheriff. So most
areas of his life were fine. He was just going to rope off that
little disaster labeled Sadie and avoid it for the time being. Pay
attention to the good and ignore the wreckage.

The incredible, mind-blowing wreckage.

He took a bite of pizza, even though he wasn't hungry. Tomorrow he was back to work. And with any luck, that would
help keep his mind off things he had no business thinking about.

CAMPAIGN SIGNS AND posters weren't enough, it seemed. Not
for the general election. TV ads and radio spots were needed.
According to Lydia at least.

He knew those things were probably necessary, and he'd
done some checking into it already, but there was something

about the way Lydia talked about the election, filled with spark and enthusiasm, that made it seem like a very daunting reality.

Made him fear it was just too damn much to take on. The feeling he was sinking beneath a pile of endless work was one he'd had for most of his life, so it wasn't new. But it didn't mean he had to like it.

He ought to slap a campaign manager button on her chest and hire her right here in the coffee shop. But that would mean constant exposure to this level of energy and ideas, and he wasn't sure he could handle that now.

Not with hurricane Sadie encroaching on his borders.

Eli was starting to think he needed to buy coffee somewhere else. But other than The Grind the closest place with decent caffeine was fifteen miles away and it wasn't his usual assignment. And he basically had no reason ever to drive there for a latte, even when it meant avoiding Lydia's too-keen eyes.

After what had happened with Sadie it felt exposing, and made him feel a little guilty. Which was stupid, because if Lydia was interested in him, he'd never given her a reason to be. And he shouldn't feel at all like he'd somehow led her on.

But he did. And he felt even worse because she was helping with the Independence Day Community Whatever and because she seemed so invested in his campaign.

And if she found out he'd slept with Sadie…well, the help would likely be withdrawn from both endeavors. Which, when he thought about it, was more tempting than it should be.

"I think you should do a full-color spread," Lydia was saying now.

"Excuse me?"

"Like…put your picture on the posters and the signs. I feel like you have the looks to really grab voters."

"Is that…a thing?" he asked.

She smiled. "It's always a thing. I mean, when you're as kind and dedicated as you are, handsomeness shouldn't matter. But it certainly enhances things. It's part of charisma."

He was so rarely accused of having that.

"Well, the other guy running certainly has a lot of good qualities, and has years more experience than I do."

"He isn't from Copper Ridge, though. And since this is the largest town in the county, that matters. They just work here. It's different."

It was in his mind, too. Man, it would be so much easier if he found Lydia attractive. Ferret-like levels of energy aside, she was pretty amazing. They could work together on his campaign, and hell, in spite of his gut opposition to a wife and family, he could eventually settle down with someone like her and they could be the unofficial king and queen of Logan County.

Too bad a stick in the eye sounded more appealing.

He looked away from Lydia, across the street, and saw a messy blond bun bobbing on the far side of the cars parked against the curb. And he knew, instantly, who the bun belonged to.

He'd avoided her for three days. Three days without seeing her and kissing her, or putting her up against the wall and banging her.

It had been a successful, if not entirely fun, three days.

The identity of his visual target was confirmed when she appeared through a gap in the parked cars, turning away from the street and facing the wall of one of the shops. She set a stack of papers on the ground and held a staple gun up. Pressing one sheet of paper to a bulletin board and holding the gun against it, she efficiently shot a staple into each corner, before bending and picking up the flyers again and moving on to the next shop.

They were maybe fifteen feet apart, but that didn't stop her from adding a flyer to that board, too.

"Sorry," he said to Lydia. "I have to…law enforcement business."

He walked to the end of the sidewalk, to the crosswalk, and moved quickly across to where Sadie was.

"What are you doing?" he asked.

She turned, her expression fierce as she pressed the trigger on the gun and shot a staple through the paper and cork board. "Posting posters," she said.

She lowered her hand to her side and lifted her eyebrow, the staple gun menacing in her dainty hold.

"I can see that."

He looked behind her head and read the words.

Logan County Community Barbecue
Independence Day
Come to the Garrett Ranch for food, fun and games.
Horseshoes, pie eating contest, live music
and a barbecue battle.

"Well, this is...firming up."

She looked down below his belt pointedly, raising her arm, and the staple gun with it. "Is it?"

He frowned. "Sadie..."

"Give the guy a little sex and suddenly he gets the dick jokes."

"Are you mad at me?" he asked.

"Did you expect me to be super thrilled with you?"

"I expected you to do the socially acceptable thing and pretend nothing happened while you brooded silently. That was my plan."

"Too bad for you, I've never excelled at the socially acceptable."

"Look, let's talk about this," he said, indicating the poster. "Not...the other thing. This is good. The other is bad."

"The other was actually *quite good*, if I say so myself. I am apparently not only good in bed, but good against the wall. Adding it to my résumé."

"Why are you so difficult?" he asked.

"I don't know. Character flaw? Asset? You be the judge."

"And I'm trying to be nice."

"Not doing a very good job." She propped her chin on the staple gun handle.

"So why don't you try to play nice for two seconds. Why don't you go ahead and not keep bringing up what I think is sort of an awkward moment for both of us."

"I don't think *awkward* is the word I would use," she said, frowning.

"It's not?"

"It was actually really athletic. I thought we were kind of awesome."

"Yeah, I guess we were," he said, taking a sip of his latte as an involuntary smile tugged at the corners of his mouth.

"Ah, the male ego," she said, giving him the squinty eye. "So susceptible to praise. Now suddenly The Sex exists."

"I know it exists. I just don't see the point of doing a post-mortem on something that we both know can't happen again."

"Why not?" she asked.

"Because. Because it can't," he said, feeling the conviction leak out of his words as he spoke them.

"Because why?"

"Because we don't get along. And I'm busy running for sheriff."

"Yeah, well, I'm busy, too."

"And I'm busy with cows."

"Moo," she said.

"That is absurd."

"Yep."

"And cute," he said, trying to get a handle on the heat firing through his veins.

Then her cheeks turned pink, a smile curving her lips. "Aw, you think I'm cute."

"I think puppies are cute, too. Don't go getting a big head."

"And cats?"

He shook his head. "You know I don't think cats are cute."

"Which is another reason we shouldn't have sex, is that right? Because I love cats. Not just Toby. I love every kind of cat."

"Yeah, no."

"Also, you're humorless."

"Untrue."

She crossed her arms beneath her breasts and leaned back on her heels. "Is it? Tell me a joke."

"I'm not going to tell you a joke."

"So you are humorless."

He paused for a second, genuinely considering telling her one just to get her off his back and prove that he had humor, dammit. But then for some reason, he could think of only one joke. And it was…well, not the kind of joke he should tell.

"Well?" she asked, cocking her head to the side.

"Fine," he said through gritted teeth. "What's the difference between snow boys and snow girls?"

"What?" she asked, smiling wide.

He sighed heavily. "Snowballs."

"Ha! You said balls. Also, that is a terrible joke."

"It's the only one I could think of."

"I don't think that counts toward proving your point."

"Of course you don't, because if it does, I win."

"I don't think a bad joke constitutes as a win for any involved. Are you going to stand here all day? Because I have posters to hang."

He frowned. "And I have a job to do."

"Are you not patrolling the streets?"

"I should be out doing traffic stops."

"Doesn't that just make you feel like a dick?"

"No," he said. "I've lost too many people to road accidents. If I make someone mad because I pull them over or give them a ticket, that's not really my problem. Or my concern. My concern is that they live to drive another day, as do the other people they share the highway with."

He was annoying himself with how obnoxious he sounded,

how serious and in general downbeat. Especially when talking to Sadie, who seemed to be all smiles and laughter, except when he messed with things. He was the bad guy in this scenario and he didn't particularly like it.

"Fair enough," she said, her voice softening. "I'm sorry, that was kind of insensitive of me."

"Why would you ever connect doing traffic stops with the people I've lost? It's my own particular issue. It has nothing to do with you."

"We all have issues, right? And I get that you want to take care of everyone," she said, biting her lip. "It's pretty obvious that you really do care a lot for the people in your life. And the people here, which I think I owe you an apology about, but more on that later."

"When later?"

"When I feel like eating dirt. Right now I don't really want to because I'm hanging posters and I feel bad enough for saying what I did about the traffic stops."

"Don't feel bad," he said, and he meant it.

She looked at him expectantly.

"What?" he asked.

She blinked. "What do you mean, what? I said I owed you an apology for saying bad things about you. Don't you owe me one?"

"I think you've said a lot worse things to me than I have to you," he said, frowning.

"Oh, really?"

"Yeah, and anyway, most of what I said was true."

She blinked rapidly. "Excuse me?" And she was pointing the staple gun in his direction, with what appeared to be intent.

"Sadie…"

"You said that I ran from things. And that I was on my high horse. And that the work that I do is worthless. And you're going to stand by all of that being true?"

"That's not exactly what I said."

"It's pretty much what you said."

"I'm sorry," he said. And he was feeling pretty sorry for most everything that had happened since Sadie had come to town. He'd screwed up with her. Way more times than he wanted to count. And now she was standing here calling him on it. All of it.

She huffed out a growl. "You're just saying it now."

"So?"

"So it doesn't mean anything now."

"I give up, Sadie," he said, turning away from her and walking back in the direction of the crosswalk.

"Wait," she said.

He stopped. "What?"

"Don't leave. I'm mad at you. And I feel like we haven't resolved anything."

"Do we need to?"

"I'd like to."

He turned to face her again. "Okay, what is it you want resolved?"

"I was wondering something."

"What?"

"Do you want to keep having sex?"

CHAPTER ELEVEN

SADIE COULD HAVE immediately bitten her own tongue off. Where the heck had that come from? Oh, okay, she knew where it had come from.

Sleepless nights, endless erotic dreams about his strong body, his hands, his lips, his…well, his everything. She couldn't forget him. Couldn't forget how amazing it was to be with him. How much she wanted him.

She was so annoyed with herself, too.

She didn't do the physical obsession thing. She just didn't. And here she was basically burning up her sheets alone, waking up all sweaty and tangled up in the bedding like a dolphin in a tuna net.

On the verge of orgasm and with no desire to finish the job herself. And now this. This had come out of her mouth. On a public street, during a lovely sunny day. With children most likely playing at a nearby park.

Eli had been walking away, she'd looked at his butt, a butt that was so perfect and masculine and muscular and begging for her to touch it, and the words had just fallen out of her mouth.

He was just standing there, his expression stone, his lips pressed into a firm line.

Now she was filled with regret. Swollen with it. And she was still holding a staple gun.

It was a weird moment. There was no denying it.

"What did you say?" he asked.

"Oh, you know what I said. Why do people do that? Ask you to repeat something they heard but was totally crazy. Do you think I actually want to repeat that?"

"I have to be sure you said it," he said. "Because honestly? My mind could be playing tricks on me. It's entirely possible."

"Yeah, I said it."

"Then I have to be sure you meant it."

He was frozen, every line in his body hard and firm, on high alert. Was he interested? All of his talk about how crazy it was—and it was—and the way he'd stormed out after... But maybe it was just because it was all making him feel as insane as she did.

Maybe it was because he wanted it but didn't want to want it.

Well, he could join the club.

He just kept staring at her, waiting for her answer. And dammit, she didn't know the answer. She wanted it, yes, but was she willing to engage in a purely sexual, no-strings fling with a man who made her want to pull her hair out?

"Yes." Apparently she was. "I meant it."

She could see his hard swallow, his teeth grinding as his jaw shifted. And she hoped, a good portion of her *really* hoped, that he would say no. That he would make her angry. Walk away again and say something insulting on his way down the street that would be so vile all the lust she felt for him would be knocked out of her system.

"Okay," he said. "But I need rules."

"I..." She couldn't believe he'd agreed. She'd been counting on him to be the voice of reason. That was what he did, who he was, except for that time against the wall. And she'd been counting on him to make the smart choices here, since she was very obviously not going to do it. "What kind of rules?" she asked.

If he couldn't be the voice of reason, maybe, just maybe, there was still time for him to piss her off so she'd change her mind.

He looked to each side and then walked toward her, apparently satisfied that there were no prying eyes. "Just sex," he said.

"Yeah, that's what I said."

"And no one knows about it."

She rolled her eyes. "Well, obviously. I'm not going to print it in the paper. Or march over to your brother's place like, 'Hey! Been banging Eli. Here's your rent.'"

"I'm serious. I don't like complications. This is more complicated than I like it already, so it needs to stay clean."

"You don't strike me as a player."

"I'm not."

"But these are player rules."

"They're the rules of a man who generally doesn't date women who live within walking distance of his house. Or even the same town. Or really…a man who doesn't date much at all. But I'm still not a player. I'm just a guy who has too much to do. I don't want a wife, kids or exes all over where I have to patrol every day, so that means I do the best I can to keep things separate."

She hadn't really thought of it like that. Eli moved around town, around the whole area, all the time. Talked to random people, responded to calls. Having exes right in town had the potential to be a mess. She tended to move states away from hers, and she was never all that attached to any of them, so it wouldn't have much mattered anyway.

"Okay," she said. "And ultimately it doesn't really matter to me one way or the other. I like it casual, and no, I don't normally go in for sex only. In fact, I never do. But my relationships have all been very…nonserious."

"I just don't want you to get hurt," he said.

"Pfft. Eli, I've yet to fall in love with any man who touched me. Good in bed or not. Even if the guy is prone to giving me flowers and taking me out, I tend to remain fairly distant. It's hardly going to change with you. Remember? I don't even like you. I just want your body. And that means that this will be the best sex-only relationship ever. Plus, we live close. Late-night booty calls will be a breeze and there will be no temptation at all to develop finer feelings."

He lifted his coffee cup and took a drink. "Okay, I have to get back to work. Then I have to bring Connor food to ensure he does more than ingest alcohol today."

"Sure," she said, feeling a little like shrieking or scurrying in circles or something. Not with joy or anything, but with... panic, excitement and a pulse of adrenaline that seemed more appropriate for scaling a mountain than propositioning a guy for no-strings sex.

"I'll see you after."

"My place?" she asked, her throat dry.

"Probably for the best."

"Bring condoms," she said, looking around, suddenly concerned people might have started milling around since Eli last looked. "I am lacking, currently. And that would be a shame."

He nodded. "I'll come prepared." The black radio on his shoulder buzzed and he put his hand up over the top of it. "I have to go. See you tonight. Good luck with the posters."

Then he turned and walked away. Like some badass action movie star with a surprisingly poor exit line.

Oh, dear Lord, what had she done?

She bent and picked up her stack of posters again, holding them to her chest, the staple gun braced against the back of them.

There was no reason to panic. None at all. She'd propositioned Eli Garrett. And he'd said yes. They were going to have a no-strings fling that would result in many orgasms for both of them.

Putting it like that, it didn't seem like a big deal at all.

No, it sounded awesome.

A slow grin spread across her face and she turned and started walking down the sidewalk, beneath the covered walkway that ran along the row of little shops.

She paused at the next bulletin board, her heart beating fast, excitement building now.

Things had just gotten a whole lot more interesting.

"DAMMIT, ELI. THERE'S mustard on this."

"What?" Eli looked at his brother for a full ten seconds before he processed what he was saying.

"My burger. There's mustard. You know I don't like mustard."

"Sorry," he said, taking a French fry out of his carton and eating it, looking across the kitchen counter at his brother, who was looking grumpier than normal.

"How the hell do you forget something like that?"

Oh, good, Connor was hell-bent on being an ass. This would be fun.

"I just did," Eli said.

Because his mind was on Sadie. Because his brother could starve for all he cared, except he couldn't really let that happen.

So he was here, pretending like he was invested in the meal he'd brought in for the two of them, listening to Connor bitch about condiments.

"Ace knows I don't like mustard," Connor said, glaring and getting up from his seat, going to the counter to get paper towels and a knife.

"He didn't ask if the burger was for you."

"Who else would it have been for?"

Fair question. "Kate. She likes mustard."

"And you remember that, apparently," he said.

"Shut up, Connor," Eli said, watching him flick the bulk of the mustard off the top bun with a knife before wiping it, seriously wiping it, with the paper towel, then scraping it thoroughly with the knife.

"You don't normally forget."

"If you want a flawless hamburger order, have Liss do it, since she actually likes taking care of you. Or better yet, why don't you go and order your own damn food."

Connor took a bite of the hamburger. "Because you do it for me," he said.

"I should stop," he said, putting another fry in his mouth.

He heard footsteps in the doorway and for a moment, his heart leaped up into his throat, his body tensing as he wondered if it was Sadie with a disaster of some kind, or... Sadie for any reason, really.

But it was Liss, speaking of, walking around the corner, holding a big white box. "Pie," she said, smiling.

Connor looked at Eli. "See, I bet she got it without mustard."

"If you put that pie down in front of me I'm going to squirt mustard all over it, Liss," Eli told her.

"Connor doesn't like mustard," she said, setting it down on the counter.

"Yes. We know."

She dropped her purse onto the counter and her keys with it, sighing heavily. "Is there anything for me?" she asked, turning and facing the fridge, jerking the door open.

Liss had a tendency to act like she lived here, which didn't seem to bother Connor at all. But then, Liss had been a fixture during his marriage, since she'd been close to him and Jessie both. "Dear Lord, Connor, you need to go grocery shopping."

"Still?" Eli asked. "I told him to go two weeks ago."

"I did. I went out to fill up my truck and stopped and bought beanie weenies and beer."

Liss gave him the evil eye. "That doesn't count."

"Why not?"

"I'm eating your fries."

"That's healthy."

"Fries before pies," she said, reaching over and snagging a handful of them out of the container.

And now that Liss was here, and would probably manage to

keep Connor from drinking himself into a coma before bed, it was time for Eli to leave.

"I'm going to take off," Eli said, standing, shoving another French fry in his mouth and pushing the carton forward.

"Are you going to finish your burger?" Liss asked.

"No."

She reached out and pulled the carton over to another stool and sat down. "Thank you."

"You're welcome."

"Where are you taking off to?" Connor asked.

"Tired," he said, lying his ass off.

Connor gave him some serious side eye. "Okay. If, say, I were to send our younger sister to your house on a random errand in about an hour she wouldn't be emotionally scarred by activities conducted with female visitors, would she?"

No, because he wouldn't be at his house.

"No, but she'll wake me up and I'd be forced to come over here and shove your head in a toilet."

Connor smiled. "Interesting. Well, fine, I won't send her over. And I won't bug you."

Eli grunted and walked out of the house, feeling very much like he'd already been caught with his hand in the cookie jar. But he didn't care. He was going to go eat his damn cookies anyway.

SADIE WAS A ball of nervous energy. Adrenaline pumping through her veins, heat pooling in her stomach, arousal throbbing between her legs.

She was expecting him soon. And she'd been waiting all day. No, she'd been waiting for this all week. This was what she wanted, and now that she was finally embracing it she was free to appreciate how much she truly craved him.

She wanted more than against the wall. She wanted him naked. All the way naked. In bed. For hours. Subject to her exploration and any twisted desires she might have. She didn't usually have desires she'd consider twisted, but she hadn't ruled anything out with Eli.

Because he made her feel like a giant ball of want. Like a ticking time bomb of need that was ready to explode all over her living room—which was currently spotless, because after she'd done any and all planning she could do for the barbecue alone, and after she'd ordered bedding online for all of the bedrooms in the house, she'd had nothing better to do but clean.

You know. The floor, the wall, the kitchen counter. Just in case he wanted to bang her on unconventional surfaces. She did not need a nasty kernel of cat food right by her head while Eli was trying to satisfy her on the living room rug.

"Oh...cat," she said aloud.

Toby might not allow for sexual spontaneity.

He was currently sprawled over the blue armchair in the living room, looking like the tragic victim of a train collision, his paws out straight, head cocked back and to the side, his back legs up and spread.

"You're a sophisticated beast, Toby."

He didn't move. But of course, it was because it didn't suit him to move. If Eli started making out with her on the couch Toby would probably wake up and decide the only place in the world he wanted to be was on Eli's lap.

And she wasn't going to go locking him in the bathroom or anything just so she could have a good time in the room of her choice. The thing with Eli was physical. Toby, though he couldn't speak actual words, was her friend. Who had stuck with her through it all, mainly because his other choice was a life on the streets as a mouser and he wouldn't engage in anything so gauche.

Either way, she wasn't prioritizing her hookup over her cat's comfort.

Besides, she was having soft, luxurious bed fantasies. And that was better anyway.

The heavy knock on her front door had her scrambling to-

ward the entryway, her heart bouncing around in her chest like
a rubber ball that had been thrown at a wall as hard as possible.

She stopped for a second and looked down at the scoop-neck
dress she was wearing. Then she leaned forward, reached down
the front of the dress and cupped her breast, tugging it up in her
bra before doing the same to the other one.

She took a breath and examined her improved cleavage.
"Okay. We're good. We can do this."

She shook her head, her hair falling over her shoulders, then
walked to the door, grabbing the handle and opening it.

"Hi," she said, going for casual.

"Can we not do the talking thing?" he asked. "You just get
mad at me when we talk." He shifted, the bag he was holding
rustling with the motion.

"I'm okay with that."

He walked into the house without waiting for her to invite
him in, his presence dominating the entryway, filling it. He was
a solid wall of man, and now that she'd been naked with him,
she knew just how solid.

Knew how his skin felt beneath her hands, how his lips felt
on hers, how his stubble felt against soft skin.

And she didn't want to talk, either.

"I want you naked," he said. "Now."

"Should we go into the bedroom...?"

"No," he said, slamming the door shut, shrugging off his
jacket and hanging it on the peg.

That made her smile, because even in his dark intensity he
couldn't bring himself to make a mess. Even now, he was still
conscious of order.

But that was okay, because it was part of what made him him.

And no matter what she said about not liking him, she had
to like him at least a little bit, or any male body would do.
There was something special about this male body that went
past muscles and body hair and...well...generous physical at-
tributes down below the belt.

And that was the soul that was in the body.

The thought made her chest feel tight. Made it hard to breathe. But then, that could just be because he was looking at her like a starving man might eye a piece of very chocolaty cake.

She took a breath, banished the nerves and made eye contact with him as she reached around behind her back and tugged the zipper on her dress down.

She folded her shoulders in slightly and let it fall to the floor, left herself standing there in nothing but a lacy black bra and matching panties.

She'd never been insecure about her body. She had one small scar from her laparoscopic surgery, but nothing too noticeable. Which was good, because she rarely had to explain it, and she barely thought about it, since it was so close to invisible.

Also, she'd never seen the point in being inhibited. If a man had shown interest when she had clothes on, he wouldn't get less interested once her clothes were off. And if he did, that was about him, not her.

But right now, she cared. She really, really wanted to see interest flare in Eli's eyes. Wanted him to be crazy with desire because she felt that way about him.

Because he wasn't another naked man, as good as any other. He was the best-looking man she'd ever seen. Because just looking at him got her hotter than twenty minutes of foreplay with any of her exes. So it felt much more important that he find her more than passable.

She watched him closely, watched the color across his cheekbones heighten, watched his chest pitch with hard breath, his hands clenched into fists at his sides.

It was safe to say she had a captive audience.

She arched her back and reached behind her, putting her hands on her bra clasp and carefully separating the hooks and eyes before letting the garment drop to the floor, her black lace flag of surrender.

He kept his gaze on hers. He didn't look down at her breasts, not right away, and for some reason, that was unspeakably hot. Watching the tension increase in his frame, watching his dark eyes burning with heat, determinedly fixed on her face.

She smiled. "Are you trying to earn an award for not being too obvious?" she asked, sliding one hand up her stomach, just beneath the curve of one breast, before drawing her fingertips over her nipple, a small gasp escaping her lips.

That broke his concentration.

His eyes dropped then and she ran her hand over her other breast, pausing to tease the tightened bud. His jaw was clenched tight, his arousal pushing aggressively against the zipper of his pants.

Oh, yes, she had nothing to worry about.

"You aren't done," he bit out.

"Am I not?" she asked, stilling her hands and glancing at him, trying to look innocent. Knowing she was failing, because she wasn't innocent at all. She was a woman who knew exactly what she wanted. And she knew how to get it.

Knew she was going to get it.

"The rest," he said, the words a hard command that sent a shiver through her.

She pressed her palms against her body and slid her hands down to the waistband of her panties. Then she pushed her fingers below the lace, in the front, cupping herself as she pushed them down, watching as his breathing increased, the pulse beating so hard in his neck she could see it.

She shoved them down her legs and kicked them to the side, leaving one hand where it was, sliding her fingertip over her clit. She gasped, white-hot pleasure firing through her. She was a whole lot more sensitive than she expected to be. But a day of anticipation, combined with how it felt to have his attention, was a hell of a lot more intoxicating than she'd anticipated.

"I'm wet," she said. "If you were curious."

"Bedroom," he said. "Now."

She turned away from him and walked slowly through the

house, through the living room, casting a quick glance at Toby, who was still asleep, because obviously he couldn't be bothered to care about humans and their shenanigans.

She could hear Eli's heavy footsteps behind her. And she fought the urge to look back. But not looking was so much better than looking. Feeling his hot gaze on her without seeing him. Knowing he was watching her butt as she walked. That he was as tense with need as she was.

She led him to her bedroom. "Watch your step," she said, taking the small stair that dropped down at the entrance to the room.

She heard his boot hit the carpet behind her and she turned, her heart kicking hard against her breastbone as she looked at him.

"Can you close the door?" she asked.

"Why?"

"Trying to avoid Cattus Interruptus," she said.

"Right." He turned and shut the door behind them, setting the bag, which she assumed contained contraception, on the dresser. "This is another point in favor of keeping animals outside," he said.

"Yeah, yeah. Your anti-cat platform has no momentum here, might as well drop it. And while you're at it, drop your pants, Sheriff."

"Deputy sheriff."

"Why is that hot?" she asked, sitting on the edge of the bed and leaning back, propping herself up with her elbows. "Why is you being obnoxiously pedantic sexy? I don't even get it."

"Hell if I know."

"I mean, I know why the rest of you is sexy. Dayum."

He smiled as his hands went to his shirt collar. "Sorry about this," he said, tugging his tie from his shirt collar in one easy snap, the whole thing intact.

"Clip-on?" she asked.

"Standard issue. You can't take it off without looking like an idiot."

"All right, I'll let the tie go. But only because I'm already naked over here. And very, very horny."

"Points for me," he said, setting the tie on the edge of her vanity. Then he moved his hands to the first button on his shirt and released it, undoing it quickly, revealing a plain T-shirt the same color as his uniform underneath. "This is less of a strip show than bachelorette parties might have led you to believe," he said. "Didn't have time to go home and change."

"Are you embarrassed?" she asked.

He stilled with his hands on his belt. "No. But you went to a lot of... You had on matching underwear."

She nodded. "I did, it's true. But I am way less interested in your clothes than I am in the removal of them. So carry on."

He undid his belt and shrugged the tan T-shirt over his head. Beneath that was a thin black vest. Kevlar, she assumed. And something hit her in the stomach, a sharp pang. A realization of who he was and what it was he did on a whole new level. He wasn't just a man who cared about his town. He was a man who put his life on the line. He was a man who backed up his word.

And tonight? He was all hers.

He took the vest off, laying it neatly with everything else.

"Oh, yesss," she said, the breath hissing through her teeth. "That's what I'm here to see."

He looked at her, one dark brow arched.

"What?" she asked. "Women don't usually sing the praises of your body?"

"In my experience, it's expected for me to sing the praises of theirs." He turned to face her, working at the clasp on his pants, the muscles in his chest shifting, his abs rippling with the motion.

"Well, by all means, sing my praises. But it has to be said that you are one hell of a man."

He shoved his pants down and proved her point and then

some, his erection thick and enticing and, right now, just for her. He folded his pants carefully on top of the rest of his clothes.

"Come here," she said.

"You think you're giving the orders?" he asked.

"If you want to play," she said, raising a brow, "you might want to follow them."

"What sort of game do you want to play?" he asked, his voice rough.

"One we're both going to like. I want to taste you." His eyes darkened, his expression getting tense.

"Come on, Deputy Sheriff," she said.

He walked over to the bed and wrapped his hand around her head, gripping her hair tight and leaning down, kissing her hard on the mouth before straightening, putting all of *himself* right at eye level.

She licked her lips and looked up at him, bracing her hands on his lean hips. She wanted this. Had wanted it since well before the first time they'd been together. They'd only had urgency then. No thought, no finesse and very little time for exploration.

Now she wanted to explore.

She leaned in, gripping his shaft in her palm and squeezing tight. He groaned, his head falling back, his hand returning to her hair, tugging slightly, the stinging sensation sending a shot of pleasure down between her thighs. Making her hotter. Wetter.

Then she leaned in, blazing a trail over his hard length with the tip of her tongue, her heart hammering fast as she explored him from tip to base and back again before taking him deep inside her mouth.

He was beautiful. He was incredible. And he made this a pleasure. A gift that was truly more blessed to give. Though based on the shivering of his thigh muscles he was very happy to receive.

She pleasured him with her hands, her lips, her tongue, reveling in this strong, solid man's loss of control as he cursed and shook beneath her touch.

She'd never felt more powerful.

She'd never felt more wanted.

Such a dangerous game, but she wanted to play as long as she possibly could. To hold her hand near the flame until it burned her.

She shifted and took him in deeper and he tugged her hair hard, pulling her head up. "Not like that," he said, his words a growl.

She looked at him, at the fierce, untamed light in his eyes. Eli Garrett was never anything less than civil. He'd once put her in handcuffs while she'd clawed and spit like a mad cat, and he'd never been less than a gentleman.

That was probably where some of the strange conflicting anger-desire had come from back then. Even when she was angry at him, she'd sensed somehow that he was the closest thing to a real-life superhero. Truth, justice, the American way and all that.

Yes, civility was second nature to him, and now it was stripped away. And he was reduced to nothing more than a man who desired a woman. Desired her. Restraint folded up on the floor with his uniform.

"What do you want?" she asked, moving away from him, leaning back on the bed, conscious of how her posture displayed her breasts, of how her relaxed thighs gave him a view of everything else.

"I need to be inside you," he said, moving to the dresser and getting the bag, tugging out a box of condoms. He opened it, took out one condom, then threw the box to the bed, where it landed next to her. "You can put those in your nightstand."

"Generous of you."

"They're only for me," he said.

And she knew then that she'd only teased him at all to hear him say something like that. To hear him get proprietary and possessive and all the things she usually hated.

But being with Eli seemed to be an exploration of everything she'd previously labeled off-limits. Everything she'd always called a bad idea.

This was her chance to dip her toe into some fantasies she'd never given breath before. A man who would take charge. A man who would give as good as he got. A man who wouldn't shrug and say, "Yeah, whatever," if she called it off.

She put the box in the nightstand, not wanting to push him now. Someday she would. Just for fun. Just to see what would happen. But not now.

He tore open the packet and she watched, rapt, while he rolled the condom onto his thick length. She liked seeing that big, masculine hand wrapped around his cock. She'd love to watch him bring himself off sometime. And she'd never wanted to do that before, because what would be in it for her?

But with Eli...watching him was one of the best things she could think to do with her time.

He moved to the bed and she smiled, kissing his lips, then pushing against him with all of her weight so that he was on his back and she was straddling him, the slick entrance to her body touching his hard length.

"What are you doing?" he asked.

"Going for a ride," she said, smiling.

"Not just yet."

He angled his head up and took one nipple deep in his mouth, sucking hard. A sharp groan volunteered to be the soundtrack to her pleasure, and there was nothing she could do to stop it as his hand teased her other nipple, while he slid his other palm down over her ass, his fingertips delving into the elegant line there, sending a shock wave of sensation through her.

Then he gripped her butt hard, tugging her into position, lowering her down onto his arousal, every thick inch filling her slowly. Perfectly.

"I'm supposed to be in charge here," she said, when he was buried in her to the hilt.

"Sorry," he said, his voice rough. "Missed that memo."

"No, you didn't."

He slid his hand over her bottom again, squeezing her. "What are you going to do about it?"

"Ride you until you can't speak anymore. Until you don't have the energy to challenge me."

"We could be here all night," he said.

"Oh, I hope so."

He gripped her face, tugging her head down so he could kiss her hard, his other hand still firm on her bottom, keeping her pressed tightly against him as he flexed his hips upward, stealing her control, stealing her breath.

He was amazing. Perfect. Everything.

And never before had she assigned those adjectives to a man. But they fit him, just like he fit her.

She pushed her hips forward, butting up against his, sensation rocketing through her. He released his hold on her chin, his head falling back, his hands moving to a more relaxed position on her hips as he let her take the lead.

She braced her hands on his shoulders, moving in time with his breathing. Slow and measured at first, then faster, harder, more intense. Her orgasm started to build, a low ball of pleasure and intensity in the pit of her stomach, pulsing down to her core, her internal muscles tightening around his hard length.

She squeezed his shoulders tight, her nails digging into his skin. She hoped he felt it. The pain and pleasure. She hoped she marked him, because he was damn well marking her. This didn't feel like a game now. Not the light power struggle it had been. The fun flirtation. This was something raw. Pleasure walking a knife's edge. One wrong slip and it would cut deep. Wound. Destroy. And scar forever.

She closed her eyes, her heartbeat pounding against the backs of them, blood roaring through her ears. "Oh… Eli…"

"Not yet," he said, his voice harsh, pulling her through the haze, pushing her climax back.

He removed his hand from her hip and put it between her

legs, just near where their bodies were joined, his fingers tracing her clit, sharp, hot need assaulting her as he did.

"I want to give it to you," he said, his eyes intense on hers as he continued to stroke her. The combination of his touch along with the feeling of him inside her was almost too much to bear, but now she was fighting her orgasm.

Because she wanted to stay like this. On the edge. In this moment of beautiful torture.

He took his hand away and she gasped, then lifted his fingers, the tips touching the edge of her lips. Then she looked at him, leaned forward and sucked both deep into her mouth.

He swore, short and hard, never looking away. She ran her tongue along the edge of his forefinger and he pulled her down, hard, thrusting up inside of her as he did. That was enough. To push her from the edge into the abyss.

She shuddered, leaning forward, palms braced on the bedspread as she rode out the climax, waves rolling through her, leaving her breathless, shaking and on the verge of the kind of emotional breakdown she never allowed herself. Ever.

He let out a harsh breath, his grip on her tightening, his muscles shivering as he found his own release, his stomach muscles contracting and expanding beneath her.

She waited until it was over. Until he was relaxed. Then she rolled away from him, lying on her back, her arm over her face, her eyes shut tight behind it, trying to gain her balance. Trying to find her center or whatever. But she was firmly…off center, so that just wasn't going to happen.

He'd tromped all over her center. Left his big, standard-issue boot prints all over it.

She was wrecked.

He wrapped his arm around her and pulled her close and she moved her arm, blinking, shocked by the fact that he was touching her, that he wasn't halfway out the door. But no, he was leaning in, his head pressed to her breasts, his breath hot against her skin.

She lifted her hand and traced his jaw with the tip of her finger, his stubble rough. There was something undeniably male about it. Undeniably sexy.

What was it about him? Why did he make her feel so *much*?

She shook all that off, trying to catch her breath. Trying to pull herself out of the emotional well she'd fallen into. This wasn't like her. She didn't get moony and weird. And she didn't sleep with guys after sex. She was too busy getting dressed, saying goodbyes and getting back to her own space. Or pushing them back to theirs.

Well, she wasn't going to sleep with Eli. She was just going to rest for a second while she got her bearings, and then she would remind him that he needed to get back to his place stat.

He moved his hands over her curves until she could feel herself melting into the sheets like a candle pressed into a flame.

Man, she was pathetic.

And all she wanted to do was sleep. Or turn over and lick him. All over. Oh, yes, that was what she wanted to do. Lick every inch of Eli Garrett until he was shaking. Until he was hard again. Until…

There was a fearsome-sounding scratch and a sound that was closer to a caterwaul than a meow at the door.

She jumped, the sound breaking hard through her fantasies.

There was more scratching, this time on the carpet beneath the door, followed by more angry feline noises.

"Oh, you damn cat!" she growled, wiggling out of Eli's hold and sitting up. And she was almost grateful Toby had come to the rescue then, because it had saved her from revealing her fairly intense neediness.

She stood and looked down at Eli, who was staring at the ceiling, all naked and muscle-y and as hot as ever. Then she turned and went to the door, flinging it open. "What?"

Toby sauntered in, and his eyes seemed to go straight to Eli. "Don't judge," she said to Toby. "You don't have balls. You don't know what this kind of drive does to a person."

Eli laughed, a deep, male sound that was much more relaxed than he generally was. "Do you always talk to your cat?" He sat up and swung his legs over the side of the bed and she was sort of struck dumb by the whole display.

His body in motion, regardless of the motion, was a beautiful thing. And naked? It was mouth-dryingly, pantie-dampeningly beautiful.

"Yes, yes, Eli, I do talk to my cat. And please be advised," she said, crossing her arms beneath her bare breasts, "that I won't allow for anti-cat speech in this house."

"Anti-cat thoughts?"

"Forbidden. The thought police are here. Assimilate or be destroyed."

"I didn't understand any of that."

"It's a good thing you're nice to look at."

"Nice to touch, too, I hope," he said, standing and walking toward her.

Her heart stuttered. "Do you have to ask?"

"Doesn't hurt to be told."

"Touch. Taste. All of the above. I very much enjoy the many attractions your body has to offer."

"Possibly the strangest compliment I've ever received."

"Well, that gives me a new target to aim for. Something weirder than that."

"I look forward to it." He bent down and picked up his clothes, shaking them out, tugging his underwear and pants on.

Her heart sank. She was so much more disappointed by the fact that he was leaving than she should be. She'd just been thinking she needed to get rid of him. Reclamation of space and all that.

But now he was vacating her space. And that was different.

At least it felt different for some reason.

He tugged the tan shirt on over his head and collected the overshirt and tie, and put them into the bag the condoms had come from. Then he went for his boots. And she just stood there naked and watched, which was hugely stupid but she couldn't really bring herself to stop watching him. Or to move and get dressed. She didn't want her lacy underthings or her dress back anyway.

She wanted jammies. And she wanted to cry a little bit.

She felt like an alien being with way too many feelings had crawled into her ear and then chewed his way from her brain stem, down her neck and into her chest, where he'd made a comfy home and decided to force his emotions on her.

Yes, that was what she felt like. Foreign, and completely out of her depth. And she just wasn't used to feeling that way. She kept herself out of situations that made her feel this way for a reason.

"See you tomorrow," he said, all casual and like his skull hadn't been cracked by the thundering pleasure that had just rolled through them both.

"Uh...okay."

"I can't stay," he said, not looking at her.

"No," she said. "No, I know. I mean, I wasn't going to ask you to. I was going to ask you to leave, actually. But I didn't have to because of the cat, and then you got up, and now you're going so I didn't have to."

Sure, Sadie, ramble. That's convincing and doesn't sound at all weird.

"Okay," he said slowly.

"Don't say it like that. I'm fine. I don't sleep with guys. I like my space, just like you do. And we made rules. Rules on the street corner. In front of God and everyone."

"I'll see you tomorrow, Sadie."

Two days in a row. That was intense. It was, she realized in that moment, a violation of her usual relationship conduct. She'd never been in a relationship where she felt the need to have sex that often. It was healthy and good to have nights alone, and to have time to herself and...and...he was talking sex tomorrow. Probably the next day, too.

And she was going to say yes.

"Okay. Tomorrow. Do you work?" she asked.

He nodded. "Yeah. I'll be patrolling the highway mainly, but I always come to town for coffee and lunch."

"I was going to stop in on Alison again. So I'll be in town tomorrow, too."

"Maybe we can run into each other when I get coffee," he said.

"Elevenish, right?"

He nodded.

She shouldn't be making a coffee date with the guy. She shouldn't even have made an immediate follow-up sex date with him. And now there would be an additional meet-up. But she wasn't going to tell him no. She might not show up to coffee, though. She might not.

Toby started rubbing against her legs and she looked down at him. "What?" she asked, and got nothing but a blank cat stare in return.

"See you," Eli said.

"Yeah, bye."

He walked out of her bedroom without even kissing her goodbye, and she stood there, naked, until she heard the front door shut behind him. And she became acutely aware that she was standing naked in a room with a cat leaning against her legs, watching the blank space where Eli had been.

She shuffled to the bed and flopped onto her stomach, then shrieked when Toby followed, jumping onto the bed and walking across her back, the pads of his feet cold on her skin.

"Boundaries!" she shouted, mainly at Toby but also partly at herself.

If this Eli thing was going to work there would have to be boundaries. Because he'd left her feeling hollow and emotional. She rolled to her side and curled her knees up to her chest, her heart thudding dully.

It was all because she'd been celibate for too long. She was out of practice. The sex had been easy. More than easy, it had been so much better than she'd ever remembered it being. But the surrounding stuff all seemed harder. Deeper. Weirder.

But she would work it out. They would work it out. Because this was way too good to give up.

But she was not meeting him for coffee tomorrow.

SHE COULD NOT believe she was meeting Eli for coffee. Sadie frowned deeply so that she would appear as angry with herself as she felt and tugged on her sweater sleeves, crossing her arms beneath her breasts as she stormed across the street and into the coffee shop.

Where he was not.

Well, eff him and his effing coffee break. Was he not coming? Was that the game? Make Sadie think you were coming to coffee and then not come to coffee the day after you banged her senseless and left her curled up alone in bed with a cat?

As if he could make her feel more pathetic.

No, she wasn't pathetic. And he wasn't allowed to make her feel pathetic because she forbade it. She withdrew permission. She was the keeper of her own life, blah blah blah.

She leaned against the counter, tapping her fingertips together while she looked over her shoulder at the closed door, then into the empty dining room.

There was a girl who had to be in high school working behind the counter, pulling espresso shots and chatting with another boy who really was no more than an infant. Or…sixteen, but whatever.

They were flirting. Ugh. Well, someday he would leave her standing in an empty coffee shop. So flirt away, little children. Bah.

Sadie didn't know how Cassie, the owner of The Grind, could stand to be around the heady teenage hormones all day. But there she was, smiling away at the register and seemingly unannoyed by her employees.

It was because Cassie was in love herself, probably, as Sadie had learned during her frequent visits to get coffee. Because Cassie was so in love, she radiated joy and spent much of her time talking about her man, Jake. That love nonsense seemed to blind otherwise rational people to related stupidity.

The door behind her opened, the wind rushing in. She turned and the breath rushed out of her. Eli. He was here. He hadn't stood her up.

And it shouldn't matter.

Feeling a bond with him post-sex is okay. It's not like you've ever done it quite like this before.

Ah, yes, her running internal monologue had a point.

Before him she'd always been in an actual dating relationship with the men she slept with. And with that had come companionship and coffee dates and nice talks. And it had all gone a long way in reinforcing her and her ego.

But this was different and so the fact that she didn't have a firm handle on it really was understandable.

There, pep talk managed. And now she would just enjoy her coffee.

"You came," she said.

"I'm on time."

Yes, dammit, he was. And she had been flailing around for no reason at all.

"Of course," she said. "Coffee?"

"That's what we're here for." He walked to the counter and Cassie smiled.

"Deputy Garrett, the usual?"

"Yep," he said. "And whatever Sadie would like."

Her eyebrows shot upward but she didn't say anything. He was buying her coffee in public. That seemed like a…thing. Like a public declaration, even. Or maybe it was just coffee. Probably it was.

"I'll have just a coffee. Room for cream. Two raw sugars," she said.

Eli pulled out his wallet and paid with cash and she almost laughed. He, and everything about the town, was about eight years behind everything else. In fact, now that she looked, she didn't think the store was set up to take a debit or credit card. Good thing he'd treated, because she didn't have any cash.

"And how has your day been?" she asked.

"Good. Gave out some speeding tickets, so the answers of those I've encountered could be different."

"I would say," she said. "I've gotten a lot of speeding tickets."

"Have you?" he asked.

"What can I say? I'm a rebel." Too late she realized she was making jokes about not driving safe again. Bah. She should have gotten a biscotti to gnaw on so her stupid mouth would be occupied. Talking to Eli wasn't safe.

And why was that? Why was she such a mess with him? She was usually really good with men. All small talky and light and flirty like the barista babies behind the counter.

But not now. And not with him.

"Here you go," Cassie said, handing the cups to Eli. "Have a nice day, Deputy Garrett. You, too, Sadie." The other woman's expression was far too meaningful for Sadie's liking.

"Same to you, Cassie. Tell Jake hi." He turned and started to walk out of the shop, her coffee in his hand.

"Wait! I need my cream." He stopped and handed her the cup, which she took from him before turning to face the little bar, popping the white lid off and picking up the thermos to dump a healthy amount of half-and-half into her drink.

She put the lid back on, managing to avoid spilling and looking like a total dork, which, with her shaky sweaty hands, had been a distinct possibility. "Okay, now we can go."

He shook his head slightly and pushed the door open, holding it for her. It should not have made her stomach feel warm and fuzzy, but it did. She had a serious fuzziness issue where that man was concerned.

"So," she said, once the door closed behind them. "How did *you* sleep last night?"

He turned, his shoulder stiff, his cup paused midsip. "Fine," he said.

Fine. Well. Fine. She'd been fine. Totally fine. Not at all shivery or lonely or horny. "Oh, good. Me, too."

"The way you said it made it seem like maybe *you* didn't sleep well."

"That's a lot of…meaning you read into my very simple question."

"Your very simple question with what sounded like specific emphasis."

"Fine," she said. "It had emphasis. Specific emphasis. But you're lying."

He raised a brow and stopped walking, the wind ruffling his short dark hair. "Really?"

She wasn't going to stand there and wallow in indignation. She was going to take a chance. To take a chance on the fact that last night had been as amazing for him as it had been for her.

"Uh-huh. Lying. You didn't sleep well." She leaned in. "You slept terrible. Naked. Sweaty and tangled up in your blankets. Wishing I was there to touch you. Wishing it was me putting my hand around your cock instead of you."

She could see the tension work its way through his body, tightening his shoulders, tightening his jaw. The gamble had paid off.

"That's enough," he said.

"Oh, no, it's not nearly enough."

"I am on patrol."

She winked. "Yeah, you are."

"Euphemism?"

She lifted her shoulders. "Could be."

"For what?"

"Just messing with you."

"Don't you have somewhere to be?"

"Well, sort of," she said. "I was going to swing by the diner to talk to Alison about pie."

And also kind of to check in on Alison, since Sadie was feeling twitchy about the entire situation. Unless someone came into her office to talk touchy situations, she didn't normally seek them out. But Alison used to be a friend. And this was different.

Though she felt she could be talked out of involvement very easily since it sorely tested her comfort zone.

But then, just about everything she'd done for the past couple of months—signing a long-term lease, sleeping with a man who gave her feelings and dealing with spiderwebs in a house that had been long empty—had tested her comfort zone.

So why not continue the theme?

"Right. You were going to, but...?"

"What is your stance on ride-alongs?" she asked, looking at his patrol car parked down the street.

"It depends on who the person is."

"Me. Me is the person."

"Heavily against."

"Why?" she asked, knowing she sounded whiny, knowing she was using him to help her avoid the Alison thing.

"Because. I'm not going to let a known criminal sit in the front seat of my car."

"Ha-ha-ha," she said drily, "you are a clever, clever man. And fine. I'll go off and do my actual stuff instead of forcing you to spend any more of your precious time in the presence of my adorableness."

He let out a long breath. "Fine. Come on."

"I can go?"

"If you promise not to mess with things."

"I can't promise that, Eli."

"Why?" he asked, looking long-suffering now.

"Because if there are buttons, I may not be able to resist the urge to push them."

"I'll dump your ass on the roadside and leave you to hitch-hike back to town."

"No, you won't," she said, breezing past him. "You're too nice."

"I am not."

"Sure you are," she said, waiting by the passenger-side door of the car. "You're so nice you're letting me come on a ride-along."

He opened his door and unlocked hers from that side, then got in without waiting for her. She opened the door and climbed in. There was a laptop mounted to the dash, and in the center console were all the buttons, radios and things she generally wanted to mess with, but didn't, because the car wasn't moving yet, and at this point he probably would still kick her out.

"That is not evidence of any particular niceness," he said, starting the car and putting his drink in the cup holder.

"You don't like it that I think you're nice?"

"I don't want you to get the wrong idea," he said.

"You're just annoyed because I have the right idea."

He pulled the car away from the curb and onto the mostly vacant streets. It wasn't quite lunchtime and it wasn't peak tourist season, so the main street of Copper Ridge was quiet.

"So how did you sleep?" he asked. "Real answer this time."

"Like a baby."

"So you woke up every few hours crying?"

"Meh," she said, taking a sip of her coffee.

"Or maybe just…wet and aching and wishing it was my hand between your legs instead of your own."

She snorted, coffee spurting over the hole in the cup lid and down her chin. She lowered the cup and wiped at her face.

"What?" he asked. "Was that not a nice question?"

She was wet and throbbing now. And not just from the slight dribble of hot coffee on her chin.

"No, it was not nice. Or polite. Or gentlemanly."

"I warned you. Good, sure. Nice, no. Also, not a gentleman."

"I feel like I'm learning a lesson about still waters running deep. And a little dirtier than expected, to be honest."

"Are you sad about that?"

She thought back to last night. To his much-better-than-average bedroom skills. "Uh, no. Can't say that I am."

"I thought you seemed to enjoy it."

"Are we allowed to talk about this on a ride-along? Shouldn't we be talking official sheriff's department business?"

"We could. Do you have questions?"

"Funniest call you've ever gotten?"

"Concerning piglets who scattered in the elementary school."

"Wow. That is…way to break small-town stereotypes, Copper Ridge."

He laughed. "A student had brought them in for show-and-tell. And I happened to be there for a Say No to Drugs assembly. So when all hell broke loose I took the call over the radio. So I was the official first responder to the pig debacle."

"Legend," she said.

"Pretty much."

"Did you always know you wanted to do this?"

"Sort of. I mean, at first I thought maybe I'd do state police. Or head up to Portland and work there. Do something in the city. But I always had my eye on law enforcement because I liked the idea that I could…make people follow the rules." His voice halted a little on the last part.

"You wanted everyone to behave?" she asked.

He cleared his throat. "When I was a teenager I thought… I thought maybe if I were a cop I could make my mom come back. Make my dad quit drinking. It was power to me. Authority that I didn't have. I mean, I got over the fantasy really quick, but the desire to be able to change things stayed with me."

She clutched her coffee to her chest, her eyes on the thinning buildings and the increasing trees, the waves in the distance. Something about his words had made her feel raw. Like the admittance of his own childhood fantasies, of change and control, had scratched against hers.

Interesting how those two desires had put them on such different paths. She'd thrown up her hands and let it all go. Walked away and never looked back because when she'd realized that nothing in her family would change, she'd realized that she couldn't stay. That she couldn't even tempt herself to try.

And yet Eli had stayed. And he'd made changes here that were concrete. He'd done what he'd always dreamed, in many ways. Even though he still hadn't saved his family. It made her feel like the flake she'd been accused of being more than once.

Especially next to this solid man who had dug his heels in and stayed, even when it was hard. Even when it seemed like there was no point.

But then, she had no brothers and sisters. She'd had no one to stay and fight for.

What about your friends? Alison?

But then they would have known. They would have known what had happened to her and the simple fact was, she hadn't been able to take the humiliation.

She'd lost her spleen and her family, so it had seemed a bit much to also lose her pride by letting everyone know that her dad had beaten the shit out of her and her mother had sided with him.

No, thank you. Internal bleeding was enough.

Man, what a massively horrible train of thought that was. She was done with it in three, two...

"I think it's amazing you did what you set out to do," she said.

"And what about you?" he asked.

Well, darn. She wasn't in the market to talk about her.

"What about me?"

"Did you always want to be a therapist?"

"No," she said. "I'm not even sure I wanted to be one when I was one. Which is why I typically did other things on the side. Painting, working part-time in coffeehouses, that kind of thing."

"Then why did you do it?"

"I was able to get financial aid for school with the help of a guidance counselor." That counselor and Jenny, her therapist, were the only two people she'd ever talked to about her dad. "And then from there it was recommended I see a therapist. And it was part of being a student at the school, so I went. Jenny listened to me. It made me feel good. I realized that having someone to listen was important."

She'd never spoken with honesty before. Not even to her high school friends. They'd spoken in veiled terms about how bad it was. Some had unexplained bruises. Some had drugs they'd stolen from their parents' dresser drawers. They were all escaping, supporting each other, but none of them had ever wanted to detail what their home life was like. If they spent their time away doing that, what was the point of leaving?

She cleared her throat. "Anyway, it was different with Jenny. She made me feel like my words had value. Like I mattered. Like my experiences mattered and like I'd solved something by talking about them. I wanted to do that. And I had to choose a course of study so... I ended up getting a master's in social work. I figured I would find a way to help people."

"And you chose crisis counseling."

"That's partly because I move so often. It makes more sense for me to work with people who are dealing with a sudden, isolated event, rather than people who need long-term care. I like to help people. But it's not an easy job. I mean, people in crisis are...well, they're in crisis. And hearing about those problems isn't always the most fun." She drummed her fingers on the door handle. "Though I imagine I'm preaching to the choir."

"Yeah," he said. "Law enforcement isn't all locking up bad guys and being the hero. It's a whole lot of sad reality."

"Reality is lame. It's basically my least favorite."

"Too bad there's so much of it around."

"Man, I feel like you *get* me," she said, laughing and letting her head fall back against the seat. She was happy being with him. And she didn't want to examine that too closely.

"We're going to park up here," he said.

She sat up straighter, her heart thundering. "And make out?"

"And wait for speeding cars to go by."

"Uh. Boo. I like mine better."

"This," he said, waving his hand between them, "has to stay in your bedroom."

"Then why did you meet me for coffee?"

"Why did you meet me?" he asked, pulling over and turning to look at her.

"Because it seems like I should know you a little. And that we should talk without fighting. If we're going to sleep together."

"I thought the same thing."

"Well, so then this makes sense," she said, biting her lip.

"Yep."

"And we're not making out in the patrol car."

"No," he said. "Please tell me you aren't a badge bunny."

"A badge bunny?" She turned to face him. "Is that a thing? Tell me that is not a thing."

"It's a thing."

"Wow. You sound so regretful about it. It's like a badge-related groupie, right?"

"Yes, yes, it is."

"And you don't sound thrilled."

He let out a sigh. "It's weird. I'm not a rock star or anything. Women who are hyper into the whole uniform thing... it's weird."

"Most guys wouldn't question it."

"Jack wouldn't. Jack doesn't," Eli said. "The other bunny we get is the buckle bunny. They like cowboys. They go after Jack and Connor."

"Connor obviously doesn't go back."

"No. He was never much of a player. And he's less of one now. Jack, on the other hand..."

"That's your friend. The one I met briefly the night I burst the pipes. And he was with you in the bar, too, right?"

"Yeah. That's him. He's more like a degenerate brother. But he's never taken anything half as seriously as Connor or I do. Which is probably why he's happier."

"If more sex is equal to more happiness, then sure. Though you should be bucking up by now."

"We've only had sex twice," he said.

"We probably could have doubled that if you would have stuck around for a while last night."

"Not the best time to have this conversation."

"Well, just don't go scuttling off into the cold tonight and you're likely to get a little more action."

He cleared his throat. "I didn't want to assume."

"Oh, I can go all night, buddy," she said. Which wasn't a theory she'd tested. Because usually one and done for the evening was fine with her. One orgasm basically put her under the table. She was a sexual lightweight in that way.

"Good to know," he said, sounding a little strained.

She liked that she could affect him this way. Because he was so solid. So stoic and serious and *good*. She liked that a little naughtiness got him hot under the uniform collar. And clip-on tie.

"So now we wait in semi-camouflage," she mused, looking into the woods on the passenger side of the car, "for an unsuspecting speeder to go by?"

"Basically," he said.

"I'm drunk with power," she said. "And I don't even have ticket-writing powers. How the hell do you do this without succumbing to the urge to abuse your authority?" She wiggled her eyebrows.

"Humorless response coming, beware."

"I expected nothing less," she said, rolling her eyes.

"If I abused my power, my entire reason for wanting it wouldn't be the same. I want to fix things, remember?"

"So you're not going to go breaking them further."

"Not exactly."

The radio buzzed and Eli held up his hand, putting his hand on the black button. A woman's voice filled the car, along with a decent amount of feedback. "Disturbance at Oak and Scotchbroom. Suspect appears to be unarmed but is threatening diner patrons."

"Copy. En route."

He put his hand back on the shifter and put the car in Drive, flipping a U-turn before turning on the lights and heading back toward town. "More than you bargained for?" he asked.

"Yes," she said, hanging on to the door handle. "The diner."

"Yep."

"We would have been meeting up even if I hadn't gone with you," she said, suddenly very glad she was on this end of the call, and not the other. Because men—violent men—did scare her. There was a place down in her soul that went cold when she saw violence in a man's eyes. That same part curled up in a ball and cried like a little girl getting kicked, over and over again, by her father.

A memory that was never buried as deep as she wished it were.

Suddenly she felt tense. Tense and transparent. He would know that she was afraid. That heading toward whatever was happening was like walking back into a fractured memory she never wanted to revisit.

Calm the hell down, Sadie. It's a man creating a disturbance and you're with a man who has a gun.

She took a deep breath and let her internal pep talk bolster her a little.

"Everything will be okay, right?" she asked, in spite of herself, looking over at him.

"I have a 100 percent success rate on making it through the day. I don't expect today to be any different."

She didn't argue with him about how everyone on earth had

the same success rate he did, right up until they didn't. Because it was too nice to hear him say that. Too encouraging. And it made her warm all the way through. Banished that ice-cold fear. And for now she was going to let it, because it was so much better than being afraid.

They entered the town and her tension rose, metallic fear flooding her mouth, like her internal thermometer had broken, poisoning her with a wave of mercury. Or possibly she was being overdramatic. Hard to tell, what with the fact that she was panicking.

He pulled into the lot of the diner and she saw a group of men standing in the parking lot, and Alison on the fringes, wringing her hands.

"Stay in the car," Eli said.

"But Alison—"

"Stay. In. The. Car," he repeated, his words terse as he got out, his hand resting on the top of his gun.

ELI SURVEYED THE CROWD, assessing exactly what was happening. It was what he suspected—a late-morning drunken dispute, which was something that shouldn't happen, but did—and he doubted anyone's life was in danger today.

But then, those kinds of thoughts got people killed, and he well knew it, which meant his hand was staying on his gun. He didn't want to come in looking like a threat, but he wasn't going to be passive, either.

He knew these guys. Loggers mainly, and unsurprisingly, at the center, Alison's husband, Jared. He was the drunk one from the looks of things, and the one causing trouble.

"What's going on here?" he asked, walking over to the knot of men.

"Jared being an asshole," said Randy, a middle-aged man with a long beard and a tobacco habit that had taken a toll on his teeth.

"Typical day, then," Mark, a fisherman, added.

"I'm just defending what's mine," Jared growled, his expression mutinous and unfocused.

"Jared..." Alison said.

"Shut up. Shut the fuck up," Jared spat in his wife's direction. "I wouldn't have to be down here if you weren't acting like a slut. So shut your whore mouth."

Eli let out a long slow breath. Because otherwise he would be tempted to get violent. And that wasn't what he was here for. But the temptation to move in and shut Jared's mouth with his fist was a lot stronger than he'd expected.

"There's no need to talk like that," he said, his tone hard.

"Free speech, Deputy," he said.

"We could take a vote on whether or not we like your kind of speech," Bud, not the one from the gas station, said. "I, for one, would cast my vote with my fist."

"That's enough," Eli said. "Is anyone hurt?"

He looked around the group. There was no blood or visible bruising. But there was no way he could say there was no harm done. Alison was ashen. Terrified. And it churned his gut.

"Is anyone wanting to press charges?" he asked.

"Nah," Mark said. "No one got hurt."

Dammit.

He could escort Jared home, but that was about it. State laws regarding public drunkenness were essentially nonexistent. A public health concern, not a misdemeanor. And given that no punches had been thrown, he was back at sending Jared back to his house, where Alison would be later. And that gave him no small amount of concern.

"Jared, I'm going to make sure you get home okay."

"No, thank you, Deputy," he spat.

"Oh, well, see, that's not your choice. Get in on your own, or get in in handcuffs." He turned back to his car and opened the passenger door. "Out, Sadie, I have to make a delivery, and I'd rather you weren't with me."

She looked at him with big worried eyes and it made something in his chest twist. She'd been afraid on the way to this call, and he'd dismissed it as normal, civilian fear, but right now he had a feeling it was something different.

Especially when she got out of the car without argument and headed to the side, not approaching the crowd.

"Stay here and eat pie, I'll be back for you," he said.

"I… I could walk to my car."

"Wait for me," he said. "You'll be fine."

He looked pointedly at Jared, who chose that moment to obey him. "Backseat," Eli said, then he walked over to Alison. "Call me," he said. "Call someone if he gives you any trouble, do you understand me?"

She shook her head. "He doesn't."

"You're lying to me," Eli said, his voice low and soft.

"I'm not." She met his gaze, her brown eyes defiant.

And he wanted to punch something again. A wall. Jared's face. Why did she protect him? Why did they always protect them?

"Well, even so…" He reached into his jacket and took out his card. "Call me."

He walked back to the patrol car, back to his drunken, asshole backseat tenant. He would drive Jared home. The guy would sober up for a while. And the cycle would go on and on.

He knew it would. It was what he saw in a town this size, over and over.

Times like this he could understand why Sadie didn't stay.

CHAPTER TWELVE

SADIE SAT IN the booth, a cup of coffee and a piece of pie in front of her. The fishermen were back in their corner booth, and Alison was pacing behind the counter.

She took a bite of the lemon meringue. "It really is good pie," she said, loud enough for Alison to hear.

Alison tried to smile. "Thank you."

"Could I get more coffee?" She didn't need more coffee, but she needed Alison to come to where she was sitting, and to stop hiding.

So yeah, this wasn't her favorite thing, but obviously she wasn't avoiding Alison, or the facts about Alison's life today. Fate had handily intervened even when she was trying to jump ship.

She felt a little like Jonah. Thrown overboard, swallowed by a giant fish and vomited into the diner, the very diner she'd been avoiding. Yes, it was an analogy of Biblical proportions, but appropriate, she felt.

Alison walked across the diner and looked into Sadie's full cup.

"Just kidding. I lied. Sit down."

"I'm working," Alison said.

"Yeah, and I'm eating pie. Sit."

Alison did, her hands folded tightly in her lap, the carafe placed in front of her on the table.

"So, hi," Sadie said. "It's been a while. Or since last week. But you know."

"Yeah," Alison said.

"I feel… I feel like I should apologize."

Alison looked startled by that.

"For dropping off the earth after high school. For never calling. For never coming back. Because we were a team, in some ways. We laughed together, and I don't think we laughed very much when we were apart. You spent all those years sticking by me. All of you did. Josh Grayson was my first kiss. Hell, my first…everything. And I just left you all. Without looking back. I had to leave… I had to. But I should have thought of you."

"Sadie…we never knew what happened to you really. Your mom just said you'd run off. And…"

"You believed her because I used to say I would," Sadie finished. "And I did run off. It's true. I mean, I ran off to college. And a career and things. It's not like I was pole dancing, not that there's anything wrong with that. It's just…the long and the short of it is, I ran."

"We missed you," Alison said.

She looked so tired and sad. A sharp contrast to the Alison whom Sadie remembered. A girl in black clothes, with a fierce light of determination in her eyes.

A girl who'd looked ready to fight.

The fight was gone from her now. Drained out of her slowly over the years. Years when Sadie had been gone.

But if Sadie had stayed…the same thing might have happened to her. She and Alison had started out in the same place. A couple of teenage girls who'd never had innocence. Who'd always seen the hard, ugly side of life. Neither of them had illusions about love.

And still Alison had ended up with that man. Sadie was very

aware that it could very well have been her sitting there, sad-eyed and defeated.

Sadie sucked in a sharp breath, feeling like something had cracked in her chest. "I... I didn't expect to be missed."

"I don't think any of us would have," Alison said.

"That's a problem," Sadie said. "It's not...healthy, that's for sure. So... Josh left?"

"Yeah, he's doing business somewhere. Washington first, and I haven't heard anything about him in a while."

"Hmm." Sadie allowed herself a brief, nice memory of him. He'd been hot, at least in her teenage estimation. But the memory of him didn't make her shiver or anything. Not like Eli.

"You stayed," she said, turning her focus back to Alison.

"I thought about leaving, but my mom's health wasn't good. Then right after she died, I met Jared."

"Ah, yes," Sadie said, the ache in her chest inverting, splintering and sinking down to her stomach. "I believe I met him today."

Alison cleared her throat and looked determinedly at the carafe. "I know it looks bad."

"It is bad," Sadie said. "Don't BS me. I'm a therapist by trade, when I'm not renovating bed-and-breakfasts. I see women who have come out of abusive relationships all the time. I see men who are afraid they might be abusers. And more than that, I lived with a man who solved problems with violence for my entire childhood. So, I repeat, do not BS me. I am the wrong person to try that on."

"He's not that bad."

"We can skip that part. We can skip the part where you tell me why you make him do it. And he's a good guy. And his past was hard. Because I've heard it. Just...five months ago maybe, I saw a woman who was in the hospital. Recovering from the wounds her husband had inflicted on her. I've seen where it ends, Alison. Unless you make the decision to leave."

Alison grabbed the napkin to her left and started twisting it, her hands shaking.

"I'm not talking to you as a therapist," Sadie said. "I'm talking to you as an old friend. As someone who knew you before him. You're not the only one. And you don't have to be embarrassed."

"I don't have to be embarrassed?" Alison asked. "I think I do, actually. Because...because I think you have to be pretty stupid to get pulled into something like this."

"That's not true," she said. "It's not. It doesn't matter how smart you are. It's not your brain making these decisions. It's your emotions. It's the things he's done to you. The things he's told you. The stuff he's twisted all up so slowly over the years you barely realized what was happening."

The other woman shook her head. "It's too late for me," she said. "I don't have anyone else. I don't have anything else. Just this job. And that man."

"Then get more," Sadie said, frustration burning through her. "Want more."

Alison stood up. "I don't remember how. Coffee and pie are on me. Thank you," she said. "Just...thank you."

Alison turned, slight shoulders hunched, and walked back to the counter, just as Eli walked through the door.

Sadie stood, not having any of the appetite to finish her pie, even if it was free pie, and walked toward him, shepherding him back out the door before he could ask why.

"Did you get him home?" she asked, barely meeting Eli's eyes when they were out in the parking lot.

"Yeah," Eli said. "Do you see what it's like?"

"He deserved to be hit. He deserved to have his head shoved into the pavement."

"Yeah, and I can't do that, Sadie. The minute I act like I can, I'm not a whole lot better than he is. Because I have authority and I have to be careful never to abuse that. But I might have let

Mark and the other guys off with a warning if they would have done it. Or if someone would have…said anything."

"Given you a reason to arrest him," she said.

"That's the problem with situations like this," Eli said, putting his hands on his lean hips and looking back toward the diner. "She's an adult. I can't drag her out of that house any more than I can put handcuffs on him for something I suspect but have never seen." He turned and hit the top of his patrol car with his open palm, a rough growl escaping his lips. "Sometimes the more power you have the less powerful you feel."

"She won't… I tried to talk to her," Sadie said. "But…"

"I know." He took a deep breath. "Listen, I'm on for a while longer. I'll take you to your car."

"Okay. We'll see each other tonight?"

He nodded slowly. "Yeah. I think I need to."

SHE WASN'T LESS nervous than she'd been the night before. If anything, she was more nervous. Because now she knew for a fact the intensity between Eli and herself wasn't a fluke.

Because she was kind of going all in tonight, knowing full well what she was getting herself into. It was a dangerous game and she liked it. That surprised her more than anything.

But today had been beyond upsetting and she was looking forward to something just as strong to help take away some of the unsettled feelings that remained.

At least for a while.

You can't fix things for people when they don't want them fixed.

She'd reminded herself of that countless times over the years. Every time she hadn't called her mother. Checked in on her to see if her father was still ruling the house with a fist of iron. Because she'd tried to help. And her mother had chosen to stay. Her mother had chosen the man who'd put her daughter in the hospital. So Sadie had accepted that she couldn't change things for her mom and had set about changing them for herself.

She was going to have to let this go, too. Even though it sucked. It was a lot harder when you couldn't physically let it go by driving into another city and never looking back.

"Bah." She stalked into the kitchen and hauled herself up onto the counter, her knees planted firmly on the granite surface as she rummaged through one of the cabinets for a bottle of wine. Probably she would have to get a real fancy-ass wine rack for when guests were here. Luckily, she had a little time.

She took two glasses down, along with the wine, because in all honesty, Eli probably needed a drink, too.

She wondered if he would get more relaxed if he had a glass or two. If she could get him to smile. If his lips would taste like merlot and sin and the *smile* that was the rarest thing she could think of.

She licked her own lips in anticipation and carried the objects she now considered her fantasy aids into the living room.

She was still in the same clothes she'd been wearing earlier—sad for Eli, no matching bra and panties for him today. But after the incident at the diner, she'd thrown herself into B and B things, including looking at website proofs, which were fan-freaking-tastic, and choosing the stain for her deck, which was very nearly done because a whole team of burly men could handle decks like no one's business.

She hummed as she set the glasses on the old-fashioned captain's trunk she was using for a coffee table and sat on the couch, her feet tucked up under her.

And for one heart-crinkling moment she really wanted Eli to just come and sit next to her. To release his stress while she let go of hers. To share in a calm moment.

She blinked. No. That wasn't what this was about. It wasn't supposed to be about sharing emotions. It was supposed to be about sharing nakedness and orgasms.

The heavy knock on her front door saved her from her thoughts. "It's open!" she shouted.

She heard the door open, then close, the heavy shoes on

the wood floor, and finally Eli appeared in the living room entryway.

"Hiya," she said, surveying his tall, lean frame. He'd changed. Dark jeans conforming to muscular thighs, a tight black T-shirt giving hints of all the fun that lay beneath the fabric.

"Hi," he said.

"You can come in," she said, patting the empty spot beside her.

"Right." He cast a long look at a sleeping Toby, who was in the chair he'd claimed as his own, before walking across the room and joining her on the couch, keeping a healthy distance between them.

"Wine?" she asked.

"I don't really care for it."

Well, dammit. There went her merlot-flavored fantasy. She'd just drink enough for both of them. "Well, I hope you don't mind if I drink," she said, tugging the already-popped cork out. She poured herself a generous amount, then picked the glass up and clinked the edge against the empty one still sitting on the trunk. "Cheers to me, then." She took a sip and sat back, feeling distinctly broody now. Because she'd gotten a picture in her head that shouldn't have been there, and now she was disappointed for him not conforming to said ill-advised picture.

"Are you mad at me now?" he asked.

She looked up over her glass and at him, at serious brown eyes that made her stomach do tricks. "A little."

"Why?" he asked, the corners of his mouth turning up.

There was her smile. A small one, but she'd gotten it. "Because you were supposed to drink wine and be cozy with me."

"That doesn't sound like what we agreed on," he said, his tone gentle. Why was he being so nice? She was trying to be peeved.

"No, I know it doesn't. But I was sort of hoping for it. Because I am a fickle and difficult creature."

"Yeah, you are."

"You weren't supposed to agree so readily."

"Sadie," he said, his dark eyes burning hotter now. He reached out and gently touched her glass, lowering it. "You know what this is."

"I know," she said. "You don't need to worry about me."

"Then why are you angry?"

"Because," she said, setting her wineglass down on the trunk and standing, moving over to where Eli sat and standing in front of him, "I had a little fantasy."

"Did you?" he asked, his focus sharpening.

"Mmm-hmm." She put her knee on the couch, next to his thigh, and then the other one, straddling his lap. "It had to do with getting you to relax a little."

"This is not the way to relax me," he said, putting his hands on her hips. "You realize that, right?"

"I was going to relax you," she said. "Lick the wine flavor off your lips." She leaned in and traced the outline of his top lip with the tip of her tongue. "But I have to say you taste pretty good all on your own."

He took a deep breath, his hold on her tightening, his head falling back. "You're dangerous. Do you know that?"

"I've never been accused of being dangerous." She planted her hands on his chest and leaned forward, kissing him hard. "Flaky. Fun. Fluttery. Lots of *F* words, none too naughty. Never dangerous."

"Then the men you've been with before were blind."

"Or maybe we just didn't have this kind of chemistry. It's definitely a little bit more combustible than the norm."

"True," he said, sliding his hand upward, forking his fingers through her hair, his thumb teasing the edge of her lips. "You still mad at me?"

"Not really," she said.

"Good. Because I didn't come here to fight."

"I'm hoping you came for another one of those *F* words."

"Yep," he said, "and I stand by my original statement. You, Sadie Miller, are dangerous as hell."

"You're not exactly a kitten, Deputy Garrett." She arched her hips forward and gasped as she came into contact with his erection, rock-hard and obviously ready for her.

Really, she was becoming less and less disappointed in the loss of her brief domestic fantasy.

He tightened his hold on her hair and tugged her face down to his, kissing her deep and long. Leaving her gasping for breath. "Not exactly," he said.

Just like that the intensity was back. The need that hit hard like a punch to the stomach and made it hard to breathe. The desire that verged on pain, her core already so slick with need for him, so sensitized, one more calculated move against his cock would send her straight over the edge.

But the releases Eli offered weren't easy. Not a sweet relief like the opening of a flower, they were like going through a storm. And she was charging in willingly, knowing full well how it would be. Knowing that this time might be the time that saw her washed overboard, completely adrift.

It was worth the risk. Every time it was worth the risk.

She kissed him back, bit his lower lip as she tugged his T-shirt up over his head. Then she put her hands on his chest, all that hard, hot muscle for her to explore. Just for her.

"You, too," he growled.

And she hastened to obey, tugging her shirt up over her head, undoing the front clasp on her bra. She leaned forward, a short, sharp sound escaping her lips when her nipples came into contact with all that hot bare skin.

He moved his hands over her back, his touch firm and sure. He touched her with the kind of authority she had no issue with at all.

He tightened his hold on her and picked her up, switching their positions so that she was lying sideways on the couch, on her back, with him over her, his hands on the snap of his jeans.

Heat flooded her face, her body, anticipation coursing along her veins as she waited for him to get his pants off.

She undid her jeans and pushed them and her underwear down her legs. "Come on," she said, "you're going to kill me."

"I don't think you're going to die," he said, leaning in, tracing the outline of her nipple with his tongue.

"Yes," she said, the breath rushing from her lungs, "I really think I might."

"I didn't realize you were so fragile," he said, kissing her lightly on the breast before moving downward, pressing another kiss to her stomach.

"I am not fragile."

"You sure, baby? Another one of those *F* words."

"You turn into such a bad man when your dick is hard," she said, her voice shaky.

"And you like it," he said.

"Hell yes, I like it."

"Then we don't have a problem." He took hold of her leg, his fingertips sliding along her inner thigh, her muscles quivering in response.

"Except the little problem where I die because you won't give me what I want."

"What do you want?" he asked, pressing his lips along the path his fingers had just traced.

"Oh... I... You know."

"You want this," he said, leaning in, hot breath blowing across her clit.

"Oh...yes. Please."

"You're going to have to ask me by name."

"Please, Eli," she said. She wasn't above taking orders. Hell, at this point, she was so desperate for release she wasn't above begging. "Oh, please."

"Please what?"

"Please do...you know."

"You want me to lick you until you scream?"

Heat shot through her, her face burning hot. She was not a prude, but she'd never had a man talk to her like this before, either. And the fact that it was Eli, straight-arrow Eli Garrett who didn't get double entendres and who'd once put her in handcuffs in an un-fun way, made it feel all the more illicit and shocking.

"Eli…"

"Do you?" he asked.

"Yes," she said.

He curved his hands around both of her thighs and tugged her down hard, his lips meeting her tender flesh, his tongue stroking her clit. She threw one arm over the back of the couch, putting the other one on his shoulder as he teased her, as he pushed her, mercilessly, straight over the edge into a climax she wasn't even remotely prepared for.

Pleasure poured through her, threatening to drown her, and all she could do was cling to Eli. Cling to him and hope she survived the storm.

"Turn over," he said, his voice rough.

"What?"

"On your knees, babe," he said.

She sat up and obeyed, resting part of her body against the arm of the couch, her knees pressing into the cushions.

She could hear him getting his wallet out, tearing the condom packet. Her throat was dry, her body throbbing. She could not need to come again this bad less than a minute after that last orgasm. It wasn't even possible.

But it was happening.

She was shaking, she needed him so bad. And shaking with fear because this level of need was terrifying. But she couldn't stop him. Which only made it scarier. Because she didn't want to. She should be running. She should be in her Toyota and halfway to the Washington border. But she was here, bracing herself on the couch, waiting for Eli. Needing Eli.

She didn't have to wait long.

He pushed inside her, and she lowered her head, her forehead pressing against the arm of the couch, the brocade pattern biting into her skin.

He gripped her hips and established a steady rhythm, his hand drifting between her thighs, stroking her clit, making her shiver. She was powerless in this position, at his mercy. And she loved it.

It was so different from the last time they'd been together, when she'd ridden him until they both lost their minds. This was his game. He set the pace, and he had total control. She'd never liked this, submitting to a guy like this. But she liked it with him.

She more than liked it.

He pulled her back against him and increased the intensity, her whole body tightening up, pleasure twisting around her, reaching that unbearable point where she knew something had to give.

He pressed down hard between her thighs, the added pressure the final straw that snapped the tension, sending waves of release pounding through her.

He put both hands on her hips, his fingers digging into her skin as he rode her hard, chasing his own release. He found it on a harsh growl as he stiffened against her, then relaxed, his head resting against the curve of her back.

He moved away from her, her skin prickling in the cool air after he removed his warmth. "I'll be right back," he said.

She lay flat on her stomach, her knees and arms like wilted kale. She tried to catch her breath, to catch a thought, before he came back. So she didn't do something dumb and needy like crawl into his lap and bury her head in his chest.

But she kind of felt dumb and needy. Which was really aggravating.

She pushed herself into a sitting position so that she would look a little less pathetic upon his return.

He walked back into the room, beautifully naked, his eyes most definitely focused on her breasts. "Hi," he said.

"I'm having déjà vu. Except you were wearing clothes last time you walked in and said that."

"So were you."

"Yes, well. Not now."

"Obviously."

"Don't leave," she said, and she could have bitten her tongue off.

"I won't," he said. "Just yet."

"Yeah, that's what I meant. Just not...right now. We could... We could go into the bedroom, and..."

Toby chose that moment to jump onto the floor between them and look at them both, judgment gleaming in his golden cat eyes.

"Oh, you," she said, "go make yourself useful. Catch vermin!"

"You said he didn't catch vermin," Eli said, a smile curving his lips.

"He needs a hobby. One that is not staring at us after we have sex. Over it, cat. I'm over it."

Toby meowed and walked over to Eli, rubbing against his bare legs and winding his tail around his calf. Eli looked pointedly at Sadie, his eyebrows arched.

"He can smell your disdain. It's...well, it's like catnip to him. He feeds off hatred."

"Why do you like him again?"

"Don't take this the wrong way, but I think for reasons similar to the ones I like you for."

He looked back down at the cat, who was winding himself around his ankles, then back at her. "Excuse me?"

"We don't always get along. You can be grumpy. Standoffish. Judge-y as hell. But there is just something about you."

"You're really selling my personality."

"Hey, I know what I like. Grumpy, judgmental cats and... grumpy, judgmental men in uniform."

"I'm not judgmental," he said.

"Sure you're not."

"I'm not."

"You seem upset. Are you going to punish me to the fullest extent of the law?" She wiggled her brows and stood up, her legs wobbling beneath her.

"I might," he said, his voice getting deeper, huskier.

Oh, yes, this was better than the alternative. Desire was better than that other stuff. The intense aftershocks of sex with him. The deep need that it seemed to expose, without ever satisfying it.

"I think it's time for us to go to bed."

And for once, he didn't argue with her.

CHAPTER THIRTEEN

IT WAS EARLY. It was cold. And it was fence repairing time.

All things that, in many ways, Eli found enjoyable. All right, so fence repair wasn't the most fun thing he could think of to do on a Saturday, but it was quiet work. And he and Connor had thermoses of coffee set on the fence posts, their breath putting out bursts of condensation in the cold air, and there was something about it that was familiar. Constant.

Of course, his brain was back in bed with Sadie. He'd gone to her place every night that week. He hadn't slept there any of the nights, but last night he'd stayed until the sky had started to lighten, slept for an hour, and now, here he was out in the field.

It was jarring. To go from this sort of out-of-reality experience with Sadie, in her arms, in her bed. He had the kind of sex with her he'd barely even fantasized about. Because he hadn't thought it was real. Or even a possibility.

What they had was hot, on a level he hadn't known existed. He wasn't used to sex consuming him like this, but he sure as hell wasn't arguing.

But yeah, the transition from there, to sleep, to this had him a little off his game.

"Hand me the wire cutters," Connor said, his voice still rough from sleep.

"Sure," Eli said, reaching out and taking the cutters from the ground, and placing them in Connor's outstretched hand.

"You're quiet this morning," Connor said.

"And you appear to have woken up with an estrogen surge."

"What the hell?" Connor asked.

"Seriously, what was that? 'You're quiet this morning.'" Eli knew he was being a jackass, because he *was* tired, because he'd been up all night having sex. Which he felt kind of smug about, but also which he didn't want his brother to know about. "Only women say crap like that."

"You seem to have woken up on the asshole side of the bed this morning and stepped in a pile of sexist on your way out to the barn," Connor said.

"You make a similar trek every morning. Why should it bother you if I'm trying to speak your language?"

"Because you don't normally. You are normally very well-adjusted, which actually kind of pisses me off, because you're my younger brother and your shit is way more together than mine. In fact, no matter what's going on, it all seems together for you. Which makes me very suspicious of why you're acting this way." Connor straightened and tugged off his glove, leaning against the wooden fence post and picking up his thermos, unscrewing the cap. "Yeah, very suspicious." He poured himself a cup, black, no sugar. "Either you're still mad because you want to screw Sadie, or...oh, no," he said, a smile curving his lips. Eli groaned internally. "No, that's not it. You said you weren't going to sleep with her, so even if you were in full monk vow of celibacy mode you wouldn't be grumpy like this. You did sleep with her. And you're mad because you broke your little vow."

Wrong. He was not mad about sleeping with Sadie. He loved every minute of it. He was, however, more than a little pissed that his brother had guessed so close to the truth.

"Shut up, Connor," he said, reaching for his own thermos and pouring himself a cup, with cream and sugar.

"You did. You slept with her."

"I *am* sleeping with her," he corrected, his tone hard. He hadn't intended to admit it, because it just wasn't Connor's damn business. It felt like something that was just for him and Sadie. And it felt wrong to talk about it. Like it violated what they had. Like it violated her.

"Well," Connor said, pushing his hat back on his forehead. "I did not expect that."

"What?"

"To be right, for you to admit it if I was, and for it to have happened more than once."

"I can't even count how many times it's happened." And there he was putting male ego over decency, which he rarely did, but he was only human.

Connor shook his head and took another sip of his coffee. "For a second, I was jealous of you," he said.

"Only for a second?" Eli asked.

"Yeah, then I remembered how much I don't want to screw with any of that stuff ever again."

Eli let out a long, slow breath. He didn't want to have this conversation with Connor, but they were apparently having it. "You're never going to sleep with anyone again?" he asked.

"Not planning on it." He took another sip of coffee.

"That's not... You're thirty-four years old, Connor. That's not healthy."

"You don't still believe in blue balls, do you?" Connor asked.

"No. Look, I just..." He swallowed. "I don't like to tell you how to deal with this. To deal with Jessie, and the loss of her, because who am I? I've never loved a woman, Connor. I don't plan on ever marrying one. It's just not in the cards for me. But *you* have to move on."

Connor shook his head, his jaw tight. "No, Eli, I don't. I don't have to move on. I don't have to do anything I don't want to do."

"So you're going to be like this forever?"

"Maybe. I run my ranch. I get the work done. What the hell else do I need to do?"

"Be okay?" Eli asked.

Connor laughed. "I'm not okay," he said. "Why should I bother acting like I am?"

Eli looked down. "It's been three years," he said, his tone soft.

"And it was supposed to be a lifetime." Connor put the lid back on his thermos. "When is the appropriate time to get over the loss of your whole life? Answer that question, Deputy."

"I can't," Eli said.

"Yeah, I didn't think so. You don't want to get married."

"Give me one reason why I should," Eli said, leaning forward on the fence, propping his boot up on the bottom slat. "Love comes here to die." It seemed a weird thing to say, with the pine trees in the distance tipped in gold from the sun, and the breeze coming in from the sea, mixing with the scent of earth, trees and livestock. With all these things that made the ranch look like heaven, it was hard to see it for what it was.

But the simple fact was, no one in his family had ever managed to hold on to love. The house, the Catalog House that he was starting to think of as Sadie's, was the original monument to that. A gift for a woman who wouldn't stay.

And on it had gone, all the way to Connor.

No, Eli had no plans to get married. He'd never seen a good reason to want love, and he'd seen plenty of reasons to avoid it.

"Yeah," Connor said. "Sometimes it feels that way. But my point is, you already don't want marriage. With the way things were for Dad after Mom left... I did, and look where it got me? Don't you think I have enough of a reason to not want to get married again?"

"Sure, but not to never have sex again."

"Let me worry about that."

"Yeah, I promise I'll never think about it again. Or ask you about it again."

"Sounds like a plan. So there. You had the talk with me. You said the thing that's been brewing. And I spoke my piece. You can call your brotherly duty done."

"Good," Eli said, but none of it felt good.

"The sex good?" Connor asked.

"What?"

"With Sadie. Is the sex good? Tell me that at least."

"Damn good."

Connor groaned. "Okay, well, we got that out of the way, too. World's most awkward conversation?"

"Very."

"Did you want to talk about religion or politics next?"

"I'll pass," Eli said.

"I guess we just fix the fence and mind our own business, then."

"I'm okay with that."

Eli went back to work, his eyes on the pale blue sky extending above lush green mountains. He tried not to replay the conversation he'd had with Connor. Tried not to remember the bleakness in his brother's eyes. It was everything he'd been afraid was in him, said out loud. That Connor wasn't okay at all.

And he couldn't fix it. Dammit, he hated when he couldn't fix it.

It was like his dad all over again. Watching somebody drown in sorrow, doing their best to manage their addiction until just once…just once you weren't there to stop them. To care for them.

At least Connor wasn't drinking as much as their father used to. But Eli worried. His brother sure as hell drank more now than he had before Jessie's death.

The thought gave him heartburn. More than that, it made him want to get back into Sadie's bed. At least there things were good.

Mind-bendingly good.

There, he didn't think so much about the things he needed to fix that couldn't be fixed. He could just think about himself. Just a hell of a lot more length of fence to fix, some calf vaccinations to deal with, and he'd be back with her.

That would be his happy thought for the day. It was rare he had a happy thought, and no one was more surprised than he was that today Sadie Miller was his.

"THANK YOU FOR COMING, Kate," Sadie said, standing with one hand outstretched, an apron dangling from her fingertips.

Kate looked from side to side. "I see no half-naked deck builders."

"You're not here to ogle, sweetheart. You're here to bake."

Kate crossed her arms beneath her breasts, her dark eyebrows shooting upward. "I am?"

"Yep. We're going to make dinner rolls. I mean, if you want to. I thought we could hang out. And since I'm trying to learn how to get some recipes perfected I thought this might be fun." Sadie really hoped this might be Kate's idea of fun. Otherwise she feared hanging out with Kate might involve intensive horseback riding, or something equally outdoorsy. Not that Sadie was opposed. She just needed to work up to it.

Much to her relief, Kate brightened and took the apron. "Sounds great." She started putting the apron on. "Not that I really need to protect my clothes," she said, indicating her plain white T-shirt and high-waisted jeans.

"Better than wearing flour for the rest of the day."

Sadie started getting out mixing bowls and ingredients while Kate stood in the center of the kitchen, obviously slightly out of place in the environment.

"Let me guess," Sadie said. "You don't have much cooking experience."

"Not really. Eli's always done that. Throw meat on the grill, bring home pizza or whatever. Why are you cooking rolls for a bed-and-breakfast?"

"Well, I have to eat so I thought I would offer additional meals for an additional price a few days a week," Sadie said. "Anyway, I like cooking."

"Oh." Kate moved in closer and stood at the counter.

"You sound surprised."

"Eli never seemed to like it. But, I mean, he did it. And his food is edible. Unlike Connor's..."

"So Eli did all the cooking for you guys?" Sadie asked, unbearably curious and slightly guilty. She should not be interrogating Kate about her brother. Especially because Kate's brother was her secret lover. And if Kate knew that Sadie and Eli were sleeping together, she would probably make a horror face and run screaming from the room and never speak to Sadie again.

And thus, Sadie would lose one of the very few friends she had.

"Yeah. He did. Connor kept the money coming in, and, I mean, Lord knows that was important, but... Eli was the one who made sure I was ready for school. He learned to braid my hair," she said, her hand going to the hairstyle she still wore.

Sadie's stomach squeezed tight, her eyes stinging. Eli's strength was sexy, no question, but this? This was even sexier. It was a part of the strength, really. A part that most people wouldn't see.

Braiding a little girl's hair.

Sadie saw it, though. An older brother, a teenager, getting his little sister ready for school. Cooking meals. All things that would never be public, but that had shaped Kate into the woman she was.

Eli was all that had stood between Kate growing up to feel safe and secure...and growing up feeling like Sadie had. Like no one cared. Like she was better off cutting ties and leaving parents who didn't want her anyway.

It was Eli who'd protected Kate's trust. Her openness. Eli who'd given her her strength.

Sadie couldn't help but be envious. And she realized then that the little fascination she'd had for him when she was a teenager hadn't been about a bad girl wanting a cop. It had been about wanting a man with that kind of strength to protect her. Care for her.

Well, he didn't. No one did. Deal with it.

"That's…really sweet," she said, grabbing a measuring cup and pushing it down into the flour bag, a white cloud rising up around them.

Kate smiled. "Well, don't let him hear you say that. But then, if he's still avoiding you, that shouldn't be a problem."

Sadie felt a twinge of guilt, which made a sucky companion to the envy. "Yeah," she said. "Not sure when I'll see him again. So, let's make rolls."

"POTATO SACK RACING."

"Lame," he said, lying back on the bed, keeping his focus on Sadie, who was sitting next to him, completely naked, her hair tumbling over her shoulders.

"It is not lame. Not for kids."

"Three-legged race is better."

"Unless you have to run with a boy who is stupid, doesn't listen and stinks."

"But what if you get to run with the cute girl that you have a crush on?" he asked, leaning in and kissing her shoulder.

"Did you have crushes?" she asked, cocking her head to the side.

"Sure, didn't everyone?"

"I don't know. Sometimes I kind of picture you like you sprang out of the ground wearing your uniform and a frown."

"Your flattery is almost embarrassing."

"Sorry if it didn't sound complimentary," she said. "I wouldn't be here if I didn't like you. Scratch that, I would be here, you wouldn't be. And I would be alone."

"Well, I wasn't born in uniform."

"And I wasn't born running," she said, smiling faintly.

"Life has a lot to answer for."

"Sure does."

She flopped backward, raising her arms above her head, and his eyes fell to the little silver scar on her side. A surgical scar. Sometimes he wanted to ask her about it, but ultimately, her medical history wasn't really his business. So he didn't ask.

"Where are you at on your big barbecue plans in terms of booths? We'll put three-legged races to the side for now," he said, shifting so that he was lying on his side.

"I've got pony rides. Cookie decorating, face painting. John from the Farm and Garden is going to bring over one of those mini-sheds that looks like a playhouse for the kids. And the pie eating. There will be pie eating."

She ran her fingers through her hair and the temptation for him to do the same was too much. He wanted to pull her close. Play with the silky blond strands. Braid it. Which was not something he'd ever done for his lovers, but something about the idea appealed to him.

He wanted to take care of her.

He wrapped his hand around her hair, about to separate it into three separate sections, but she turned her head. He dropped his hands back down to his sides, the strange tightness in his chest dissipating a little.

He'd had a moment of temporary insanity. Sadie was good at doing that to him.

"What are you going to do about Alison?" he asked.

"Nothing," she said, chewing her lip. "What can I do? I can buy pie from her. Hope she feels proud of her accomplishment. Hope she wants something different for herself, but really, there is nothing else I can do."

He moved his hand over her breast, down over her stomach, his conscience tugging at him. "I told Connor," he said.

"About Alison?" she asked, frowning.

"About you and me."

She sat up, blinking. "Why?"

A damn good question. A weird impulse, as weird as the one he'd just had to braid her hair.

"I just... He sort of asked. Well, he tried guessing. He

guessed I slept with you once, and I…corrected him. I'm not a very good liar."

She leaned forward, covering her mouth, a giggle trapped behind it. "Oh, my gosh. No, I bet you aren't." She looked down at him, her hair sliding over her shoulders, over her breasts, covering pale pink nipples. She was such a tempting picture. Naughtier because she was smiling, because she was covered. He wanted her again. So soon. And it didn't even shock him anymore. "You're way too straitlaced."

"I'm straitlaced?" he asked.

"Yeah, you kind of are."

He pushed her onto her back and she shrieked, then he kissed her neck, feeling her pulse quicken beneath his lips. "How many straitlaced men do you know who can make you come so hard?"

He never talked to his lovers like this. Ever. Hell, he never really talked in bed at all. But she brought it out in him. He didn't worry. He didn't overthink. He told her what he wanted. And she loved it. And that did things to him. Things he hadn't known he wanted to have done to him.

In truth, he'd never been this consumed by sex. Because his mind was always somewhere else. Because taking care of things was still in the forefront, but here, there wasn't room for anyone but her and him.

"None. But then, I think this might be colored by the fact that I haven't exactly tested the sexual prowess of every straitlaced man I've known."

"Fair point."

"I like that you don't lie," she said, her blue eyes on his. "I like that when I look at you, I feel like I really see *you*. Not just the man you want the world to see."

That made him feel a little guilty. Since, in so many ways, he felt like he did just put on a good front. The man who seemed unruffled on the surface, hiding the festering pool of worry beneath. The gut-churning terror all the responsibility he took on built in him.

"Sadie..."

"No. If you're going to tell me you have secrets, just don't. Because I want to think I know. What's the harm in thinking that for now? It's not like this is forever."

"No," he said. "It's not."

For some reason, her words and the agreement made his chest feel like it was full of lead.

"So let's have the fantasy. You be the straitlaced badass who rocks my world. I'll be comfortable here with you, trusting you. All well-adjusted and stuff." She smiled and kissed his chin, wrapped her legs around his calves.

"Are you saying you aren't well-adjusted?"

"Shh. In the fantasy, I am."

"Are you drunk?"

"A little," she said. "You won't share the wine with me so it's not my fault I have to drink more than normal."

"Connor won't tell anyone," he said. He was sure of that. Because the information Connor had given in exchange was too precious. Connor wouldn't want anyone to know how bad he was hurting. How hopeless he felt.

Eli didn't even really want to know, but he did. And now he had to try to fix it. Make it right.

He could never escape that feeling.

He pushed it aside, though, because Sadie was beneath him, and devoting everything to that sensation was, right now, more important.

"It's for the best. We don't need everyone all up in our business. And besides, Lydia is a good ally. She keeps the Chamber of Commerce on my side. And I have a feeling she might cut me if she knew I was sleeping with you."

"Really?"

"She's very smiley. I find that concerning."

"Maybe she's friendly."

"Maybe," Sadie said. "You are just something else."

"Am I?"

"How have you seen so much of the crap you have, and still... How are you so good, Eli Garrett?"

"I have to be," he said, the words slipping out before he had a chance to think them through.

"Why?" she asked, pushing his hair off his forehead.

"If I'm not...who will be?"

"Not enough people," she said.

"You are," he said.

"Me? You mean me, who runs away from everything and everyone?"

"I should never have said that to you. I'm sorry." Regret tightened his stomach.

She shook her head. "You weren't wrong. And the more I see you here, the more I realize how much harder it is to deal with people when you have to watch them not learn. And not listen."

"Regardless, it doesn't mean that you haven't helped people. You listen to people."

"For money," she said.

"So? Some people would pay to *not* listen to people's problems."

She laughed. "Okay, so maybe we're both okay?"

"Sure. We're both okay."

"Right now anyway." She arched against him, sending a shock of pleasure down his spine.

"Right now I'm more than okay."

SADIE CLOSED HER laptop and looked out the window at the row of buildings across the street. The sky was bright blue, clear, the breeze pushing waves over the American flag that rose up from the two-story restaurant behind the main street, just off the harbor. She imagined it was creating matching waves on the sea beyond the buildings, too.

She'd managed to touch base with Alison, awkwardly, about

the pies and confirmed that she would make some for the contest and sell some in the booth. But it didn't really make her feel much better about the situation as a whole.

She'd spent most of the day in the coffee shop approving the mock-up of the B and B's website. She'd ventured out briefly to go to the Wagon Wheel, a local home store, and special order curtains for the house, and some quilts. Then she'd stopped in at the glass studio Brooke, her old friend from school, now owned.

Brooke's life seemed to be going better than Alison's. So that was a comfort at least. She'd been enthusiastic about the barbecue and had asked for brochures for it, and for the B and B, to put in her shop. They'd parted with plans to do lunch, and unlike most times vague lunch plans were made, Sadie had a feeling they really would get together.

She tapped her fingers across the top of the computer. Eli was off today. Well, working on the ranch. Putting in his part-time cowboy hours. Which was his definition of a day off. And she'd decided to leave the ranch and come to town because it was better and less embarrassing than hanging out and hoping to catch glimpses of him walking around all sweaty and sexy and *everything* that a man should be.

Yeah, she needed an Eli hiatus. Which was why she'd asked Kate to drop her off at the coffee shop this morning, so she could do all her online work for the B and B from a remote location.

She wouldn't be taking a hiatus from him at night, of course, because heaven knew how many nights they had left together. And she would not be skipping a single night of orgasmic bliss. Apparently, pleasure was the price she'd willingly pay for her sanity. And she couldn't even be bothered to feel bad about it.

Nope. All she felt was pleasantly aroused, thank you very much.

But the issue with being around him all day was that he made things other than her lady parts fluttery. He made her chest area feel fluttery. And that was not something that needed to be indulged.

In fact, quite the opposite.

It was harder still after nights like last night. Where they'd sort of wound around each other, naked, and talked, and laughed. And he'd told Connor about them.

That had made her breath hitch. Made all the questions about what that could possibly mean float to the forefront of her brain. The logical part of her knew it meant that he was too honest to lie to Connor. But then there was this weird, previously dormant girlie part of her that seemed to want to pull it apart further to assign labels and meaning to every little piece and part of what he'd said.

This was not a good time to get all freaky about that stuff. Well, okay, there was never a time for that. She sighed and stood up, tucking her laptop into her purse, chucking her cup into the trash can and waving at Baby Barista Number One before stepping outside.

She shook her head and lifted her face toward the sun, taking a deep breath before crossing the street and cutting through two buildings on her way down to the wharf.

The water was a deep gray blue, pitching and rolling against the rocks on the jetty. She turned and looked down toward the bar, and saw a patrol car, parked across the narrow street in the do-it-yourself car wash.

"He's at the ranch," she said to herself. "And not on duty, so that isn't him." She was already walking toward the car, her internal commentary not doing anything at all to deter her.

She got closer, and her view shifted, and then she saw him. In blue jeans and a T-shirt, washing the patrol car in one of those do-it-yourself car wash spots. It was like some sort of fantasy delivered to her at a very unexpected time.

All that was left was for him to spray his chest with the water so the shirt stuck to his muscles...

"Hello, stranger," she said, feeling like a total dork the moment it left her mouth. "I mean, hi, Eli." She knew the amendment hadn't done much to cover up the original silliness, but oh well.

His eyebrows shot up. "What are you doing here?"

"I am a hallucination," she said. "Your subconscious mind brought me to you."

"Oh, really?" he asked.

"Yes. Don't you want to know what I mean?"

"I suppose you're going to tell me."

"I mean that you're extremely—" she wiggled her brows "—randy. And you're feeling sexually frustrated. Taking it out on your car, too. Wax on, wax off. Very suggestive."

"Is that all, hallucination Sadie?"

"No. I'm also here to warn you. You're in graaaave danger."

"Is that all?"

"And I would like a sandwich?"

"Do you evaporate soon?" he asked.

"Nope." She approached the car and him, her heartbeat speeding up a bit when she got near him. "Because I'm real. Surprise."

He smiled then, and her heart did a full turn in her chest. "In that case, what are you doing here?"

"I was in town working. Your sister dropped me off."

"Are you ready to head back?"

"Sure. Are there sandwiches?"

"There could be sandwiches," he said.

"What kind?"

"Get in the car."

There was something about that authoritative tone that made her shiver all the way down to her toes. He was magic like that.

"Only because you asked so nicely." She opened the door and got in, and he did the same. "So, you wash your car on your days off?"

"Yes," he said. "It's either that or leave for shift early, or leave late. And I keep the car parked at the house, so it gets a lot of stuff dropped onto it from the trees."

"You are so cute," she said.

"I'm not sure how I feel about that."

"What? I like that you don't lie and you take care of your things. My gosh, except for your lack of inhibition in bed, you're like a flashback to a black-and-white film."

"And what is my lack of inhibition like?"

"A flashback to spam emails often found in my inbox. But, like, in a good way."

He smiled, started the car engine and pulled forward through the car wash, and around, out toward the street. "I haven't really been to the beach since I've been back," she said, looking out at the ocean.

"Do you want to go?"

"Eh. Sand has its place. It also gets in *places*, so there's that."

He snorted. "What the hell sort of things do you do on the beach?"

"Not *that*. *That* we saved for the woods. It's more private. Actually most of my teenage shenanigans were saved for the woods. We conducted very few on the beaches."

"Likely why you got away with them. Especially back when I worked nights, I did a lot of drive-by spotlighting on the beaches."

"Oh, man, that would have been awkward."

They needed to change the conversation topic since she was starting to get a bit hot around the shirt collar talking sex with him in an enclosed space.

Something about the car turned her on. And granted, she'd been existing in a perpetual state of arousal since Eli had first kissed her, but this was different. It had an edge to it. Maybe it was the fact that, while she was sure it wasn't this exact car, he'd put her in the backseat of one very similar to it ten years ago, her hands in cuffs.

And maybe it had something to do with the fact that the memory had morphed into something sexy since she'd begun sleeping with him.

Strange, since before it had been such a horrible one. Not because of what he'd done, but because of what had happened after.

Something about the car fantasy seemed like a reclamation of that night. And maybe that was assigning too high of a purpose to her sexual fantasies, but she kind of liked it.

"So you've never had sex in your car?" So much for changing the subject.

He whipped his head to the side to look at her. "What? That's...random."

"Not really. We were talking about my sex life...in the woods, not on the beach, thanks. And I was wondering about you."

"No. That's edging into... Like I was saying, I was with a woman once who was a badge bunny. Which was fine in some ways, but in others got really weird. And...no, I haven't."

"So it only seems *weird* to you?" she asked, biting her lip, feeling disappointed. "Not even a little hot?"

"I feel like you're leading me somewhere."

"I want you to do it with me in the back of your car."

He applied the brakes, hard, sending her jerking forward, the belt catching her. "Ow. Glad to know I succeeded in shocking."

"I didn't expect that."

"I guess not." She looked over at him, his jaw clenched tight, his knuckles white on the steering wheel. "What are you doing?"

"Thinking of all the places I could pull over and not get caught. I know where I have caught people having sex in cars before, so I'm trying to be original."

"Are you serious?" she asked, eyes wide.

He took his hand off the wheel and curved it around her arm, drawing it over to his lap, to his erection, hard and thick beneath his jeans.

She moved her palm over him. "Serious indeed."

That he was doing this for her, that he wanted to do it when it had put him off before, was a thrill she hadn't realized it would be.

"You have that effect on me."

He turned away from town, onto a service road that led out into the forest. It wasn't the preferred location she and her friends had used, but it was similar, she imagined. A pocket deep enough in the woods that people rarely bothered to drive in, especially when it wasn't hunting season.

Her stomach tightened and she squeezed his cock through his jeans.

"It'll be over before it starts if you keep doing that," he said, his teeth gritted.

"Well, we can't have that. I want my reward."

"Your reward?"

"I was arrested by you, and put in the back of a car. And it was one of the least fun backseat experiences I've ever had." They were driving over dirt and pine needles now, the pavement ending abruptly as the trees thickened. "Scratch that, it was the worst backseat experience I've ever had. Given all that, don't you think you owe me a better one?"

"I damn well think I do," he said, pulling into an alcove of trees just off the road. "Get in the backseat."

She unbuckled slowly, keeping her eyes on him as she did, before opening the door and getting out of the car. It was so quiet the silence seemed to close in around her, around them. It was a strange, intimate openness. Somehow much more public than being in a bedroom, but also much more secluded.

She closed her door, then opened the back door, climbing inside before closing herself in.

He got out of the car and she watched him through the windows as he moved to the back and opened the door, his hands on his belt, sliding it through the loops before joining her inside, closing the door.

"This is way more like it," she said, leaning back, resting her head on the window.

"Yeah?" He moved over her, leaning in and kissing her deep.

"Mmm. Yeah. Much better than being back here all by myself."

"I'm surprised you remember it," he said, and this time, there was no judgment in his voice. No disdain.

"I was pretty drunk, right?"

"Yeah, you and everyone else. They kind of scattered and left you to it." He brushed his knuckles over her cheeks. "I never thought that was very fair."

"I survived," she said. "The charges didn't stick anyway. My rap sheet remains somewhat mythical."

"Well, you left town anyway. Probably would have ended up getting charged with failure to appear."

"I needed to leave," she said, her heart tightening.

His dark eyes turned serious. "I'm sure you did."

She looked over to the side and saw a glint of silver in the center console of the car. She knew what they were, remembered what it had been like to wear them in the back of the patrol car. Feeling trapped. At his mercy. How different that thought was now. How different it was with Eli, the man as she knew him now.

"Are those handcuffs?" she asked, reaching out and snagging them. "Well, indeed. You just leave these lying around?"

He took them out of her hand. "Not usually."

"You put these on me that night."

Emotion passed over his face. Something like regret wrapped in horror. "I had to."

She smiled. "I know. But in the interest of re-creating things..."

ELI LOOKED DOWN at Sadie, his heart thudding dully in his throat, making him feel like he might choke. He was so turned on he couldn't see straight, and somewhere, in the middle of just trying to remember to breathe, he was trying to parse exactly why when his ex had done this, it had turned him off. And why now, with Sadie, it didn't just seem sexy, it seemed impossible to resist. And heavy with some kind of meaning he was having trouble guessing.

That again had to do with body parts shifting. Heart to throat, blood to cock. Things like that.

And then the handcuffs.

"You really want me to handcuff you?" he asked.

She bit her lips, the action so unconsciously sexy it sent a jolt through his body and down to his dick. "I really do."

"Why?"

"Do I have to know why something turns me on?" she asked. "If so, I like the idea of putting myself here, of my own free will. Letting you keep me, because I want you to. Because that first time I didn't have a choice...well, I didn't have a choice once I'd made the several bad ones I made that got me arrested in the first place."

"That's a little twisted," he said, even as his gut tightened.

"And what's your point? Isn't it a little twisted that I came back to town and fell into your arms?" She traced his jawline with her forefinger, a wicked smile on her face. "To tell you the truth, I think you like twisted a little bit."

He wrapped his arm around her waist and tugged her down so that she was lying flat on the seat, then he gripped her hands, deftly putting the cuffs on. In many ways, he was more confident in his ability to handcuff a woman than he was in seducing her. He'd just never wanted to combine the two.

"Maybe I do," he said, his words rough.

She saw things in him. The dark things. The secret things. And he couldn't deny, something in him liked it. Because it meant he didn't have to hide. Didn't have to try so hard to be upstanding.

Very few people would call what he was doing now upstanding, and he knew that. But they didn't matter. Nothing mattered but her.

"Now what?" he asked.

"I think you're the one in charge," she said, blue eyes wide.

"I guess I am." He traced her lower lip with the edge of his thumb, his eyes intent on hers, watching to make sure she wasn't nervous or afraid. "You okay with that?"

Her mouth curved upward beneath his thumb. "It's kinda what I asked for, right?"

"I promise to make it worth it."

He lowered his hand to her stomach, pushing her shirt upward, watching the muscles contract as she took a short, sharp breath. He pushed it up higher, his fingers brushing the rounded underside of her breast before sliding up farther, the fabric of her T-shirt folding over his hand as he moved his thumb across her tightened nipple, barely covered by her whisper-thin bra.

Her head fell back, her hands lifted upward, bound by the cuffs.

"Good?" he asked.

"Mmm."

"I'll take that as a yes."

He moved his hands to her jeans, unsnapped them, cursing the stiff denim as he hauled it down her thighs and pushed it, and her shoes and socks, off her legs.

"This was just an excuse to get me to do all the work, wasn't it?" he asked.

"Ah, darn," she said. "You're onto me."

He looked at her, her top pushed up, barely covering her breasts, bright blue panties low on her hips, standing out against her pale skin. "I'm finding it hard to be too upset about it."

He slipped his finger beneath the waistband of her panties, his breath hissing through his teeth as he felt the soft hair beneath the silken fabric. As he moved lower and felt how wet she was for him. How much she liked this game.

Well, he liked it, too. It was everything he never thought he'd do, things he'd never thought he'd want, and now he was all in, shaking with need. Unable to turn back.

He didn't even want to.

He leaned in and pressed a kiss to her stomach, her skin soft beneath his lips. He breathed in deep, taking in the scent of her arousal, the scent of *her*.

He lifted his head and looked at her, at her flushed cheeks, her blond hair tumbling over her shoulders. This was not his life. This was not the kind of thing that happened to him. Not the kind of beauty he was allowed to indulge in.

He almost couldn't breathe. Everything in him was bound up, suspended in the moment.

He reached into his pocket and took out a condom, shrugging his pants and underwear down his legs while holding tight to the plastic condom packet. "I did this out of order." He tugged his T-shirt up over his head, fighting with the tight space of the car.

She giggled. "I'm suddenly remembering why, since becoming an adult with my own bed, I haven't revisited my backseat days."

"I never had to use one."

"Oh, am I your first?" she asked.

"You are. My first for quite a few things in this particular instance. And now, my first woman in handcuffs in more than one way."

He tore open the condom and rolled it over his cock, his chest muscles seizing up as his fist squeezed his aching flesh tight.

She arched her hips upward and he positioned himself, pressing his arousal against her cloth-covered sex, heat shooting up through his teeth when he made contact with her. He rocked against her and she gasped, arching upward, pressing her breasts to his chest, the metal handcuffs clanking against the window.

"Oh...please," she said.

He didn't need any encouragement, not when he felt like he needed to be inside her five minutes ago. But he loved to hear her beg. Loved that she was at his mercy.

Who the hell was he?

Right now, he didn't know, and he didn't care.

All he knew was that watching her, seeing how much she wanted him, making her wait, was the best damn feeling he'd ever had. This was for him. It wouldn't fix anyone, it wouldn't save a damn thing. But it would feel good. And he wanted it.

Wanted her.

"Take my panties off," she said, her words coming out short, harsh.

"Not yet," he said, rocking against her, watching the color in her cheeks deepen.

"You bastard," she said, and wrapped her legs around his hips, tugging him down harder.

"I think you called me that last time I had you in handcuffs."

"It was true then, it's true now." She shifted. "And you didn't make me come either time."

"We still have time." He slipped his hand around beneath her and cupped her ass, tugging her hard against him.

She whimpered, her breath hot on his neck. "Please... I need you."

He shifted his hand and tugged her panties to the side, positioning himself at her entrance and sliding in slowly. He cursed, short and sharp. She was so slick and tight, he thought he might go over the edge the moment he was buried inside her to the hilt.

"Eli," she whispered, his name broken on her breath, the splinters lodging deep inside him, burning his soul. Branding him.

"I've got you, baby." Her eyes clashed with his, wide and... shocked? Almost afraid? It made his stomach clench tight. "Hey, hey, I've got you."

She nodded wordlessly, her eyes never leaving his. He leaned in and kissed her lips, long and slow, withdrawing from her body, just an inch, before pushing back inside.

Then he was lost completely, chasing the liquid heat that was raging through him, building, bringing him closer to the edge. His blood roaring through his ears, canceling out everything, his vision going dark, nothing remaining but the hot, hard bite of pleasure, twisting and turning in his gut, ready to savage him, ready to squeeze everything inside of him into dust, the pressure building, threatening destruction if he didn't find release soon.

"Come for me, Sadie," he said, the words hard-won, almost impossible to push through his tightened throat. "Baby, I'm on the edge. Come for me."

She arched against him, flexing her hips, the motion twisting everything in him even tighter. He tightened his hold on her ass, his other hand braced flat on the window behind her head as he circled his hips slowly, grinding against her clit.

Finally, he felt her give, heard the hoarse cry escape her lips, felt her internal muscles squeezing him tight. And he let himself go.

His release roared through him like a wildfire, scorching everything that had been contorted inside him, hollowing him out completely and leaving him devastated in its wake.

He tried to catch his breath, his muscles shaking, sweat rolling between his shoulder blades. He felt like he'd just run five miles in the desert. And found an oasis at the end of the race.

Sadie.

He let out a harsh breath and moved away from her. "Well," he said, leaning back against the seat, dimly aware that sitting bare-assed in his patrol car was probably not the most professional thing, but he didn't think he could move much farther right at the moment. "I didn't think the condom thing through," he said, looking down, feeling vaguely embarrassed that he hadn't quickly dealt with it out of her sight, like he would normally do.

"Oh, dear," she said, wiggling slightly then giving him a hard stare. "I need releasing."

"Oh, sorry," he said, leaning forward and pulling the key out of the cup holder, undoing the handcuffs as quickly as possible.

She smiled, almost shyly, which was unusual, if not unheard of, for Sadie. She rubbed her wrists, looking around. "Yeah, I think you have to bury it."

He let out a long breath. "This is more complicated than I thought."

"Well, you can't litter. That's a crime and you're, like...running for sheriff. Can you imagine the scandal?"

"You're right. We can't have that," he said, opening the passenger door, one bare foot hitting the pine-needle-covered ground. "This is the most awkward thing I've ever experienced."

He heard a giggle behind him and turned and gave her a hard look.

"The view is good anyway," she said.

He rolled his eyes and shut the door, hurrying, naked and in broad daylight, into the trees, where he dug a small hole in the soft dirt and disposed of the condom. Then walked as quickly as he could back to the car, taking light steps, trying to avoid majorly sharp rocks and any particularly crunchy sticks.

When he returned to the car, Sadie was sitting there with the door open, her legs sticking out, jeans back on and T-shirt tugged back down. And she was smiling. Far too broadly.

"You look all back to normal," he said.

She stood, her legs wobbling. "Looks can be deceiving. Are you ready to head back?"

"Well, I'd like to get dressed."

She swallowed visibly and nodded slowly, moving to the side so that he could reach in and grab his clothes. He shrugged his underwear on, making sure none of the pine needles that were sticking to his feet flaked off inside the underwear, then grabbed his jeans, tugging them on as quickly as possible.

And now he felt at least marginally less ridiculous. He turned back to Sadie, who wasn't smiling anymore. She had her arms folded beneath her breasts, a blank stare on her face, her lower lips trembling.

He flashed back to that moment she'd looked at him. That calm before the storm when she'd looked almost terrified in his arms.

"Sadie? Did I... Did I hurt you?" he asked, regret slamming into him, making his face feel numb and his stomach sick.

"No," she said, shaking her head, "I'm fine." A tear trailed down her cheek, leaving a streak of glitter on her skin.

"You are not fine," he said. "What did I do?"

"Nothing," she bit out. "It's just... I don't know, it was more intense than I anticipated, is all."

"I should never have agreed to this. To the handcuffs and..."

"No, it's not that. Well, it is that. It's just... I can't stop thinking about what happened that night."

"I'm sure it's scary to get arrested," he said, feeling like he was treading on thin ice, unsure of what to say next. "I'm sure..."

"Not the arrest," she said. "It's what... Eli, that night after I left the police station...my father picked me up." She leaned against the patrol car and picked up a twig that had fallen onto the trunk. She gripped it, pushed on it with her thumb and snapped it in half, the sound echoing in the dense silence around them. "And when we got home...he beat me so badly I ended up in the hospital."

CHAPTER FOURTEEN

OH, DAMMIT, SHE was crying. And not just a few tears, but the honest-to-God beginnings of a flash flood. She could feel the dams eroding, so much emotion building, pressing against the already-compromised structure, and she knew the minute it gave way, she was going to cry until she was dry inside.

Because it had been building for years. And now it was all falling apart in front of the man she…the man she'd spent a long time blaming in so many ways. The man who'd just taken her to heaven and back in his car, with what could very well be the same handcuffs on her wrists.

It was fitting he was the one to witness this. When he hadn't witnessed it then.

Why didn't you protect me, Eli? You protect everyone. Why couldn't you see I needed it?

But she didn't say that out loud. Instead, she continued on, ignoring the tears that slid down her cheeks.

"He was angry at me. For the arrest. And…oh, he said I'd been daring him for a long time. And he wasn't wrong about that," she said, swallowing hard, imagining how her father had looked that night. His face red, the vein in his forehead standing out as he'd screamed at her. As he'd landed his first blow, knocking her to the ground. And after that she hadn't seen him at all. She'd just wound herself into a ball while it continued. Unable to defend herself. Unable to move. While she heard nothing. Nothing but the sound of his knees, boots and fists hitting her body.

When she'd imagined him doing this, she'd heard her mother screaming for him to stop.

But in reality, she hadn't. In reality, her mother had been silent.

"Anyway," she said. "It was the last straw. I'd finally set him on me. After years of watching him go after my mother I finally managed to turn it onto myself. She didn't call 911. So you would never have heard it over dispatch. She drove me to the hospital in Tolowa. We were far enough out that it was just as close as the one on the other end of Copper Ridge."

"Sadie," he said, his voice rough. "I had no idea…"

"I know," she said. "But please let me finish. I had to go into surgery. I know you've seen the little scar." So funny that it was so small, when the scars beneath were so massive. "My spleen had ruptured."

"Shit," he said, the word harsh in the silence of the forest, so much heavier with emotion than her own blank retelling.

"My mother told them I had gotten into a fight. She didn't tell them my father had done it. When I was alone with the nurse she said that I could press charges. But that it was going to be difficult because my mother was adamant I'd gotten into a fight with a group of boys," she snorted. "She said if I were a minor I could be removed while investigations were done, but I was eighteen and that meant there was nothing they could do. So she asked me what I wanted. My father had come to pick my mother up. My car was in the parking lot. My mother had left the keys. And that was when I realized that people don't change. So I figured… I'd just change everything around me."

He covered his mouth with his hand and took a step back, his complexion waxen. "Sadie, I don't—" He dropped his hands to his sides. "That happened because I arrested you?"

"Don't," she said. "Don't do that. I've done that. I... I do it still sometimes. It was my choice that got me arrested. It was his choice to beat me. It was..."

Suddenly she was pulled tight against his chest, all of the resistance pulled from her by his tight embrace, all of the emotion wringing out of her, tears falling down her cheeks.

He moved his hand over her back, warm and comforting. And way too much.

She buried her face in his chest, the tears hot now, angry. "Why didn't you protect me?" she asked, the words slipping out before she could process them. Before she could analyze just how unfair they were. He didn't know. He couldn't have known. But it was the question that had screamed inside of her for ten years, even when the pain was buried so far beneath years of rocks and rubble and dirt she'd thrown on top of it in an effort to keep it quiet. In an effort to blot it out.

He tightened his hold on her and she curled her hands into fists, pressed against his bare chest as she let him hold her. Her shoulders jerked upward on the sob that filled her throat, forcing her to suck a sharp breath of air.

"You said it's your job to protect everyone," she said, the words muffled by his chest. "Everyone in your town. But you didn't protect me."

He gripped her shoulders tight, tugging her backward and looking down at her face, his dark eyes sincere, intense. She wanted to look away from him. Hide her weakness, her emotion. Every insecurity and stupid thought.

"Never mind, it's not your fault..." she began again.

"Sadie, listen to me," he said. "I would never have given you to him. Ever. I would never have let you go home. If I'd had any idea..." He shook his head. "I should have seen it."

"Why would you?" she asked, stepping back, feeling so embarrassed she wanted to crawl under the patrol car and curl up into a ball.

"It's my job. And...sometimes I think I don't look long

enough or hard enough. Because…well, like with Alison. My hands are tied because she won't tell. She won't ask for help. She won't leave. I hate knowing that. That, no matter what, I can't help. But I could have helped you. If I had asked…you would have told me, wouldn't you?"

She studied his handsome face, the deep grooves around his mouth that spoke of years of frowns. The lines between his brows that told the story of just how many nights he'd sat up worrying. "I was angry, drunk and belligerent. There was no reason for you to offer me anything. I deserved to be arrested and I—"

"You said something to me when you first came to town," he said, interrupting her.

"What?" she asked, feeling gritty and watery at the same time, and not really enjoying either sensation.

"You said that…that there were people like me who just put people away, and people like you who listen, and try to change things. You're right. I wouldn't have listened, not then. I didn't listen. I figured I was doing the right thing. The legal thing was all the protection that was needed, but it wasn't."

"Eli, don't. Don't take it on yourself. You wouldn't have listened, but I wouldn't have told you. I wanted him to do it. For years… For years and years I watched him hit her. And then I finally decided I was sick of walking on eggshells. That I was going to go ahead and dare him to do the same to me. Because in my head I figured I could take it. Because I figured she would stop it. Well, it turns out I'm not as tough as I thought. And it turns out she didn't care as much as I thought, either."

"Sadie, you said—"

"I shouldn't have said it. But I needed to say it," she said. "I don't… I've thought it before. I… Look, I really hate talking about this but I needed to tell you because, well…hello, post-sex emotional breakdown, and you did need to know why. I've… I was hammered that night, okay? But when you grabbed me and put me in the car, all I could think was you were really strong.

The kind of guy who could put a jackass like my dad in his place. The kind of guy who would. You were good, Eli, and I knew it then. I know it now."

"I'm sorry I didn't stop him."

"I'm sorry I ever blamed you."

"Don't apologize to me," he said. "Not for that." He looked grim, and she knew she'd pushed the worst button she could have ever pushed.

Other men might have shouted and said there was nothing they could have done, and they would have had a right. She'd given Eli a new sin that didn't belong to him, to add to the long list of other people's transgressions he seemed to be trying to atone for.

He released his hold on her and turned back toward the car and she just stared at his broad back, his strong shoulders.

All the better to carry the weight of the world on them.

She moved over to him and wrapped her arms around him, resting her head against his bare skin. "Don't carry this," she said, kissing the deep groove beneath his shoulder blade. "Please don't."

He lifted his hand and covered hers with it, pressing it against his chest. "No one's going to hurt you again," he said. "I promise."

Another tear trailed down her cheek. Because it was everything she'd ever wanted to hear from someone, and it terrified her how much it meant to hear from him now.

Even more terrifying was just how much the words meant, and how cold she felt in her chest when she had to acknowledge that the only person who really had the power to hurt her was him.

No matter how much she'd wanted to keep her feelings for him neutral, he'd burrowed beneath her protective layer. At some point "just sex" had become a hell of a lot more. And she had no idea how that was possible.

She'd had relationships with men, whole relationships based on more than just sex, that hadn't been like this.

At least, she thought that was what they'd been. They'd gone on dates and chatted, and some nights they hadn't even slept together, which proved that they had a deeper connection than just the physical. Or that's what it was supposed to prove.

But this was supposed to be sex. Hot, sweaty, ill-advised cop-cowboy sex. Like some kind of alpha-male female fantasy on steroids. With handcuffs. On a horse.

So why hadn't it stayed that way? Why did she feel like things were changing? How in the hell had a romp in the backseat of a patrol car turned into the most exposing, soul-baring experience of her life?

"I guess we should get back," she said, stepping away from him, wishing that separating the feelings that she had for him from her heart was as easy as breaking contact with his skin.

"Yeah," he said, bending down and retrieving his shirt from the backseat of the car and tugging it on.

Something had changed between them. It was good and bad. She could feel it. He was all tension now, and she couldn't blame him. But at the same time she felt like the bond had tightened between them.

Because he was the only person who knew. The only one who knew the whole story. Who knew that she wished, more than anything, she'd had someone to protect her.

She hadn't even let herself in on that, not really, until the moment she'd told him.

"That was fun," she said, wiping the moisture from beneath her eyes.

"Yeah," he said, slamming the back door shut before jerking open the front door. "Fun."

ELI SLAMMED THE maul down on the splitter and two pieces of wood went flying onto the dirt, the physical energy doing very little to relieve the raging…whatever the hell these feelings were that were roaring through his veins.

He didn't know what he was feeling. So he was chopping wood instead of feeling. Or at least, that was the plan. And if that didn't work, eventually he would be exhausted enough that he would just forget he had feelings that didn't involve his screaming muscles.

Barring that, he'd drink them away, but considering that was the way most other men in his family handled Unpleasant Things No One Wanted to Handle, he was averse. But not entirely opposed. Desperate times, et cetera.

"You have enough wood to keep all of Copper Ridge toasty through the wet season. Why are you chopping more?"

Eli turned and saw Kate standing just behind him, her hands on her hips, her weight resting on one leg. "Because," he said, bending over and picking up one of the log halves, "I'm expecting it to be a cold year."

"Oh, okay. Hey, have you talked to Sadie lately?"

Oh, good, that was what he needed. To talk about Sadie with his sister when he was trying to forget the woman via manual labor. In that way that he just wanted to forget about her for long enough to make himself feel comfortable again.

Enough to make himself forget the look on her face. The way she'd shivered in his arms.

Why didn't you protect me?

He bent and picked up the other log half, scowling deeply. "I talked to her this morning. Why?"

"I wanted to tell her that I made rolls."

"What?"

"I made rolls by myself. And they're edible. She showed me how yesterday, so I was… Hey, how are you?"

"Fine," he said, gritting his teeth and walking over to the wood pile to stack the pieces on top.

"You don't seem fine," she said, frowning. "Is this about the people coming for the barbecue next week?"

Weirdly, that bothered him a hell of a lot less than it had in the beginning. In fact, in a very strange way he was looking forward to it. Looking forward to seeing Sadie's vision come to life. To seeing her hard work become a real, tangible thing.

He shouldn't care. He did.

Don't carry this.

Too damn late, Sadiepants.

"Nope," he said. "I am fine."

"You are growly."

"And?"

"That's Connor's job. What is up?"

"Just thinking about things," he said, putting another log on the stump. "Dad."

"Oh," she said, looking down.

He positioned the splitter, then lifted the maul again, bringing it down hard. "It's that time of the year."

"Yeah, I guess it is." She bit her lip and looked down, then back up, her dark eyes fierce. "I don't think about him very much."

"You don't?"

"No."

He looked at Kate and fully realized—maybe for the first time—that she had never, ever known the good parts of their mother or father. And they had existed. Their mother hadn't always been despondent and unable to cope. Their father hadn't always been a man viewing life through an alcohol haze.

He'd gotten to know the people they were. So had Connor.

"He was a good man at one time, Katie," he said.

"That's fine," she said. "For him. For you and Connor. But I never knew that man. I never saw him any way but falling on his ass drunk. You and Connor loved me. Then Jessie, when she married Connor. Jack was there, and Liss, our friends who always made our house feel less empty. But I can't miss the person who made the house seem sad."

She didn't understand, because she didn't realize what really made him think of their father. She didn't know that he was trying to cope with the feelings Sadie's words had triggered.

That they had brought to mind all he'd failed to protect.

And that was the crux of the problem. He wanted to protect the people he loved, the people of Copper Ridge. And his track record was hit or miss at best.

"Hello." He turned and saw Sadie standing in the driveway, her hands in her back pockets, tugging the T-shirt she was wearing tight across her breasts, her expression sheepish. "Hopefully I'm not interrupting anything."

"Not anything important," Kate said, forcing a smile.

She looked a whole lot like him when she faked okay, and he wasn't sure what he thought about that.

"How is everything, Kate?" Sadie asked, smiling. Sadie's smile, regardless of her feelings, always seemed genuine. And that was even more concerning. He was starting to realize that everything about Sadie, all of her ease and lightness, wasn't what it seemed.

Ruptured spleen. Hospitalization. Her mother wouldn't defend her...

He couldn't imagine it. Couldn't believe this bright, amazing woman had been subjected to horrors that topped the Garrett Ranch's Greatest Hits by a mile. He hadn't even guessed at her pain, and today she'd poured it out onto his chest.

And he felt it now. The weight of it. Of what he hadn't done. Of what he always left undone.

"Good," Kate said. "I was actually just asking about you."

"Well, here I am! Things are really moving along for the barbecue. Though I wanted to ask you, and I know it's really last minute, but are you interested in doing any type of rodeo demonstration?"

Kate brightened visibly. "Yes. I'd love to. I could do some barrel racing in the arena, or even some calf roping."

"Both if you want."

"Maybe Jack will be interested in helping out," she said.

"That would be great."

"I'll go and call him," Kate said. "See you." She waved and then bounded off in the direction of her little cabin.

"She is quite something," Sadie said, moving in closer to him.

"She is. Sometimes I'm afraid she really lost out having to be raised by us. We're not exactly a soft touch."

"No," Sadie said, "but you're a pretty darn satisfying touch if I say so myself."

"Well, thanks for that."

"Actually, that's what I'm here to talk to you about."

"Oh?" he asked, feeling the scowl forming from the inside out. He'd come to cut wood and escape her and here she was.

Wanting to talk about the feelings he was pretending not to have.

"I'm sorry about what I said. I wanted to make sure we were okay."

She didn't meet his eyes when she said any of that. And he knew she really was sorry, and that she was afraid that she'd overstepped. But he also knew she'd meant it all. And it had hit its mark.

"We're fine," he told her, because it was the thing he had to say to get sex. And whatever he felt, he knew he still wanted that.

"Good. I don't normally spill my guts like that. Normally I listen to other people do it. That's kind of why I do it. Did it."

"Therapy?"

"Yes. Because I got to give it to other people and sort of turn over their own issues and never think of mine. I mean…it hurts. That memory hurts. I think it always will. And I'm projecting. I know that. I…wished someone would have seen, Eli, and in my head, because you were so tangled up in that night, something in me made that person you. My patients do the same thing and I know better. But you know…it's a 'doctors are terrible patients' kind of a thing."

He could hear what she was saying, and he even believed

her to an extent. But it didn't change the way that heavy mass of emotion felt in his chest. Didn't make breathing easier or his throat less tight.

"Let's forget that it happened," she said. "You know. You're basically the only person who knows. And... I think we should just...go to bed."

"It's six o'clock."

"So?" she asked.

They were standing outside his house. And he'd never had her in his house before. But he'd had her in his patrol car. And that was, in some ways, more intimate.

"I guess I can't think of a reason." Mainly because the blood had all rushed down south of his belt. A chronic, Sadie-related issue.

"Oh, good," she said, looking relieved. "I don't want things to change."

Neither did he, but he was afraid that they had.

"We're on the same page, then."

"Your house or the car?"

"House," he said.

"Probably for the best. In hindsight, it was a pretty poor use of the people's property. Doing it in a county-owned vehicle."

"Excuse me," he said, the tension in his chest easing slightly, though not the tension in his cock, "you started it."

"True. But then," she said, putting her hand on his chest, a smile curving her lips, "I am a criminal. A very bad girl. And you are so good."

He wrapped his hand around her wrist and drew her fingertips up to his lips, sucking one into his mouth, swirling his tongue around the tip. Then he closed his teeth lightly over her skin and released her. "Am I?" he asked.

He didn't feel good. He felt like a failure. Like a man who'd let another man beat this woman near to death. Like a man who couldn't protect the weaker people around him, even though he tried with everything in him.

There were tons of people who never let their fathers drive off in a drunken stupor and die. And those people probably didn't try half as hard as he did.

Sometimes he wondered if he was destined to fail everyone around him, no matter how hard he tried to be acceptable. To be good enough.

So if he was going to be bad, maybe he should just embrace it.

"I think you're underestimating me," he said. "Still. And I've had you in handcuffs."

"I don't know, Eli."

"Sadie," he said, gripping her chin, kissing her firmly on the lips. "Get your ass in my bed."

CHAPTER FIFTEEN

SADIE WASN'T SURE what was happening, or why it felt so different. It wasn't about sex. She knew that much. Well, it was about sex, but it was about something more, too. Something deeper. Something she really didn't want to guess at.

Eli had only let her in his house that night she'd used his shower when she'd burst the pipes. Never since.

They had sex at her house. And then he returned to his space. His neat and ordered space.

She walked through the front door, her heart hammering hard. Everything was like she remembered, identical, really, to the only other time she'd ever been here.

Neat, clean. Verging on shiny.

For a man who worked with farm animals and criminals, he sure kept his space spotless.

Maybe that was why.

"You know where my bedroom is," he said.

"Yes."

"Get upstairs." There was a hard, determined light in his dark eyes. Like a switch had been flipped. There was so much electricity arching between them. So much heat. And so much intense meaning.

Things had changed. She'd changed them by telling him her story. By telling him he should have protected her.

She wasn't sure yet if she'd made things better or ruined them, but she was sure she'd changed them. She'd felt it then, standing isolated in the woods with him, and she felt it now.

"Okay," she said, because whatever was happening she wasn't going to tell him no.

She turned and headed up the stairs, her footsteps loud on the wooden floor, her heart hammering louder in her ears, sounding over her feet.

"I like to watch you walk," he said. "Though I like it better when you aren't wearing anything."

She heard him behind her, following her, his voice rough. "Well, I'm hardly going to walk through your kitchen naked," she said.

"I walked through the woods naked for you," he said. "And that's not my usual thing."

"No," she said, tossing a look over her shoulder, her stomach knotting tighter as she saw the hungry look on his face. "I don't suppose."

"But I don't do any of the usual things with you," he said.

She pushed open his bedroom door and tugged her shirt over her head, ditching her bra just as quickly before crossing one arm over her breasts and turning, giving him her best saucy smile. "Oh, really?"

"No," he said, his voice lowering. "I don't."

"Well," she said, spreading her fingers, giving him a slight peek at her nipple, knowing that she was driving him crazy, "maybe we can see what else I might tempt you to do."

He advanced on her, his expression dark. He extended his hands and cupped her face, tilting her head backward, his fingers forked through her hair. "Don't make this a joke, Sadie."

"I'm not," she said, her heart tightening, like he'd grabbed hold of that instead of her face and squeezed tight.

"You're trying to make light of it so you don't feel it. I can't

do that. As you pointed out, I'm a pretty humorless bastard."
He traced the edge of her lower lip with his thumb. "So no
more talking. Don't try to make it funny. I have to feel it. So
you damn well have to feel it, too."

Her heart lurched into her throat, made a response impossible. But it didn't matter because then he was kissing her, his
lips hard and firm on hers, stubble scraping her chin, her cheeks,
as things intensified between them.

Their little love scene in the car had been intense, driven by
her need to wash something out of the past. To make it different. But this was different still. He was different.

And he was right. She wanted to do exactly what he had accused her of. She wanted to do a striptease and laugh and make
it fun. She wanted it to be the kind of sex she knew, the kind
she could control.

But Eli was in charge now. And for some reason, she felt
more helpless now than when her wrists had been in handcuffs.

Because that had been her idea, her plan. But this was about
his demons, not hers.

He pushed her back onto the bed, stripping her jeans, underwear and shoes from her body before he shoved his jeans down
his hips, leaving him naked, bare for her.

"I'll be right back." He turned and walked into the bathroom
and returned a moment later, rolling the condom onto his length
as he moved back to the bed.

He positioned himself between her thighs, kissing her deep.
There was no foreplay, no preamble at all, but she didn't care.
She was ready. She'd been ready since the last time he was in-
side her.

There was just something about him.

He pushed inside of her, deep, thick, filling her completely. A
sharp gasp escaped her lips as he pushed his hips forward, going
impossibly deeper. She wrapped her legs around his thighs,
opening herself to him, allowing him better access.

She smoothed her hands over his hair, down his shoulders

and back, her eyes never leaving his, the impact hitting her deep, sparking off the protective shields she'd built up around her chest, making her burn. Making her feel like she was on the verge of an attack that might bring the walls down forever.

He ground himself against her, pleasure rushing through her, her orgasm taking her by surprise, taking her over completely. Rushing through her and eclipsing all of the emotions that had been knotting up in her chest, leaving her feeling clean, new. Relieved.

Above her, Eli lowered his head, his body shaking as he shuddered out his own release. He let out a hard breath and moved away from her, rolling onto his back. She just stayed where she was, staring at the ceiling, at the slats of wood, knotted and imperfect, but somehow orderly. Like the man himself.

The only sound was his harsh breathing. Probably hers, too, but for some reason she was much more aware of him than of herself. Possibly because she didn't want to be aware of herself, all things considered.

The things considered being the fact that it felt like there was a potential avalanche of feelings about to crash down inside of her. A veritable rock slide of emotions.

No, thank you, sir.

She closed her eyes and tried to capture the post-orgasmic warmth that she was counting on coming to the rescue. She felt decidedly less glowy than normal.

She was far too aware of everything. The burn on her cheeks from his whiskers, the blood still throbbing hot through her body, her heart beating unevenly. How cold her breasts felt now that he'd moved away from her.

The shifting of the mattress as he got up and the sound of his feet slapping on the wood floor as he headed back into the bathroom. She shivered, then looked around the room, pushing herself into a sitting position.

He didn't have pictures on the walls. The wood-paneled walls were broken up by large windows that overlooked the dense trees that backed the house. The sun was sinking outside, golden rays filtering through the green, casting everything in a hazy filtered light.

She suddenly felt completely exhausted, her eyelids ready to sink like the sun. She crawled up to the head of the bed and slipped beneath the covers, lying on her side, watching the tree branches outside wave in the breeze. She heard Eli walking back through the room, felt the mattress sink just across from her.

The covers slipped down and she felt his warmth beneath the covers. Wordlessly, he wrapped his arms around her and pulled her close. She relaxed, head resting against the solid wall of his chest.

She would just close her eyes for a second.

Then she would go.

WHEN SADIE OPENED her eyes, gray light was bathing the bedroom, and Eli's arms were still wrapped tightly around her.

She scrubbed her eyes, rolling onto her back, his hands drifting over her breasts as she did. Then she craned her neck to look over him, and at the bedside clock.

It was five-thirty, and she sure as hell knew she hadn't gone back in time, which meant she'd slept here all night.

She sat up, pulling the covers up to her chest. Eli made a deep noise, then rolled over.

Her heart was hammering, her hands a little sweaty. She'd never done that before. Never slept beside another person like that. There was something so impossibly intimate about it. Something sort of terrifying.

She waited for her muscles to spring into action, for her legs to get her out of bed and her feet to run her out the door.

But it didn't happen.

She breathed in deep, and the panic started to subside, her breath normalizing. She didn't want to leave. That was the most startling revelation that came from her subsiding panic. Other startling revelations included that she actually felt happy that he'd let her stay the night. That he'd invited her into his home and his bedroom.

He'd shared something with her last night. Like she'd shared with him after they'd made love in the car. But he'd done it wordlessly, and she had no idea what exactly she was supposed to extrapolate from it, but she still felt it.

She slipped out of bed and hunted for her clothes, tugging them on before she went downstairs and helped herself to Eli's mugs and his coffeemaker, humming absently as she did.

She remembered that he ordered lattes and pulled some milk out of the fridge, nuking it in the microwave, then whisking it while the coffee brewed. Then she added a generous helping to his coffee, along with some sugar. Leaving her own coffee fairly underdressed with a dollop of warm milk and a little sugar. When she got back upstairs, Eli was out of bed, standing in the center of the room, naked and looking a little lost.

"You're still here," he said, when she walked in.

"Yes, I am. And I come bearing caffeine."

"Well, then, I'm very glad you stayed," he said.

"Is that the only reason?"

"No."

"Well, good. A woman hates to be wanted only for her bean-brewing skills. Though mine are legend. And no man has ever benefited from them. But they will at the B and B."

Eli frowned and set his mug on the nightstand, grabbing his black boxer briefs and T-shirt from the ground, throwing both on, then retrieving his mug. "What do you mean no man has ever benefited from your skills?"

"I'm not into sleepovers," she said, smiling, trying to keep it a little lighter than things had been between them. She turned away from him, and he caught her arm, turning her back.

"What does that mean?"

Oh, damn Eli. Why did he always want to know what something meant?

"It means that I like to sleep alone, which I've told you before. And it means that I've always slept alone. Whiz, whir, thank you, sir, if you will."

"Why, Sadie?"

"Because I don't do close, okay?" she said, realizing as the words slipped out of her mouth, cranky, curt and very pre-coffee in attitude, that they were true.

It was easy to pretend she was fine. That she had normal relationships and let them go when they weren't working because she didn't need conflict, because she wasn't going to submit to a life of unhappiness and violence under the guise of sick, twisted love, like her mother had done.

But the simple truth was, she didn't do heavy, because she didn't want to get close to anyone. She didn't let her boyfriends spend the night for the same reason she lived in a place for only a couple of years at a time.

She didn't want to bond with anything. She didn't want to need anyone.

She blinked, standing there frozen in the middle of Eli's bedroom having an epiphany. "I don't like to let people get close to me," she repeated, the words making the back of her neck prickle.

"Why?" he asked.

"Because people hurt you." That was true, too. She was filled with truth. She needed to be filled with coffee, so her truth could stay in. In and buried, like it normally was.

He nodded slowly and walked toward the French doors, undoing the latch on one and opening it out, and onto the deck that wrapped around the second floor of the house.

"Care to take your unheard-of morning-after coffee out on the deck?"

"Oh, why not?" she said, lifting a shoulder and following him outside. He set his mug on the railing, and she did the same, resting her elbows on the rough wood and looking out at the view.

She tried to see through the trees, past the closest branches, to see what was beyond, but they were like a dark blot of green ink, bleeding together to cover the blankness.

"I'm sort of mad at you," she said, looking down into her coffee, listening to the wind rustle through the trees, to the birds that were just starting to wake up.

"Why?"

"I thought I was really well-adjusted before I met you."

"Did I…maladjust you?"

"No, you just had the balls to point out that I'm a total head case. No man before you has dared."

"Every man before me got the boot out the door too quickly."

She waved her hand. "Eh. Granted. All right," she said. "Why is your house so clean?"

"Because otherwise it gets chaotic. And out of control. And I've lived that way before. I won't live that way again."

"Your dad?"

"Yes. He was a mess, Sadie. I took care of Kate, but my dad was like another child at a certain point. He made bad decisions, and it was up to me to clean it up. Cover it up. Before my mom left he was okay."

"He never got over your mom?"

He lifted a shoulder. "Probably at some point he was just an alcoholic who liked booze. Probably there was a point where he'd forgotten why he ever started drinking. But that's just a theory. There was always so much to take care of."

"It explains you."

He looked at her, his eyes blank. "I failed him, though. In the end."

"What?"

"The night he died. Whenever Dad got drunk, I used to take his keys and hide them. That was my routine. Dad was drunk every night, for the record, so I knew to hide his keys every night."

"Eli, you should have never had to deal with all that."

"But I did. We don't get to choose our lot, we choose what we do with it. Except…the night my dad died I decided not to go home after my shift. I was out. Connor and Jessie lived in the cabin Kate lives in now. My dad and I were in the main house. I hadn't moved out because he needed someone. And I knew he needed someone. But that night, I figured he was probably passed out so I didn't need to go home. Went out with a bunch of guys from the department instead. And a call came in over the radio."

"Oh… Eli."

"Yeah, well…it's been a long time. And my dad was not a father to me, not really. But that doesn't change the fact that I let him down. He was impaired, always. And he needed some-one to help manage his decisions. I wasn't there and he died."

"You can't honestly blame yourself…"

"You blame me for not saving you from abuse I didn't even know about. Of course I blame myself for this."

"Eli, I don't really blame you…"

"You do," he said. "And I understand. It's because I've prom-ised to protect people. If I just said screw it like…like Connor does, then I wouldn't expect better. And no one else would, ei-ther. But if I say I'll take care of it, I better. And I haven't al-ways. I've failed a lot of people."

"I'm sure you've helped more people," she said, her stom-ach clenching.

"But I failed where it really matters."

"But it was his fault."

"Does it matter?" he asked, turning his back to the view, leaning against the railing. "Does it matter if you know you should feel a different way about it?"

She thought about how she'd felt when her blame had poured out of her back in the woods. About how she'd been carrying that feeling around, buried deep and low, for years.

"I guess not," she said. "But…you shouldn't feel that way."

He lifted a shoulder. "Sure."

"Do we get some sort of…accolades for exposing just how

screwed up we both are?" she asked. "Because I figured this just-sex thing would involve a lot less talking."

"Then why are we talking?" he asked.

"Because. I spent a lot of years listening for a living and never met anyone I wanted to talk to. And... I want to talk to you. But I don't always like the things that get said."

"Neither do I."

"Maybe we should stop talking, then," she said, moving to him and curling her hand around his neck, kissing him.

"I have to be at work in an hour."

"I can get a lot done with twenty minutes. Just you wait and see."

SADIE WAS ACTUALLY NERVOUS. Like...upchucking nervous. The barbecue was today. Booths were being set up. Volunteers were on hand, paid workers were on hand, individual vendors were on hand.

Over the past week she'd finalized everything for the barbecue, bought new linens for the B and B, and perfected her menu, and also during that past week, she'd been sleeping with Eli, either at his place or hers.

She liked to think that had something to do with how well things were going. If for no other reason than being with him made her feel very good.

She paced the open field area where everything was being set up. The good thing about getting local businesses to participate was that everyone basically saw to their own booth once she directed them.

Barbecues were already being fired up for the cook-off, very large pots of beans and potato salad were either heating or chilling. Beer on tap was at hand. Kate and Jack were in the large uncovered arena ready to do some rodeo work and to show some basic roping techniques.

And Jack was even coordinating a round of mutton busting, with prizes donated from the Farm and Garden. She wondered if Connor had checked with his insurance about that. She imagined not.

Jack and Kate had proven to be enthusiastic additions, and their passion for the events was contagious. It was also enticing a whole new segment of the county to the barbecue.

The only booth that was empty was Alison's. And it was starting to make Sadie wring her hands in despair. Well, she could get pies from the grocery store for the contest if she had to. But she doubted it would make for as special a dessert booth as she'd planned. In fact, without the homemade stuff, it felt like a "why bother."

But considering what had happened the last time she'd seen Alison, she wasn't that surprised.

"Sadie!"

Sadie turned and saw Lydia, her favorite intrepid Chamber of Commerce representative and fellow admirer of Eli's butt. "Hi, Lydia. You're out early."

The other woman smiled. "Yes, I am. I thought I would see how it was all shaping up."

"Nicely," Sadie said, surveying the grounds. "It just might not fail."

"Eli would never let it fail," Lydia said. "Not to say you would," she quickly amended. "Only that I've known Eli for the past six years and he's always been so stable and organized. Just one of the many reasons I'm wholeheartedly endorsing his bid for sheriff."

Sadie scanned the field, looking for Eli. She didn't see him. "Yeah, I definitely think he's the man for the job," she said.

She thought back to last week's conversation on his porch. About how he felt like he failed when it came to caring for people.

She couldn't understand it.

Maybe because you suck and you threw a bunch of your issues at him?

Maybe because I really feel that way, she argued back with herself. *Because maybe...if I ever thought there was such a thing as a knight in shining armor, it would have been him.*

She didn't even bother to push the thought away.

Didn't bother to pretend there wasn't more swirling around inside of her than simple lust.

Somehow, in the space of a month and a half, she'd gone from disliking Eli immensely to...well, whatever this thing was where she felt like the sun hadn't really risen until she saw his face.

Whatever you called that.

"Sadie." Lydia interrupted her train of thought. "I was wondering if you wanted to get brochures for the B and B down to the Chamber. And also, I was wondering if we could put some brochures in the B and B for some other businesses. Tourist attractions, whale-watching excursions, things like that."

"That would be great!" Sadie said, feeling strangely warm toward Lydia at the moment. Not that she was cold toward her normally, but it was a little awkward to talk to the woman you knew had a thing for the guy you were semi-secretly sleeping with.

"Beneficial for all," Lydia said. "Oh, there he is!" Her smile broadened when she saw Eli, and Sadie felt a sliver of guilt push its way beneath her skin. Lydia was more Eli's type. They made sense. She was organized, passionate about the community. Caring.

She wasn't terrified of interpersonal connection and more likely than your average startled house cat to tear off and hide under the furniture than forge any kind of meaningful relationship with someone.

Except...she and Eli did have a meaningful relationship. She could feel it. She was carrying it around in her chest, and it weighed a ton. And it was effing inconvenient.

"Eli!" Lydia called, waving.

Oh, man. Like it couldn't get more awkward. Because she and Eli were not a couple, and when she stood near him in front of the general public she didn't know what to do with her hands. Because they were itching to touch him but she knew she couldn't.

He walked over to them, looking generally awkward, as awkward as you would expect the guy to feel in the situation.

"Hi," she said, shoving her hands into her back pockets so they wouldn't get all feelsy with him.

"Sadie," he said. "Lydia. How are things going?"

"Great," Sadie said. "And on your end?"

"Parking area is set. Connor is sober. I consider that a win."

Sadie winced. "Is Connor going to come?"

Eli shrugged. "I don't know. I kind of doubt it. Families and things...he doesn't handle this stuff well."

"Man," Sadie said. "I didn't think of it from that angle. I feel like crap now."

"Don't," he said. "Connor objectively realizes the value in this. Okay, he didn't say that, but I know he does. He'll hide away. It's his deal. Though Liss might be able to draw him out for a while when Jack and Kate ride."

"I can't wait to see them," Lydia said. "Really exciting. It'll be very fun. We've had a lot of calls about this down at the Chamber."

"That's great," Sadie said. "And goes a long way in eliminating my deep fear that I will end up here alone, eating all of the food myself. Which is, in many ways, not a bad fantasy, but... you know. People are investing a lot of time and money in this, and there has to be a good turnout or it just won't be worth it."

Eli surprised her by putting his hand on her shoulder. "There will be a big turnout. Because you've done an amazing job. And I know I was kind of grumpy about it for a while, but this is great. You did great. And people have already started pouring in." He slid his palm down her arm, the gesture going from casual encouragement to something that revealed a deeper level of intimacy between them.

And Lydia noticed. Her smile faltered for a moment, and Sadie inwardly cringed.

"Thank you," Sadie said. "Thank you both for all your help and thanks… Eli, for saying that. I really…tried." And in spite of herself, she had bonded with this place.

She looked around the picnic area, at the people there. Bud from the gas station sitting with his wife and smiling. Cassie from The Grind was with a very nice-looking man Sadie assumed was the same Jake she talked about with a dreamy smile on her face.

The group of fishermen from Rona's were there with their families, and their beer. Her old high school friend Brooke with a group of women dressed in cutoff shorts and American-flag T-shirts.

It wasn't just this place. It was these people.

This man.

And if she was going to do this, be here, she wanted to do it right. She wanted to do it all well.

She sort of hated the pressure that came with it all. The crushing need. So different than a life that wasn't tied to anything. No anchors holding you back. Nothing to entice you to try. She missed it, in a way. But then, going back to it seemed impossible.

Because…big, cowboy-in-a-uniform-shaped anchor. No matter what looked better or easier, it would never really be easy again. Cutting ties with Eli would be something she regretted. But being with him was damn hard. Because he called her on her BS and made her be serious, made her look in his eyes when she climaxed. Forced her not to joke about her pain, but to speak about it honestly.

He added an uncomfortable level of depth to her life. Discomfiting when she'd tried for so long to stay in the shallows. Bastard.

"You did more than try," he said. "You succeeded. Now we just need to wait for the place to fill up."

And it did fill up. It was unbelievable. By the early afternoon they had people everywhere. Eating, laughing, talking.

There was a band playing. Ace, the sexy bartender, was serving beer from the portable tap. The barbecues were going strong and adults were laughing while kids danced in the grass with bare feet.

Eli's three-legged race was a serious hit, and everyone was anxiously awaiting the official barbecue judging, and Jack and Kate's demonstration.

She noticed Eli standing on the perimeter and walked over to where he was, jabbing him lightly with her elbow. Since, you know, she probably couldn't kiss him in public.

"You hungry yet?" she asked.

"Starving."

"Let's get food. There's obviously enough. And we earned it."

"We did," he said. "Well, you did."

"Stop it," she said, leaning into him again and shoving him with her shoulder. "This is your place. And you've been a big support. Stop being so nice to me. It's freaking me out."

"Am I not nice to you?" he asked.

"You are," she said. "I think you've officially crossed over into being mainly nice to me. Which, considering where we came from, is kind of a huge deal."

"Well, I know you now. Instead of just thinking I know about you."

"Same," she said. "Shall we get our barbecue on?"

They walked through the crowd, Eli periodically smiling and waving at those who called out a greeting, and all she could do was just walk next to him in awe of all that he was to these people. He was a cornerstone, her man. The kind of guy who did good all the time. The kind of guy who'd affected many of the people here in amazing ways.

It was daunting. Daunting that a man like him could have clearly done so much and still feel like he hadn't done enough.

It was extra daunting because she wasn't sure if she'd ever made half that impact, even if you cobbled together the things she'd done across all the places she'd lived.

"Chicken or beef?" she asked, when they approached the barbecue line.

"Any," he said. "Any and all."

"All right, we'll fill your plate with meats."

He smiled and right then she didn't really care about impact and other deep things like that. Because Eli was smiling right at her, and that meant a hell of a lot.

"What about you?" he asked.

"I want steak, and I hear it's fantastic because it's Garrett beef. And I want copious amounts of potato salad because who doesn't love a mayonnaise and starch party in their mouth?"

"Well, you obviously do," he said.

She smiled at him, then had to look away to avoid kissing him. She noticed that Alison was at her pie booth, looking harassed and serving pieces of pie onto plates as quickly as possible. Then she noticed that Jared was standing right next to her, his large arms folded over his chest, looking every inch the threatening, Neanderthal jackass he was.

"Uh-oh," she said, "I think we might have a problem."

Eli frowned, then followed her line of sight over to the pie booth. "Oh. That asshole."

"Yeah."

A muscle in Eli's jaw ticked. "I'm feeling pretty short on patience with him."

"I know. But I do understand that there's…" Suddenly Eli was moving out of line and heading toward the booth. "Oh," she said, hurrying after him.

Jared was leaning in near Alison, saying something, and Alison was looking increasingly distressed. And Eli was starting to walk faster.

"Do we have a problem here?" Eli asked.

Jared was a big guy, and scary enough if you were a woman. But Eli stood about four inches taller and had to outweigh him by thirty pounds of pure muscle. Even without the badge and the gun, Eli was an intimidating sight.

In many ways he was more terrifying without the uniform than he was with it on. Because in the uniform, you could see his boundaries. Clearly. Deputy Garrett was a lawman. He was a man who would see justice done in accordance with the legal system.

Right now in his cowboy hat, tight black T-shirt and jeans he looked more likely to dispense a different kind of justice entirely.

And she didn't really know what he might do.

And that was funny because he was predictable and good. Except...except he wasn't all that predictable, not really. When they were in bed, he was a different man, a dangerous man.

When they were together he was something a lot more authentic.

Just now, as he was standing there ready to do God knew what, she realized that the man he was in bed wasn't an anomaly. It was him.

"No problem, Deputy Garrett," Jared said, not drunk today, just hella mean, apparently. "Just talking to my wife." Alison's shoulders shrunk in when he said the word. "That's not a problem, is it?"

"It depends on what words were being used."

"Eli..." Alison said. "It's okay..."

"You on a first-name basis with him?" Jared asked, his tone hard. "Is that why he always seems so worried about you? Are you sleeping with him, you stupid whore?"

And that was when Eli moved.

He leaned in and grabbed Jared by the back of his neck at the same time he brought his fist in to meet the other man's nose. Then he shoved him downward, bending him at the waist while he brought his knee up into Jared's stomach.

Before stepping back and letting the other man fall to the ground at his feet.

People were looking now, craning their necks, wide-eyed. Sadie just stood frozen, almost unable to believe that Eli had done it. And yet, at the same time…she wasn't shocked. No, she wasn't shocked at all.

But she was proud.

"I don't take kindly to the words *bitch* and *whore*," Eli said, keeping his voice low so that the families nearby couldn't hear him. "Especially not when you're talking to your wife. Now stand the fuck up." He gripped the back of Jared's neck and brought him to his feet. "You want to hit someone, why don't you hit me? Or is it not as much fun to go toe-to-toe with someone who outweighs you? I'll bet you're okay with hitting women. But that's not going to play today, so why don't you go ahead and hit me instead?"

Jared spat and blood dribbled down his chin. He wiped it with the back of his hand. "You prick," he said, his eyes blazing.

"Yep," Eli said, "and let me tell you something, this prick is not on duty today. Today, I'm just the owner of this property, and you're the bottom-feeder who isn't welcome on it. You're not welcome in my town, either, but there's nothing I can do about that. But I'll tell you this. I'm going to be looking for you to make a mistake. And then I'll lock your ass up. You put one finger out of line?" He gestured to Alison. "You touch her again? I will see that you stay in a jail cell for a very, very long time. So step carefully. And right now? Step. The hell. Off my property."

Jared stumbled forward and headed away from the stand. Then he turned to Eli, shouting obscenities that all ran together in a blur, before he stopped, like he intended to come back. Until Connor walked into view, from the direction of the main house.

He wrapped his hand around the back of Jared's neck, holding him steady. Eli was pretty big. Eli was threatening. But bearded Connor, who was broad and thick, every bit of him heavily muscled and with rage pouring off him, was terrifying. "I think my brother asked you to go," he said. If Eli hadn't been deterrent enough, Connor was there for backup.

Jared looked back at Eli one more time before turning and walking away, spitting profanities as he went.

Connor moved forward and joined the group. "Well, what an asshole. Sorry." He directed the apology to Alison, who was wide-eyed and shaking. "But seriously."

"Are you okay?" Sadie asked Alison.

Alison nodded, then shook her head, closing her eyes. "I don't know."

"Fair enough," Sadie said.

"I'm embarrassed. I'm so embarrassed that I'm still married to him," she said, her voice breaking. "But it's…"

"I know," Sadie said. "And trust me, I have spoken to a lot of women who've dealt with this, professionally. And unprofessionally…my mother has never left, Alison. She's stayed and stayed. For more than thirty years. I've seen what it does to someone. I've seen what they can make you think about yourself. But you have to know, whatever he's said, it's a lie."

She nodded. "I know. I do."

"Please don't go back to him. Don't go home tonight."

Connor shifted his stance. "Especially don't go home tonight. He's a coward with us, and that means he'll take it out on you."

"Is there somewhere you can go?" Eli asked.

She nodded. "My…my mom and dad live in Tolowa. I can go there. Not sure what they'll think when I show up, since I don't really… I've been so embarrassed."

"You can call them if you like," Sadie said.

Alison shook her head. "Right now? I just want to serve pie. Because that's what I'm here for. And now that… I have a feeling I'm going to need this. This business. The pie."

"Well, I'll buy a few a week at least for my B and B," Sadie said, determined. No matter how good her cooking skills were, she wasn't going to produce a pie as amazing as Alison's. "And I'll be around. Whatever you need."

"And if he ever comes near you again," Eli said, "if he hits you or threatens you…"

"I'll report him," she said. "I promise I will." She took a deep breath and straightened, and for the first time, Sadie saw an echo of the girl she'd known in the woman who stood before her. Someone a little scrappy. A lot angry. Someone who was ready to fight. "Now, I have pie to serve."

She turned and went back to slicing her pies and Eli, Connor and Sadie moved away.

"What are you doing out?" Eli asked Connor.

Connor shrugged. "Liss is going to meet me to watch Kate ride. You know I like to watch her do her thing."

"Yeah," Eli said. "She's great."

Sadie looked behind Connor's shoulder and saw red waves bouncing just before Liss came into view, jogging up behind him. "I made it. I'm late but I made it."

"You're chronically late," Connor said, turning to face her. "It's an illness."

"I'm bizay, Connor," she said, poking him in the side. "You don't know anything about that, obviously."

"No," Connor said, "I just run a whole fricking ranch, Liss. I know nothing of your busyness. I bet all that paperwork is a real strain. Wanna trade?"

"Eff no. I am not roping cows."

The ghost of a smile touched Connor's lips when he looked at his friend. "The cows don't like you much, either, honey."

"Glad to know it's mutual. The cows and I can go on giving each other the evil eye. Then I'll eat a burger because I'm human and I win."

"Come on, then, let's go," Connor said, putting his hands in his pockets and jerking his head in the direction of the arena.

"We haven't eaten yet," Eli said, and his referring to them as a "we" made Sadie feel a little warm and fuzzy.

"Go get some food, then. We'll see you over there," Connor said, eyeing them both, and Sadie felt her cheeks heat a little.

"So that was Connor in a good mood?" Sadie asked, when he and Liss were out of earshot.

"Pretty much. He got to threaten bodily harm to someone so I fail to see how he could have had a better day."

She started back over to the barbecue line, chewing on her lip. "Are you worried?" she asked. "About how all that might affect your campaign?"

He frowned. "I didn't even think of that. Which is...weird. I usually think of everything."

"Well, I don't want to add concerns that you don't really need."

"No," he said, "I think it's interesting. I don't care," he said, meeting her gaze. "I just don't care. Because I still want to be sheriff. I still think I'd do a damn good job, but I do a good job at what I do now. And...whether or not it was a popular thing or easy thing or good thing...punching that asshole in the face was the right thing to do."

She wrapped her arms around his neck and hugged him, then quickly stepped back, embarrassed by her public demonstration. "It was," she said.

"Somehow, knowing that, believing that, makes me not care very much what the consequences are."

"I think you're amazing," she said, looking ahead, smiling. "I mean, if that matters."

"It does," he said.

"And...thank you. Because she's my friend. Because she reminded me too much of my mom. And... I'm always afraid people like that will never leave."

"A lot of times they go back," he said, his voice rough.

"I know. But we'll help her."

"Yes," he said, "we will."

Yet again, she didn't know what to do with him. She felt so close to him right now, and she couldn't kiss him here. She wanted to ask him to hold her. She wanted to tell him something about herself. Wanted him to decide that, much like punching a guy in front of the whole town, she was okay, too.

And right then, she thought of the one place she hadn't been yet. She'd driven by the house where she'd grown up, but she hadn't been back to her clearing. Even though it was within walking distance of the B and B. She'd avoided serious thoughts of it since the first day back.

Again, a prickling sensation dotted the back of her neck.

There are no ghosts there. And if there are…maybe this will put some of them to rest.

She let out a long, slow breath, trying to gather her nerve. "Can I show you something?"

"My mom warned me about girls like you," he said, a smile teasing the corners of his lips.

"Did she?"

"No, my mom wasn't here."

"That's a dire punch line."

He lifted a shoulder. "Sometimes life is so dire you have to make a joke about it, right?"

"I think you've learned too much from me."

"Or not enough," he said.

"Hey, I'll get our food. Can you get a blanket for us to sit on?" she asked.

"Yeah."

She finished waiting through the line and got small portions of everything on offer, making small talk with the men and women manning the grills and scooping up sides. It was hard to do, though, since she was all jittery and fluttery inside over what she was about to do.

And there was no real logical reason why. Just that it seemed like a big deal. Bigger in some ways than what she'd shared about her father.

Because this was something she'd avoided. The last bit of Copper Ridge she hadn't revisited. And she wasn't going to test it alone to be sure she was okay. To be certain she could visit it without betraying her emotions.

She was going to let him see. All of it.

She wandered over to where he stood on the edge of the

lawn, where people were sitting at the tables that had been set up, and on blankets spread out like a rainbow patchwork over the green grass.

"Okay," he said, "what do you have to show me?"

"I hope you're ready for a hike."

IT WAS ONLY a five-minute walk, through the trees behind the B and B, just over the Garretts' property line. But the path was thick with brush and branches, the narrow trail overgrown in the years since Sadie and her friends had used it.

She and Eli wound through the evergreens, needles reaching out and grabbing her T-shirt. Then the grove thinned out, and beyond that was her clearing.

It was overgrown now, moss covering the ground, ferns encroaching. There was still a fire ring. Stumps, some on their sides, some still positioned like stools.

It had definitely been used by other people in the past decade, but not, it appeared, very recently.

"This," she said, "was my home away from home."

Her chest swelled up with emotion just looking at it, being in it. She wasn't sure why. She wasn't sure why this felt so big. Why she felt so naked.

But, like all her big feelings concerning Eli, the flip side was that as much as it hurt, she wanted him to know this part of her.

She wanted him to know her. There wasn't, she realized, another person on the whole planet—except Toby—who did.

"Alison, Matt, Josh, Brooke and a few others and I all hung out here in the afternoons. Sometimes when we were supposed to be in school. Usually on weekends."

"Doing what?" he asked.

"Drinking. Smoking…things of varying degrees of legality. Like you do. Well, not like *you* do, but like a lot of teenage ne'er-do-wells do."

He looked up at the canopy of trees overheard, then back at her. "I bet it was a great place for that."

'Perfect," she said. "You never arrested me here."

"I didn't."

"But then, in fairness, I never lit the woods on fire."

"That is true enough."

He set the blanket down in the middle of the clearing and they sat, putting their food in front of them. Sadie sat on her knees and started to poke at her potato salad.

"I lost my virginity here." Next to her Eli made a choking sound and she laughed. "Sorry," she said, "just a Sadie fun fact." It wasn't, though. She was minimizing it again. Minimizing why she'd told him. She always did that. So that if what she'd offered was rejected, she could pretend it didn't hurt.

She shoved her plate to the side and took a deep breath. "Sorry." She started over. "I told you because it seemed… This is where I learned to run," she said. "Where I learned to escape. None of us could handle the things that were happening at home and so we came here. Did a bunch of things that made us feel good. Sex was just another thing to do. But that's changing for me. All the way until I met you, sex was just a part of the logical steps in a relationship. A way to pretend that I was intimate with someone without ever really having to be. And this? Telling you this, showing you this, it's more intimate than anything I've ever done. But that's fitting, because when we're together…when we… It was never part of a logical step. It was just a thing we couldn't *not* do. And that's different, too."

"You're…different for me, too," he said.

She wanted him to say more. And she didn't know what more, but she did. She wanted to say more, but again, she wasn't sure what else. Wasn't sure what she could say that wouldn't scare her off.

She was a flight risk of the highest order, putting herself in a situation that scared her to death.

"Eli… I…" She wanted to say something big. She wanted to try to express what she was feeling but she couldn't even quantify it to herself.

The thing she wanted to say was the thing she couldn't say. Because to say it was too much. And way more than this was ever supposed to be.

The one thing she knew for sure, and the thing that terrified her to her bones, was that she wanted to have him here. In this place. The moments of weighted silence, punctuated by heavy sighs and long drags on cigarettes. Days when they'd come and sat in the rain and talked and swore as loud as they wanted, because screw the world. They were in their own world. When she'd come alone with Josh and kissed him and, eventually, taken things further because they'd both just needed someone to touch.

In this place where she'd been with her first guy, she wanted to be with Eli. The last one.

Shock skittered over her skin in an electric current. At the weight of the thought, the depth of it, the truth of it.

So she just said what she could.

"I want you."

"I thought you wanted potato salad."

She tried to laugh, shaking from the inside out. "No. Just you."

He seemed to sense the shift in tone. Another luxury of being with him. Of having him know her. He seemed to know what was happening inside her without her having to say it.

He set his plate off the blanket, too, cupping her cheek and leaning in for a kiss. She returned it, her chest filling, swelling, making it impossible to breathe. But breathing seemed secondary at the moment. Because of Eli.

She wrapped her arms around his neck and he slipped one hand down her back, holding her waist tight as he lowered her to the blanket, his body solid and warm above her. They sat together, his hands stroking her face, her hair.

He kissed her deeper and she laced her fingers through his hair. She felt everything happening on the surface of her skin. The scrape of his stubble against her neck as he kissed her there.

As his hands moved over her T-shirt, the warmth of his touch seeping through to her skin.

But it was the echo beneath the surface that really hit. That anchored her to him, to the world. It was like a deep bass note that resonated through her, vibrating along every vein, moving deep to the core of her being.

They broke the kiss, looking at each other, and her eyes met his, emotion building in her chest, bigger and stronger than any sexual climax.

It was painful and beautiful. She didn't think she could stand it for another moment, and she didn't want it to end. In that moment, she felt it all, the good, bad and scary, bound together, inescapable.

She was drowning in it, drowning in *him*. In what he made her feel. She couldn't run from it, couldn't make light of it. Couldn't shove it to the side.

All she could do was embrace it.

She held on to him, hoping his strength would hold her together because at this point, she didn't trust her own. And that was a damn scary place to be. But she was with Eli, so it had to be safe, too.

"When I'm with you, I don't want to be anywhere else," he said, moving his hand over her hair, sliding his fingers through the strands.

"Me, either," she said.

It was true. And for a woman who was always so keen to move on to the next place, the next thing, it was a huge and frightening admission.

He shifted their positions so that she was sitting between his thighs, her back to his chest, his fingers gentle as he laced them through her hair. She closed her eyes, a tightening moving from her chest, up her throat, making it hard to breathe. Making her ache.

"Is this what you used to do here?" he asked.

She laughed, a shaky sound that didn't do anything to loosen the knot of emotion inside her. "Not exactly. I've never done anything quite like this."

"Me, either."

He tugged lightly on her hair, once, then again. She turned and looked at him, and he kept hold of her. "What are you doing?" she asked.

He cocked his head to the side, a rueful smile on his face. "Braiding your hair." He kept his eyes on hers as he wove another section together. "Is that okay?"

She looked at his face, at the sincerity in his eyes. Sincerity and caring she'd never had directed at her before, and that she'd never hoped to deserve. The walls inside her cracked and she had to fight to keep the tears that welled up in her eyes from spilling down her cheeks.

Because when he said that, what she heard was *I'm taking care of you*.

"Yeah," she said, the word a whisper. "It's okay."

She closed her eyes while he finished, focusing on breathing. On not breaking down completely over this moment. On not betraying everything she felt.

He slid his thumb down the side of her neck, his touch gentle. "Done."

She turned back to him again. She wanted to say so much. And nothing, and everything.

He leaned in slowly, his breath fanning across her cheek. Then he kissed her, and she let herself get lost in it. In a kiss that wasn't meant to start anything, wasn't meant to arouse. A kiss that was meant to forge a connection. An outpouring of all the emotion their joining had brought to the surface.

Panic clawed at her as she realized the kiss would have to end. This moment would have to end.

She didn't want the kiss to end, because when it did, they would have to deal with what happened next. And part of her was already panicking about that. Part of her was feeling the need to run.

This was deep. And it was real. And the most terrifying four-letter word she could think of was pushing into her consciousness, hovering on the edge of her lips, burrowing into her heart.

And that was the one thing she hadn't wanted. The thing she feared more than anything.

But the kiss had to end. And it did. When they parted he slid his thumb over the edge of her lip. "Sadie…"

"We should go," she said, terror gnawing at her. Terror that he was going to say what she was trying not to think. That he wouldn't say it. That he would never say it. Or that he would now when she wasn't sure she could deal with hearing it.

She reached back and touched her hair, ran her fingertips over the imperfect braid. "We really should go," she repeated.

"Uh…yeah," he said, letting out a big gust of air. "You're right. The barbecue. It's your baby. You…you should be there for it."

"Well, yeah," she said, wrapping her arms around her midsection. "I kind of should. Sorry about… Not much of a seduction, I guess."

He met her gaze, his eyes intense. "I don't know if I'd say that."

She breathed in deeply through her nose, smoke burning her nostrils, and frowned. "I would have thought they'd be powering down the grills about now. It's getting dark."

"Maybe that many more people showed up," he said, sounding slightly grim and serious, and it was probably her fault. For cutting him off. For bringing him out here and spilling her guts and then basically telling him nothing of what she was feeling because it all scared her too much.

"We can hope," she said, rounding up the blanket and holding it tight against her chest. Like she was trying to apply pressure to a wound, and in some ways, she felt like that's exactly what she was doing.

Eli picked up the uneaten food, and Sadie mourned it slightly, because she didn't feel like eating at all now. She was too full.

Of feelings she didn't want to sort through. Emotions she didn't want to have.

They headed back toward the ranch, cutting through the trees, Sadie taking the lead and not walking hand in hand with Eli, like she sort of wished she could.

You can't bolt if he's holding on to you.

The smoke got thicker as they got closer to the ranch, the wind bringing a wall of it their direction. "What the hell?" he asked.

"I don't know," she said. "That's not... That's not normal."

Eli picked up the pace, passing her, before he moved into a dead run. She followed after him, clutching the blanket against her pounding heart.

She was saying things. Worried things. Things with swearing. But she couldn't really make sense of them. They were just pouring out of her mouth without any kind of specific order or reason. Fear, irrational at this point, but intuitively driving her on.

She knew something had gone wrong. She knew it as certainly as anything she'd seen with her own eyes.

And she knew it was bad.

They crossed the dirt road and back into the Garrett property line to see flames rising up above the trees.

"Oh, no. Oh, no," she said, running after Eli, releasing her hold on the blanket and letting it fall to the ground as she picked up her pace.

They ran back to the main area to find the picnickers standing facing the barn. The beautiful barn that Connor had poured his money into. Now on fire. A wicked blaze that was eating through the beautifully stained wood, the newly shingled roof.

"The horses," she said, gasping for air. "Animals?" She couldn't think. She couldn't remember the layout of things, not now. Her brain was just swimming.

"No animals in there," Eli said, his brow creased, his mouth turned down. "Just the equipment. The feed. All Connor's equipment," he repeated. "Did someone call the fire department?" Eli asked.

"Yeah." Sadie turned and saw Liss standing there, a tear rolling down her cheek. "I did."

"Is there anyone inside?"

"Not as far as we know," Liss said, her eyes not on Eli, but on Connor, who was standing nearer to the blaze than anyone else, his posture stiff, staring right at it. Watching so much of his livelihood burn.

"There's insurance," Eli said.

"Of course," Liss said. "It'll be okay." She didn't sound convinced, not at all.

A group of boys, who must have been twelve, walked up to Eli, their faces ashen, their eyes wide. "We didn't mean to, Deputy Garrett," the smallest one said. "But it's a Fourth of July thing and we were messing with fireworks…"

"In the barn?" Eli asked, his tone hard.

"Well, yeah, because we didn't want our moms to see. And we didn't think…"

"About the hay," Eli said.

"We thought," one of the other boys said, "that we'd gotten all the sparks doused and we left…"

And they'd left a smoldering firework in the hay, to burn it all from the inside out so that by the time anyone realized, the blaze inside had consumed the fuel and moved on to the structure.

Sadie was starting to shake. It was too similar to her last night in Copper Ridge. Too close to sins she'd already committed. Eli hadn't wanted this on his property, Connor hadn't wanted it and she'd pushed. She'd come onto their property, into their lives and destroyed their order.

And this was the result.

This is what happens when you try. You can't fix it. You never could.

She was watching the Garretts' world burn in front of her. Her handiwork. No, she wasn't going to fall prostrate to the ground and take total fault. She wasn't an idiot. It had been little boys with firecrackers, not her with a match. Not her at a party knocking over a lantern.

But it didn't change how horrible she felt. Didn't change the way it was unfolding. Or the fact that the boys were only here because of her.

"Eli…"

"Not now, Sadie," he said, his voice rough.

"I'm so sorry… I…"

"I said not fucking now, Sadie," he bit out, forking his fingers through his hair, his eyes on the scene in front of them. Sadie's heart curled in tight around the edges, like it had been set on fire, too.

She took a step back from him, her head swimming. She wondered if she should do something with the crowd? Try to manage? But everyone was frozen, staring at what was happening, and she just felt useless. Helpless. Like she'd been as a child in her home growing up. Watching sick, unending horror playing out before her eyes while she cowered, powerless to stop it.

The fire department came, en masse, sirens rising up over the sound of the blaze. And when it was over, there was no question as to what was left: nothing.

Nothing but a charred husk. Unusable, unsalvageable. The crowd had thinned by then, families with small children taking them away from the upsetting scene. They'd all moved on to the main fireworks display down at the beach. Though mainly they'd left so quickly to escape the smoke and debris. Sadie wished she could get carried away from it, too, but she had to watch, her own eyes gritty with ashes. She felt honor bound in so many ways.

Finally, all that remained were Liss, Jack, Kate, Eli, Lydia, Ace, Bud and the fishermen.

And Connor. Who stood alone, silent and in sharp contrast to the blackened ruins in front of him. Unmoving.

Liss was the one who broke from the small crowd and went to him, her hand going to his shoulder. He jerked away from her and walked back toward the main house, leaving Liss standing there with her arms folded beneath her breasts.

A moment later she took a deep breath and marched after him, a stubborn set to her jaw and shoulders, and for a moment, Sadie could only admire the other woman's strength. Liss was a woman who stayed. A woman who went the tough rounds.

It made Sadie feel painfully inadequate, standing there in the semi-darkness, with cooling ashes just in front of her.

"Whatever you need, Eli," Ace said. "You know we're here to help out."

"I know," Eli said.

"Anything," Lydia said. And Sadie knew she was ready to offer comfort as well, and Sadie couldn't even be mad because she felt so unequal to the task.

"Probably we all just need sleep right now," Eli said, forcing a smile.

Kate was standing silent, tears streaming down her cheeks, her shoulders shaking. Sadie moved nearer to her and put her arm around her. Feeling so inadequate to do anything to stanch the flow of grief around her.

"Of course," Ace said. "We'll get out of your hair. I'll come by tomorrow if you want, help assess the damage?"

"Thanks. I imagine we'll just be making an insurance claim. And they'll have to send someone out. Best we leave it untouched for now."

"Fair point. Come by for a drink, though," Ace said, touching the brim of his ball cap before walking away.

"Guess I better let you get rest, too," Lydia said, putting her hand on Eli's shoulder in a decidedly nonsisterly way. "I'll come by and check in on you tomorrow."

Eli didn't protest.

Lydia squeezed Sadie's shoulder, too, as she walked by her. "I'm happy to check in on you, too."

That tipped her over into utter misery. Because she didn't deserve that kindness. Not at all. "Thanks," she said, her throat raw.

"I'll go talk to the firemen," Jack said, "see if there's anything we need to know. I'll report back."

"I'm going to go find Connor," Kate said, her voice thick as she pulled away from Sadie and walked in the direction of the main house.

That left Sadie and Eli, and a pile of glowing, charred wood, alone in the darkness.

She swallowed and tried again. "Eli, I…"

"We have to be done," Eli said, cutting her off.

"What?"

"This. Us. It has to… I can't do this," he said.

ELI'S HEART TWISTED into a knot in his chest, but it had to be said. It had to be done. Because yet again, while he'd been out enjoying himself, the whole world had fallen apart. All of this, the time spent with Sadie, had been an illusion.

When he didn't keep control, the world burned. In this case, literally.

It was just too damn close to his other failures. Too damn close.

"When I'm with you, I forget what I'm doing. I forget other people. I forget myself. No, I don't forget myself, because myself is all I think of. Myself and my dick, and it can't happen like this. There is a reason that I've lived my life the way that I have. A reason that I can't ignore for good sex."

Sadie blinked rapidly, her eyes glossy in the dim light. And his stomach twisted, sick regret forming. But there was nothing else he could do. He needed to stay on top of this stuff and he wasn't doing it.

His sister had just stood there in tears, his brother watching the one thing he'd held on to since losing his wife burn to nothing.

It was all way too reminiscent of the night when he hadn't taken the keys. Of the last time Eli had let himself become distracted.

And it didn't matter what Sadie said, because in the end, this was the result. It didn't matter if he shouldn't feel at fault. He did. And it didn't change the fact that when he wasn't holding up the world around him, it all seemed to fall apart.

For a second today, he'd thought he could be something different, have something different. And then all this had swooped in and reminded him just why that wasn't possible.

Why he had to forget their moment in the woods, and every moment before. Why he had to stop wanting more, when more would never be in the cards for him. He knew that. He'd known that before Sadie Miller had blown into his life like a windstorm and rearranged his existence. Made him think that maybe everything he'd believed about his life, about himself, had been a lie.

Which was a whole lot crueler than never having hope had ever been.

For one moment, he'd thought he could do it. Thought he could punch the hell out of a guy who deserved it, thought he could sneak into the woods for a moment alone with the only woman who'd ever driven him that crazy.

Thought he could go to sleep with her every night and wake up with her every morning.

"Good sex, Eli?" she asked. "Really? Good sex? Because I think, I mean, I pretty freaking well think what we have is a lot more than that. I mean, I think we'd both had good sex before we ever met each other, and that…this is something else entirely. What we share is something else."

"It doesn't matter," he said. "It can't happen." He wanted to lash out. To blame someone other than himself. He was so tired of carrying it all. And this was just another failure. "It seems like when you're around barns tend to burn down," he said. "You have a knack for spreading disaster, I guess."

"Eli, please don't do this. Not now, not… Please."

"Sadie, I can't afford any more distractions," he said, the words scraping his throat raw. "And that's all this was. All you are to me is a distraction."

She stumbled backward and he felt like his heart lurched through his chest to follow her, leaving nothing but a bloody, vacant hole behind. This felt like he thought dying might. But he couldn't take the words back now.

He wouldn't.

It was the right thing to do. Other men could have wives and kids. Other men with other lives.

Not him. Never him.

"Well," she said, her voice thick as she put distance between them. "Don't let me distract you any longer."

She turned and walked back in the direction of the B and B, which he only thought of as hers now. What a difference a few weeks made.

But he couldn't afford the difference, and neither could any of the people who depended on him.

CHAPTER SIXTEEN

SADIE DIDN'T SLEEP at all. She spent the whole night out on her newly stained deck, a mug of coffee clutched tightly in her hand, tears rolling down her face as she slowly accepted what had happened. As she slowly accepted what she'd let herself do.

She loved Eli Garrett.

He was the first person she'd loved since she'd lost hope in her family a decade ago and run out of town.

He was the first person she'd been close to in as many years, if not more. If not ever.

She stayed on the deck, wrapped in her blanket and her misery, Toby snuggled in her lap, until pink started to bleed into the sky, extending up above the tree line.

Well, damn. There went her theory about the world stopping because she was devastated.

She deposited Toby gently onto the deck, then went into the house with him following behind her. She went upstairs, undressed and stepped into the shower, letting the hot water wash away the stiffness, the misery.

In the end, some of the stiffness got worked out, but the misery remained.

She brushed her teeth, which were fuzzy after an evening of nursing coffees, then made herself another in her single-serving brewer, bought especially so that her guests could have a fresh cup at any point in the day.

She let out a heavy sigh. Her guests. She'd had several people get in touch since the night before, inquiring about availability through her website. So soon there would be guests. She had a five-year contract.

She lowered her head, feeling very much like she was sinking into the mire. A mire she couldn't just cut and run from.

And suddenly she felt claustrophobic. She wanted to claw her clothes off, claw her skin off, step out of her body and just run from all of it.

Get away and start fresh. Away from that man, away from the feelings he made her feel.

She looked around the B and B, at her attempt to build something permanent. To make something stable. She should have known it was never about her surroundings. It was about her. It always had been.

She couldn't sign a five-year lease and expect it to make her different.

The simple truth was, she'd never been important enough for anyone to change for her. That was the painful heart of it. Her mother would rather spend her life being beaten by a man, the same man who beat her child, than leave him for the good of them both.

Her love for a husband who dealt out pain and misery was stronger than her love for Sadie. And that made it impossible to imagine anyone changing their life drastically for the sake of her love.

And Eli was proving that no one would.

This was why she always left. Because if she left first, if she never let anyone close, if she never asked anyone to know her and accept her anyway, she couldn't get hurt.

But she'd come back to Copper Ridge. She'd given of herself. She'd fallen in love and dared to hope for it back.

And now she was broken. And she had no idea how long it would take to glue the pieces back together.

One thing was for sure. She couldn't do it here.

"Toby," she said, looking at her little gray friend, the only friend she really had, "I think it's time for us to go."

ELI PACED THE length of the living room, eyeing his brother, who was passed out on the couch. He was going to hate life a whole hell of a lot when Eli woke him up.

Which was going to be now, because Eli hated life, so Connor might as well join the living.

In hell.

"Wake up, Connor," he said, clapping his hands and watching his brother go from blissfully conked out to awake and in a world of pain in an instant.

"Dammit all!" he said, then winced, his hand on his forehead. "Ow."

"Yeah, I would think *ow*. You drank roughly the amount of alcohol it would take to cleanse all the wounds on a frontier battlefield."

"Oh...shut up, Eli. Honestly."

"We have things to do."

"Like?" he asked. "Work? Because I think all my tools are gone."

"You have animals that might want to get fed."

"I don't have hay," Connor mumbled.

"So get off your ass and get some," Eli said, feeling angry. At himself, mainly, but yelling at Connor was more convenient than dealing with that.

"What the hell is your issue this morning?" Connor asked, moving into a sitting position, running his hands over his beard.

"Maybe I'm tired of watching you wallow while I take care of you," Eli said, resentment flaring up, rage burning hot in his chest.

He'd resigned himself to this last night.

To caring for other people and putting himself on hold. But this morning? This morning he'd woken up alone. And it hurt worse than he'd imagined it could. Thirty-two years of it. He should be used to it. But this morning his bed had felt so empty it had mimicked the damn hole in his chest.

And he was forgetting already why a burned-out barn had mattered more than Sadie next to him.

"What?" Connor asked.

"You are my older brother. You're a grown man."

"I never asked you to take care of me," Connor said.

"You expect it," Eli bit out.

Connor shook his head. "Look, man, I don't know what the hell your problem is, but I've never asked you for anything. I'm glad you're here, I won't lie, but if you weren't? I would be happy to just stay drunk and live in filth. You're the one who—"

"And it's things like that, Connor, that mean I can't leave you to it. Because you don't think I know you'd sink in it? I do, and I won't let it happen."

"And so what, Eli? I'm supposed to get myself together the way you see fit so you don't have to deal?"

"Yeah," Eli said. "Yeah. Just…could you? Because I can't work a job, and work on the ranch, and run for sheriff, and file your insurance claim and not lose my fucking mind. I can't… I can't do it all."

That was the first time he'd ever admitted that. To himself. To anyone else. That he couldn't shoulder everything. That he didn't even want to.

"I didn't know, Eli," Connor said, looking straight ahead. "I've had a hard time caring about anything other than myself. For the record, I mostly still don't care about anything else, but… I'm damn sorry you felt that way."

"It wasn't ever just you," Eli said. "But you know you've added to it."

"Well," Connor drawled. "I do what I can."

"You make me feel like a dick for complaining since you've been through hell."

"Yeah. Still in it most days," he mumbled. "But I guess I don't have to bring you with me."

"Sometimes I think I brought myself on purpose."

"Well, stop," Connor said.

"What?"

"Stop. Being unhappy is stupid. If there's any way you can fix it? Fix it. I can't bring my wife back. I can't...fix anything that happened. I can't make my life better just by making a different choice."

"I'm not sure I can, either," Eli said.

"Does it have to do with Sadie?"

Eli breathed in deep. "Yeah."

"She's not dead, is she?"

"No," Eli said, his voice rough.

"Then there's still hope."

CHAPTER SEVENTEEN

SADIE FINISHED PILING her personal belongings into the car. She was violating her lease agreement and she knew it. It sucked, but she just… She couldn't stay. She didn't know much about what would happen next, but she knew that much.

She sighed and put Toby's cat carrier in the backseat, safely on the floorboards, before shutting the back door.

She heard a car driving up the driveway and swore copiously under her breath. She didn't want to deal with a crestfallen Kate, a pissed-off Connor or…worse than them all, an Eli, in whatever form he chose to present.

But instead of a Garrett vehicle, it was a shiny black car making its way down the driveway.

"Lydia," she grumbled, leaning against her car and looking down. Oh, well, the other woman could give her a send-off. Hell, she'd probably be thrilled to do it.

Lydia stopped her car and got out, a stack of brochures in her hand and a frown crossing her fine features. "What's going on?" she asked.

"I'm heading out," Sadie said. "It's…kind of what I do. Don't be alarmed."

"Too late," Lydia said. "I am. Eli didn't tell you to—"

"Oh, no, he's too much of a gentleman for that." Not too

much of one to break her heart and say she wasn't important, but he'd never ask her to violate a lease agreement. That shit was legally binding.

"Does he know you're leaving?" she asked.

"No, I didn't tell him. Though it's really more relevant to Connor since he's the one who sort of headed up the lease thingy..."

"Oh, what a bunch of baloney," Lydia said. "It is not more relevant to Connor than it is to Eli if you go. And I think you know it."

She averted her eyes. "Do you know it?"

Lydia sighed. "I'm not stupid. Possibly a little bit...mmm... too hopeful? But yeah, not stupid. I've seen the way you look at each other."

Sadie cleared her throat. "But have you heard the way we talk to each other? Because that might be a better indicator of where we're at."

"Do you love him?" she asked.

Sadie's heart squeezed tight. "It doesn't matter."

"It matters. Eli Garrett is the best man I know. The best man I've ever known. And you know, I realized he's not that into me. Sure, it's sort of been a die-hard crush, even with that in mind, but pretty much the minute you showed up I knew I was screwed." She smiled, the expression tinged with sadness. "Not in a fun way, either. But ultimately, I know I won't be happy with a guy I have to coerce into a relationship. And I have a sneaking suspicion he won't be happy *without* you."

Sadie laughed. "Tell him that. He told me he didn't want me."

"He's lying," she said. "You realize that, right?"

"I don't think Eli knows how to lie."

"Well, maybe not on purpose. But he's lying even if he doesn't know he is. One benefit of watching someone more closely than you should, you get to know them. The way he looks at you? That's special. If I were you? I wouldn't walk away from that. I'd fight for it. And I'll be honest, Sadie, I took you for kind of a badass, so…if you run now, I'm going to have to retract that."

"I'm not a badass," Sadie said. "I'm basically whatever is the opposite of that. And I've never pretended to be much more. I'm a runner. And it's my cue to go."

"That sucks, because I think if you stayed, and if we weren't competing for the same guy, we could be friends. And I think if you stayed, and you married him, eventually, we would be friends. You know, after I got over my seething jealousy."

"You don't seem to be seething all that much," Sadie said.

"It's a quiet seethe. Like I said, I know he's not mine." She smiled a little more genuinely now. "Kind of bummed I never got to…"

Sadie coughed. "Yeah…that's kind of… He's good at the sex."

Lydia cleared her throat, her cheeks turning pink. "I was going to say kiss him. But sure."

Sadie winced. "Well, he's good at that, too."

"I can't decide if it sucks to know that or if it's gratifying to realize my fantasies were on track."

"It sucks to know. Because I know it sucks that I know. Because it's over. And I wish it weren't."

"So fight for it, badass," Lydia said. "Fight for *him*."

"I don't think there's anything to fight for."

"Well, then, maybe you should go. Because I happen to think he deserves someone who will fight. I thought that might be you."

"Maybe you should fight for him," Sadie said, feeling mean, small and not at all in the mood to watch another woman fight for the man she loved. But not brave enough to go and get him herself.

Lydia looked at her sadly. "It was nice to meet you, Sadie. I hope you find whatever you're looking for. And I really hope that you don't realize it was here when it's too late for you to come back."

Sadie watched Lydia toss the brochures on her passenger seat and drive away and felt a whole hot ball of rage grow in her chest. Who was Lydia to tell her what she should do? Seriously. She hadn't been there. She hadn't heard the way Eli talked to her. What he'd said.

Lydia probably had no idea what it was like to be certain that the only way attachment could end was rejection.

And hell, he'd rejected her. Why subject herself to it twice? *Because for the first time, you felt complete. Because for the first time you want to stay. Really, really.*

Well, it didn't really matter. Because he'd pushed her away. *You're just too pathetic to fight for him. Too afraid.*

Yeah, well, because what if she was wrong? Sure, maybe Eli was as afraid as she was. Maybe that was half of why he'd pushed her away. Maybe.

She jerked the backseat door open and pulled out the pet carrier, depositing it on the porch, checking to make sure Toby's food, water and litter weren't disturbed.

Then she looked out into the forest.

The place she'd always gone to escape, before she'd run for real.

She took a deep breath of the pine and salt air. And then she ran.

THE WAY ELI saw it, he had two options. The Connor option—really, the Garrett option—that meant drinking until you couldn't remember why you were sad.

Or the handle-your-shit option, which was a lot harder.

He stared at the bottle of Jack on the counter and placed his palms flat on the marble surface, looking at the bottle. As if it might tell him what to do.

"Drink it and it might," he said.

Then he shoved off from the counter and started pacing the room. What was he doing? He felt like hell. Or something worse than hell, whatever that was.

But he had order. He didn't have a blonde whirlwind with a strange emotional connection to a cat. He didn't have distractions. He had what he'd spent a lifetime cultivating.

"Loneliness," he said to the empty room. "You have loneliness. Give the man a prize."

And it was all he ever had to look forward to. An orderly life and an empty bed. All because he was too afraid to let someone in.

All because it was so much easier to keep everyone out and to never lose anyone or anything again. All because it was easier to blame himself so he could pretend he had some control in the universe when the simple fact was he didn't have control over any of it.

Mothers left. People died. Barns burned. And no amount of diligence on his part would ever stop it.

He slammed his fist down onto the counter and swore as pain shot up his arm, straight through to his heart.

What a terrible realization. And too late. Dammit, if he was going to have to deal with the fact that he had no control over his life, over anything, the least he could have done was grasped the concept before he'd lost her.

Sadie...

He looked at the spotless counter, where she'd once put her damned tennis shoes. Who did shit like that? And even though the shoes were gone, and there was not a speck of dust from the tread left behind, the memory lingered so strongly there might as well have been a muddy footprint there.

It would have been easier to erase.

He turned away from the counter and looked out the front window, and his heart about burst. Her azalea. Her apology azalea with its pink flowers. Another Sadie invasion that had been obnoxious at first, but that he couldn't imagine life without now.

She was everywhere in his house. At the counter, drinking a beer. In his bed. His shower. His yard. His heart.

Dammit, she was in his heart.

He loved her.

The realization sent warmth blooming through him. Like a burst blood vessel around his heart, flooding his chest and making him feel weak.

He *loved her*.

He hadn't loved anyone but Kate and Connor in…ever. Hadn't wanted to because he'd been so busy trying to hold the world together. Trying to make sense of things that just didn't make sense.

Trying to keep his family from falling apart, so that no one else would leave. So that he would matter.

But Sadie had always acted like he mattered, even when he was screwing things up. Sadie had held him, stripped him of his inhibitions in a way nothing and no one else ever had, accepted him when he confessed his shortcomings. Sadie, who had shared herself with him when she hadn't shared with anyone else.

An offering of herself, but also a demonstration of the trust she put in him.

And he had turned her away to keep wandering through life, holding on with an iron fist, trying desperately to earn the trust of strangers. To be seen as good enough.

When she'd already seen him that way.

"Probably not now, asshole," he said into the empty room.

No, probably not now.

And he couldn't blame her.

But he had to ask. He had to try. He had to beg forgiveness.

He had to tell her he loved her.

And damn the consequences.

Order meant nothing without her, control meant nothing without her. And the only acceptance that mattered was hers.

He shoved the Jack Daniel's bottle back into its place in the cupboard and walked out of his house. He strode toward the B and B, his heart in his throat, his hands honest-to-God shaking. Everything in him was shaking.

He'd never loved anyone. And he'd never asked anyone to love him back.

He'd tried to earn it, every day. But he'd never asked.

Today he had to ask.

He walked across the driveway and into the clearing in front of her house, and saw her car, the back door open, suitcases inside.

"What the hell?"

Just then, Sadie came down the stairs, a couple of pine needles stuck in her hair, tears on her cheeks, her face pale. Her eyes widened and she froze, staring at him like he was some kind of ghost. He walked toward her.

She was packed. She was leaving.

She was leaving him.

Hell no.

He reached out and wrapped his arm around her waist, tugging her to him, his lips crashing down on hers. He tried to make her feel what he did. To understand what he'd just started to understand. That he loved her. That she'd changed him.

She clung to him, grabbing his T-shirt and holding it tight, holding him tight.

When they parted, they were both breathing hard, and her cheeks were wet, tears tracking down her pale skin.

"Don't leave me," he said, his tone a command. "Don't go."

"Eli..."

"I am an idiot. You *are* distracting. And you did change things. But dammit, Sadie, I want to be distracted by you. I want to be changed by you. Hell, baby, I need it. And I was just about to drink a whole bottle of liquor to try to forget how much of an ass I am. But then I saw my counter."

"Your counter?"

"It's clean. Your shoes aren't sitting on it. Everything's in order. Everything. You're not there saying some...sexual innuendo I barely understand, and you know what? I hate it. I hate the order if it means I can't have you. I love you, Sadie."

"I'm not leaving," she said, her voice trembling.

"Then why are you packed?"

"Because. Because I was going to leave but I went and did some thinking. And now I'm not," she said.

"Why?" he asked.

"You know…it's hard to say. Because leaving is what I do. And even when I knew I would miss you like hell it seemed easier than this. Easier than standing in front of you and telling you I want more. But I'm going to do it anyway. I went back to my clearing. It was where I used to go when things got to be too much. When I needed to escape. But I didn't find oblivion there. I found you instead. And whatever power there was in escape, whatever I used to enjoy about it…it was gone. I don't want to run anymore. I want to stand and fight. I want to stay. I want more. Because I want you. I want everything. Good and bad and stick up your ass. I love you and I want to fight for that love like I've never fought for anything."

He felt like he'd been punched in the chest. It was one thing to confess his love to her, but he didn't think for a damn minute he deserved to have it returned. Not after the things he'd said to her.

"How can you love *me*?" he asked. "I failed you."

"That's the thing, though, Eli, you didn't. I wished that someone would have stepped in and saved me. Of course I did. And I think…it was easy to wish it had been you. But what I really needed was to save myself."

"You did, Sadie," he said, his chest tightening. "You left."

She shook her head. "No. That's not when I saved myself. That's when I learned to run. Which is the first step sometimes. But I realized something today, when I was ready to leave this place, to leave you. I realized it's not enough to have a life. You have to have all of life. And I haven't let myself do that."

"Sadie…" His throat closed up. "I haven't, either. I wanted to believe that I could control things. That somehow I could stop bad things from happening. But the problem with that is that…

I can't. I thought if I could, if I got things in order... But it's not in my power. And admitting that is one of the scariest damn things I can think of because control is everything to me. Being the one taking care of things is everything to me. So that..." He felt like an ass even thinking this, much less admitting it. But it was time to say it. And it was time to let it go. "People leave me, Sadie. I thought someday I'd make myself so important it wouldn't happen again."

"Well—" Sadie wiped the tears from her cheeks and smiled "—Eli Garrett, future sheriff of Copper Ridge, you have made yourself so important to me that this woman, who always has her running shoes on hand, can't leave you."

SADIE LOOKED UP at Eli, at the deep concern in his dark eyes, at the sincerity. And the insecurity. And any remaining walls around her heart crumbled completely.

She threw her arms around his neck and held him close, stroking her fingers through his hair. "You're the best reason in the world to stop running. And you don't have to work to get me to stay. I'm offering to. Because you're the best man there is. And anyone who made you feel like less deserves to be dragged behind a horse."

"I love you, Sadie. More than a clean house, more than stability. If you kept running, I'd run after you. Even if I had to leave all this behind. Because it doesn't mean a thing without you. And I'm sorry. Sorry for all the crap I said to you. Everything I put us through. I couldn't run, so I guess the best I could do was try to make you run. Because you scare the hell out of me, woman. But I'm even more scared of living without you."

A tear rolled down Sadie's cheek, emotion filling her, so full she thought she might break with it. "Then it's a good thing I'm staying."

"Oh, hell, does this mean I'm part of the bed-and-breakfast?"

"Only if you spend the night."

"Yeah," he said, "about that… Do you think you could run it if you mainly slept at my place?"

"Mainly?"

"Always."

"I have a cat," she reminded him. "And he sleeps indoors. He basically lives indoors."

"I will give him his own bedroom."

"Holy crap, you do love me!" she said, laughing, another tear sliding down her cheek.

"I really do," he said, leaning in to kiss her. "I really, really do."

Sadie kissed him back, the feeling of completion when their lips touched unlike anything she'd ever experienced.

Whoever said you couldn't go home again had never been to Copper Ridge. The place hadn't changed at all.

But Sadie had. And for the first time, she was home, and she was ready to stay.

* * * * *

ACKNOWLEDGMENTS

THEY SAY IT takes a village to raise a child. Sometimes I feel like it takes a village to create a book. A huge thank-you to Margo Lipschultz, who encouraged me to send this series to HQN and who has put in so many tireless hours to make it the best it can be. Kate Dresser, my fantastic editor on this book, I only wish we could have done more together. You're amazing. I always owe thanks to my wonderful agent, Helen Breitwieser, who has believed in me from the beginning. To Jackie Ashenden for reading every word I write and serving up hard truths wrapped in encouragement. Many thanks to Nicole Helm for her insider knowledge on police uniforms and how they are removed, velcro belts, clip-on ties and all. And I owe the biggest thank-you of all to Victoria Austin for the snowballs joke that Eli tells in the book. You are a goddess of the corny joke, and for that I am grateful.

Subscribe and fall in love with a Mills & Boon series today!

You'll be among the first to read stories delivered to your door monthly and enjoy great savings.

WE SIMPLY LOVE ROMANCE